A choice between vengeance and love…

BONDED *by* BLOOD

LAURIE LONDON

Dear Reader,

I'm thrilled to present *Bonded By Blood*, the first book of my paranormal series with Mills & Boon® Nocturne™. The Sweetblood world is a deadly and seductive one, where the forces of good and evil battle secretly around us, and the power of love can change everything.

The kernel of this story and my love for the ultimate bad boy began years ago, when my sister and I saw *Fright Night* eight times in the movie theater. Chris Sarandon played a dangerously handsome vampire whose intense magnetism literally sucked me in. Although he was the villain, I dreamed of being Amy, the girl he'd loved for centuries. The scene at the club still gets my heart pounding...

Okay, where was I?

Far beneath the streets of the city, in an unknown part of Underground Seattle, a team of vampire Guardians fights to protect humans from Darkbloods—vicious members of their race who kill like their ancestors and sell the blood on the black market. The rarest, called Sweetblood, commands the highest price.

Tortured by his need for vengeance, Dominic Serrano will stop at nothing in order to kill his enemy...until one forbidden taste of Mackenzie's sweet blood turns his world upside down. Seeing this fierce warrior struggle to restrain himself with a woman who brings him to his knees got my heart pounding. Just like it did in that theater.

Come with me and explore the Sweetblood world, one dangerously seductive romance at a time.

All my best,

Laurie London

BONDED by BLOOD

LAURIE LONDON

MILLS & BOON

All the characters in this book have no existence outside the imagination of
the author, and have no relation whatsoever to anyone bearing the same name
or names. They are not even distantly inspired by any individual known or
unknown to the author, and all the incidents are pure invention.

First published in Great Britain 2012
by Mills & Boon, an imprint of Harlequin (UK) Limited,
Eton House, 18-24 Paradise Road, Richmond, Surrey TW9 1SR

© Laurie Thompson 2011

ISBN: 978 0 263 89718 0

089-0212

Harlequin (UK) policy is to use papers that are natural, renewable and
recyclable products and made from wood grown in sustainable forests. The
logging and manufacturing processes conform to the legal environmental
regulations of the country of origin.

Printed and bound
by CPI Group (UK) Ltd, Croydon, CR0 4YY

ACKNOWLEDGMENTS:

Because this is my debut novel, I have so many people to thank.

First and foremost, thank you to my sister, talented author Rebecca Clark, for her unwavering encouragement, even when I thought she and her "feelings" about this story's potential were crazy.

Thank you to my agent Emmanuelle Morgen and my editor Margo Lipschultz for taking a chance on this new author and for their enthusiastic support of this series. To all the people at HQN, including the uber-talented art department, thank you.

To Alexis Morgan, thanks for your friendship and for telling me, early on, to write the story I want to write.

Thank you, Cherry Adair, for your encouragement, your wisdom, your generosity, and your belief in me. I'm truly humbled.

To my dear friends and beta readers, Shelley, Mandy, Kandis, Kathy, and Janna: your friendship and feedback mean the world to me. You made this reader think she wasn't nuts when she nervously told you she'd been writing. Barb, *muchas gracias* for your help with Spanish words and cultural details. Thanks to my GIAM friends, my Lex buddies, the writing community of Greater Seattle RWA, and the Bookinville ladies for your hearty enthusiasm.

Hugs and kisses to my two awesome children for their love and support, and for picking up the slack around the house because Mom had to write "just one more page."

Last, but not least, thank you to my real life hero, my husband Ted, for supporting my dreams and managing more than his share of the chaos so that I can write. Oh, and for agreeing with Emmanuelle that a guy wouldn't use such expressive words in a particular scene. The final version is much better.

BONDED *by* BLOOD

To my husband, Ted,
for a zillion reasons, starting with I love you

CHAPTER ONE

MACKENZIE FOSTER-SHAW spotted the cemetery sign at the last minute and squeezed the brakes, spinning out her white Triumph motorcycle in a spray of dirt and gravel. She meant to lean into a sharp, controlled turn, but the back tire lost traction and she almost had to lay the thing down.

Crap, the rocks hadn't looked that loose. Irritation at her carelessness momentarily replaced the uncertainty *riding* in with her as she sprang from the bike. After examining the chrome for chips and seeing no damage, she felt the hard lump of anticipation return, but she swallowed and tried to ignore it.

She yanked off her helmet and squinted into the shadowed interior of the cemetery. Even in the late afternoon sun, little light penetrated the heavy canopy of fir trees.

"I'm liking this so far," she said to herself as she tossed her sunglasses on the seat. But she knew better than to get her hopes up too soon. Hope didn't pay the bills, nor did wishful thinking.

Situated on a forest access road, miles from the main highway, the cemetery was certainly ancient enough. The county register listed it as one of the oldest in the region. How long had it been since anyone visited this place? Ages ago, probably.

She started to unzip her leather jacket, then hesitated.

Like most people in the Pacific Northwest after months of gray skies and the unending wetness of winter, she didn't need much of an excuse to strip off the layers. But with one glance at the bushes she'd need to traipse through, she zipped it back up. Those vivid green leaves couldn't camouflage the barb-covered vines eager to hook anything within reach. Especially bare skin. Besides, it was probably cooler and wetter inside the trees.

She grabbed her camera from the saddlebag and fiddled with the settings, not bothering with the flash attachment. The client was adamant the pictures needed to portray the ambient lighting and convey an oppressive, haunted feeling.

"Hopefully, *this* location will work for them." It was the fourth or fifth graveyard she'd visited in the past two weeks. If it didn't, she was screwed because she was totally out of ideas.

Bear Creek Pioneer Cemetery was etched in once-white paint on a crooked sign at the side of the road. After shooting a few pictures, she scanned the area for a pathway and noticed a slight indentation in the underbrush. She'd do her sketches and take measurements of the road later.

Her boots crunched on the gravel as she slung the camera strap over her shoulder and plunged into the blackberry bushes. Good thing she'd kept her riding leathers on. Both the jacket and the pants. Sharp thorns and stickers grabbed hungrily at her arms and legs, but they weren't able to gain purchase on the thick hide.

As she stepped into the small clearing, the still, dank air clung to her face. Tufts of tangled grasses crowded around the crumbling headstones in the middle of the cemetery, but at the edge, the bushes covered them completely. Oppressive? Most definitely. Her stomach lurched with excitement, but again, she quickly tamped it down and got to work.

Opening the tripod, she balanced it on the uneven ground next to a stone cross. Something about it made her hesitate. The name was no longer legible and she paused to run a finger over the weathered, rough surface. Who was buried here, gone and forgotten? A man? A woman? A child?

She must have stared a little too long because her sinuses began to itch. She wrinkled her nose, tried to sniff away the sudden heavy weight pulling at her heart, but it didn't quite work. Would someone wonder about her, too? What she looked like. What kind of a person she was. How long from now? Months? Years, maybe? If she were lucky. But the thing was, there'd be no body in her grave.

Stop. Just stop it. Quit being so damn morbid. Normally she was pretty good at not thinking much about the future. Why worry about something completely out of her control? It had to be all these depressing cemeteries she'd been visiting lately.

She took a deep breath to change the unproductive air in her lungs, screwed the camera in place and exhaled, wrenching her mind back to the present where it needed to stay.

With every satisfying click of the shutter, the outside world became only what she could see through the viewfinder. The gravestones, the trees and the quiet loneliness.

When she finally stopped to examine the results, her pulse jumped like it always did when she captured something magical through the lens. They were good. Really good. Much better than the other locations. When she got to one particular image, she hesitated. The lengthening shadows stretched out over the headstones and mounds of grass like the distorted, tortured lines of Munch's painting, *The Scream,* and her spine prickled.

Or maybe it was the wind.

A slight breeze found its way into the open collar of her jacket, tickling her neck and ears, and stirring the branches of the watchful trees. She shivered and brushed her hair away from the lens.

Zombies? Dead eyes and insatiable cravings? She could totally visualize rotting hands stretching out of their graves here. Would Hollywood think so? That was the fifteen hundred dollar bonus question.

She twisted her hair up, clipped it off her neck, and dropped to the forest floor. Although it hadn't rained, moisture lingered everywhere and the ground smelled woodsy beneath her. She rolled over onto her back, again thankful she'd decided to keep the jacket on. A few wispy fronds of grass brushed her cheek and she batted them away. Twisting the lens to focus on the treetops, she—

A sound sliced through the silence of the graveyard and she froze.

A cry? A growl?

She patted her jacket pocket and felt the reassuring hard lump of her handgun.

Maybe it was just the squeak of tree limbs protesting against the wind. Of course it was. With shaking hands, she pushed herself to a sitting position just to make sure.

When she heard it again, she scrambled to her feet.

An animal. Definitely not a tree limb.

She held her breath and fixated on the spot at the edge of the cemetery where the noise originated.

A mound of leaves and branches moved. Twenty feet or so in front of her.

Her pulse thundered behind her eardrums. It was probably just a raccoon. But didn't they hiss? She took a step backwards, her gaze unwavering.

A badger? They were mean sons of bitches. No, this definitely didn't sound like the one that crawled into their tent on the last camping trip with her father all those years ago. This sounded bigger, different.

Her breath came out in shallow bursts as she glanced behind her. Okay. Her bike was about thirty steps away then up that slight embankment through the sticker bushes. If she ran, would the thing chase her? If she moved slowly, would it even follow? No, it was probably even more scared of her. She eased the camera strap around her neck and—

She heard it again.

This time it was unmistakable.

"Help me."

The pile of leaves shuffled, falling away to reveal a man hidden underneath. With a hand outstretched to her, he writhed as if in pain.

A man? What the hell? Here in the middle of nowhere? Should she run for help? Should she walk closer?

Even from this distance, she could see his brow furrowed in agony, his eyes desperate and hollow. He didn't appear to be in any shape to harm her. Besides, she had her gun.

Recalling her mother's stern warnings over the years, she paused. This couldn't have anything to do with her family, could it? Her cousin Stacy's face flashed in her memory along with the faded one of her father. But this wasn't the big city, nor was it summer. Two critical elements. Usually.

She placed a cool hand to her throat, the racing tempo of her heart slowed just a little, and she considered her options. Maybe this was his version of "here little girl, help me with my puppy." Clear out here though? It wasn't like this place got a lot of foot traffic.

He dropped his arm and his mouth moved silently. God, he really seemed hurt. She had to do something; she couldn't just leave him.

She pulled out her cell phone, punched 911, and kept a finger above the Send button. Shaking off myriad notions of zombies and cemeteries, she strode forward to the edge of the trees.

The man lay on his back, half-hidden under the leaves and branches, his clothes covered in dirt. Given his disheveled appearance, he looked like a vagrant. But as she raked her eyes over him, she noted his expensive-looking boots and pale blue dress shirt, and he, too, was wearing leather pants. Most definitely not homeless.

Torn and muddy, his shirt was unbuttoned, ripped open actually, revealing a dirt-smeared but well-defined chest. Some of his shoulder-length dark hair, tangled with bits of leaves and debris, seemed to be partially captured in a ponytail, but she couldn't be sure from this angle. His eyes, an electrifying shade of ice blue, pierced through her. She stopped a few feet away.

"What happened to you? Are you hurt?"

"I need...your help." His voice, slightly accented, was clearly laced with pain.

At that moment, the wind picked up and swirled at her feet as if urging her to move. The leaves around him danced on the air and settled slowly back to the ground. Stepping closer, she heard his sharp intake of breath. His eyes widened at first then narrowed to slits, and he shrank backwards into the leaves.

He couldn't be scared of her, could he? He was a tall man, athletic and powerfully built. Why would he be afraid of her?

"Stay away," he ordered. Given his condition, his forceful tone surprised her.

She didn't understand. Why the sudden turnabout? He clearly needed her help. He had to be hallucinating. How long had he been here anyway? Squatting down to appear less intimidating, she tucked her phone in her pocket and stretched out her hands like she would to a frightened dog. "It's okay. I won't hurt you. I can help."

Then she saw it. A hole in his mud-encrusted shirt. She hadn't noticed it right away because it was fairly small, the size of a quarter maybe, and he cradled his arm as if it were injured.

"Oh my God. Is that...blood? Have you been shot?"

As she sprang to his side, the last thing she remembered was the way his pupils suddenly dilated. Like a shark rolling back its eyes when it bites.

DIOS MIO. What have I done?

Even in his weakened condition, his senses dulled from the blood loss and the daylight, Dominic Serrano had caught the woman's scent before he saw her or sensed her energy trail. A mesmerizing fragrance wafted in the air around him and woke him from his stupor. He should have known though. He'd been in and out of consciousness all day, but he still should've known. Should have recognized it. *What an idiot.*

He had kicked off some of the branches when he spotted her, not more than a few paces away, and watched as the tall, slender woman took pictures of the old headstones. Her movements were graceful, almost feline, as she swung her body around for different camera angles. When she recklessly flipped those loose curls behind her shoulders to reveal a long shapely neck and large hoop earrings, he almost stopped breathing.

His eyes were glued to her; he was powerless to peel them away. But his heart thundered against his ribs and he hardened instantly when she bent forward and wrestled with her hair. Closing his eyes for a moment, he imagined her standing over him, straddling his body with those long legs.

What the hell was he thinking? For God's sake, he needed to ditch the fantasy shit and figure out how to—
She fell to the ground and all he could do was stare.

With a knee bent and a boot heel wedged into the forest floor for traction, she shimmied and wriggled, aiming the lens at the distant treetops above. And, sweet Jesus, he imagined her body squirming like that beneath him.

His sudden erection surged like a battering ram against the seams of his pants and he hurried to adjust the tight-fitting leather. But the minute he moved, scorching jolts of pain shot from his injured shoulder and he cried out in agony.

The woman sat up and looked in his direction.

Shit. He held his breath, remained motionless, and hoped she'd leave without seeing him. What the hell was wrong with him? He certainly didn't need another goddamn complication. But his arm lay awkwardly at his side, the throbbing intensity getting worse.

Sucking air through his teeth with a hiss, he inched his

good arm over his stomach to reposition the bad one, but the instant shattered bones grated against torn muscles and infected tissue, he couldn't help it.

He groaned again and she stared right at him.

Think. Think. It was getting late. Not much time before the Darkbloods would be back. They knew they'd shot him and they knew what he'd stolen.

With his barely functioning willpower, the woman was vulnerable to him. He would require more than the use of her cell phone as powerful urges simmered below the taut surface of his sensibilities. He tried not to feed from humans much, but at this point he was out of options. He had no other choice.

He called out to her and licked his dry lips. With that long hair cascading past her shoulder blades, it would encase his face as he drank from her, tickling his nose and giving his hands a luxurious anchor. He'd take just enough of her blood and energies, then send her away with memories of nothing. God, he was parched.

Although he sensed her fear, she came toward him with purpose in her stride. She moved with confidence, stepping over obstacles with a strong, even pace, unaccustomed to being afraid. Her curious green eyes locked onto his and he could think of little else except the mesmerizing sway of her hips. She stopped several feet away and appraised him.

He was about to ask her about her phone when his world caved in around him. The wind picked up and with it came her scent, swirling innocently in the leaves at first, then bashing him across the forehead like a lead pipe.

Dios mio. Sangre Dulce.

He wanted to pump his legs. To scramble away from

her. But his muscles were like stone. He was virtually paralyzed.

She was more than just vulnerable, he realized. She was in terrible danger. Not just from him, but from the Darkbloods. She had to run. Get away. Now.

He clamped his eyes shut, tried to block out this nightmare. What were the odds a rare sweetblood would be the one to find him? Their blood was almost irresistible to his kind. Yes, how goddamn ironic was that? He wouldn't drink from her. He couldn't.

Once he tasted the blood of Sangre Dulce, especially in his present condition, there'd be little hope of a successful Stop and Release, a fact he knew only too well. Baser, primitive instincts would take over and the immunity training, required of all Guardians with the Agency, wouldn't do him any good.

"Leave me alone." He clenched his teeth to keep his fangs from elongating, but it was no use. As they stretched from his gums, his control ebbed away.

When she leaned close and he smelled her sweet breath on his face, all rational thought vanished. The animal lying dormant inside knew just what to do. A hidden store of energy coursed through his veins and he pounced with the practiced grace of a tiger, rolled her to her back and enveloped her body with his. Before she could scream, he pressed his palms to her temples, entrancing her in the age-old trick of his kind to subdue its prey.

She would remember nothing of the terror. Nothing of the pain. Nothing of him. That is, if she survived.

Her eyes closed and her head lolled backward, exposing the smooth delicate skin of her neck to him. In one swift movement, he tossed aside her camera, yanked the jacket off one shoulder and tore the neck of her T-shirt.

With a growl, he plunged his teeth into her flesh.

Pulling hard at her vein, he consumed mouthful after mouthful of her warm, beautiful nectar. He'd never tasted anything so glorious. So sweet. So utterly perfect. Good God, it was as if she were created solely to nourish him. Her fresh scent overpowered his nostrils as her blood filled his mouth and danced on his tongue. Suckling like a baby at the breast, his whole body shuddered in ecstasy and euphoria embraced him as a lover.

Without breaking their contact, he slipped a practiced hand to her cheek and temple, and her concentrated warm energies sluiced into his body, rejuvenating him with shocking speed. The cocoon of her fragrant hair captured his breath against her neck, making a heated and welcoming hollow for his face, and he pushed her deeper into the pile of forest debris with the weight of his body.

A small voice at the back of his head told him to stop, but he shoved it aside.

He'd fed directly from humans before, probably more than he cared to admit, and he'd absorbed the energies of thousands, but never were any of them like this. He heard about the taste of sweetblood, all of them had, but no verbal description even came close to this delicious reality. And her energies? He'd never experienced anything like them before. There was nothing he couldn't do with her in his body, he realized. Impossible no longer existed.

Darkness licked at his soul as the fragile barrier between strongly held beliefs and suppressed instincts threatened to shatter around him. That voice again, deep inside, roared out like a freight train, calling him back.

Stop. You're killing her. You're not an animal.

Oh God, he did have to stop. Her pulse weakened under

his lips and he sensed her life energy slipping away. This was wrong. He knew it was.

Releasing her vein, he crouched over her and rubbed his mouth with the back of an unsteady hand. Her scent, her sweet scent, clung to every fiber of his being, seducing him back like an addiction.

A junkie desperate for another fix, he needed more of her. The blood, the warm energies. All of it. No one would know. It'd be easy to keep this secret from everyone. He'd dispose of the body so it wouldn't be found and she'd be just another missing person. Yes, that could work.

Move away from her. Remember Alfonso.

He pinched his eyes shut, scrambled backward and collapsed next to a tree. With his head cradled between his knees, he pulled at his hair and wished she had never found him.

He raised his head and forced himself to look at what he had done. There she was, nestled innocently in the leaves, unaware of the monster at her feet, her mouth ajar, hair billowing out behind her, and long dark lashes contrasting against the pale softness of her cheeks. He noticed a small mole on her upper lip, or maybe it was a dark freckle. It looked just like the one his mother used to draw on for vanity purposes.

Dios mio. What have I become?

His parents had fought so hard to elevate their kind to more than the thoughtless killers their ancestors had been. And now look at him. If his mother were alive, she'd be horrified at what he had done and everything it represented.

Another gust of wind blew through the forest, stirring the fir boughs into a rhythmic, fanning motion around him. Cool, fresh air brushed against his face, aerating him slightly and clearing out a tiny corner of his mind.

He forced himself to stand and staggered to the edge of the creek rollicking a few feet away. She was a magnet and it took every ounce of willpower to pry himself from her presence. His body cried out, wanting more, but his mind pulled him away.

He peeled off his shirt, thrust his head into the icy cold water, and pulled the tie from his ponytail. The rushing sound filled his ears and refreshed his head. Over and over he rinsed his mouth, trying to rid himself of her taste. He scrubbed his hair, his face, his neck, washing away her smell.

He rocked back on his heels, water dripping onto his bare shoulders, and he took a deep cleansing breath. He knew what he had to do. He was not going to end up like Alfonso. No way. He'd kill himself before he let what happened to his brother happen to him. His parents' memory deserved more than that.

He doused his shirt in the creek, rubbed the fibers of the fabric together as if he had soap. Then he wrung it out and wrapped it around his nose and mouth like a makeshift bandanna.

When he scooped the woman up, his sudden strength stunned him. She was hardly a wisp of air in his arms. Her lips had a bluish cast to them and her pulse was weak, but she was alive. Thank God. He barely noticed that the agonizing pain from the silver bullet was gone.

There was no time to think about what a monster he was. That he was actually capable of such a despicable atrocity. He would deal with that later. Right now, he had to get her away.

With her scent all over this place, he had no doubt

the Darkbloods would instantly abandon their search for him and focus on finding her instead. They'd go ape-shit when they smelled Sangre Dulce. And they had no qualms about killing. None.

He fished her keys from her tight leather pocket and stifled a bitter smile when he saw her juvenile key ring. Then, pausing to retrieve her camera, he cradled her body as gently as he could.

When her head rolled back, he saw two puncture holes on her graceful neck. He had backed away from her so quickly, he hadn't sealed the wound. Without much thought, he lifted the shirt from his mouth and touched his lips to her skin.

When they drank from a human, they were never to leave an unhealed mark, no trace, no memory. He might be a rebel in the Agency, but he was no fool. Shock registered a moment later, when he realized he'd somehow controlled the urge to feed from her again. Good, maybe he could do this thing.

As he emerged from the forest into the sun of the dead, his pupils tightened and he dipped his head to shield his eyes. He started to step back into the shadows before he realized he felt none of the expected burn and no measurable energy drain. When had he last been outside willingly during this restless time of day when the sun died and his people awaited its disappearance beyond the horizon? Except as a vampire youthling prior to the Time of Change, maybe never. After that point, the cravings began and they lived out their lives away from the weakening effects of sunlight.

Just through the trees, the cemetery signpost leaned into the bushes, its wooden placard dangling in the wind, jeering, mocking him. He bit down on his defiance and strode past. There was a time when he would've made the sign of the cross and offered up a prayer, but not any longer. And certainly not today.

He glanced up the dirt road, expecting to see a sassy little sports car or even a truck. Not a freaking white motorcycle. Who was this woman with a Hello Kitty keychain?

Hell, this was going to be interesting.

CHAPTER TWO

MACKENZIE COULDN'T REMEMBER ever having a migraine this bad. Her temples pounded like mallets as blazing sunlight penetrated her eyelids. She rolled over, covered her head with her pillow, but the throbbing pulse continued over and over in her skull.

Oh God, she felt like puking.

She dragged herself from the bed toward the bathroom, sheets tangled around her, but she took only a few steps before her head began spinning even faster and her knees buckled. She expected to hit the floor, and weakly stretched out her hands, but somehow she fell onto the bed instead.

She must've slept again, drifting in and out of consciousness in an endless stream of time. Damp coldness touched her forehead and neck. It felt so good. Drops of liquid touched the back of her tongue and slid down her throat. The deafening pounding in her head receded beat by beat as the pain fibers loosened their grip from behind her eyes.

When she opened her lids, probably much later, the room was darker than before. But given the small amount of light filtering in through the margins of the closed blinds, she knew it was still daytime.

Hadn't the blinds been open earlier? Stretching her arms up, she yawned and heard her shoulders crack. Was that migraine only a bad dream? She felt wonderfully refreshed now.

Several washcloths lay neatly folded on her night-stand and a glass of ice water sat on a coaster. That was strange. It wasn't like Samantha to look after her like this. Her housemate kept strange hours and was rarely home lately.

She looked around but couldn't quite put her finger on it. Everything looked the same and yet things felt… different. As though something had happened and she'd become aware of it after the fact. The little hairs on the nape of her neck prickled. Change hung invisibly in the air, like perfume lingering in an empty elevator.

How long had she slept? Glancing at her alarm clock, her jaw dropped.

What the…that couldn't be right. Three o'clock?

She grabbed her cell phone and flipped it open.

A full day gone? She racked her brain for any detail, something that would remind her of how she'd spent the last twenty-four hours.

She remembered riding out to the lonely cemetery, but that's where everything fogged. Crumbling headstones? Towering trees? Piles of leaves? Yes, she could almost feel them swirling around her legs, hear the wind rustling through branches.

She dug deep and massaged her scalp with her fingers, determined to loosen the memory. There had to be more. An almost faded feeling of dread and sadness wavered somewhere inside. And oddly enough, so did pleasure. She recalled taking a few pictures then…nothing. Could it all have been a dream?

She leaped from the bed, grabbed her camera and snapped the memory stick into the card reader of her computer. She sank into the chair and waited a few impatient moments for all the pictures to transfer. With a click, she opened her photo-editing software and sucked in a tentative breath. The first ones to pop up were of the old cemetery sign. Thank God, she hadn't imagined riding out there. She blew the air from her lungs in a quick burst of relief.

One by one, she scrolled through the images then emailed them to her boss. Wow, they were pretty damn good. So why couldn't she remember taking them?

She pinched her upper lip, massaged it between her thumb and forefinger, and rested her elbows on the top of the desk. There had to be a completely rational explanation. She paced around the room, then picked up her cell phone.

"Steve, yeah, it's me. I just emailed you the pics I took of that location yesterday."

She heard his fingers flying over the keyboard. "Got 'em." He paused and she held her breath. Would he like them or would he hate them?

"Hey, nice work. Are the specs here somewhere, too?" He spoke slowly, as if he were concentrating on the pictures.

The specs? Did she even take any measurements or assess the surroundings? "Uh, not yet. I had the mother of all migraines and just now got the chance to send the pictures. I'll get the specs to you as soon as I can."

"You're not sick, are you?" He was probably thankful they were talking on the phone. He had a major germ phobia.

"I don't think so, but…I sort of blacked out yesterday. I don't remember taking any of the photos I just sent you."

"Well, let's hope the pictures are good enough, then." He clearly wasn't concerned about her missing time. "Talked to Patsy at the production company. Turns out they're considering shooting the film up in Vancouver instead. Something about an actual haunted cemetery."

Crap. There went her bonus if they went to Canada. Steve talked about several other potential projects, but Mackenzie didn't really listen. The zombie picture, backed by a major studio, was the only one that promised decent money up front.

Maybe she shouldn't worry about her long-gone migraine and instead should think about how she was going to make her brother's tuition payment and get the damn car fixed. Why did big expenses always seem to happen at the same time?

She examined her face in the bathroom mirror, lifted her chin and moved her head from side to side. No dark circles under her eyes, no tired lids. Just refreshed, as if she'd had a great night's sleep. She reached into the top drawer and grabbed a handful of peanut M&M's. A large unopened package of candy lay next to the opened one. When had she bought that?

She padded out to the bedroom door and cracked it an inch.

"Sam? You there?"

No answer. She waited a moment then called again. Nothing. The house was silent. What would her roommate be doing digging through her bathroom drawers? Had she eaten the candy, then felt guilty and bought more?

In one bite, she crammed the chocolate pieces into her mouth, turned back to the bathroom and stepped into the shower. Maybe she'd gotten sick and blacked out. Food poisoning? What had she eaten yesterday? Cold pizza?

As she shampooed her hair, her mind ran through the gamut of possibilities. At twenty-six, Mackenzie doubted she had Alzheimer's like her mother, but losing an entire day with no recollection plucked at the tight order of her life.

She stretched her arms overhead and flexed her muscles. Her temples tingled, probably just remnants of the migraine, but the sensation wasn't painful. It made her feel…happy? Content? How weird.

She rinsed off and debated hitting the gym, something she rarely felt like doing. With the photos emailed and no classes to teach at the art school, she had the rest of the day free. She should probably go visit her mother, but maybe she'd organize her bedroom closet instead.

Then it struck her. How the hell had she gotten home?

She turned the water off with a jarring crank of old pipes, grabbed a bath towel and ran down the stairs, dripping wet, almost slipping on the bottom step. She skidded through the kitchen and wrenched open the garage door.

Thank God. It was there. But a niggling feeling tugged at the back of her neck as she stared. Her bike was parked on Sam's side of the garage.

What was going on? Had she lost her mind?

Organized to the point that her brother called her anal, she wasn't used to feeling so out of control. Maybe she really was going a little crazy. Maybe she did need to see a doctor.

Water from her hair dripped down her back. She wrapped her head with the towel, genie-style, and imagined what Samantha would think if she walked in right now. She'd certainly think Mackenzie was nuts. Although

Sam worked at a spa and wasn't a stranger to seeing naked women's bodies, she just hadn't seen this particular one before.

Mackenzie had started back inside when she had a thought.

She approached the bike, opened one of the saddlebags, and sifted through the contents. Where was her tripod? Normally she kept it stored there. Less of a chance she'd forget to bring it on a shoot if she happened to need one. And she hadn't seen the thing in her room, either.

She noticed her field notebook tucked on its side and flipped through the pages. There were no notes pertaining to the Bear Creek Pioneer Cemetery. No measurements, no sketches, nothing. What the hell happened? Had she forgotten to do them?

She wandered back inside and pressed a few buttons on the espresso maker next to the kitchen window. The high-pitched sound of the grinder echoed in the room and the air filled with the aroma of coffee beans. With a hand on her toweled head, she leaned over the sink to get a better view of her mother's bird feeder hanging just outside the window overlooking the backyard. The thing was almost empty again. Stupid squirrels.

Her temples began to vibrate, the tingling suddenly replaced by a low buzzing hum. The migraine wasn't coming back, was it? She put the heel of her hand to her forehead, pressing up on her eyebrows. No. Her head didn't hurt. Just felt a little strange. She stretched on her tiptoes, reached into the cupboard on the other side of the window and grabbed a coffee cup.

Sweet Jesus.

The oath rang through her head, deep and hoarse. A man's voice.

She spun around in confusion, the mug slipping from her fingers and clattering to the counter. Where did that come from?

I could just…damn…she's so…

Words and sentence fragments tumbled into her head from elsewhere but it made no sense. God, what was happening to her? Was she really losing her mind?

"Hello? Sam?" Barely able to eke the words out, she knew her roommate was gone, but she called to her anyway, hoping Sam would answer, though the voice was clearly male. "Who's there?"

She yanked the towel from her hair and wrapped it around herself in an attempt to cover up. Her heart hammered out a deafening staccato in her chest, while the atmosphere seemed to shift around her as if someone was near. She pulled a large knife from the cutting block, held her other palm to the hilt as she'd been taught and backed up until the edge of the countertop stopped her from going farther.

The words felt as if they had been projected into her head rather than spoken aloud. With the noise from the espresso machine, someone would need to shout for her to even hear them. And what she heard was crystal clear. It just didn't make sense. She must be going crazy or—

Exquisite…so frightened…I wish…can she hear…

She ran into the dining room, pointing the blade out wildly in front of her. Her temples continued to vibrate and she rubbed her forehead with the back of her knife hand.

Oh God, was this it? Was this what had happened to her father when he disappeared all those years ago? And Stacy?

A surge of strangling heat started at her toes and rose

upward, clutching at her chest and pythoning her airways. She could hardly breathe.

It couldn't be. It couldn't be happening. Good Lord, no.

Then, like the snap of an off-switch, the vibration in her head stopped. Gone.

Relief flooded over her and she dropped the knife on the dining room table. She drew in a few raspy breaths and the constricting panic disappeared, fading into a calm assurance that she was safe.

What happened to her father had nothing to do with this. She didn't know why. She just knew.

Seconds ticked into minutes and her breath eventually evened out.

Although she didn't hear the voice again, something tangible still called to her. A silent longing tugged at her heart as an ache settled into her bones.

Her lips throbbed, felt swollen, and she detected a slow rhythmic sensation in her head. Not painful, just strange. It didn't seem to match that of her own heart doing cartwheels and clanging around her rib cage. The sound in her temples was steady and quietly reassuring.

Two heartbeats? Okay, think. Well, she knew she couldn't be pregnant. It took a man as well as a body capable of carrying a child. Two things she didn't have. No, definitely not pregnant.

What about the missing chunk of time? What if… She felt between her legs and rubbed her hands over her breasts. Nothing. She'd know if she'd had sex last night, especially since it had been ages. No, she was positive she hadn't been with a man.

Could the migraine be coming back? What the hell was happening to her? She needed to seriously calm down and figure this out. There had to be a completely rational explanation for this…this…whatever this was.

Air. She needed fresh air. She flung open the French doors of the dining room, and a rush of coolness whispered over her damp skin and hair as she scanned the perimeter of her backyard. For what, she had no idea.

The dewy green of spring was everywhere and her cherry tree was starting to blossom. Ceramic pots on the patio waited to be filled with flowers, and a swallow swooped under the eaves, its beak filled with bits of dried grass. Everything seemed the same, normal, but she knew things weren't.

She concentrated on the slow thumping beat in her head, rather than her racing heart and was startled to find that the more she focused on it, the more comforting it became. Gradually, the tempo of the two beats got closer together and eventually meshed into one.

One rhythm. One sound. One heartbeat.

She leaned against the doorjamb, her skin flushed hot, and for some crazy reason, she imagined the crush of a man's muscular body against hers. She closed her eyes, wrapped her arms around her toweled body, and could almost feel the strong muscles of his shoulders moving beneath her hands. The musky fragrance of his passion in her lungs. Wetness surged between her legs as if her body were readying itself for him.

Her breath came in short bursts, and drawn to the backyard by an invisible thread, she stepped onto the patio. Like an electric charge, an unseen yet shimmering presence in the air, something called to her. She wanted to respond, to answer, but she didn't know how.

Then, just as it had started, the second heartbeat was gone. Not a gradual fading, but a tearing away. A bandage ripped from a wound. She waited a few moments, but it was gone.

Shuffling back inside, she collapsed into a chair.

What the hell just happened?

She had to be losing it. Or going completely mental—as her mother's British friend at the nursing home would say. Imaginary orgasmic sensations? Oh great, how would she explain that one to a doctor?

"Well, I was home alone, when I heard an imaginary guy talking to me, and then I almost had a real orgasm."

Yeah, right. Can you say crazy? She forced herself to laugh, hoping to lighten her mood so she could think more clearly.

But there was something about the voice in her head that nagged at her. Like she should know it. Like she had heard it before. She racked her brain but came up with nothing.

And what about her missing day? What the heck was going on?

She took a deep breath, squared her shoulders and pushed away from the table. No sense wasting time worrying or pondering. She would do what she always did—she'd either find some answers or she'd quit dwelling on things she had no control over and move on. She'd had a lot of practice with that.

After mopping up all the water she'd tracked in from her shower, she finished getting ready and jumped on the Triumph. Armed with a plan, she roared out of the garage.

THIS CAN'T be happening. It's just a Hill Country legend. An old Cantabrian myth. Not real.

Dom swung his silver Porsche away from the curb and followed the woman—Mackenzie—through her neighborhood and onto a major thoroughfare. With a bandanna on her head and two braided pigtails bouncing on her back, she handled the bike deftly. Where was her goddamn helmet?

Of course, he had heard the old stories told during the Feast of the Longest Day. But that was all they were. Stories. No one actually knew anyone who became telepathic and bonded through blood sharing. And certainly not with a human. It was just a tale about sex and love told by the elders late at night around the bonfires. A gothic romance causing girls to swoon and boys to snicker. No one thought it had any basis in reality.

But what else could it be? She clearly heard his thoughts and he had heard hers. If he hadn't made that realization and shut his mind off to her, who knew what she would have done with that knife. There were stories of that, as well. And for God's sake, they'd practically made love from a distance. His balls still ached.

After he had nursed her through the night and most of the day, when he was confident her condition had improved enough, he planned to drive out of her life. He didn't have time for this. So why was he following her?

He really should turn around, head home. She looked fine now. But when he lifted his foot off the accelerator, a pain cut into his gut like a blunt knife. He needed to flick the turn signal, crank the steering wheel, but he couldn't make himself do it. He rubbed a hand over his chest, which actually ached. When he pressed down on the pedal again and the vehicle moved a little closer, the pain faded away.

What the hell was going on? This seemed much more

than just a sweetblood attraction. Alfonso had never mentioned any of this shit happening to him.

And where was she going? He didn't dare probe her mind to find out. If things felt to her as they did to him, the sounds in her head might cause her to run off the road. Could she feel him, too, and just not understand the sensation? Unlike his thoughts, his presence was something he couldn't block from her.

She turned the bike onto the freeway on-ramp and headed north. The aching pit in his gut expanded and he knew it was worry.

Then his phone rang. Santiago. The Region Commander.

And the pit stretched wider.

"Dom, how'd it go? Get it locked up with that woman?"

"A little too locked up, I'd say."

She wove in and out of cars like a lunatic on that bike. It was the tail-end of rush hour and traffic was still heavy on the wet roadways.

"How so?" Santiago sounded apprehensive, like he was ready to get pissed off. "Wait. Are you in the car? At this hour?"

"Uh, yes." Dom gritted his teeth, preparing himself for the inevitable verbal onslaught. "Remember when we talked last night and I told you the woman was dying? Lips turning blue? Vital signs weakening?"

"Don't fuckin' tell me. Don't you say it. I told you to just walk away."

"Well, I didn't."

"And you—" Dom turned down the volume as his boss yelled.

He knew Santiago would freak out. What did he

expect? Dom would be lucky not to be hauled in front of the Council. What he'd done this time was more than just a simple infraction.

Although she was five or six cars ahead of him, he could see the exposed skin on her back between her jacket and the low waistband of her jeans. Was everyone else on the road staring at the same tantalizing inch he was? White-knuckling it, he accelerated and the Porsche surged forward.

"Listen. She was going downhill fast and I thought she wouldn't make it. It was a small amount. Just a couple drops of my blood. She appears to be doing fine now, so it worked. But there's a little problem."

"More than an illegal blood transfer? What could be worse than that, Dom? What in God's name could possibly be worse?"

Mackenzie changed lanes, spraying an arc of standing water and causing the car behind her to slam on its brakes. What the hell was she doing riding a motorcycle with these road conditions anyway? He eased up on the gas and the Porsche downshifted automatically. Seeing an opening ahead, he cranked the wheel and accelerated into the next lane.

"In addition to a sudden lack of UV sensitivity, I am— She is— We're telepathic." There, he said it.

"You're what?"

"I can hear her and she can hear me. Thank God I was able to set up a mental barrier when I realized she could hear my thoughts, but there was nothing I could do about her feeling my presence until I left."

Santiago was uncharacteristically quiet.

"You still there?"

"You're not shitting me, are you?"

"This isn't a damn joke. I'd walk away right now and forget all about this mind-reading bullshit, but she's still in danger." That wasn't the only reason he didn't want to walk away, but he wasn't about to tell Santiago about the stabbing feeling inside when he thought about leaving her. Hell, he didn't understand it himself.

"Goddamn it. You never should've done it in the first place. You know better than to blood-share with a human. And now you put me in a position where I should report your actions to the Council. Then you'll really be screwed. What the hell is wrong with you?"

"Whatever. Do what you need to do. Screw them."

"At this rate, you're going to be stuck up here forever. I thought you wanted to get back to one of the southern field offices. Where all the Darkblood action is."

"She would've died without it."

"Humans die every day. We can't get involved in their affairs beyond just covert protection from Darkbloods."

"Yes, well, they don't die because of me." Dom jabbed the climate control button and cranked the A/C, but the cold air did little to cool him off.

If Santiago launched into his standard lecture about there being billions of humans on this earth, but very few vampires, or that humans represent the grains of sand on a beach whereas the number of vampires could be sifted through your fingers, Dom was going to need another new phone. He'd been a Guardian almost as long as Santiago and he sure as hell didn't need to hear another patronizing sermon outlining the concerns of the Council and reminding him what he should and shouldn't do.

Santiago was silent for a few moments. "Where are you headed now?"

"She's going back to the cemetery where she found

me, if she gets there alive. She drives like a goddamn maniac." His jaw ached from clenching it so tightly. "I think she's trying to piece together why she blacked out. Her last memory is from there."

"Did you sweep it yet?"

"No, and her scent is all over that place. When I brought her home, I took evasive measures and hid our trail. If the Darkbloods showed up at the cemetery last night, they wouldn't have been able to follow us. But, if they're slow and track me there tonight, her new scent will lead straight back to her house. I've got to do something to cover it up again."

He eased up on the accelerator and concentrated on hanging back a little farther. It made him inexplicably nervous having her too far away.

"Seems a little excessive. Didn't you use any scent neutralizing granules? They do an adequate job of absorbing the trace of a sweetblood."

Dom choked back a few swearwords. Was he serious? "That carbon crap works only temporarily and only if the Darkblood forgets to breathe or has a sudden allergy attack."

"Oh for chrissake, they're effective enough. Why don't you call someone for backup then, if you're so worried about them tracking her? Who do you have on duty tonight?"

There weren't many choices. They ran a lean operation.

"Foss." But the thought of having the biggest manwhore in the Guardian ranks anywhere near the woman made him nauseous as hell.

"Hey, where the hell is that data? I've been waiting for you to upload it."

Dom steeled his shoulders to prepare himself for Santiago's inevitable reaction. "As soon as I can locate the phone I downloaded it to. I dropped it sometime after I was shot and because I floated so far downstream, the phone could be anywhere. And, most likely, it's no longer functioning." He should have searched for it immediately, but strangely enough, it hadn't crossed his mind until now. "I'll find it."

Santiago let loose with a volley of foreign profanity Dom had never heard before. Yes, his boss definitely had a way with words.

"I'll see if we can pick up its GPS signal. You'd better pray you find it. That mission cost us a lot. Stryker was hit after the two of you split up."

Oh, shit. His new guy. "Is he okay? What happened?" He shouldn't have allowed someone as inexperienced as Mitchell Stryker in the kill zone, but when they hacked into the Darkblood system, they'd been so focused on copying everything, he'd forgotten all about protocol.

"Yeah, you cut out on our conversation last night before I could tell you. He's still in the clinic. Shot by a silvie, just like you were. But he didn't hit pay dirt and run into a sweetblood."

Clamping his teeth together, Dom's pulse jackhammered behind his eyeballs. He took a couple of deep breaths and willed himself to calm down. He wanted to acquaint his boss with some of his own favorite swearwords, foreign and domestic, but biting Santiago's head off would only anger him more and Dom needed him on his side. The Council could kick his ass to a really remote location if he wasn't careful.

Then he'd be even farther from *him*. From the whole reason he joined the Agency.

In a scene he'd pictured in his mind every night for the past century, Dom visualized his hands around *his* neck, choking the air from stale lungs, before he crammed a stake into his black heart and spit on the ashes. Being a field team leader all the way up here was bad enough. Where else could they send him? Anchorage?

He mentally shook off those images and forced himself to think about Stryker. "What's his prognosis? Will he be all right?" Mitchell was a good guy. A little over-eager, but he reminded Dom of himself when he first started with the Agency. He'd visit him when he finished to-night.

"He'll be fine in a week or two. Bullet got him in the thigh. Staff tells me he's been asking about you. So how's the shoulder doing?"

Dom had actually forgotten all about it. Reaching a hand into the open collar of his shirt, he shrugged, half-expecting to feel a twinge, a pull, something. But he felt nothing. Even the skin of his shoulder was smooth, as if he'd never been shot. He kneaded the muscle a few times just to make sure. "Fine, I guess."

"Sangre Dulce blood is very healing in addition to the incredible rush, right?" Santiago dropped his voice. "So how was it? I've only heard the stories. I still can't believe you did a Stop and Release on a sweetblood in your condition. A goddamn S and R." He whistled into the phone.

"You can't imagine. Drinking from her was so…" He searched for the right word. *Utterly exquisite* and *complete perfection* came to mind. But these were private recollections and he didn't want to share them. "Amazing." Generic enough, he supposed.

"What's up with you? I can't remember when I've ever

heard you so affected by a woman. Sure you didn't prong her with the sharps *and* the blunt?"

"Fuck no. That's the last thing on my mind." Did he sound convincing?

Santiago's laugh reflected his apparent disbelief. Guess not. Oh well, his boss could think what he wanted.

"Given just its taste, can you understand why there's such a huge black market for the shit?"

"Unfortunately, yes, I can." And that's what worried him. Now that he knew what it was like, he didn't want to be tempted again. It was one thing to wonder, but it was completely different to know for sure.

CHAPTER THREE

AT THE CEMETERY, Mackenzie retied the red bandanna, flung her thick braids in front of her shoulders and grabbed her notepad. With the sun already dipping below the tops of the trees, she had only an hour or so to wrap things up.

Squinting in the direction she came, she estimated the distance from the paved road to the cemetery entrance. It was too far to pace off. A mile? Two miles? She'd clock it on the odometer when she left. After measuring the width of the gravel road, she scribbled the figures in her notebook. The camera and equipment trucks took up a lot of space, as did the large special effects trailer, but this road had no shoulder. Where would they all park? They'd have to drive the rigs in single-file. Would there even be enough room to pass another vehicle if they needed to move one closer? Access might be the real problem here.

Her research seemed correct that this was an old logging road, but she jumped back on her bike to explore a little farther.

Just around the corner, a rickety bridge spanned what was probably Bear Creek and her stomach sank. With a missing railing and cracked wooden slats, it couldn't accommodate a heavy vehicle. The crew wouldn't be able to park beyond the bridge, which didn't give them a lot of room. After snapping a couple of pictures anyway, she climbed on the bike and headed back to the cemetery entrance.

At least it was only a one- or two-day shoot with none of the main actors and only a handful of extras. They didn't need to accommodate a huge catering facility and provide private dressing rooms. Most of it was just special effects stuff. Yeah, maybe it could still work.

She licked a fingertip and flipped through the pages of her notebook. It looked like she'd gotten everything. After she tucked the pad and camera into the saddlebag, she grabbed her gun and stuffed it into her pocket. Now it was time for a different set of answers. Maybe something in the cemetery would jump-start her memory.

The clearing was cool and damp and the wind whispered through the branches of the trees, lifting them in an orchestrated wave as if welcoming her back. She took a deep breath and shivered, nervous about what she may find.

Stepping over the headstones, she swept her gaze over the pale green mounds of tufted grass and weeds that seemed to cover everything. She spied a familiar marker but wasn't sure if she recognized it from being here yesterday or from the photos she'd reviewed back home today.

Then she spotted it. Her portable tripod. It lay on its side, still fully extended, as if she had removed the camera and left it there. How could that have happened? It was almost second nature to grab it when she did a shoot. *Camera strap around the neck, unhook the camera, grab the tripod, fold up the legs.* She'd done it so many times and she'd never left it behind before. Had she been distracted or startled yesterday? A chill snaked up her spine.

Distracted or startled by what?

She turned slowly, making a complete circle as her eyes combed the forest perimeter. Did this look familiar? Yes, maybe.

Drawn to the sound of water, she zigzagged around the crumbled tombstones to the edge of the cemetery. Beneath the canopy of a huge old cedar, she saw a large pile of leaves and the hairs on the back of her neck prickled. She slipped a hand into her pocket and touched the gun for reassurance.

Something crunched underneath her boot when she shuffled through the leaves. She stooped and found a hair clip. Hers? The plastic was cracked, the spring was broken, and it looked like the type she wore. But if she'd been right here, why couldn't she remember? Had she fallen and hit her head?

She stared at the leaves and brushed her hand over the surface, stirring them up. Unlike the other piles, these were dry, protected under the thick canopy of the cedar tree. She picked up a handful. They smelled like the forest. With her eyes closed, she rubbed them against her cheek. Stiff, crisp…and familiar. But the memory was just beyond her reach—she couldn't determine how to pluck it out. Crunching the leaves in her hand, she blew the pieces into the air and they fluttered to the ground.

She stepped through the bushes and down to the creek. Six or seven feet across and only a foot or two deep, the crystal-clear water flowed over a layer of dark-colored stones.

A small sandbar, bathed in sunlight, lined the bank on the far side and looked inviting. With the gentle sound of the running water, the hard knots of tension lodged between her shoulder blades seemed to loosen. She turned to walk upstream along the edge, but the undergrowth was thick with thorny blackberries and waist-high marsh grasses that looked like giant mop heads.

She stripped off her boots and socks, rolled up her jeans and sloshed to the other side. When she plopped down onto the sand, a gust of wind, warm with the promise of summer, ruffled her hair. She closed her eyes, just for a minute, and the ever-present tingling—an almost constant sensation since she'd woken up this afternoon—fluttered against her temples.

A twig snapped on the other side of the creek and she sat up. God, had she actually dozed off? She noticed the shadows had lengthened and the sun had dropped lower in the sky. When she bent to pick up her boots and tripod, the sun glinted off an object half-submerged in the sand.

A cell phone.

How did that get here? Even after she brushed off the sand, she had a hard time sliding it open. The touchpad screen was shattered. With a little bit of effort, she forced the phone closed again and rolled it around in her hands. Probably water damaged. She held it to her cheek; the molded plastic felt warm from the sun.

Small and sleek, it had to be a fairly new model. Maybe the contact numbers could still be extracted. Those were always a bitch to re-create. She'd take it to a cell phone store to see if they could find the owner.

With the tripod in one hand and her boots in the other, she stepped back into the creek and hurriedly sloshed through the water. But before she reached the far side, her foot slipped on the smooth river stones and she shrieked.

Helicoptering her arms, she tried to catch herself, but she fell to her knees, submerging her boots and tripod.

She patted her pocket. The gun and the phone were safe. But crap, the ride home was going to be frigid.

"JACKSON, YOU all set? She's coming."

"Yep, I'm ready, although I think you're going way overboard with this convoluted scent-masking scheme."

"Just do as I say." If only Dom could let her go straight home. Or better yet, invite her into his warm car with its heated seats. But it was crucial to confuse her trail if any Darkbloods got to the cemetery looking for him. They'd pick up her scent and follow her like bloodhounds. This was the only way to make sure they couldn't track her.

He sensed her discomfort and wished there was something he could do. When he saw her fall in the creek, he had jumped to help, but he had to stop himself and could only watch as she got drenched.

After her bike roared past his location in the trees, he waited a few impatient moments before following.

"Where do you have the first detour?" Dom gritted his teeth as he glanced at the speedometer. Did she even know what a speed limit was?

"At Maple Grove Road. She'll want to turn right, but I've got the road closure barricade set up and she'll have to turn left. Hope there isn't much traffic."

"There shouldn't be. Just don't lose her, all right? And don't get too close. Don't forget she's a sweetblood." Why in the hell had he let Foss set up the detours anyway? He should've done it himself.

"Yeah, yeah, yeah. Here she comes now." Jackson paused and Dom heard the low rumble of her bike through the phone. "Oh shit, dude, she's pissed." As Foss erupted in snorts of laughter, Dom bristled. "She didn't see the sign until she was almost on it. She pulled a Uey and kicked the damn thing over. You should've seen her whip that bike around. And when she drove away... Man, she's hot."

Dom nearly ran the Porsche off the road. Cursing under his breath, he told himself to stay calm.

"Gotta get the next one ready." Jackson laughed and the line went dead.

Dom drove straight to Mackenzie's house, laying down masking scent as Jackson did on the long route. After parking down the block, he reclined the seat and popped in a CD. His shoulders ached and he reached back to rub the knotted muscles. Taking a deep breath, he tried to relax. The circuitous route home should put her back here in thirty or forty minutes. No big deal.

But what about that phone? Her finding it screwed up everything. How was he going to get it back? The data might not be retrievable, the device might be too damaged, but he still had to try. He'd just let himself into her house tonight and take it. That's all there was to it. Then he'd be done with this.

He glanced at his watch, ran his fingers through his hair. She should be pulling in soon but he didn't sense her presence yet. What the hell? His fingers drummed the back of his headrest, then the steering wheel, and he inspected his watch again. Technically, they weren't really late. The half-hour timeframe was merely an approximation.

Fifteen minutes later, he texted Jackson. *Be there soon,* was the reply. After goose bumps prickled his arms and he shivered, he realized he was sensing her chills.

He couldn't bear to sit inside any longer. When he

climbed out of the car, the peppery smell of wet pavement and the sound of spring frogs hidden in the dark reminded him he was among the calm energies of the Seattle area, not the volatile ones he was used to in the South.

He paced the sidewalk for what seemed like a millennium, memorizing every crack, every stray weed, and the license plate numbers of every car on her block. Picking up snippets of her neighbors' lives, he heard a blaring television, an argument with kids about bath-time, and one neighbor was fucking someone who wasn't his wife. Christ.

When he didn't think he could take it a moment longer, a single headlight flashed in the distance and he heard the low rumble of her motorcycle. He leaned on the hood of the car and his head slumped with relief. Finally, he could breathe again. Although he sensed how cold she was, she was here. She was fine. She pulled into her garage and disappeared into the house.

Minutes later, two headlights appeared and a jacked-up black 4x4 pulled in behind the Porsche. He had Foss by the neck before he could put the vehicle in Park. Dom leaned in close, his fangs extended.

"What the hell did you do to her?"

"Jesus, Dom, what's wrong with you? Get off me."

"Did you touch her?" His thumb and fingers tightened around his friend's larynx as he took a deep whiff, sniffing for any sign of *her*. Nothing.

"No. What the hell's your problem?" Jackson choked.

Relieved on one level, but still pissed off, Dom loosened his grip and Jackson shoved him away.

"What took you so long? You should have had her back thirty minutes ago."

"It's not like I'm some weakass Darkblood wanting to

suck anything with two legs and a pulse," Jackson said as he rubbed his neck, "even if she is a sweetblood. She got pulled over by the cops. No helmet. Talked her way out of a ticket though. Since when did you become so protective?"

"Why didn't you call or text me?"

"I had a few more detours to set up. You should've seen her. Every time she'd come to one, she'd kick at it. God, it was hilarious. This one time—"

"You were only supposed to do three. She's freezing, for God's sake. Did that ever cross your mind?"

"Sorry, man, you're right. But if you could have seen her…" Foss looked up with a dreamy smile, and Dom wanted to wipe it from his face.

Rage boiled just below the surface, threatening to overflow, and his fangs ached. He never should've let Foss get so close to her.

Jackson cocked an eyebrow. "What is *wrong* with you? I swear I didn't touch her. She's a hottie, but she's yours. I get that."

"She's not mine." Dom wrenched open the door of the Porsche.

"Could've fuckin' fooled me."

CHAPTER FOUR

THE BAND AT Big Daddy's was getting ready to play their final set and most of the patrons were on their third or fourth pitcher of Friday night refreshment. People crowded the pool tables and lines formed at every dartboard.

"Can I get you anything else, sugar?" The waitress leaned over Dom's table to adjust the location of the salt shaker and her large breasts dangled in his face.

He pushed himself back slightly and saw her tongue dart from the corner of her over-glossed lips. She was offering him more than just beer, but he was definitely not interested.

"Two Hefeweizens."

"Two? How 'bout a pitcher. It's a better deal." She put her hand on his shoulder. The rose tattoo on her right breast hovered at eye level, the name Lenny entwined in the stem. "Expecting company?"

"Yes, and here she is. Two beers. And a straw."

"Alrighty, then." She pulled one from her apron pocket and turned around as a lanky woman approached the table with a swagger that belonged on a Fashion Week runway. "Day-um," the waitress muttered under her breath and walked away.

The blonde's painted-on low-rise jeans barely covered her ass and her red heels screamed "come fuck me." One guy fell over in his chair, gaping, as she sauntered past him, her belly-button chain swinging with each step. Dom rolled his eyes and smiled when he saw it was a diamond-encrusted arrow pointing down. Shock and awe had always been her motto. Some things never changed.

"Lily." Dom stood and hugged her. She air-kissed him on both cheeks and rested her hands, with red-tipped fingernails, lightly on his biceps. Holding her at arm's length, his eyes raked her up and down. She loved the admiration and, as a good friend he needed a favor from, he wanted to feed her ego. "Stunning as usual. I think there's a collective heart attack going on in here."

"Thanks, love." Her breathy just-out-of-bed voice always caught him off guard. She ran a hand down her stick-straight, shoulder-length hair, flicking the ends through her fingers. Leaning in close, she inhaled with half-closed eyes. He stiffened his shoulders and got ready for what he knew was coming.

"Mmm. You smell positively mouthwatering." She slid a hand down to his ass and, with a grunt, yanked his hips close then let go.

"Thanks." He laughed and pulled out her chair.

She hung her purse on the seat back and sat down just as the waitress returned with their drinks.

"May I? That's a beautiful tattoo." Lily stretched her palms out and took the woman's hand. She ignored the colorful Lenny tattoo and pretended to be engrossed in the plain barbed wire one on the woman's arm, but Dom knew better. "Nice. Very nice." Lily's eyes fluttered and the corners of her mouth turned up.

"Uh, thanks." The waitress lifted her free hand to her mouth and yawned.

Lily loosened her grip and the woman pulled away, blinked a few times and walked slowly back to the bar.

"Shit, Lily. You couldn't wait?"

"Sorry. Been with the fam all week up in Whistler and I was low on energy. I was slogging." She reached her arms overhead and her shoulders cracked. "Ahhh, much better. So what's the job, love? Your text was cryptic." She unwrapped the straw, put it in her beer and took a long sip.

"I need your help to close an assignment."

The driving beat of a bass drum filled the air, followed by a screeching guitar. The lead singer straddled the microphone stand and began to sing. Not bad. Dom hadn't heard a cover of this song before. With the loud background noise, no one would be able to hear their conversation.

"Three days ago, my team uncovered a Darkblood den. I had just uploaded some data from their computer when they surprised us. We managed to take a couple of them out, but Stryker and I were shot. With silvies."

"You obviously had on your gear, eh?"

Dom took a drink and shook his head. "No. Didn't see the need. Our intel hasn't confirmed the usage of silver-tipped bullets by any Northwest cells yet. These boys are pretty unsophisticated up here. Didn't know they had them."

"Yet? Are you all pigheaded idiots? It was just a matter of time. All the DBs in the South are using them—you know that. Didn't you get the Agency directive instructing all agents to wear protection when out on patrol?"

"Yes. And your point is…?"

"My point is that you could've been killed, or worse. Some body parts don't regenerate as completely as others. Didn't you hear about Eddie Bale in Costa Rica? Almost got his head shot off with a silvie and they've had a heck of a time with the skin grafts. Even after they flew him to that burn center in New York."

"I hate those damn vests. Besides, a vest wouldn't have helped Eddie anyway. Next thing you know, the Agency's going to make us wear helmets. What we do is dangerous. If that bothered me in the slightest, I'd have chosen another line of work. Like owning a bar."

A loud ruckus broke out near the pool tables as a couple of cops cuffed an old guy with a long, thinning comb-over and hauled him through the crowd. When he refused to walk, they grabbed him by each arm and dragged him outside to a waiting patrol car. Dom turned his attention back to Lily.

"Three days ago you were shot with a silvie?" She pursed her lips, obviously contemplating what he had said. "Impossible. You'd still be flat on your ass."

"That's why I called you here. A couple of DBs came after me, but I managed to dodge them early in the morning and bury myself in the woods. Then a sweetblood found me. And you don't have to guess to know what happened next."

Lily whistled. "Shit, Dom. Did you drain him? Her? That explains the speedy recovery. And your fabulous smell." She grabbed his arm and pressed her nose to the inside of his wrist. "Her, right?"

He pointedly ignored her question and withdrew his hand. "I need your help. Foss and I covered up the scent trail, but in order to wrap up the assignment, I wanted to see if you could detect any lingering traces. To make sure the Darkbloods can't track the scent back."

She played with her straw and scowled into her glass. When she met his gaze, his gut clenched. He really didn't want to explain it to her when he didn't understand it himself. Besides, the whole experience seemed too personal, too intimate to discuss. He wasn't like Jackson, or Lily, for that matter, who loved recounting their exploits to anyone with a set of ears. Not his style. Or at least it wasn't now.

"Seems like a bit of an overkill, don't you think? I'm sure you and Jackson covered the trail well enough." Her hawkish eyes appraised him. He wasn't going to get anything past her.

"I just want to be sure." Leaning back in his seat, he forced himself to tap his fingers to the music, pretending to be focused on the band. He could almost hear the cogs in Lily's head turning. *No goddamn questions. Just take the assignment.*

"It's a woman, eh?" She reached over and put her hand on his wrist. She was too perceptive. Or maybe he was just a poor actor. He attempted to keep his face expressionless, hard. "And you have feelings for her. I'm right, aren't I?"

He didn't know what he was feeling. "It's a woman." He tried to sound emotionless.

"What's going on? Talk. I can tell something's up. I know you too well."

For chrissake. Running a hand through his hair, he took a deep breath and resigned himself to the inevitable *Oprah*-like scrutiny. Feelings and talking and shit.

"The strangest thing happened. I almost drained her so I had to do a blood transfer." She sat up straight and her eyes widened. "Spare me the lecture, Lil. Santiago knows about it and is probably going to report it to the Council. The bigger problem is now she and I have this weird connection, some kind of strange bond, yet we've never talked. She's never seen me, or at least she doesn't remember seeing me. I wiped her memory."

As he recounted the incident at Mackenzie's house, Lily listened with her head bowed, nodding at times, and picked at her red-tipped nails. He braced himself for twenty questions, but she remained silent.

"Have you ever heard of such crap? I had some unusual sensations with just her blood in my system. But now that she's had a little of mine, it's even more heightened. I even heard her dreams when she slept. I thought the old stories were a bunch of superstitious nonsense."

"*Enlazado por la Sangre.*" Lily dropped her voice so low he could barely hear even though the band was now playing a slow ballad.

Her subdued reaction surprised him. "What?"

"Bonded by blood. My grandparents shared a blood bond, have I never told you that?"

Dom shook his head. Never heard of it.

"Hardly anyone outside the family knew. In fact, not many inside the family did, either. I'm the only grandchild my grandmother told."

"I don't believe it. You? Keeping secrets?"

"Yeah, well, she ended up staking herself. So we don't talk about it much."

"God, Lil, I'm sorry."

"No problem. You didn't know." Lily took another sip of beer from her straw. "She described the bond as a joining of body, soul and spirit. They knew each other's thoughts. Could sense each other's energy and emotions. Kind of like tuning into a private radio signal of someone's life force. Prana, I think she called it. Not only did they share blood, but they also shared energies and could absorb it from each other just by touching. They thrived off it."

"What's so earth-shattering about energy transfers?" Dom nodded his head toward their waitress still leaning on the bar.

"Between two vampires? As much as I like your prana, Dom, what's yours is yours and what's mine is mine. I'd take a little bit of yours if I could, though." She flashed him a playful smile. "But my grandparents—they could share it between the two of them with just a simple touch."

He supposed he had inadvertently absorbed some of Mackenzie's energy at some point, although he had been careful not to touch his palms to her hands or her face. Well, when he had his wits about him, he didn't. Had he unknowingly given her some of his? Was that even possible?

"And their emotions?" he asked.

"Yeah. My grandparents could sense how the other was feeling even from a distance. Many years ago, when my grandmother worked at a medical clinic, a DB or maybe just a run-of-the-mill freak came in demanding Sweet. Said if she didn't get him some sweetblood, he was going to kill her. Of course she was scared. A short time later my grandfather burst through the entrance with a couple of Guardians and they staked the loser. Said he felt her fear as if it were his own and knew she needed his help. That story is one of the reasons I joined the Agency. I thought it was so heroic. Still do. And very romantic."

Dom ran his fingers against his scalp and tugged at the roots of his hair. This was bullshit. Could it get any worse? "Anything else?"

"Well, apart from the fact that the sex is like an awakening of sorts, that's about all I know."

"You and your grandmother talked about sex?"

"What can I say? She was a very enlightened woman, comfortable with her sexuality. Over cocktails once, she told me that intimate relations were much more enhanced. But, no, she didn't go into detail." She grasped his hand, gave a reassuring squeeze, then released it. "They were so completely bonded to each other that when my grandfather died, she couldn't bear to live without him."

Every nerve ending seemed to shut down as his body numbed and the bar noise faded into the background. He stared at the amber liquid in his glass, twirling it gently, watching the foam cling to the sides. Was that what he was craving from her as well? Her prana? Sex? That certainly explained why he couldn't stop thinking about her.

"But, like I said, they were both vamps. I've never heard of it happening with a human. Blood-bonded to a sweetblood? That sucks." She barked out an unflattering laugh. "And you've never spoken?"

"No."

"Don't know what else I can tell you. Why don't you go introduce yourself? What woman can resist your charms? I know I have a hard time." She blew him an air kiss, obviously trying to lighten his mood.

"Ha. *'Excuse me, but you're my soul mate. Pardon me while I kill you.'* Riiiight."

"I'd see if she'd go horizontal first, eh?" One perfectly plucked eyebrow lifted into a naughty arch.

"Very funny. For all I know, she's a raging bitch. I've seen her lists, her alphabetized DVD collection, her antiseptic refrigerator."

Not that a pretty girl's personality quirks had ever mattered to him before. Most of the time he spent with them was between the sheets and what they did involved little talking. Maybe if they had sex, he could get her out of his system.

"I'm guessing you're enticed by more than her blood, even if she is Sangre Dulce. My grandmother told me she was made for my grandfather and he was made for her. Not sure what that means in terms of sex, but all I know is that it's a soul mate thing."

"That's insane."

Lily fished a tube of shimmery pink lipstick from her purse, applied it without a mirror, and tossed it back into her bag. She shook her head slowly as she rubbed her lips together, and when she looked at him again, she flashed him an all-knowing grin.

From across the room, a whoop of laughter erupted above the music, momentarily distracting him. The singer had jumped onto the dance floor and stroked the microphone stand between his lycra-clad legs like a giant hard-on while an orgasmic-like guitar riff went on and on. A woman with an animal-print thong teeing above the waistband of her jeans hopped onto a man's back and dry-humped him while the crowd cheered.

Oh, for God's sake. He turned his attention back to Lily who was still smiling, although he knew she despised this kind of music.

"No. I'm serious, Lil. I just need to be sure the DBs can't track her. Then I'll close the assignment and be done with it. I need to be in Portland."

"Suit yourself, but I think you're hosed, love."

"Need some help, Sam?" Mackenzie's roommate struggled through the front door holding a precarious stack of cardboard boxes. "Here, let me—"

Dropping her paintbrush, Mackenzie jumped up and they hefted the boxes to the dining room table. "What do you have in here? These weigh a ton."

"It's for my new internet jewelry business. It's a bunch of supplies I ordered." Sam shrugged out of her jacket and started to put it on the chair across the table from Mackenzie, but she pivoted back to the entryway and hung it in the hall closet instead. Fluffing her short dark hair, Sam rewound her long, hand-knit scarf a couple times around her neck before she returned to the dining room and started opening boxes.

"When did you start that? Aren't you still working at the hotel spa?"

Sam wasn't quitting her job to start a business, was she? Giving up a regular paycheck? It had been a while since they'd been home at the same time. But still... wouldn't she have let Mackenzie know? She eyed Sam warily over the top of the canvas. Mackenzie had liked Sam's company this past year, but help with the mortgage was sort of the point in getting a roommate in the first place.

"Oh, I'm still working down there, but my clients kept asking me about all the jewelry I wear, so I decided to sell the stuff online. I've had a ton of hits on my website already and can't believe all the orders I've gotten."

"That's exciting. How long has it been?" Thank God for regular paychecks.

"Only a couple weeks." As Sam reached inside a box, several large medallions hanging under her scarf clanked together like gaudy wind chimes. One-of-a-kind pieces. Definitely. Missing were her trademark dangly chandelier earrings and all the bracelets she usually had stacked on each wrist. She must even be selling the jewelry she wore because she never took the stuff off.

"You still on for Friday night?" Mackenzie asked.

"The auction? You bet. But I prolly won't bid on anything. Been spending all my extra funds on my jewelry stuff."

"Yeah, I'm not sure I will, either, but these things are still fun to attend. It's at the top of the Columbia Center. You know, the one with the amazing women's bathroom?"

"Isn't that the one where each stall has its own individual view of the city with floor-to-ceiling windows?"

"Yup. That's the one." Mackenzie picked up her brush and turned her attention back to her painting as Sam sifted through the contents. "You haven't been home much lately. So this is what you've been up to." Mackenzie fanned the canvas with her hand as if it would speed up the drying of oil paint. She knew it wouldn't help, but she did it anyway because the piece needed to be finished by the weekend.

"Yeah, and, well, I've been seeing someone new."

"What happened to Ethan?"

"He's long gone. Started getting too serious so I broke up with him. Talking marriage and stuff."

Oh, to be that cavalier. "So who's the new guy? Don't tell me you picked one up at the club again." Mackenzie didn't begrudge her roommate's dating habits, but she did like to tease her.

"He's a client, actually. Been staying at his place a lot but he works the graveyard shift, so we…ah…sleep a lot during the day. Don't say anything if Gretchen calls. If my manager knew I was sleeping with a client, she'd have a shit-fit."

"How'd that happen? You ask the guy if he wanted a happy ending?"

"Something like that. Said I had magical hands."

"How original."

Sam laughed, but it sounded a bit hollow.

Mackenzie looked up. Sam was rubbing the backs of her arms, a strained expression on her face. "You okay?"

"Of course." But the words came out a little too fast.

Sam's eyes drooped slightly at the corners and her posture lacked its usual energetic stance. She usually was so perky. Annoyingly perky. Had she not been sleeping well? Mackenzie decided not to ask. What woman wants to know she looks tired?

Over the top of her canvas, Mackenzie watched her roommate pull item after item from the boxes. Several large spools of wire, a bunch of hand tools and an item that looked like a freestanding, oversized butane lighter.

"What's that for?" Mackenzie had seen a smaller, yet similar, device at Corey's, but somehow she didn't think Sam had bought it to light doobies.

"It's a torch. You melt the ends of silver wire to make headpins. You know, the danglies on earrings, necklaces and bracelets? It can also fire small bits of precious metal clay. Like these." She twisted her empty wrists and laughed. "Oops. I'm so used to wearing those bracelets, I forgot I didn't have them on. I made these silver Celtic crosses with that clay, too, but they have to be fired in a kiln at the bead store. Too big for that little thing to work."

"What are those going for? That's a lot of silver. And they're so ornate."

"Two hundred bucks apiece."

Mackenzie whistled and reached over. "May I? Have you sold any?" Sam came around the table and moved her scarf aside for Mackenzie to examine them more closely.

"Yeah, quite a few. I take orders for them online. Four or five should be out of the kiln today. Damn. That's right. I need to pick them up and mail them out."

With the scarf out of the way, Mackenzie's eyes zeroed in not on the jewelry, but on several dark bruises marring the skin on Sam's neck. She snapped her head up, but Sam turned away and hastily covered them with her scarf again. What the hell was going on?

"Sam? You okay?"

"Yeah, sure." Still not meeting her gaze, Sam held both palms up and shook her head as if to say she didn't want to talk about anything.

"You're not okay. What happened to you?"

"Mackenzie, please. I'm fine. Really I am." Her brown eyes met Mackenzie's and she made a sound of exasperation. "Oh, all right. Things with my new boyfriend get a little kinky, but I'm totally fine. Really. I'm not hurt. You should see what he has me do to him."

Mackenzie kept her eyes narrowed. She wasn't sure she was buying Sam's story. What the hell was this new guy doing to her?

"I'm happy. See?" Sam twirled around the dining room with her hands outstretched as if to prove her point. "I'm a strong girl. I wouldn't put up with what you're thinking of. Promise. Now come on. I'm detecting a little envy with all your questions about my business. You totally want to set up something online, too, don't you?"

Mackenzie tried to protest, to find out more about what was going on, but Sam interrupted. "Come on. I totally think you should get a website with all those paintings you do. They're awesome. You should try to sell them. Maybe you could even take commissioned orders online. You know, someone likes your stuff, but wants certain colors to go in a particular room in their house or their business."

"Yeah, I know how commissioned art works." All right, she'd let Sam change the subject for now, but she wasn't going to forget this.

"Well, it's easy. Took only an hour or two to get my website up and running. Gonna be around for a while? I can show you how."

Several hours later, although the painting wasn't finished and she'd gotten no additional answers from Sam, Mackenzie did have a website, complete with photographs of some of her pieces. She typed a short bio for the *About Me* page, took a deep breath and hit enter.

CHAPTER FIVE

ON A TYPICAL weekday, area business people filled the benches in the small park near Pioneer Square, sipping espresso drinks from one of a dozen nearby coffee shops and eating takeout Thai, Chinese, Indian, Italian or pre-wrapped vegan sandwiches. Even the homeless who frequented the park drank espresso.

But in the early morning hours on Friday and Saturday, when the multitude of area clubs closed down, everything changed as humanity spilled out onto damp streets. Groups of girls who'd been prettier five hours ago stumbled down cobblestone sidewalks, while frat boys and gangbangers exchanged words, fists and the occasional knife. Some hoped they weren't too drunk to drive and could blow less than a point-oh-eight, while others headed to all-night diners or after parties. And, like most nights, a few others looked for a different kind of trouble.

"Fuckin' bouncer. Just wanted to finish my drink outside. If that asshole had any idea of who he was messing with, he'd be pissin' his pants and cryin' for his mama." The man tugged his football jersey over his expansive middle and turned down an alley in Pioneer Square with his buddy.

"Shoulda taken him out. I would have. Can't let 'em treat you like that. It ain't right." His friend, wearing a black hoodie, bit at his nails and spat a hangnail on the pavement.

"Easy for you to say, but I swear I saw one of those Agency bastards at the end of the block."

"Let's wait for your bouncer friend out back and jump him when he gets off work. You can drink him in the alley and we'll see what a tough guy he is then." He pulled the hood of his sweatshirt up against the light drizzle and yanked at the strings. "If he apologizes, you can wipe his mind after it's over just like a regular law-abiding Council pussy. But if not, you can leave him with a memory that'll haunt his nightmares forever. And if he really pisses you off, well, you know what you can do. Besides, they taste better when they're scared and dying."

Football Jersey laughed. "Tempting, dude, but no. You can, though. I got a whiff of him when he had me pressed against the bricks. I'm so sick of O-positive, I could puke. Now if he were APoz, I'd be all over him."

Passing a Dumpster, Hoodie pointed to the mouth of the alley. "Hey, aren't those a couple of DBs over there?"

On the far side of the park, a man and a woman sat stiffly on a wrought-iron bench under a burned-out street-lamp.

"How can you tell?" asked Football Jersey as he stepped over a drunk passed out on a piece of flattened cardboard.

"First of all, they all wear those dorky wraparound sunglasses like those two have on. Now watch. It's said when they go through DB initiation and are assigned a partner, they sorta start acting like each other. Check it out."

The woman leaned forward and grabbed a hard-sided

suitcase at her feet and a split second later, the man did the same. She adjusted it on her lap then snapped it open. The man's actions mirrored hers perfectly. She pushed her sunglasses higher on her nose and so did the man.

"That's freaky, dude," Football Jersey said.

"Yeah, but come on. Let's see what they got."

The woman sniffed the air and a yellowed smile creased her face as they approached. "Hey, boys, what-cha need tonight?"

"Got any Sweet?" Hoodie elbowed his friend in the gut. "We're lookin' for a little sugar."

"You gotta be kidding me. No one's got that kind of shit right now. But when we do, it goes like that." She snapped her fingers. The man snapped his as well but remained silent. "At this hour you boys would be way too late for the candy anyway. Gotta get here early for any good stuff."

"Damn. When are you gettin' more in?" Hoodie asked.

"Sweet's been tight." She craned her head around, as if making sure no one could hear them. Her partner did the same. "That is, since the Overlord's coming."

"Lord Pavlos? No shit?" Hoodie elbowed his buddy, who pushed him back and cursed under his breath.

"Yeah. Only drinks the sweet stuff, so our supply is nada."

"That's bullshit. Where does that leave us?" asked Hoodie.

"He's not staying long. Hates it up here."

"Don't we all," Football Jersey said as he looked around the darkened park littered with people in various stages of drunkenness. "Why's he coming then?"

"I dunno. Doing some kind of experiment shit or something," the woman said.

"What?" Hoodie and Football Jersey asked in unison. They looked at each other, then back at the DB pair, and laughed.

The woman shrugged and the man copied her a moment later. "They don't tell us peons nothing, but it has something to do with Sweet. Better be worth it, that's all I can say. So can we interest you boys in a nice BPoz? Next best thing. Real fresh. Give you a good deal."

Laughter echoed nearby and they all looked up. Clanking dishes and the sound of stacking chairs reverberated through the back door of a nearby bar as it opened, illuminating two figures in the dark alley for a moment before slamming shut again.

Hoodie held his nose in the air and sniffed. "Dude, it's your bouncer friend. And the girl with him is APoz. What do you say? I'll take him and you can take her. Wanna use what your mama gave you?"

"My mama would be pissed if I used it like that."

Hoodie shrugged. "Let's go, then."

"Thanks, lady, but no thanks," said Football Jersey. "We're gonna score some off the hoof tonight."

"Playing with fire, boys. Better watch out. I hear there's an Agency patrol nearby. Sure you don't want the easy stuff? Fifty bucks. And I'll float it with a little APoz for an extra ten."

"No thanks. We'll save our money for the Sweet when it comes in. And fuck the Agency. Come on," Football Jersey said to his buddy. "I'm starving."

UNDER A DARK freeway overpass in a section of Portland called rough on a good night, Dom spotted a group of vampire youthlings huddled around what could only be trouble. Probably doing Sweet shots.

He glanced at the still darkening sky and cursed. It was too damn early. Usually this sort of shit happened much later in the evening, after the heavy consumption of legal and illegal substances. Someone probably just scored some Sweet and they couldn't wait to party.

In a show of intimidation, he flipped open his hip-length leather coat to put his weapons on display and hoped he wouldn't have to use force. They were just kids, barely old enough to have gone through puberty, when the blood cravings and aversion to sunlight began. "Okay, gentlemen, ladies. Break it up. Time to move along."

He pushed his way into the circle, heard a mumbled "fuck you, asshole" and "goddamn Agency pig," but at least half of the kids dispersed and left the scene. Only the hardcore losers remained.

At the center of the crowd, on the gritty pavement, a girl sat straight-legged and leaned back on her hands. With wild, unfocused eyes, she stared up at the young man straddling her as he fumbled with something in his hands.

Dom grabbed his arm. "Give it to me."

"Fuck yourself," the kid said, sounding way too jaded for his age. He stumbled over the girl's legs as he tried to shrug away from Dom's grasp.

"Doesn't work for me. Hand it over. Trust me, you don't want this to get any messier than it already is."

The young man lurched around and thrust a hand into his pocket. Weapon?

In a flash, Dom clamped him into a headlock and twisted the kid's arm behind him, shoving it upwards, and the kid howled. "I said give me the goddamn Sweet."

"I swear I don't have any." The kid's voice was raspy and he choked as Dom pressed harder on his larynx.

"Yeah, and I'm Prince Fucking Charming."

In the struggle, a small glass vial fell to the pavement, shattering and spilling its contents at their feet. With a snarl, the gawking youthlings leaped in.

For a half-second, Dom considered pulling out his blades and scattering the crowd that way, but he decided to let them act like wild animals, scratching and clawing the dirty cement until the blood was gone. Unfortunately, the micro-cuts on their mouths from the shards of glass would heal almost instantly from the effect of the Sweet. With disgust he watched them tongue the pavement, licking up every last drop.

When the frenzy died down a few minutes later, Dom cuffed the dealer with silver-lined handcuffs and yanked him to his feet.

"Everyone else—out. You've had your fun, now get the hell out of here." Turning his attention back to the dealer, he said, "I've got plans for you." He punched a couple of buttons on his cell phone and within minutes an unmarked panel van pulled up to the curb. An agent dressed in black fatigues burst through the rear doors, scruffed the dealer by the neck and waistband and threw his ass inside. Dom two-patted the side of the van and it drove away.

One down, how many more to go? He ran a hand through his hair and walked slowly back to the Porsche parked around the corner.

It was the same thing, night after night, here and in Seattle. God, he was so sick of it. He didn't know how much more of this bullshit he could take. He picked up an empty blood vial and tossed it into a nearby trash can.

These kids weren't the problem. Pavlos was the problem, and *he* was somewhere in the South.

When he opened the car door, his cell phone vibrated. He climbed in, glanced at the screen and cursed. Nice text. Where the hell did Santiago think he was?

Portland, he texted back.

The guy was a serious micromanager. Or maybe he just didn't trust Dom. Especially given what happened with *her*. He never should've told his boss. It should've been his own twisted little secret.

He cranked the seat back and closed his eyes. Not that Dom came to the Horseshoe Bay Region with glowing recommendations, but no one—not his old commander, not the other field agents he'd led or trained over the years, or even the few humans he'd worked with who knew about the Agency—questioned his effectiveness or loyalty. But then, not all of them knew about what had happened with Alfonso, either.

Dom leaned his head on the steering wheel and his mind wandered to Mackenzie again. What was she doing right now? He checked his watch. Perhaps she was home watching a movie. Or organizing something. Or cleaning. Or maybe she was in bed early on a Friday night, curled up with a book. He rubbed that ever-present ache centered in his chest and groaned.

This is bullshit. It's got to stop.

Irritated by his inability to keep her out of his thoughts, he jumped out of the car again, hit the alarm remote and jogged back to the freeway underpass. Usually he went weeks between live feedings, but maybe someone else's blood would dilute the effects of hers, still present and way too strong in his system. Hopefully, the human loser he'd spotted earlier down by the river was still there. He'd take a quick mouthful, and if the guy was as drunk as he appeared earlier, Dom might not even need to bother with wiping his memory.

The phone vibrated again. *Shit.* Santiago had decided to call this time.

He flipped the phone open. "This is Dom."

"Your old phone—you told me it was busted." No "hello" or "how's it going" for Santiago.

"Yes, and…"

"Come on, you haven't forgotten. Let me refresh your fading memory. The goddamn one with all the DB data that landed Stryker in the clinic and you with that sweet-blood."

Dom cringed. "Yes, what about it?"

"Care to explain something to me then?"

"What? The thing was busted. I told you already." Dom clicked the volume button down a few notches and held the phone away from his ear just as Santiago erupted.

"Tell me why in the hell a broken phone would suddenly go online again. Why a broken phone started pinging from a cell tower near the mall in the Northend today. Why a broken phone has been pinging on St. Francis Hill where it's been sitting for the last hour."

Mackenzie's neighborhood. Palming his keys, he turned around and sprinted back to the Porsche.

"You didn't get the phone back from that woman, did you?"

"No. But I told you. I thought it was broken."

"Thought? You thought? Goddamn it. You fucking lied to me. You know how important that data is. I'm sending Foss over to get it back from her one way or another."

He felt his pupils dilate with rage as he yanked the car door open. "You keep him away from her." He had hoped his desire for her would wane, but the thought of Jackson getting close to her filleted his guts from pelvis to sternum. His focus narrowed to a dark tunnel and her name drummed over and over in his head. He started the car and headed for the freeway.

"Jesus, Mary and Joseph. You screwed up and I'm sending him to clean up your mess. First the illegal blood transfer and now this. What the hell is going on with you?"

"No. I'll handle it. I'm leaving Portland now. Be there in two hours."

"Handle it like you did the first time? That damn phone better be back at the field office by midnight tonight or I'm sending Foss. Two hours? You're crazy. You'll be lucky to do it in four."

"I said I'll be there in two." With a snap of the phone, Dom ended the call.

Of course Santiago was right. He should've gotten the damn phone back from her that night by walking right into her house and taking it directly from her as she screamed. A simple memory wipe, and that would've been it. But he hadn't.

He engaged the radar detection, punched the accelerator and merged onto 205 North. After bypassing the bottlenosed traffic by riding the shoulder a few times, he crossed the bridge back into Washington. By the time he hit the straightaway on I-5, he'd cranked it up to a hundred and twenty.

CHAPTER SIX

PIANO MUSIC FROM the foyer wafted into the elegantly appointed ladies' room where Mackenzie fidgeted in her cocktail dress. If Sam hadn't backed out at the last minute, she'd have known she had panty lines showing through the delicate green chiffon. Why hadn't she worn a thong?

She closed herself into a stall, stepped out of her panties and stuffed them into her evening bag. She hoped she wouldn't have to open it with anyone around. It was one of those crystal-encrusted clamshell-style clutches that puts everything on display when they're opened, and it was hardly big enough to hold more than a credit card and a lipstick. How would she explain the pair of underwear and the two cell phones?

Slipping her fingers around the second phone, she thought about its owner again. Why had she felt compelled to carry it with her every day since she'd found it?

Today she had even gone to the cell phone store looking for a charger. At first the salesperson had been skeptical. Said the phone must be an advanced prototype because he hadn't seen one like it before. He was surprised when they found a charger that fit.

She'd thought about just leaving the thing at the store for them to track down the owner. But the salesperson had practically salivated over it and she suddenly didn't trust him. Or at least that's what she'd told herself. Her stomach had tied up in nervous little knots at the thought of leaving it, so she'd bought a charger and taken it back home. She was shocked when it powered up.

She opened the device now, held it to her lips and imagined it pressed to its owner's face, the cool plastic warming against his skin. She didn't question why she felt the owner was male, she just knew. After stuffing it back into her tiny purse, she exited the ladies' room.

The crowd at the annual benefit auction for the North-west Alzheimer's Foundation was the largest she had seen. Mackenzie had been attending and donating items ever since her mother was diagnosed.

"Mackenzie, I was hoping I'd run into you." A loud voice behind her caused several people to turn around. She couldn't remember the woman's name—Tammy or Terry maybe. "Wow, you're pretty brave to be wearing a dress like that."

Mackenzie smoothed a hand over the skirt. It couldn't be see-through—she'd double-checked that in the rest-room. "Is there a problem with it?"

"Totally personal preference, but a simple, non-revealing black is so much more traditional at affairs like this."

Mackenzie bristled at her patronizing tone of voice. The woman spoke as though she were giving advice to someone who'd never attended a charity auction before. Glancing around, Mackenzie saw plenty of brightly-colored gowns. Most were long, but a few women wore cocktail dresses that fell a few inches above the knee, as well. So what was the big deal?

A waiter walked by with a tray of glasses filled with

red wine. Mackenzie grabbed one and swallowed the contents in one gulp as the woman continued talking. Were they serving any appetizers before dinner? She could really use—

"Mackenzie?"

"Sorry, what?" Her mind had been wandering so much lately, probably because she hadn't been sleeping well.

"I asked if you donated another one of your pieces this year. Landon, darling, Mackenzie here likes to paint horses."

A tall, balding man stifled a yawn with the back of his hand as he slowly turned around. From the looks of it, he had no idea what Tammy-Terry had said, nor did he care. Mackenzie twirled the stem of the empty wine glass and coughed.

"Um, yes, I did. No horses this time, though. Just a couple of whimsical landscapes and some art lessons."

"Isn't that sweet? Speaking of paintings, I'm dying to know. Mrs. Thorn-Steuben tells me you were the model for the nude that Martin Johanovich donated. Is that true? I could never do something like that—take my clothes off for an artist to paint."

Mackenzie's face prickled with heat. "Nude painting? I'm not sure I know what you're talking about. Martin's a good friend, that's all." She pointedly avoided the question. "Oh, I think I see him now. Will you excuse me? Nice meeting you," she called to Landon as she slipped away.

How had Tammy-Terry heard that? Martin was very discreet and had promised not to reveal that she'd posed as his model. He'd sworn the piece wouldn't be realistic enough for her to be recognized.

As she made her way across the crowded room, she

grabbed another glass of wine. That first one had helped ease the tension she'd been feeling all afternoon. Taking a sip, she felt a calming sensation as the liquid slid down her throat.

Surrounded by a bunch of his adoring fans, Martin smiled at her and excused himself. His work was highly regarded and with his charming personality, he was a darling of the vibrant Seattle art scene and a very popular fixture at local charity events.

"Oh, honey, aren't you a sight for the visually astute." He took her hand and spun her around. She was careful to hold the skirt of her dress down. "You look positively radiant. You must share your beauty secrets with me, darling. It's not fair for you to hoard them all to yourself. And that color screams you, you, you."

"Not too shockingly green or revealing?"

"Good Lord, no. How'd you get a silly idea like that in your head? You look fab."

"Thanks, Martin. You're looking pretty smashing yourself." He beamed and adjusted his bow tie. Lowering her voice, she said, "Where is that nude? I thought you said I wouldn't be recognizable."

"You aren't, honey. Promise. Why do you ask?"

Mackenzie relayed what Tammy-Terry said.

"Oh, for crying out loud. It must be that gossip, Mrs. Thorn-Steuben. She arrived at my studio right after you left our last sitting. Did you see her? When she saw the painting I was working on, she must've put two and two together. It really is not noticeable that it's you…only someone who knows your lovely back would recognize it. Go see for yourself. It's right over there." He nodded his head to the right. "Are you here alone?"

"Yes, my roommate dogged me at the last minute. Her

new boyfriend called and— Well, you know how that is. So it's just me tonight."

"Well, then you must join us at our table. We have a few extra seats. Jerry and Craig weren't able to make it, either. Table Three. Right up front."

Mackenzie meandered through the silent auction tables, and although she hadn't planned on bidding, she wrote her auction number on a couple of items. If she was fortunate enough to get something, she'd be excited. If not, then at least she'd have succeeded in bumping up the price and making more money for the Foundation. She saw that her two paintings and the art lessons she'd donated had several bidders already.

The live auction items were set up in the front of the room. A trip for two to Tuscany, a walk-on part in a popular sitcom, a winemaker's dinner for twelve at a winery. Next to the display for a culinary trip to Paris was the painting of the nude.

Almost life-sized, it had been done on a large canvas using warm-hued oils applied with a palette knife. Martin was right—none of the details were very clear, and for that she was relieved. A group of people had just moved away from it and she stood there alone.

The naked figure on the canvas posed with her back to the viewer, one arm resting on the floor behind her, the other hand entwined in her hair. A gossamer cloth draped over one shoulder, pooling on the foreground in front of her backside. Just a hint of the right breast was visible and the face, turned down, was masked by a cascade of long brown hair.

Although she wasn't recognizable in the painting, she still felt her temperature rise. Why had she worn this bare-backed dress tonight and pinned her hair to the side over one shoulder? Was everyone noticing the similarities between her back and the one in the painting?

Feeling the heat of someone's stare, she wished she could loosen her hair and hide behind it. She was about to step away when she felt a tingling, almost a purring, flutter against her temples and the little hairs on the back of her neck stood up. She rubbed her shoulders but realized the sensation was sort of relaxing.

"It's quite lovely." The accented voice was deep and rich, and brought to mind dark chocolate melting on the back of her tongue. Goose bumps formed on her arms and she turned to see a man standing a few feet away.

He stood at least a head taller than her, and had dark, shoulder-length hair pulled back by a leather tie. A thick strand in the front had slipped free, as if it had been tied with the nonchalance of someone who knew perfection wasn't important. She found herself wanting to twist it around her finger and see the tips of her nails peek out from under that thick mane. The crystalline blue of his eyes was a stark contrast to a dark fringe of lashes as he looked down at her with an air of familiarity.

God, did she know him from somewhere? Surely she'd remember meeting a man like him if she had.

Those eyes, those beautiful eyes, flanked by a few lines that suggested living rather than time, raked the inner recesses of her mind. They were gentle now, but somehow she knew they could be cruel. She took a step backward on her teetering heels, her heart hammering two staccatos—one in her head and the other in her chest.

Although his attire was more casual than the stiff tuxedos sported by most of the men in attendance, he carried himself with a grace and ease that exuded confidence. He wore a brushed silk T-shirt that draped luxuriously over tailored charcoal slacks. With a black leather coat tossed easily over one arm and a hint of stubble peppering his jaw, he looked more like he belonged on a movie screen than at a charity event. Her mouth went suddenly dry and she licked her lips.

With one brow lifted, he looked at her quizzically. God, had he asked her something?

"The painting?"

"Oh, yes." What about the painting?

"I find it very lovely." As he stepped closer, the heat from his body warmed her bare shoulders and the two internal drumbeats evolved into one sound. She reached a hand up and rubbed her neck. Wasn't this the same—

"Are you familiar with the piece?" He nodded toward the canvas but didn't take his eyes off of her.

If she stretched out her hand, she could touch his chest, he was that close. Stroke his jaw, brush a thumb over his lips. Oh God, what was she thinking? She dug her nails into the palms of her hands to keep her thoughts from wandering where they shouldn't.

His warm breath lifted a stray wisp of her hair on the back of her neck as she turned toward the painting. When his fingertips grazed down the back of her arm to guide her forward, a jolt of electricity left a trail of heat on her skin. She found herself inching closer to him, almost instinctively, as if her body knew this man though her mind did not.

"Um, yes. My friend Martin painted it."

"I find it absolutely captivating. It's gorgeous. I'm Dominic Serrano, but please call me Dom." He extended his hand and she noted he wore a thick, filigree ring on each thumb.

"Mackenzie Foster-Shaw. It's nice to meet you. Yes,

Martin is an amazingly gifted artist." The bracelets on her wrist jingled together as she took his hand in hers.

With the touch, she felt instantly alive. Every nerve ending danced as her palm pressed to his. The background piano music, which she'd hardly noticed before, seemed to morph into a tender melody. The room sparkled with prisms of candlelight reflected off the chandeliers above. Everything looked so different. How could she not have seen the room like this before?

He released her abruptly and turned back toward the painting, his expression composed, measured.

Normally, she'd have filled the void with some sort of mindless chatter, but now she felt no need. Calm and relaxed, she waited.

"Such rich colors he used. The ethereal light." She could get lost in the sound of his voice. "The echoing lines of the composition. From the arc of her neck, along her back to the draping fabric over her shoulder." As he spoke, he reached his hand out and traced the lines in the air, his long fingers caressing the space in front of them. Her breath rasped unevenly in her chest. It was as if he were running his hands over her bare skin. "From her breast to the curve of her legs and buttocks. I find it very enchanting. Almost seductive. Yes, your friend Martin is very talented, but he had an equally exquisite subject."

She stepped forward and silently read the title of the piece.

"What is it called?"

He was right there. He could read it himself, but she did what he asked.

"Where Are You, My Love."

I am where you are. The words chimed in her head. She glanced at him but his face was unreadable.

How would his arms feel around her? Would she fit beneath his chin like a puzzle piece? He sucked in a deep breath and let it out slowly, his stare never dropping from her face. Feeling a tiny trickle of heat between her legs, she cursed inwardly for not wearing a thong.

Sweet Jesus.

That voice again. Although his lips didn't move, she knew it was his. It rang in her head and echoed in her ears. The darkened room seemed to spin as if they were in the middle of a vortex. The clinking of wineglasses, the low din of conversation, the lovely chords of the piano—everything faded around them.

As if in slow motion, he stepped in front of her so she had to tilt her chin up to meet his gaze. Another inch or two and her nipples, covered only in thin folds of green chiffon, would have brushed against the fabric of his shirt. Her body trembled in anticipation.

"I know you, don't I?"

His jaw flexed as he stared at her, his eyes an unfathomable glacier blue, terrifying and beautiful at the same time.

Without thinking, she reached up to brush a stray lock of hair from his face, her fingertips a whisper against his temple, and her palm molded softly to his cheek.

He caught her wrist roughly, lowering it to her side, and his mouth hardened as if he were biting back the urge to say something cruel. Fury and something else smoldered in his eyes as his pupils dilated, leaving only a ring of that icy blue.

What the hell? Don't pupils usually shrink to pinpricks when you're pissed?

Danger lurked behind those now-dark eyes, and she took a step back. He looked almost inhuman for a moment. Part of her knew she should be afraid. But she wasn't. Instead, anger boiled up in her veins, matching what she felt in him.

Why had he grabbed her like that? Why was he looking at her with such intensity? It stirred her dander, like the wind fanning a flame. Evidently it was okay for him to touch her, but not the other way around. Was that it?

Squaring her shoulders, she jerked her hand away. How dare he react to her that way? If there was one thing she'd learned about men from her mother, it was not to take any crap from them. With a huff, she spun on her heel and melted into the crowd.

Forgive me, she imagined him saying.

Go screw yourself, was her imagined reply.

In a daze, she meandered over to the now-closed silent auction tables. People milled about, checking various items to see if their numbers were the winning bids. Three women dressed in sparkling dresses and precarious heels jumped up and down, squealing like schoolgirls. They'd evidently gotten the auction item they had wanted.

What the hell just happened? She felt like she knew this Dom Serrano, had met him before, had encountered his voice, even his thoughts, which was completely insane and made no sense. He was somehow familiar and yet a stranger. The thrumming in her head and chest became more and more mismatched and she almost felt nauseous.

One minute he was making love to her with his words and the next minute he changed into something wild and uncontrollable. Her actions obviously caught him off-guard and pissed him off. What had she done? It was just an innocent touch.

Although she couldn't deny the attraction, she certainly

didn't have the fortitude for these stupid dating-scene games spurred on by misread sexual desires and hypocritical reactions. She hadn't behaved too forwardly, had she? Maybe going pantyless had given her some balls.

Her bid number wasn't the highest on any of the items she'd wanted. She would've especially loved that spa day at Ummelina downtown, but she couldn't justify paying that kind of money for her own indulgence, only for charity. However, given the state of her financial affairs, it was probably a good thing she wasn't the winning bidder.

She ran into a few more people she knew, friends of her mother's whom she hadn't seen in ages. Politely, they inquired about her mother. They continued chatting until the master of ceremonies announced dinner was being served and asked the guests to find their seats.

She zigzagged around the tables, looking for Number Three. Martin had said it was up front. She stiffened and nearly turned around when she saw a familiar figure seated at a table near the stage. Martin jumped up and ran toward her.

"Darling, I hope you don't mind, but I asked your dishy friend to sit with us. He was stuck clear in the back and was just about to sit next to Mrs. Thorn-Steuben when I rescued him." He grabbed her elbow and urged her forward. "He tried to protest, but I insisted. Here, right this way."

Dom stood up as she approached, pulling out the chair next to him. As she took her seat, she jutted her chin out and ignored him. He held her napkin out for her and she yanked it from his grasp. Did he think she was a ditzy fool? That she could be swayed by a momentary act of politeness? She'd make him regret his bad attitude.

With her back to him, she offered her hand to the

woman on her right. "I'm Mackenzie Foster-Shaw. You must be a friend of Martin's?"

"Janet Forrest." The woman gripped Mackenzie's fingertips in the gentle handshake of the upper class. "And this is my husband, Ernie." Mackenzie reached a hand over and the portly man clasped it in the same manner. "It's so nice to meet you. Yes, we're friends of Martin's. We've got many of his pieces in our collection, don't we, dear?"

"Which ones? I'm quite familiar with his entire body of work."

As they ate their salads, the woman told her about each piece in detail and Mackenzie nodded appreciatively. She felt the heat from Dom's eyes on her back and she purposely played with a lock of her hair and twirled the stem of her wineglass. She was so not going to turn around.

"I'm sorry," Mrs. Forrest said. "Here I am droning on and on about myself. How about you? How do you know Martin?"

Before Mackenzie could reply, Martin's voice boomed from behind her. She turned around and saw Dom staring at her through lowered lids. He looked dreamy and way too sensuous. Dragging her gaze away, she concentrated on Martin.

"Mackenzie was one of my best students at the University of Washington. She's a talented young artist and I couldn't bear to let her go at the end of the term. A few years ago I made her an offer she couldn't refuse." He tilted his head back with an infectious laugh that invited company, and a few others at the table joined in, including Dom. "Right, darling?" Martin asked.

Mackenzie bit back her laughter and smiled awkwardly.

All eyes at the table turned to her, but the only set she was aware of was the ice blue pair to her left.

"Martin was kind enough to offer me a job teaching beginning art students—"

"Yes, and she came up with a brilliant lesson plan where she takes them on a walking tour of the various local galleries, then puts what they've observed into their own work in the studio. In addition to that—"

"Martin, please."

Ignoring her protest, he continued. "In addition to being an artist, she's also a skilled photographer. She works for a location scout in town. You know—movie locations." Excitement tinged his voice and he sat forward in his seat. Like everyone else, he thought her part-time job was glamorous. If only she felt the same way.

"Oh, how wonderful. That sounds so exciting. Just what does a location photographer do?" Mrs. Forrest leaned forward as well, clasping her gnarled fingers under her chin.

Mackenzie squirmed in her chair and rearranged the food on her plate.

"We get a spec sheet from the production company, spelling out what they're looking for at each shooting location. I research possible sites, taking pictures and measurements and my boss—my other boss, not him—" she inclined her head in Martin's direction "—handles all the permits and permissions. Sometimes he has ideas for me but other times, I do the research myself."

"So what film are you working on now?"

"I'm not allowed to say specifically, but a potential client wants to shoot some scenes at a cemetery. So that's what I've been working on based on their specific needs. I've got a few more sites to photograph before I'm done.

The port. A beach with a cityscape in the background—
I'll head over to West Seattle for that one. But it's the
cemetery I'm having the most trouble with." She touched
a finger to her forehead, remembering the migraine.

"You'd think that'd be easy," Dom said. "There are
plenty of cemeteries around here."

Determined to ignore him, she turned to Mrs. Forrest
and continued. "It needs to be somewhat dark, very oppressive, and not too far from the city. It's expensive to
take all the film equipment too far."

"That's a little frightening, don't you think?" asked
Mrs. Forrest. "How do you do it, dear?"

Mackenzie leaned in and lowered her voice. "When
I'm out shooting remote locations, I carry a gun."

Mrs. Forrest gasped. "Oh, goodness. Do you know
how to use the thing?"

"Well, yes. I've been using one for years. My mother
started taking both me and my brother to the shooting
range when we were old enough to legally carry a gun."

*Please stop and move onto someone else. Surely some-
one else at this table would be more interesting to talk
to.*

"You must be a terrific shot. Do you have it with you
now?"

"No. Not enough room in this little thing." She winked
at Mrs. Forrest and shook her clutch. "And nowhere to
strap a holster on this outfit."

Everyone at the table laughed. Good, now maybe the
conversation would turn elsewhere. She threw a glance
in Dom's direction and he looked down his nose at her,
his lips turned up as if he was trying not to give her a
haughty smile. He was so irritating. She wondered if he
practiced. She flipped her hair and turned away.

Words like *fascinating* and *exciting* swirled around the table. She shifted her water glass, aligned her fork next to her plate. Taking compliments was not something she was comfortable with, and neither was being the center of attention.

When the conversation thankfully turned to other things, she relaxed against her seat and felt the sudden warmth of Dom's hand. Every nerve ending jumped to attention. He had casually, maybe even conveniently, laid his arm on the back of her chair. Before she could sit forward, she could've sworn he brushed his thumb across her shoulder blade. A trail of sparks lingered on her skin and she shivered involuntarily.

Mrs. Forrest whispered into her ear. "What's your date's name? I'm sorry, but I've forgotten."

"Dominic…Serrano, I think. But he's not my date."

Louder now, Mrs. Forrest said, "Mr. Serrano, what is it that you do? I detect a bit of an accent, though not much. Spanish, is it?"

"My family is originally from Northern Spain—yes. But I've lived in the States for years now. I'm surprised you even picked up on it."

"Ernie and I made the mistake of visiting Madrid during the summer months a few years ago. Remember that, honey? It was so humid…" While Mrs. Forrest continued, Mackenzie sipped her wine, not paying much attention until Dom began to speak.

"I work for a multinational corporation that has contracts with the U.S. government. We have a small presence here locally, but it's classified, so I really can't say much about it."

"Goodness. We've got exciting here—" she patted

Mackenzie's hand "—and mysterious there. What a couple you two make. Is your office here in the city?"

Mackenzie bristled. "Careful, he might have to kill you if he tells you."

Everyone laughed, including Dom, who rested an arm easily over the back of her chair again. She made sure not to lean back this time.

"We maintain a small field office downtown, but the majority of the region's work is out of British Columbia. I'm in charge of things here in Seattle, and I occasionally work in Portland, Spokane and Boise. But I'm afraid that's about all I can tell you." Dom's smile stretched to his eyes and seemed genuine.

Why did he have to be so charismatic? It'd be much easier to ignore him if he wasn't. She toyed with the evening bag on her lap, turning it over and over, and the prongs of an embedded crystal caught the chiffon of her skirt. Damn. While Martin talked about one of his recent projects, she picked it loose, but the stupid thing snagged the fabric.

"Why don't you just put that on the floor beneath your chair?" Dom said. "I'll make sure no one steals it."

"Everyone knows it's bad feng shui to put your purse on the floor."

"Pardon me?" He sounded amused.

"Purses are never to go on the floor. It encourages money to fly out."

His faux pained look told her that was the dumbest thing he'd ever heard. "Who told you that?"

What an asshole. "My mother."

"And you believe it?"

She gritted her teeth. "It's a habit, okay. Is that better?"

"Well, here, let me set it on the empty chair beside me, then. We certainly don't want anything flying out of your purse unexpectedly."

Oh my God. Even though she was irritated, she almost snorted out loud and had to bite her lip to keep quiet. If only he knew about the panties tucked inside.

"Fine." Without looking at him, she held out her purse and hoped she came across as indifferent, bored and completely disinterested. She couldn't care less that he was sitting just inches away from her, that she could feel the heat of his stare on her back and neck, that he was so damn hot. No, she didn't care at all.

"Did you find any interesting silent auction items?" She directed her attention to the woman sitting across from her. As she replied, Mackenzie found her mind wandering.

You want me, the imaginary voice whispered melodically in her ear, *almost as much as I want you.*

She stiffened her spine and popped a roasted vegetable into her mouth. What was it with that damned voice in her head? Her stupid wishful thinking. Who cared that she found Dom massively attractive? That she longed to feel his hand sliding along her skin again. His lips against her throat. What the hell was wrong with her? Yes, he was gorgeous, but—

She glanced at him again. He twirled a few strands of pasta on his fork and lifted it to his mouth. As his lips closed over the utensil, he looked up at her and their eyes locked. His jaw flexed as he chewed slowly, then swallowed, never dropping his gaze from her face.

The fluttering of her heart belied her cool exterior.

Too much wine. She pushed the glass away to reach for her water, but the base of the stemware caught on a fold of the tablecloth and slipped from her fingers. In an instant, Dom's hand was there and caught the glass before a drop was spilled.

How did he move so fast? I've had way too much to drink.

"Finished?"

She nodded her head. With a lift of his brow, he held the wineglass in front of him in a silent toast.

To the most enticingly beautiful female I've ever met, the imaginary voice spoke in her head.

To the most infuriating male.

She thought she saw the corner of his mouth twitch just before he took a sip from her glass, which really made no sense. Better switch to water only.

When the live auction started, the energy in the room ratcheted up. As the auctioneer called out dollar amounts in a dizzying frenzy, people laughed and shrieked, urging the bidding higher and higher. Mackenzie's head began to swim with too much wine and thoughts of the exorbitant amounts of money people were spending.

After excusing herself, she skirted around the tables, a little wobbly on her heels, and headed to the ladies' room. She dampened a hand cloth with cool water and held it to her neck and wrists. She leaned against the basin and waited until the cloth was no longer cold. Although refreshed, she still felt a little light-headed. A glance in the mirror showed she needed lipstick, but she'd left that damn little purse back at the table. Hopefully Martin was keeping an eye on it, because she really needed some fresh air. She straightened her dress, smoothed her hair and left the restroom.

THE AUCTIONEER'S SING-SONG voice clipped along at a rapid pace, barking out increasingly higher dollar amounts, and with every lift of a bidder's paddle, the crowd whooped even louder.

Dom kept an eye on the archway leading toward the restrooms and the rooftop terrace and sensed Mackenzie wasn't far away.

"Sold to number one-ninety-three."

While the next item was being readied, Dom leaned toward Martin and casually slipped his leather coat over Mackenzie's evening bag on the chair beside him.

"So tell me about your painting, Martin. It's her, isn't it?"

Before he could reply, two burly men in tuxedos lifted the nude painting up at the front of the room so that everyone could see, and the auctioneer began to read the description. Martin stood up as the spotlight trained on him and when he bowed to the applause, Dom reached a hand under his coat and opened Mackenzie's purse.

Quickly locating the damaged phone, his hand touched upon a silky piece of fabric. She didn't seem like a handkerchief sort of woman, so he peered under the coat. Sweet Jesus. A pair of dark purple lace panties were wrapped around his phone. His cock shifted against his thigh for the millionth time tonight. So that was what she'd meant when he detected her thoughts about panties. He rubbed his fingers briefly against the lace before he snapped the purse shut, tucked the phone away and discreetly rearranged himself. Again. She wasn't planning on going home with one of these bozos, was she? His pupils dilated and he ran a finger under the suddenly tight collar of his shirt.

"How did you know?" Martin sat down as the bidding started. "Did she tell you? Or did Mrs. Thorn-Steuben?"

"Who? No. Those sweeping, graceful lines of the composition could only belong to her. Although your piece is gorgeous and you're quite talented, it's not even a fraction as beautiful as the real thing."

Several people around the room raised their bidders' paddles as the tempo of the auctioneer's calls increased, and Dom glanced around. A horse-faced letch with oversized teeth, a slovenly old man with a blond trophy wife, a barely-out-of-puberty dot-com geek. Damn if he was going to let anyone else have that painting.

He raised his paddle, doubled the current amount, and the crowd went wild. The Bill Gates lookalike had the nerve to bid again and when Dom doubled the amount a second time, the whole place gasped in a collective orgasm.

"Sold to number three-twenty-two."

It's about time. He tossed his number on Mackenzie's empty chair, gathered up his coat and her purse, and put a hand on Martin's shoulder. "Do me a favor. Don't tell her it was me."

"Why? She'll be thrilled it went for so much. The Alzheimer's Foundation is a cause she cares deeply about."

"Trust me. I can sense these things. She'd be angry and would think I— Just don't, all right? I'm going to be out of town for a while. Can you arrange delivery in a couple of weeks?"

"You bet." Martin flipped him a business card. "Just call when you get back and I'll have everything arranged with our installation boys."

ON THE DECK of the rooftop terrace, the lights of the Space Needle twinkled against the ink black sky. Sea air from Elliott Bay blew into Mackenzie's face, cooling her heat-flushed cheeks, and her hair swirled around wildly. The melancholy cawing of a seagull sounded in the distance and a ferry with its lights ablaze headed toward one of the islands. She heard footsteps behind her and her neck began to tingle.

"It's lovely, isn't it?"

She turned and faced Dom. His eyes were shadowed, unreadable.

"That's the second time you've said that tonight. Need a thesaurus?"

He laughed then—a deep resonant laugh, the kind she imagined she'd never tire of hearing—and handed over her evening bag.

"Here, you left this at the table."

Well, that was considerate. She took it from him and set it on a nearby cocktail table, not wanting the thing to snag her dress again.

"And I've said it many more times in my head tonight," he continued. "I don't have a problem with redundancy. Would you prefer gorgeous, exquisite, beautiful, magnificent?"

"Whatever. Is this the part where you suddenly get mad again and look like you could eat me alive? You must have some serious anger management issues. That, or you're totally manic."

"Perhaps, but I do know what I want." He slid his hands down the backs of her arms and grasped her balled fists. Her knees almost buckled as he slowly brought her hands to his lips and kissed the inside of each wrist.

"Just so you know, in case you're wondering," she said huskily, "I find pricks really unattractive."

He rubbed the tip of his nose against the delicate flesh

and she shivered. She should pull away, right now, leave the terrace, get back to the auction.

With his eyes closed, he took a deep breath, as if he was savoring the fresh sea air. When he opened them, his pupils were dilated again. How strange—she'd never seen eyes like his before. He looked eager, and yes, almost hungry, but not angry like he had before. His expression was softer, almost gentle.

"I'm terribly sorry if I came off as rude earlier. I know I did. You are just so startlingly beautiful, it caught me off-guard and I lost my head for a moment. Normally I'm much more…in control of myself than that."

She raised her eyebrows. What an odd thing to say. "I had no idea I'd elicit such bizarre responses from people with what I wore tonight. Maybe I should've come in jeans."

"That wouldn't have made a difference. Forgive me." There was an edge to his voice and the moment the words tumbled out, he scowled.

In a sudden burst of courage, she steeled her shoulders and turned away to face the city lights again. Forgive him? "I'll think about it."

Neither spoke for a moment, just looked out at the water and the lights twinkling on the distant shore of Bainbridge Island and the peninsula. But her brain didn't register much except for a strange but delightful sound flickering in her head and the warmth emanating from his body. The little hairs on her skin stood on end as if they were reaching out, pulling her toward him.

"Will this take long? Your thinking?" His voice whispered roughly in her ear. "Is there anything I can do to change your mind?"

The backs of his fingers brushed aside a few wind-whipped pieces of hair from her shoulder and when his warm breath heated her skin and his lips grazed her neck, she had to lock her knees to keep from wobbling.

She was strong, but not that strong. He was so damn hot and she hadn't felt a man against her in ages. What harm would there be in a little kiss? Even though it really wasn't like her, she turned to face him again and snaked her arms around his neck. What the hell. She could suspend her better judgment for tonight and imagine his apology was sincere.

His mouth crushed against hers, parting her lips, and she felt the tip of his tongue. Oh God, he tasted so good. She melted into him, her fingers twining around his ponytail, as if they operated independently of her brain.

Through the haze of all the wine, she knew she was capable of getting carried away, succumbing to more than just his kisses. Maybe she should just walk away. Right now, before things got really out of hand.

Yeah, right. Everything about him was perfect. The taste of him, the smell of his hair, the feel of his chest against hers and the way his urgent hands caressed the bare skin of her back. Although she remembered drinking only a couple glasses of wine, she had to be drunk because his overwhelming presence muddled her rational sensibilities until she doubted she possessed the strength to pull away from him.

Not that she really wanted to. If she couldn't have long-term happiness, what would be the harm in a little short-term fun? She might be tipsy, but at least she was still practical. And who better to be practical with than someone like Dom?

His warm palm slipped down her back, lower until it cupped her bottom, molding her body to his. His length was a steel ridge against her stomach, and for some outrageous reason, she rocked her hips, imagining no fabric between them.

He froze. His hands and lips stopped moving along her skin. With her eyes closed, she could sense the tension in his face, in his body, as if it was her own. "What is it? What's wrong?"

"Shhh. Hold very still." His voice came out in a ragged whisper.

They stood that way, clasped together, for what seemed like an eternity. She barely felt him breathing. Then it hit her. Was he about to have an orgasm? Fully clothed? Was that even possible for a man?

She could've sworn she felt the rumble of laughter in his chest. The tension seemed to melt away beneath her fingertips, and when his lips caressed her skin more fervently than before, it was as if he'd been rejuvenated. She ran her hands through his hair, the leather cord loosened, and his dark locks spilled down around her upturned face.

He kissed her neck, her hair, her shoulders with such intensity, she wasn't entirely sure she could get him to stop if she wanted him to. A delicious chill, almost a numbness, radiated outward wherever his lips touched. Did he just graze his teeth along her sensitive skin? The blood sped through her veins and she clutched the muscles of his arms a little tighter, felt her nails dig into him, drawing him even closer. With a swift movement, he cupped her buttocks again, but this time he lifted her up and she wrapped her legs around his waist. She was vaguely aware of her no-panty situation but didn't care at that point. She was hungry for him and any misgivings had thawed with that first kiss.

He stepped toward a darkened back wall, ran his hand up her thigh and hesitated. "Are you okay with this?"

How could she not be? Did she act like she wasn't? "Yes," she mumbled against his lips and grabbed his hair in her fist. "I want you. I want *this*."

He didn't act surprised when he encountered no panties, his fingers easily finding her delicate cleft, slipping carefully inside. She moaned into his mouth as he explored her sensitive folds, the pad of his thumb massaging her flesh. The feeling was so sudden, so intense, it almost hurt.

The night air, the city sounds, the cold wall against her back. Gone. The only sensations she was conscious of were those caused by him as he touched her.

"*Dios mio*." He spoke so softly, almost to himself. "I can hardly believe…"

Her body rocked automatically against his hand and he mirrored her movement. Already slickened and ready from the drawn-out foreplay of the evening, she sighed as the night began to crescendo around her.

He pressed his thumb more tightly against her, circled it ever so slightly. "Yes," he whispered into her ear. "There you go. Give in to what you're feeling." *Give in to me*.

And something inside her broke loose.

An intense surge of pleasure, unlike anything she'd ever felt before, crashed through her. Starting in the center of her body, where his fingers were, it shot upward, outward until she felt she might burst. Somehow, through it all, her legs with their silver-heeled shoes stayed clasped around his waist.

When she finished trembling, he gently lowered her to the ground, as if he knew her knees were capable of buckling. She wasn't entirely sure she could stand on her own after that. He brushed a few loose strands of hair from her shoulder and placed his lips there—not moving, not kissing. In small little circles, he ran the tip of his tongue along her flesh like he was tasting her and when he pulled away, cool air chilled the lingering moistness. Needing him to stay close, she ran her fingers along his scalp to keep his mouth there. She wasn't done with him, but she wasn't sure what she was craving. Only that she needed more. He raised his head, his shoulders stiffened slightly and he held her out at arm's length.

Apart from him, she was cold. She wanted to see his expression, read what he was thinking, but his face was hidden in shadow.

Of course. It was his turn now. How could she be so completely absorbed in her own needs? She bent to unzip his pants but he clasped her wrists and straightened her up.

"Just you tonight. I can wait."

"Wait?" *What does he mean by wait? As in not right now? As in yes, but later?*

A hint of anxiety gnawed at her stomach—her conscience? She'd never gone home with someone she just met, let alone experienced an orgasm like that, or offered oral sex to a man who was a perfect stranger mere hours ago.

The muscles of his arms bulged beneath her palms and strange feelings tightened around her insides like a fist. Maybe she wasn't reading him correctly. He was apprehensive for some reason.

Was it simply an excuse to get her to stop? God, he wasn't married, was he?

At that moment, the door opened with a bang and two couples stumbled onto the rooftop terrace. One of the women erupted with laughter when her companion dropped his wineglass onto the concrete floor with a crash. Sounds of music and clinking silverware wafted through the opening.

Mackenzie tore away from his embrace and grabbed her handbag. "I should go. Martin's probably wondering where I am."

She cast a glance over her shoulder as she reached for the door handle. Dom remained near the back wall, the orange light from an overhead infrared heater giving his features an eerie glow while the rest of his body all but faded into the shadows. It was obvious he wasn't going to stop her, so she swallowed her disappointment and pulled open the door.

"There is no one else," she thought he said, although she could've sworn she didn't see his lips move.

UNDER A BURNED-OUT streetlight on the other side of Fifth Avenue, Dom leaned a hip on the hood of the Porsche parked halfway down the block and watched as Mackenzie stepped through the revolving doors of the Columbia Center building and into the taxi line. Perfect. He'd wait for her to jump into one of the yellow cabs, then get the phone to the Agency's tech lab only an hour late. Santiago should be satisfied with that.

He took a deep breath to filter the smells and detected nothing unusual. His olfactory receptors weren't nearly as sensitive as Lily's—he smelled only the salty air rolling off the bay and the wet roadway—but he wouldn't relax until he knew Mackenzie was safely on her way home. His hair whipped across his face, still loose from when she pulled out the leather tie. When he brushed it away, he caught a whiff of her musky, exotic scent still on his fingers and the blood rushed to his cock yet again.

Another chilly burst of wind whistled up the city street and the skirt of her flimsy dress Marilyn Monroed. With a little shriek, she caught it just in time and laughed with the people standing around her. Something tugged at his insides and for an instant he wished he were over there, sharing in that silly moment with her. She flung her wool coat around her shoulders and when a taxi pulled away, she moved to the front of the line.

Aware of a faint throbbing, like the pulse of a vein behind his eyes, he shook his head to clear away the sensation, but it didn't change. It neither lessened nor intensified. *Of course.* He jammed his hands into his pockets. This was her headache, not his. Her blood levels still weren't what they should be. Combined with the several glasses of wine she'd drunk tonight, she undoubtedly felt like hell. All because of him.

Finally, another cab pulled up, blocking everything but her face from his view. He could stretch out his senses to her, get her to look down here, her gaze meeting his one last time. But he didn't .

Goodbye, Mackenzie.

And her taxi drove away.

CHAPTER SEVEN

"THE THING IS smashed to hell. It's amazing it holds a charge." Dom leaned in as Cordell Kincade, the Agency's tech engineer, opened the back of the cell phone and pulled out the data card with a small pair of tweezers.

"Holds a charge? Dom, I'm shocked it even powers up. Look at the damage within the internal casing. The sim card reader assembly is completely shot. Who knows about the circuit board. Let's hope the read/write flash…"

As Cordell's voice droned on with a bunch of tech bullshit, Dom thought about a wispy dress, a fragrant hollow behind delicate ears, a flash of spunky green eyes and a pair of long legs that encircled him and refused to let go.

Should he have chased after her? Begged her to come home with him? Would he be with her now, making love to her in his bed? He yearned for the impossible. To see her naked again, but not as her nursemaid or a lascivious spy outside her kitchen window.

Cordell paused, yanking Dom from his daydream.

"Yes, yes. That's all fine, but can you get the data?"

"I'm afraid the flash memory is corrupt, but let's see if I can get it fired up enough to extract something." Cordell plugged the tiny card into a reader device hooked to his computer. "Cross your fingers. I'll get only one shot.

Every time a damaged drive is accessed, it lessens the chance of being able to retrieve the data. I'd have a better chance if they made these next generation flash memory chips—"

Dom pinched the bridge of his nose, trying to block out Cordell's geek-speak.

Although he had felt himself slipping a few times tonight, overall he was pleased he'd been able to control the urge to drink from Mackenzie again, even when she was in his arms. God, she felt so good.

But her reactions were the most shocking. Most humans instinctively reacted with the flight instinct, sensing the innate danger of a predator. When she witnessed his physiological hunger changes, he felt her fear at first, but she shoved it away with anger. He'd never seen a human do that before. And she thought he was having an orgasm? Good God. If she only knew.

But almost more than the desire to drink from her—hell, he'd have that kind of urge around a sweetblooded male—was a deep-seated longing to get to know her on a deeper level. What made her happy? What made her sad? What did she dream of doing one day? If she could travel to anywhere in the world, where would she go and why? He imagined that as she told him these things, she'd be absently twisting a piece of his hair around her fingers because it helped her think. With his eyes closed, he'd listen, letting her words soak in until they became a part of him, too.

God, he really needed to focus here. He straddled an empty chair and tried to listen to the yapping, but it was no use.

"You're losing me," Dom said, which got an eyebrow

raise from Cordell. "All I want to know is if you can get that data off the phone."

"Sorry. It's just that— Okay, here we go." Cordell punched several keys and they waited as the light on the device blinked red. "Come on, come on. This could take a few moments."

The big man wheeled back and absently kneaded his thighs. Cordell would be embarrassed to know how much he did that. Dom knew it was from the spinal cord injury he'd suffered as a human. It was only after he changed that the cord had rejuvenated and he was able to walk again. But he still had a sort of phantom limb-like pain. Dom guessed it bothered him more than he let on.

"Sorry, Dom, but it's not looking good. It'll blink green if it's reading the card. Oh, great. This isn't good at all." Cordell's fingers flew across the keyboard and an error message popped up. "'Inability to read external Drive G.' I was afraid of that. Okay, okay, I know you're corrupt. But just give me what I want and I'll let you roll over and go to sleep."

Dom managed a grim smile. Cordell talked to his tech devices when he wanted them to do something. Strange thing was they usually complied.

"Don't ask me why this works, but sometimes it does. In fact, when Lily's hard drive crashed—" He glanced at Dom. "Sorry, sorry. Okay, I'm unhooking all my peripherals and we'll see if this puppy fires up." Cordell disconnected all the other devices attached to the various data ports on his computer. "Here's where we pray to God, promise to be good from now on and sacrifice our firstborn."

Dom held his breath as the device continued to blink red. He was a fool not to have gotten the phone from her earlier. The thing paused for a moment, beeped once, then started to blink green. A bunch of encrypted shit popped up on the screen.

"Is that it? Is that the data?"

"Yep. You got it."

"Nice work." Hopefully, they'd be able to determine what those Darkblood idiots had been up to before they shot him. Now maybe Santiago would back off, let Dom do his job.

"That's my girl." Cordell patted the top of the huge curved monitor and skimmed over a few more keys.

"Your computer is a she?"

"Hell, yeah. If I'm running my hands over something all day long expecting it to put out, it better be female. It may take me a while to decode this stuff. You going to be around? I'll call you when I get it up. Well, when I get the data up, that is."

"Yes, I'll be home before going out on second shift. Call me when you have something."

BACK AT THE loft, Dom rummaged through the refrigerator, looking for something to snack on. Nothing. He grabbed a handful of almonds and a beer, plodded down the hallway and flipped on the light to his office. His in-box was probably jammed as he'd not checked email the entire time he'd been in Portland.

He slumped in his desk chair, knowing he should be thrilled the phone data had been recovered, but all he could focus on was a vague sense of emptiness inside.

Amidst the lottery notifications and the penile enlargement offers, an email from the Baja Region caught his eye. He read it quickly—a job offer—and glanced at his wall calendar. Yes, it had been just about five years since he'd been sent up here in forced exile after that mess in Florida. Officially, he wasn't eligible for a transfer for another couple of months, but evidently others had been waiting for his punishment, or cooling-off period or whatever else they wanted to call it, to end, as well. Maybe they could push it through early, because it was definitely time to move on. He rubbed his chest and told himself the dull ache was simply a beer bubble that hadn't made it to the surface yet. Maybe Perdido Bay wouldn't want him back, but it looked like Baja did. He fired off an inquiry about the job description then took another long draught.

His thoughts drifted back to the auction again. He recalled the way Mackenzie stared at him through her impossibly long lashes then bristled when she got caught, how she squared her lovely shoulders against him as if she knew how much he was dying to run the tips of his fingers over her flesh. As he remembered her sweet scent, her fiery green eyes and her silky softness upon his hand, his cock swelled.

The desk chair creaked when he reached into his pants to adjust himself. This was the same hand he'd used to touch her just a short time ago. He hardened further and stroked himself in a slow rhythm, up and down his length, thinking about her sassy spirit, the taste of her mouth and how her body responded to his touch like a beautiful instrument in his hands. He gripped himself tighter. Ah, yes. Naked underneath that flirty skirt with purple panties in her purse. Oh God, and out there in the taxi line. He closed his eyes and imagined pushing himself into her warmth, feeling her tighten around him. As he strained his head back, a powerful surge of pleasure pulsed out over his belly. He held himself a few moments longer as his cock softened in his hand.

Maybe he could— For chrissake, who was he fooling? There was no way any sort of a relationship would work. Just being around her would put her life in danger. He couldn't possibly take that risk.

He shoved the chair away from the desk, marched down the hallway and took a quick shower to wash away the idiotic fantasy. He had retrieved his cell phone from her and had fun doing it. End of story. It would be best if he simply forgot about her. Blood tie or no blood tie. She hadn't had much of his blood so the effects should fade away quickly for her.

Cordell texted him just as he finished dressing. When he returned to the computer lab a few minutes later, he stared at the data on the large screen, organized into tables and charts.

"What is that?" He had a bad feeling about this.

"It's a list of known sweetbloods in this sector. Looks like they're doing blood collections without killing. Or at least that's what it looks they're doing," Cordell said.

"A catch and release?" Since when had they been doing that? An icy chill ran through his body, erasing any of the remaining warmth from his evening memories. This kind of premeditation required planning, organization and restraint. Much more than the haphazard draining and killing the DBs' cells normally did. This was something new.

"Yeah, and look. It appears they've got them on a three-week rotation. That window is much too short. Those people have probably been wondering why they're always so tired."

"Yes, until one day when they don't return home. When

the DBs fuck up and drain them completely like they normally do. Scroll down."

Dom held his breath as Cordell clicked through the list of names, ages, addresses and collection dates. Shit. They were all so young. Decker, Marsha, age 21; Dinsmore, Scott, age 17; Grant, Crystal, age 14. No Foster-Shaw. He blew the air out in a quiet breath of relief. The Darkbloods didn't know about her. "Wait. Keep going." Cordell paged through the rest of the list. No Shaws, either. Thank God. "We'll set up regular patrols around these people in order to catch the DBs who come to pick them up. What do you think—twenty or thirty of them in the Seattle area?"

Cordell clicked through the list and said something about the team being spread too thin, but Dom ignored him.

"Let Santiago know what's going on," Dom said. "The other regions need to know about this change in Darkblood operations. I've never heard of them doing this before. They usually just sell the blood when they get their hands on a sweetblood. This is way too organized. If they're doing it up here, they're probably either doing it or planning to in other regions."

Down in the weapons center, Dom grabbed a couple of handguns, a set of silver-tipped brass knuckles and several pairs of silver-lined handcuffs, taking care to handle them only from their steel clips. The downtown clubs were closing soon and a whole horde of losers would be out looking for trouble. Or at least that's why he told himself he was going out. To put his mind at ease, he wanted to run up to the Northend and double-check she made it home, before he focused on what his team needed to do.

On his way out the door, he paused. What the hell. He grabbed his protection vest then hit the lights.

CHAPTER EIGHT

"MACKENZIE, BE A peach." Martin crooned over the phone. "Please? For me?"

"You know I'd do it in a heartbeat, but I've been feeling like crap lately." Not really, but she didn't know how else to explain it. Restless maybe? "I think I'm coming down with something. You can't find anyone else to do it?"

"Although I love these installation guys, I don't trust them to hang the piece correctly. They need supervision, otherwise the thing will be slapped up on any old wall. I'd do it, but I completely forgot my teaching schedule is different this term. I'm in class in less than an hour." She heard him sniff away a couple of fake tears through the phone connection.

"Yeah, Martin, talk about embarrassing. I'm helping hang a picture of my naked self."

"If you're not up to it, I understand. I'll just reschedule."

It would give her a chance to see the painting one last time. To see its new home. "Oh, all right. So if I need you to cover for one of my classes, you won't bitch about it, will you?"

"Of course not. I knew I could count on you."

"Where do they live? One of the suburbs? Traffic getting over there will be a nightmare at this time of the morning."

"Nope. One of the artist lofts in Pioneer Square. Shouldn't take you too long to get there from the studio."

She hung up the phone and finished getting ready. She'd planned to shoot some pictures of the docks this afternoon anyway, and Pioneer Square wasn't far. She packed her camera into the Triumph's saddlebag and met the workers at the studio. When the painting was loaded into the delivery van, she followed them over the Ballard Bridge and along the waterfront into the downtown area.

The loft was located in one of the oldest and most historic parts of the city, near the sports stadiums and overlooking Elliott Bay. Since many of the buildings were in the National Historic Register, none were very tall. This was an artsy part of town with trendy stores, art galleries and a funky coffee shop every few feet or so.

Her heart beat with anticipation. She'd always wondered what the lofts looked like from the inside and imagined how exciting it would be to live in the heart of everything. Forgetting how out of sorts she had been feeling, she practically skipped into the building foyer.

The doorman, though polite, evaluated her with the efficiency and no-bullshit air of a seasoned security professional as he checked a logbook, punched something on his keyboard and made a phone call. Although she wasn't positive, she thought she passed through at least two different metal detectors and the guy put her bag through an X-ray machine. It felt like the airport.

As she waited for more direction from him, she scanned her surroundings. All the high-tech security gadgetry couldn't hide the rich old-world beauty of the building itself, with its gleaming inlaid marble floors, ornately carved moldings and corbels and intricate wrought-iron details.

Things went from a little odd to downright bizarre when she stepped through a narrow opening into a cylindrical-shaped mini-room and the door slammed shut behind her.

"One moment, miss." The guard's voice piped through a speaker.

Good thing she wasn't claustrophobic. Little lights bordering the edges flashed orange before a short burst of dry mist surrounded her and she coughed. When they blinked green, a door in front opened and the man motioned her forward, handing her the satchel.

What would he have done if she had strapped on her handgun today? Hauled her ass to a holding area for interrogation? Her knife—

She dug into her bag, her fingers sifting through the loose contents at the bottom. Where was her Kershaw folding knife?

As if reading her mind, the doorman—no—guard held it up for her to see.

"Sorry, ma'am. You'll get it back when you leave."

I don't care if Martin pays me for overtime. He is so going to owe me for this.

As she rode the slow, clunky elevator to the top floor, she wondered what kind of important paranoid people lived here. Pulling out her paperwork, she examined Martin's chicken scratch. For a talented artist, he had the handwriting of a doctor.

Would she be able to see any of the San Juan Islands from up here? With a ding, the elevator doors opened into an expansive hallway. She glanced around but saw no windows and walked toward the only door. Guess she'd have to wait to see the view until she got inside. The building might not be quite tall enough, but she'd surely be able to see West Seattle and maybe even Vashon Island. She wondered if the Olympic Mountains on the peninsula were visible. Sunsets had to be—

"Goddamn it." Although the voice was somewhat muffled, obviously coming from deep inside the loft, it still boomed through the cracked door. "Does everyone in San Diego have to follow every damn procedure like they were friggin' boy scouts?"

A prickly heat started in her toes and rushed upwards with the force of a broken fire hydrant, burning her cheeks and setting every hair on edge.

Martin. I'm going to positively kill him this time.

"It's open," the voice called. "I'll be right there."

Like electricity in the air before a lightning storm, the atmosphere felt charged as she pushed the door wider with her foot. She stood frozen as heavy footsteps echoed on the planks of the wood floor.

"Have Gibson call me back, then." A cell phone clicked shut.

Clad only in a pair of low-riding jeans clearly pulled on in haste as the top of his fly hung open, Dom was towel-drying his hair when he emerged from the hallway into the foyer. "Martin, thanks so much for coming on short notice. I—" He hesitated midstep when their eyes met, and Mackenzie could smell the cedarlike scent of a man's soap.

Wrinkling her nose, she tried not to notice his bare, well-developed upper body, the hanks of dark wet hair hanging in clumps around his face, and the ridges of his stomach muscles making a pathway into the waistband of his black boxer-briefs. No, she desperately tried not to notice any of these things.

"Mackenzie." He expelled her name like an expletive.

"You." Her voice sounded too breathy and the thin fabric of her T-shirt fluttered with her pounding heart. The memory of what he'd done to her on the terrace made her cheeks heat with embarrassment. She'd been intimate with a man—this man—though she hardly knew him. Many times over the past week, thoughts of him had invaded her head, and she wished he was more than just a stranger who'd shown her a good time. She'd wondered if she'd ever see him again but doubted she ever would. "I didn't know…how did you—" Totally unprepared, she willed the floor to swallow her up and disappear.

She clamped her eyes shut, sucked a deep breath through her teeth and tried to get ahold of herself. Then it dawned on her. Was this what he meant by "not tonight" when they were on the terrace, because he knew she'd be coming here later? Had he set this whole damn thing up? Mortification gave way as a flood of anger roared in her ears.

Steeling herself for a confrontation, her eyes flew open. But now he was on the other side of the foyer. She blinked a few times, wondering how he could've moved so fast. With white knuckles, he clutched the wrought-iron railing and his towel-draped head hung down between the straining muscles of his shoulders.

Was he sick? Outrage dissolved into concern and she approached him tentatively. An odd sense of déjà vu needled at her memory.

Her sneakers squeaked lightly on the smooth wooden floor of the foyer. She stopped and slipped them off her feet. "Are you okay? What just happened? I heard you on the phone. Is something wrong?"

He continued leaning on the railing and remained silent until she moved closer.

"Stay there." He threw a hand back and she hesitated again.

"I'll just come back later, then." She turned to leave.

"No." DOM HELD the towel tighter around his head, a desperate barrier between the two of them. If he'd had the slightest idea Mackenzie was delivering the painting, he would've been ready for the overwhelming force of her presence. How could he have missed picking up her energy trail? He'd assumed the knot in his chest was because he was so pissed off with San Diego's ineptness. There was certainly no mistaking that she was inches from him now.

Heat from her body ignited his bare skin, while the rush of blood through her veins seduced the beast inside him. A familiar throbbing vibrated his gums. He bit down hard, but it was no use. Razor-sharp fangs pushed through, cutting his lips, and he was forced to open his mouth to accommodate them. With every muscle tensed, his body prepared to spring, straining against his will. He gripped the railing with such force that it compressed beneath his fingers.

She hesitated, he could hear the breath catch in her throat, then, with one final step, she was at his side, and impossibly cool fingers grazed his shoulder. A thrill surged through his body, yet calmed him at the same time and in the span of a heartbeat, the violent tension left his muscles like water pouring from a glass.

"Dom?" She dipped her head close, her voice velvety in his ear.

Her fingers caressed his back so subtly, like the automatic touch of a lover, and he doubted she realized her hand was moving. His fangs retracted, but he was powerless to control the needs of a man. When his erection threatened to emerge from the top of his briefs, he shifted his stance and Mackenzie dropped her hand.

No fear emanated from her pores, nor could he taste it in the air. He perceived only her concern for him along with the remnants of anger. What the hell? It made no sense. Why wasn't she freaked out like most people would be? And how was he able to control himself?

With his back to her, he straightened up and scrubbed his face with the towel. "I'm fine. Head rush." What a pathetic explanation. "You caught me off— I was expecting one of Martin's people. Not you." He stumbled into the kitchen and carefully zipped his fly.

"I am one of Martin's people." She sounded irritated now. "I work for him, remember? But of course, you knew that. I'll come back another time. Or better yet, Martin can."

"No. I want the painting installed today." His tone was harsher than he'd intended, but he didn't want her to leave.

Getting nothing but silence from the foyer, he was about to blurt out "latte or mocha?" when he heard a rustling of fabric. Was she leaving?

Through the doorway, he spotted her bag near her shoes on the floor, and watched as she stepped down, sock-footed, into the living room and disappeared from view. What had drawn her attention? After he licked his lips to make sure the cuts from his fangs had closed, he marched past the kitchen island, still conscious of the heavy throbbing between his legs.

With her back to him, she stood before the wall of windows. Careful to stay out of the direct sunlight, he moved closer to better observe her. Jeans hugged her shapely legs and bottom as if they were custom-made. A colorful knit scarf draped around her neck hinted at a carefree attitude, and the sun on her long, dark hair gave it a rich, auburn cast. With her mouth agape, she stared at the view.

And he stared at her.

"I knew it," she whispered.

"What?" She jumped at his question, evidently not expecting him to have heard her. He felt her raw emotion, the eager thumping of her heart in his head.

Excitement flickered in her expression, but was gone a moment later. "Nothing." With her eyebrows slightly lifted as if to better control herself, she dropped her eyes and turned toward the foyer.

He stepped in front of her, blocking her way. "No, tell me." For some reason, he needed to hear her verbalize what she was feeling when she looked out the window.

She frowned, stared at her hands. "Well…I've always wondered whether the islands and the peninsula could be seen from one of these lofts on a clear day." She met his gaze with damp eyes, then abruptly turned away. "Sorry. I'm a little overwhelmed by your view. Should we—"

"No, please go on." Was she crying? He sifted through the air but detected no sadness. Why were there tears?

Her eyes narrowed. Clearly, she doubted his sincerity.

"I'm serious. I've lived here on and off for so long that I'm rather immune to the view, I'm afraid. Tell me what you think when you look out. What you see." As if watching a conductor raise his baton, he held his breath in anticipation.

"It's stunning, of course. Magnificent." She stood at the window with her arms crossed.

"Come on. You can do better than that. That's not what you were thinking when you first looked out. Tell me."

She seemed to come alive then, hopefully noting the sincerity in his voice. "Well, all right." She cleared her throat and faced the view again. "I see how the Olympic Mountains seem to stretch out forever to the north and south and wonder how much has never been walked on by human feet." Wide-eyed, she glanced over at him and he nodded his encouragement. As if to get more serious, she gathered her hair into a loose ponytail, using a hair band around her wrist. She took a deep breath and continued.

"The jagged peaks against the unusually clear sky remind me of a torn strip of paper glued into place. A contrast of shapes and textures, very different, yet united by color."

His heart thumped unevenly at first, then as he tuned in to her voice, it seemed to blend in with the beating in his head as she continued.

"Today, it's a study of blues. The misty mountains. The indigo water. The pale, cloud-strewn sky. But tonight it may be pinks and tomorrow it may be grays. It honestly takes my breath away."

"You have an artist's eye for description. What else?"

She wiggled a finger around and pointed at the distant peaks. "Could there be a person exactly right there? Or a bear? Or a mountain goat? Or Bigfoot?" Her laughter tickled his ears. "Pretty silly. Not really an artist's description."

"Mmm, not at all. You see and imagine more than an average person would when confronted with the same scenario."

When she looked over at him, her full upper lip puckered into a playful smile, and a strange sensation, as well as a few familiar ones, tugged at his insides. Seeing the view had lighted her mood and that made him...happy.

He longed to pull her into his arms, to mold her body against his and to bury himself inside her with more than just his fingers. Instead, he plunged his hands into his pockets to hide his still hard erection and took a step away.

"Let's say you knew someone was standing in that exact spot you're pointing to. How would that make you feel?" He was utterly captivated by her imagination and didn't want her to stop.

She stared through the glass and was quiet for such a long time, he wasn't sure she was going to answer.

"Less lonely, I guess."

He suddenly needed to make her laugh again, to lift the trace of heaviness from her heart. Twirl her around the room and see her sparkling green eyes dance with excitement. To be the source of her happiness.

"That's beautiful. I've never heard it described quite so vividly. Lovely." He flashed her a devious smile. "Sorry. I'd have studied my thesaurus had I known you were coming."

Her head snapped in his direction, her cheeks flushed a bewitching shade of crimson, and her fiery glance ignited him. She spun on her heel and stormed back through the living room.

Good God, was she still embarrassed about last week? He had hoped to make her laugh again, but this might even be better. Watching her sassy ponytail bounce its delightful "go screw yourself" message against her back, he grinned.

To hell with playing nice. Yes, this could be fun.

MACKENZIE STOMPED BACK to the foyer and knew he followed, irritating her further. She dug into the satchel, rifled through the contents and pulled out a cell phone.

"Calling your boys downstairs?"

"No, I'm calling Martin to tell him to reschedule."

"But I want it installed today."

Those damn blue eyes were probably raking across her backside; she could practically feel them on her bare skin. Crap. Did her waistband dip low when she stooped? She grabbed a belt loop on the back of her jeans, stood up and hoped she looked as mad as she felt.

But when she thought about leaving, she knew the install guys would wonder why. She wasn't prepared to tell them anything. She supposed she could lie, say the client wasn't available, but what if Dom followed her down?

She decided to ignore his references to the auction and pretend this was a normal install. That was how she'd get through this. Just get the painting hung and leave. Not get sucked into his stupid game. "Fine."

He'd played her at the auction and, most likely, he was playing her now. He couldn't care less how she felt about the view. He probably just wanted to soften her up to get in her pants again.

"Can I get you something?"

She forced herself to examine the soaring open-beam

ceiling rather than the swing of his hips in those jeans as he headed for the kitchen.

"Latte, perhaps? Water?" He said something else but she couldn't make it out.

"No. I won't be long."

The open kitchen was a dream with granite and stainless steel and the high-pitched whine of the milk steamer filled the room. Four upholstered stools perched beneath the island counter, a perfect gathering place for people who liked to cook together or for a chef who liked an audience.

"Aren't you worried about things flying out? Bad feng shui?" She heard the amusement in his voice.

"It's not my purse," she said through gritted teeth. He was clearly having way too much fun tormenting her. God, she couldn't wait to get out of here.

She yanked a clipboard and measuring tape from her bag and peered down the long hallway, surprised to see so many doors. His loft had to take up half the floor. Which room had he come out of? Did anyone else live here with him? Girlfriend? The occasional weak-kneed hook-up? She heard footsteps behind her.

"Let me just take a look at the space and I'll get the workers up here. They're waiting in the van. We'll get the piece hung and be out of your hair."

"I'm in no hurry, unless you are." He handed her a large coffeehouse mug.

She tried to protest, but he shoved it at her. Taking a sip, she discovered the drink was light on the chocolate, heavy on the whipped cream. Perfect. Lucky guess.

"Let me show you the two places I had in mind. Right this way."

His fingers brushed the back of her arm and she

shivered. He guided her down into the living area again and pointed to a huge empty wall behind a cream-colored leather sectional.

"That's one place. I like the lighting, of course. Natural, not manmade, but I don't want it to compete with the view. Besides, the piece is a little intimate for a living room, don't you think?"

His breath skimmed over her ear, causing loose tendrils from her ponytail to dance on her cheek. He was closer than she'd thought. Inches away, actually. Hadn't he just been on the other side of the ottoman? She felt herself shift slightly toward him.

Hell, what was she doing? She set her mug and clipboard down, grabbed the tape measure and folded her arms tightly against her chest.

"That's up to you." She didn't want to discuss the appropriateness of her naked form in his living room. "This is a nice location. It'll work, but the wall could really use a couple of spotlights. Especially in the evening when there is no natural light. We could get an electrician in here and Martin could come back later to install the painting."

He had a strange look on his face and shook his head.

"Suit yourself. Could you hold the end of this so I can get some measurements?"

His fingers grazed hers as he reached for the end of the tape and she pretended not to notice. Had he been someone else, the insubstantial contact never would have registered with her. Why did everything with him seem so magnetized? Larger than life? After jotting down the measurements, she took another sip of the mocha, trying to keep her hands from shaking as she felt the heat from his body right behind her.

"Where's the other space?" she asked.

She turned and crystal blue eyes locked her in place. He ran a hungry gaze over her face, stopping at her mouth, which burned in response. He reached up and flicked a thumb over her lips, then put it to his mouth.

"Whipped cream." His voice was husky.

Her heart stuttered and she could hardly breathe.

Remember, he's just playing you.

She grabbed her things, stepped away from him and repeated her question. The corners of his mouth turned up slightly as if confirming her suspicions.

"This way." He touched the back of her arm again, obviously not deterred by her reaction, and guided her down the hall. She was only vaguely aware of the colorful artwork on the walls and the humming of a washer and dryer behind one of the doors as her skin tingled from the contact.

At the end of the hallway stood a pair of ornately carved wood doors, grander than the others. He grasped both handles and swung them wide.

The room was completely dark. When he stepped forward and pressed a button on the wall, natural light flooded the room as flexible metal covers retracted from the windows.

Oh God. His bedroom. He wants the painting of me in here? Is this some kind of sick joke?

Her gaze rested on the unmade bed. Rather intimate to see his bare sheets still rumpled from the night. Had he gotten up, just in time for a shower, before she arrived? Were the sheets still warm? She shuffled the papers on the clipboard and fiddled with the tape measure.

With a flourish, Dom motioned her inside while he stayed at the door. *He's just a client*, she repeated to herself as she brushed past, careful not to touch him. This was just a job.

The room was almost as big as the living area, with floor-to-ceiling windows on two of the walls. The glass met at the corner, no trim to spoil the view. With a motor-ized click, the metal blinds retracted into a narrow panel on both walls. She wasn't aware of how she'd gotten over to the glass, but she was there now. From this vantage point facing northwest, she could see the mouth of the bay. A container ship was pulling into port. Was that Bainbridge Island up there?

To wake up to this every day. To open your eyes and see this.

She imagined sitting here with a cup of coffee in the morning. Or in the evening with a glass of wine. *Is there a rooftop terrace to watch the sun as it sets behind the Olympics?*

The air shifted behind her. She whirled around, the mocha sloshing in her cup. She'd almost forgotten why she was here.

Oh God, there he was, still barely clothed, still so damned hot and still with that smug smile that grated on her nerves.

But now they were in his bedroom.

Why couldn't he just put on a shirt? Her fingers itched to splay over the defined muscles of his chest and she gripped her clipboard tighter. With his unshaven face, would his kisses sting her lips?

In the light she noticed the palest of shadows hovering under his half-hooded eyes, as if he hadn't gotten much sleep.

She glanced again at the tangled sheets, imagined a woman here, running down the hallway just hours ago, late for work in high heels and a wrinkled dress from the day before. They'd probably had sex all night long and he'd have slept longer if the painting wasn't being delivered. Why did she care? Who was he to her? Just a casual hook-up. Why did the extracurricular activities of a player like Dom even matter to her?

With him standing so close, she could hardly trust herself to say anything coherent. She skittered away from him. His presence invaded her mind and muddled up her thoughts.

"What…where did you have in mind? I mean…for the painting. Where do you want it?" Everything sounded suggestive and her cheeks burned again.

She tried to remain businesslike, but all she could see was that big damn bed right in front of her and the half-dressed man beside her. She tried to ignore the massive carved wood headboard that looked like it belonged in a castle, the lush golden silk duvet cover and the multitude of pillows tangled up in the sheets.

She shuffled her papers again, dropping her pen. As she stooped to pick it up, her eyes froze on the crotch of his jeans. She almost gasped at the outline of his length, level with her eyes, straining against the fabric. Could her face get any hotter?

She chewed on the inside of her lip as she stood up. Ever so slightly, his hips turned toward her and his stance widened. She felt a gush of warmth and a throbbing pulse between her legs.

What was happening to her? She stepped away and fanned her cheeks with the clipboard.

"Hot?"

"A little, yes." She didn't dare make eye contact, for her composure was held together only by a thread. If he touched her, raised an eyebrow, skimmed his breath on her skin, she knew it'd be all over. Her body would betray her and she wouldn't be able to resist him.

"Do you want something? Water?"

"No. I'm fine. Should we get on with it? The guys have been waiting for fifteen minutes or so. Where in here? For the painting."

She was sure his gaze rested for a moment on the sheets.

"There." He lifted an arm and pointed at the wall behind the bed.

"Really? Don't you think it'd be better over there?" She indicated the long wall near the double doors. *Just talk. Keep talking. Focus on the words and nothing else.* "Or even back in the living area? The lighting there was awfully nice and besides, no one will see it if it's in here."

"I didn't think you liked the lighting out there."

She pretended to be writing something on the clipboard and kept her eyes glued downward. "It's better than in here."

"Hmm. Now that I'm standing here, I think the wall behind the bed is my favorite place. I can look at it often." She felt the heat of his smile and looked up. It was a slow, knowing grin, as if he were daring her somehow.

"All right." *Often? He'd only be able to see it if he were right here. And how often will he be standing in this very place?*

She glanced around the room. In bed, it'd be behind him. Why was he looking at her like that?

He sauntered closer, his hands in his back pockets, taunting her. She stepped back with her clipboard clutched to her chest, a flimsy yet tangible barrier between them.

At the foot of the bed he stopped and held his palms up as if framing a picture.

"It's the perfect location."

Something about the tone of his voice tickled inside her head and she rubbed a finger against her temple. And then it dawned on her.

He'd be able to see it if he were making love.

Anger ripped at her thin resolve and she could scarcely breathe as she brushed past him and rushed from the room. He was nothing to her. Absolutely nothing.

"I'll get the guys up here with the equipment and the painting. Back in a moment." She squeaked the words and heard him laugh as she stormed down the hall.

CHAPTER NINE

ALTHOUGH DOM HAD driven out to the islands many times, he'd never made the ferry trip in the middle of the day, but then he didn't want to wait any longer than necessary. He knew this conversation wasn't going to be easy on so many levels.

When he stepped out of the car and the sun warmed his skin, he felt strangely out of place. An older woman, dressed in gardening clogs and a loud floral print dress, stepped over a row of hedges and ambled toward him.

"Hey, Shirl."

"Good heavens," she said as she pulled off her work gloves and kissed Dom on the cheek. "I could hardly believe it when Chuck told me you were coming out. Not that I don't love your visits, but look at you—out in the sunlight like this." She held him at arm's length and looked him up and down. "I want to hear what's going on, but I expect you want to explain things to Chuck first."

"Is he up yet?"

"Go on in—he's down in the pool. Back's been bothering him lately and he finds if he swims when he first wakes up, it doesn't ache so much the rest of the night. Can I bring you something to eat? How does lentil soup with homemade sourdough bread sound?"

He didn't want to give her any additional work, but he

hadn't eaten since last night and she was a fabulous cook. "Well…uh…"

She brushed the dirt off her hand shovel. "Off with you. I'll bring it down in a few minutes. Chuck's always starving when he gets out of the pool anyway."

Dom looked around, didn't see any other cars. "No guests?"

"Nope. The place is empty right now. But we're booked up come June. Oh, ouch." A thin line of blood beaded up on her palm and she hissed a breath through her teeth. "I forgot he just sharpened all my garden tools."

"May I?" Dom asked.

"Would you? Chuck would think I wasn't being careful and I really don't want to hear him go on and on about humans and blood and the fragility of life. After fifty years of marriage, you'd think I'd be used to it by now."

He licked his thumb, rubbed it over her wound, and the bleeding stopped. "He just worries about you, you know. It's in our nature to be protective of the ones we love."

"Well, it can really be a pain in the you-know-what sometimes. What a dear." She smiled as she examined her hand and flexed her fingers. "Good as new. Thank you. Now run along. I'll bring you that food in a few minutes."

On the covered porch, even before he stepped inside the lodge, he smelled the freshly baked bread and was instantly starving. He took the stairs to the basement two at a time, pushed open the double doors and when he stepped onto the sea-green tiles, Frank Sinatra blasted through the speakers. In the summer the Olympic-sized pool would be packed with vamp families wanting to play in the water away from the sun, but today it was empty except for Chuck swimming laps in one of the middle lanes. The tempo of *New York, New York* matched the man's slow, methodical crawl stroke. Figuring it'd take a while for him to make the turn and swim back, Dom sat on a nearby cedar bench, but he'd hardly made himself comfortable when Chuck gripped the edge of the pool at his feet.

"Jesus, you're like an octogenarian Michael Phelps."

"Who?" Chuck pulled off his swim goggles and scowled in that you're-an-idiot manner perfected only by the elderly.

"You know—Mark Spitz?" Nothing. "Johnny Weissmuller?"

"Tarzan?" Chuck brightened as he pulled himself up onto the pool deck. "I'll take it as a compliment, then. Put on a suit and get your ass into the Jacuzzi with me. I'm not about to talk to you if I have to crank my head up to see you. There are clean ones hanging inside the locker-room door. Just don't grab one of those banana slings you European boys seem to be so fond of."

After changing into a loose-fitting pair of swim trunks, Dom exited the locker room and stepped into the Jacuzzi. Chuck had turned off the music and sat with his eyes closed on the far side of the tub, up to his neck in the bubbling water. The temperature was a little cooler than Dom was accustomed to, but he supposed they'd be able to stay in longer. This wasn't going to be a quick little hi-how-are-you.

"Why in the hell are you taking a job down in San Diego anyway? I thought you hated Markem and his band of merry men."

So much for pussyfooting around. "Santiago told you, then."

That shouldn't surprise him. Santiago had taken over

as Region Commander when Chuck retired, and he often consulted with the man. But what else had he told Chuck?

"Markem's gone," Dom continued. "Took a transfer to the new unit in Australia. The rest of the field team is decent." He rubbed his chest, trying to ignore the persistent ache lodged deep inside. It was the opportunity he'd been waiting for, wasn't it?

"It's about time the Council pulled its head out of its ass and put some Agency personnel down there. I've been telling them for years we needed to open up a field office somewhere in the Carpentaria Region. With their UV indexes off the charts, it was only a matter of time before the Darkbloods set up shop. I'll bet those bastards have a hey day with the high levels of energy in the indigenous population. So what happened to make the Council put an office down there? A bunch of humans go missing? Bodies found mysteriously drained of blood?"

Dom shrugged. "No idea."

"When are you leaving for San Diego? I haven't told Shirl yet. She'll be devastated, you know. Thinks of you as the son she never had and was thrilled when you came up here." He cleared his throat as he examined his pruned fingers. "So why in the hell are you going? What's so goddamn appealing about California?"

Dom kept his eyes down. "I don't have a start date yet." He balanced his hand loosely on the surface of the water and watched the bubbles rise between his fingers and float his arm outward. He moved it back and it started all over again. "But I've got to go, Chuck. You know I do. Our latest intel shows *he* is somewhere in Southern California."

"Son, what happened that night in Madrid?"

When Dom didn't answer, Chuck sighed. "Keep it locked inside and it'll continue to fester like a shard from a silvie. You can't keep doing this, you know. At some point, you've got to forget about the past and start living for yourself."

"I will never forget." Dom twisted the twin rings on his thumbs, studied the intricate pattern of the filigree. His recollection of that night was as fresh as if it happened yesterday. "I saw my parents' ashed remains." The windows had been left open; the draperies flapped like untethered sails in the evening breeze, no longer gathered neatly against the wall with his mother's fussy golden tassels. "I sifted through what was left of them and retrieved their matching wedding bands—these." He had them resized so they'd be with him always. Constant reminders of what Pavlos had done and the vow Dom had made to kill him. "So, no, I can never forget."

The Jacuzzi jet timer stopped with a click, the bubbles faded into nothingness, and he stared into the water again.

"I guess what I'm saying is not to forget *them*," Chuck said, "but that it's about goddamn time you moved on. It wasn't your fault. Your father would be proud of what you're doing now. Don't scoff at me, young man. You're doing good work here in the Northwest. The cities are as safe as they've ever been thanks to your tenacity and dedication. Bringing Pavlos to justice is the Agency's number one priority. We'll catch him, son. It doesn't have to be you."

Dom slid under the water, resurfaced and pushed the dripping hair off his forehead. Chuck just didn't understand.

"It was *my* fault. My mother sent word to me that

Pavlos was threatening my father. She feared for their lives and needed my help. Even though I was on duty that night and should've been easy to locate, no one knew where I was at first. I was at an inn with a lady friend and otherwise engaged. Not really what you call dedication to my work."

"Well, you're a damned fool to blame yourself. Your father knew he faced risks. None of us predicted Pavlos would take it as far as he did."

"My father wasn't a Guardian, either. He was an optimist who failed to fully grasp that a powerful evil resides inside many of us, too strong to be swayed by reason and logic. But me? I knew better. After Alfonso fell into the Darkblood ranks, I should've realized my parents were a target. Did you know he tortured them, Chuck? That Pavlos— My mother—"

He balled his hands into fists and forced himself to say the words. "From the position of their ashes—my mother's on the bed and my father's on a chair—it's clear that he raped her and forced my father to watch. He's done that kind of thing before. When I arrived, one of my father's cigarillos was still glowing on the nightstand. Minutes, Chuck. I failed my parents by a few goddamn minutes."

It was Chuck's turn to stare into the water. "Why are you so eager to blame Alfonso? He was a young kid mixed up with some unsavory friends."

"Yes, and those unsavory friends happened to start the whole Darkblood movement. Jesus, Chuck. The correspondence from my mother all but implicated him and the house staff confirmed another person was in the carriage when they were murdered. After I kill Pavlos, I'm going after my brother."

They sat in silence for a few minutes until Shirl pushed the door open and set a tray of food on a table, breaking the somber mood. They climbed out and Chuck threw Dom a towel from a nearby shelf.

"Was that all you came to talk to me about?" Chuck asked.

"What do you mean?"

"Santiago tells me you've met a woman."

Oh for chrissake. Was nothing private anymore?

CHAPTER TEN

A FEW EARLY students filed up the stairs into one of the classrooms, some carrying fresh, unopened art supplies and crisp pads of oversized drawing paper, while others brought dog-eared sketch pads and nubs of well-used charcoals and pencils.

Mackenzie loved the beginning of a new session, the eager anticipation in their faces, the promise hidden on a blank sheet of paper. She finished setting up the last easel and was about to review the class list when Martin walked in.

"Hey, what are you doing here?" she asked. With Martin's busy schedule, he rarely popped in unannounced.

"I'm meeting Paul here and we're going out to dinner. Here. I brought you this." He handed her a Starbucks cup.

She glanced at the clock and guessed she had enough time. She followed him to the hallway and sank into one of the upholstered chairs.

"How's the new session shaping up so far?" Martin asked. "Classes full?"

"Yes, most of them are and we've got wait lists on a couple of them. I think we'll need to add another session of beginning drawing next term. Although with the school year wrapping up after this session, I'm not sure if kids are going to want to continue through the summer.

But let's remember that when we start planning the fall schedule."

"That's fantastic. Have I told you how much I appreciate all you do around here? This place wouldn't be half as successful without you." When she said nothing, he kicked the toe of her boot and she looked up. "I'm serious, Kenz."

"Thanks, I love it. Especially the beginning classes. It's exciting to see their progress from beginning to end. The kids are especially fun because they tend not to hide their enthusiasm like adults do."

"I think it's your passion and enthusiasm that gets people excited." He took a sip from his cup and leaned back in his chair. "Forgive me for sending you to Dominic's home?"

"I still can't believe you didn't give me a heads-up." She flicked him playfully with her pencil. "I thought you were my friend."

"I am, darling. Your BFF."

"Friends don't let friends show up at devastatingly gorgeous men's homes without a warning. What if I had gone to the gym first and was all sweaty and stinky? Did you ever think about that?"

"You don't work out."

"But it's the principle."

"Sorry, Kenz, but there was something about the two of you and I wanted to help ignite that spark."

"You're quite the fairy godmother."

"Don't roll your eyes at me, missy. I'm serious. I can't put my finger on it. There's like an undercurrent churning between you, just below the surface, and if you don't dive in, you'll never get swept away. I just wanted to do my part by pushing you into the water. I'm only sorry nothing came of it. "

"Very poetic. Do you make that stuff up in your sleep and try to find a way to use it?" Mackenzie took off the plastic lid of her cup and dipped a finger into the whipped cream.

"No. I'm naturally gifted that way."

"I figured Mrs. Thorn-Steuben told him I had posed for the painting. Wasn't she sitting next to him originally?"

"I rescued him before she sat down. Besides, would it be so bad if he bought it because he did know it was you?"

"In a word—yeah. It's a nude, Martin. I'm naked in that painting. It makes me feel awkward, that's all. And to show up clueless on his doorstep—I wanted to throttle you." Yet although she could barely admit it to herself, Dom's passion for the piece did excite her on some level.

"I worry about you, Mackenzie, that's all. Working two jobs, looking out for everyone but yourself. Have you had any man-fun since you gave Kyle the boot?"

"Martin, please." She glanced around but knew they were not within earshot of the classroom. She hadn't thought about her ex-fiancé in ages and preferred to keep it that way.

"Or are you still worried about what happened with your cousin last year?"

Setting her empty cup down at her feet, she folded her arms across her knees and stared at the floor before answering.

"Constantly. If you truly understood what my family has been through, you'd understand. Stacy is the third cousin of mine to disappear. Of course I worry I'm next. Wouldn't you be?"

She tugged at the hem of her skirt, thinking he couldn't fully appreciate the cloud of dread she lived under each and every day.

"It's not like I have a family history of heart disease," she continued, "where healthy living can reduce my chances of getting it. This is a very real possibility and if it's going to happen to me, it'll probably happen soon."

"You're so fatalistic. I say you live your life and if you fall in love, well, so much the better."

"Do you think it's fair to jeopardize the future happiness of a husband and children in the event something does happen to me? It's hard to imagine the overwhelming devastation you feel when you lose a parent. It's a living nightmare that you never wake from. I know what that feels like, Martin, and I just can't do that to a child. It's a choice I've made. You mentioned Kyle—I have to admit, it was the knowledge that I could never have children that ruined things between the two of us, and it made me realize what a fool I had been."

"He knew you didn't ever want kids, didn't he?"

Noticing a scuff on the top of her black boot, she licked her finger and rubbed it off. A few more students filed into the classroom and she glanced at her watch. She'd have to get going soon.

"Yeah, but I think he was hoping I'd change my mind after we were married. When I got the news from my doctor, although it was a relief to me, it was the reason he needed to call things off."

"God, that guy was an ass. I never did like him, Kenz. I'm sorry, darling, but I just didn't."

"I'm fine with it all, I really am. I don't know what

I was thinking when we got engaged in the first place. Long-term just isn't something I can have. Strictly short-term only, if anything. I was fooling myself into thinking I could have a normal life, I guess. It's actually much easier living only for yourself and not worrying about what loved ones will do when you're gone. Mom hardly remembers me any longer and Corey... Well, he's Corey."

"Isn't he worried like you are?"

"No, not really. He's in denial, whereas I...I'm a realist." She sat up and tucked a leg under herself, the leather from her tall boot sliding easily against the fabric of the chair. "What am I doing discussing all this heavy stuff with you? You're my boss."

Of course he was her boss, but he was also one of her best friends. One of the few people she could really talk to. Although she knew he didn't really understand—could anyone?—he always listened, validating her feelings whether he agreed with them or not.

"Friend first, boss last. I'd be lost without you, darling. I hate hearing you talk like this."

"Oh, Martin. Don't say that. You'd be fine without me. That's why I'm extremely organized in case something happens. You've seen the detailed notebooks and materials I have on each class. Someone could pick up right where I've left off without skipping a beat. You'd be fine."

"I'm not talking about the stupid classes, silly. I'm talking about you."

"Don't go there. Please. That's the one thing I can't control."

He reached over and patted the back of her hand. They sat there in silence as another student entered the classroom across the hall. Glancing at her watch, she made a move to stand up, but Martin held her back.

"Kenz, since you're so worried about the future, why not focus on the present? Dom Serrano is such a hottie. If he went the other way, I swear, I'd be all over him."

She stood up, grabbed her cup, and blew Martin an air-kiss over her shoulder. "I promise not to tell Paul. Thanks for the mocha."

Mackenzie had just enough time to gather a few things for the still life they'd be working on. Most of the students had arrived and the low hum of conversation filled the room. She cleared her throat and moved to a spot where everyone could see her.

"Hello and welcome to City Art School. I'm Mackenzie Foster-Shaw and I see a few familiar faces." She waggled her fingers at them as she looked around the circle of easels.

She opened her mouth to continue her standard introduction, but when she looked toward the doorway, she forgot how to speak. She had to grab the edge of the table behind her to steady herself.

With a black leather coat draped over his arm, Dom sauntered in like he owned the place.

"Dom." She managed to choke out his name after her mouth hung open for a moment. Everyone turned to the door.

She glanced around the room but wasn't sure what she was looking for. What in the hell was he doing here? All moisture inside her mouth evaporated as the temperature in the room skyrocketed. With one eyebrow raised, he looked as if he were waiting for an answer. Had he just asked her something? If so, she hadn't heard anything but the ringing in her ears.

"Can I help you?"

"I'll wait till you're free. Mind if I watch?"

Not trusting her voice, she nodded. Was this beginning drawing or watercolor? Everyone's eyes were on her, including Dom's, as they waited for her to continue.

She looked at the class list, unable to keep the paper from rattling. Beginning drawing. How did she normally start? Discuss composition? Art supplies? Her expectations?

Somehow she figured out what to say and limped through a few demonstrations. Soon everyone was focused on their drawing exercises. She walked over to where he sat near the door. His cologne had a rugged smell, like leather and sandalwood, reminding her of his condo when he'd just climbed out of the shower.

"What are you doing here?" she asked, keeping her voice low. The room was as quiet as a library.

"You left this." He tossed her tape measure onto the table. "Figured you'd be missing it. Can't find a Hello Kitty tape measure just anywhere. Mind if I stay and observe?"

She snatched it up. "Suit yourself."

Now that the initial shock of seeing him had worn off, she was just plain irritated. What did he think he was doing coming in like this? Her hands shook as she assembled the still life in the center of the room. She fiddled with a piece of white silk until she was satisfied with how it draped over a box, then, after arranging a few pieces of fruit, a blue glass and a book, she stepped back to see how it all looked.

Did he want to tease her again since he'd obviously gotten so much enjoyment out of it the last time?

With her hands on her hips, she appraised the still life.

Way too ordered, too predictable. The elements were situated with too much purpose. She shifted the book, moved the fruit and messed up the fabric. Much better.

She walked around the room, answering questions and making suggestions. When she got to Dom, she expected to meander casually past him, but she found herself stopping. He'd been doodling on a spare drawing pad she kept near the door in case someone forgot their art supplies. She was stunned to find his approach to the assignment energetic and almost whimsical.

His apple didn't quite look like an apple with its irregular shape, and yet it was. The shading was dark and unabashedly bold. His book wasn't a realistic interpretation of the still life book as it looked more like a trapezoid, but the shape was exuberant and she liked how he positioned it haphazardly on the paper. The style and composition were fabulous and she had to keep herself from putting an encouraging hand on his shoulder the way she did with her other students.

"How am I doing, teacher?"

His words yanked her back to reality. Impudent bastard.

With his back to her, his thick dark hair moved almost of its own volition as he blended a charcoal mark with his finger.

That hair. That thick, wavy hair. It wasn't pulled back in the leather thong this time. Instead, it grazed the top of his collar, the ends tousled and curled, almost windblown. Would her fingers glide through easily or get caught in the thickness?

She stopped herself just in time. She had almost leaned in to discover whether it had a concentrated sandalwood scent to it. Tugging at the hem of her T-shirt, she smoothed it over the top of her hips as she attempted to collect her wits.

"I…I love it actually." She wanted to lie. To tell him it was terrible, but she couldn't. "It's bold. A little reckless perhaps, even defiant. Skirting the rules somewhat, but not quite without abandon." She took a step forward, resting her hand on the back of his chair and leaned close. She couldn't help herself. "It's got a certain *je ne sais quoi* about it, Mr. Serrano, if you want to know what I really feel."

Slowly, and with the self-assurance of a man who knows what he wants and probably often gets it, he swiveled to face her.

She forgot about the rest of her students for a moment as her arm slipped from his chair back and glanced off his shoulder. With a warm hand, he clasped hers before it could fall to her side.

Looking down at his face, she saw the soft sparkle of his eyes and wanted to run her fingers along the square of his jaw. His mouth twisted into that playful smile she'd seen several times before and had dreamed about at night, and she suddenly realized she was positioned in the juncture of his legs. She couldn't remember how to breathe.

"What a detailed assessment of my little sketch. You do have a beautiful way with words. I'm truly flattered. Thank you." He raised an eyebrow. "Mister?"

Clearing her throat to buy herself an extra speck of time, she tried pulling away but he wouldn't release her. She searched her brain for a clever comeback, a fitting reply. Nothing. She felt jumbled inside. "You're welcome. Dom. It really is quite good. It…it makes me smile." He softened his grip, but she wasn't really relieved when she was able to pull away.

"Teacher?" She tried her best to copy his flippant tone.

After class, everyone helped stack the easels against the wall, but one student struggled to get his folded up. Before she could move to help him, Dom was at his side.

"These are rather sticky. Can I have a try at it?" With a twist, he loosened the thumb screws, collapsed the legs and handed the folded easel back. Dom rested a hand on the boy's shoulder, the gesture almost fatherly, and the two spoke quietly for a moment. Then they both laughed. "Me, too," she heard Dom say.

She was surprised. In previous terms the boy had been uncommunicative and rarely asked for or accepted help. As she shuffled through her papers and drawing samples, she wondered what Dom had said to make him feel so comfortable. She finished putting away all the supplies and turned to go.

"Good class." Dom was close behind her as they walked out the door, and the thrill of his nearness raised goose bumps on her arms.

"Thanks. I don't know what kind of game you're playing, though."

"What are you talking about?"

"First of all, you can't just waltz in anywhere you want to. I was teaching a class. These people paid good money to take it. They don't need their teacher distracted by… by an unexpected visitor."

"I distract you?"

"You know what I'm talking about."

"Actually, I am a student. At the silent auction, I was the highest bidder on this." He waved a piece of paper with the City Art School logo. "Lucky me. Again." Despite herself, she felt her face heat. "You donated a six-week session of art classes, remember?"

"Of course I remember," she snapped. Okay, now it made sense. When she'd checked to see how much money her donations had raised, she'd noticed someone had filled out the buy-now price on this item. It was *him*. She wasn't sure whether to be flattered or pissed off.

"I didn't plan on taking the classes, but—"

"Then why did you buy it if you didn't intend to use it?"

He shrugged. "It was an impulse purchase. Besides, many people buy certificates at auctions with no intention of ever using them. They simply consider it a donation."

The temperature of her blood shot up. She didn't care that he'd paid much more for the classes than what they were worth. Damn the Alzheimer's Foundation.

"So when you left the tape measure, I thought I'd drop it off. Besides, I enjoyed our conversation. The way you describe things is…intriguing."

"Intriguing?" Her anger began to fizzle. She didn't remember exactly what she'd said last week at the loft. What she did remember were his thinly veiled taunts and innuendos.

He leaned against the door frame and she almost grazed his hip when she reached for the handle.

"Thank you, I guess." Shutting the classroom door with a bang, she locked it and turned on her heel.

"HAVE DINNER WITH me," Dom called, before she got to the top of the stairs. "Tomorrow night at the loft. I want to cook for you."

Mackenzie stopped then spun around to face him. Her eyes danced in obvious anticipation of what she was about to say. He tuned in to the beat of her heart as it pounded in his ears.

"What, so you can christen the arrival of your new bedroom painting with the actual subject matter?" The words spat through her teeth, twisting his gut in a delicious fashion. She was clearly on edge. He should stop and try to calm her down, but her feistiness lit a fire inside him that he wanted to keep smoldering.

"How interesting. I hadn't thought of that."

"Oh." She scowled. "Well, I've got news for you. What happened at the auction was an anomaly. An accident. A horrible mistake."

He closed the distance between them and her eyes flashed. Toe to heel, she backed away from his advance but he continued until she could go no further. With both hands on the wall, he caged her between his arms and leaned in, stopping just before their bodies met. His eyes were drawn to the pulse fluttering below her ear and he licked his lips.

"An anomaly, yes. A horrible mistake, no."

He heard the breath catch in her throat as he dipped his head to hers. He knew she expected him to kiss her, and that's why he didn't. A brown curl tickled his cheek as he inhaled and pulled her scent into his lungs, his erection throbbing between his legs. He repositioned himself, wanted to press his length hard against her hip—God, she would feel good—but he didn't. She arched closer as if she sensed his desire, her body contradicting her words.

"What are— Who do you think— Just so you know, I don't do these sorts of things with strange men. Ever. I'm sorry I gave you that impression." Her halting voice betrayed the effect he was having on her and he grinned.

Although she was a head shorter than him, with a defiant lift of her chin, she managed to look down her nose at him through her lashes.

His gums throbbed as his fangs threatened to break through, but he willed them to stay put. "I'm not really a stranger, though, am I?"

Her green eyes were glued to his lips. Was she hoping he'd kiss her? Even the tip of her tongue darted out for a moment, but still he didn't make contact. He wanted her to touch him first and he wasn't disappointed.

Her palms were cool against the heat of his chest as she tried to push him away with an *oomph*. It was half-hearted at best. He moved away from her slightly, although he could tell she was caving and desire simmered behind her eyes.

"What do you think you're doing? I have no idea what came over me that night or what kind of a person you think I am, but it ain't happening again." She thrust her finger at his chest and he jumped back playfully. Oh, he was so loving this.

"So if you think—" She took a step forward, poking him in the chest with a short pink nail and he took a step back. "You can ask me to dinner—" Another step, another poke. "Just to get me into bed, you can forget it."

His back was now against the opposite wall and he put his hands up in a mock show of self-defense.

"I would never, not in a million years, have gone to your place last week if I had known it was you who bought that painting. Got it? And I would've figured out a way for you to take an art class from someone else had I known you were coming. And that Hello Kitty tape measure? You can buy them at practically every drugstore. What are you laughing at?"

The corners of her mouth strained, betraying her efforts not to smile. She was upset, yes, but not angry. Just because he'd surprised her? He sensed there was something more. Did he dare dip into her thoughts again while they were this close? The bond was strong for him.

Not a moment had gone by since he'd taken her blood that he hadn't thought of her. Wondered what she was doing. Where she was. What she was thinking, feeling. It was no use. He was achingly attracted to her and knew she wanted him.

He reached out with his mind, stroking hers ever so gently, then released her. She scowled and rubbed her neck. He had to be careful, he couldn't bear to wipe her memory again. He didn't want to remove himself from her even if he was leaving soon.

What he learned surprised him. She wasn't upset about what happened at the auction or that she couldn't get him off her mind. She was upset by how he regarded her as a result, that he may have a low opinion of her.

Oh God, if she only knew.

She didn't want him to think her behavior that night was indicative of her as a person even though all she was looking for was a short-term relationship.

He wanted to drag her into his arms, cover her with kisses, and convince her otherwise. That he didn't think any less of her. Quite the opposite. Their attraction for each other was powerful, almost palpable. Being aware of the blood bond had helped him to control it, but she had no idea. She really couldn't help herself that night.

One thing was clear. She wanted him now. He didn't have to probe her mind to know that. He could taste it in the air between them, smell it on her breath. Whether or not she'd admit it just depended on how hard he tried.

Everything about her compelled him and he physically ached to know her better. Short-term? Yes, he was fine with that. Wouldn't want anything more. Of course not.

"What if I told you that I find you attractive on every level? That I want to know what makes you you?" Her face softened somewhat. She was listening. "What kind of music you like. Your favorite artist. The last book you read. Your favorite dessert. I know you're much more than those fifteen minutes on the terrace. You fascinate me on every level, Mackenzie Foster-Shaw, and I simply want to know you better. That's all."

She said nothing, but the color of her eyes deepened, saying what words could not.

He ran the tip of his nose along the smooth column of her throat and felt her shiver. Instead of backing away, she tilted her chin up to give him more access, and he knew he had her. He pushed her hair aside, still careful not to touch her skin with his fingers. She moaned softly and the musky scent of her arousal filled his nostrils. He knew she wanted to feel his hands on her, but he was going to make her wait.

"Of course, I'd be lying if I said I was upset it happened. I'm not. Ever since that night on the terrace, I've dreamed what it would be like to have you in my bed." He felt heat radiate from her cheeks and she exhaled slowly. "But I also respect your feelings and simply want to cook for you. That's it. There will be no christening." The tip of her tongue darted out for a moment. *Not unless you want it*, he wanted to say, but he stopped himself.

God, he was mesmerized by her. Her large hoop earring had captured a strand of her hair. Reaching up a finger, taking care not to touch the silver, he ran it down the side of her face, releasing the curl. Her body trembled and he had to suppress a growl. His gums ached, but his fangs stayed hidden.

He wanted this woman as he had never wanted anyone before. It took every ounce of willpower he possessed not to lift up her flirty skirt, slip her tights off her hips, and push himself inside her softness here in the art school hallway. He was going to get her to make the first move and it would be so much sweeter that way.

"I'll be the perfect gentleman." He put his palms up. "Promise."

Her lips curved into a smile as she backed away and sauntered to the stairs again, her skirt swinging against her thighs in a sweet goodbye. Long, loose curls bounced on her back as she trotted down the steps.

"Tomorrow night? What time?" she called from the landing.

"How about seven?"

"I'll be there." As she got to the bottom, he heard her voice again, but it was so low he wasn't sure whether she spoke it aloud or it came from her thoughts. "Coconut cream pie."

CHAPTER ELEVEN

A FEW MINUTES before seven, Mackenzie stood in front of the heavy steel entry door of Dom's loft. She took a deep breath to quiet her pounding heart, but it ignored her and raged on.

After yesterday's impetuous decision to have dinner with Dom, she wasn't sure whether to kick herself for being swept away by his charm or congratulate herself for following Martin's advice to live in the moment. Either way, she was nervous standing here, wondering what was in store for her on the other side of the door.

Could she do it? Have sex with someone she hardly knew? Of course, she could be wrong. It was entirely possible that he intended only to cook dinner for her. But she wasn't a total fool. As she'd lain in bed last night, trying without much success to fall asleep, she'd decided she had to expect it *could* come to that. Dinner at a restaurant would be one thing, but dinner at his place was a whole different scenario.

Shifting the bottle of wine to her other hand, she checked her bag, making sure her overnight items were tucked safely at the bottom. Not sure if it was customary to spend the night after a one-night stand, she'd brought a few things just in case. And if nothing happened, well, at least she'd come prepared.

She straightened her spine and rang the bell.

Mackenzie thought she was prepared to see Dom this time. She willed herself to be strong, calm and focused. They were just two people who were going to have dinner together. But she forgot all that when the door swung open.

Barefoot, with an untucked shirt and jeans, Dom stood casually enough in the doorway, a dish towel tossed carelessly over a shoulder and his hair pulled loosely into a ponytail, but his unpolished attire only heightened his unorchestrated sexuality.

She couldn't speak, couldn't think of a thing to say; her eyes seemed to be the only body part functioning.

He wore a stack of black leather bracelets on one wrist, with those ornately carved rings she'd noticed before on each thumb, and when he reached for her to invite her in, her mouth felt as if it had been swabbed with a giant ball of cotton. The only way he could look any better was if he were naked and her hands were exploring his body. A rush of heat rose to her face and she averted her gaze for a moment in an attempt to collect herself.

"Welcome back." He dipped his head, touching his lips to her cheek, then shut the door behind her.

Her nostrils flared as she inhaled the warm scent of his cologne. She felt her body arch toward him, wanting the smell to stay as concentrated as possible in her lungs. Normally she didn't care for a man's potent aftershave but his was heavenly, almost addictive. She thrust the wine bottle into his hands.

"Thank you." His eyes raked her up and down then crinkled at the corners. "You look great. We're a matched pair."

She glanced at her lacy brown cardigan and smoothed down the fabric of her colorful dress. It coordinated perfectly with his chocolate brown shirt. She liked the way that sounded—a matched pair—and smiled up at him. "Thanks. We must be on the same wavelength tonight."

"Yes, there does seem to be an uncanny connection between us." He paused and a shiver of excitement prickled her skin. "How was parking? I hope you used my building valet."

"I…uh…had to take a cab. It's raining and I didn't want to drive the motorcycle."

"Do you not own a sedan? Is the Triumph your only mode of transportation?"

"It is right now. My mother's car is in the repair shop." She liked that he referred to her— "How did you know I drive a Triumph?"

Something flashed across his expression then was gone.

"Bonneville. I saw it parked outside the art school and assumed it was yours. A woman like you on a Bonnie is hard to forget."

She wasn't sure how to respond to that, so she smiled and looked around as he ushered her inside. Her gaze fell to an ethereal blown-glass sculpture, lit from above, displayed magnificently on a wooden stand near the windows. How could she have missed that vibrant yellow color and the unmistakable fluted shape when she was here last week?

"Oh my God. Is that a Chihuly? Is it new? I'd have noticed it before." Without waiting for him, she walked through the living room and stopped a few feet away.

"His work is unmistakable, isn't it?" he said, approaching from behind. "No, it's not new. I purchased the piece almost five years ago, right after I moved to Seattle. It was in my office, but I moved it here because I thought you'd enjoy seeing it. You can get closer to it. It won't bite, I promise."

She laughed. "Trust me. Breakables and I don't mix. This is as close as I get."

"Well, then sit here and admire it while I finish a few things in the kitchen. Can I get you a glass of wine? Red or white?"

"White, but let me help. I'm not much of a cook, but I can chop, stir, whisk and I'm pretty good at tasting."

"Good. I need help with all of the above."

He touched the small of her back, guiding her to an upholstered bar stool at the kitchen counter. Even through her clothing, his hand felt heavy and warm.

He grabbed a bottle of wine and with a few twists, it was uncorked, two glasses were filled and he was offering one to her. A small cutting board with an onion and a knife sat just out of reach on the counter.

"Can you slide that over? Do you want it chopped in little pieces or in slices?"

A strange expression flashed across his face before he smiled. "No knives for you. Is peeling in your repertoire? You can peel a few carrots, if you'd like."

"Funny you should ask, because I happen to be an expert."

He handed her a vegetable peeler, several carrots, and a bowl for scraps. With his fingers tucked under like a professional chef, he began to chop the onion with the speed and precision of someone who did it for a living.

"How long have you worked as a location scout? How did you get the job?"

"I've been working on and off for Steve about six years now. He and my father were friends. After my father…"

She cleared her throat and started peeling. "When he died, my mother eventually moved us up here and he hired me part-time because he knew I liked photography."

"Your father—how long has he been gone?"

"He passed away when I was a kid."

"So it's just you and your mother?"

"And my brother, Corey."

He retrieved a sauté pan from a lower cabinet, drizzled in some oil and set it on a burner. "Does he work for your father's friend as well?"

"No, just me. Corey's in college and it's probably best if he doesn't have to concentrate on a job till school's over."

"You've been working as a location scout for several years, then. You must enjoy it."

"Yeah, I guess. I get to see lots of beautiful places I might not otherwise have seen."

He raised an eyebrow and leveled her with a serious look. "You don't say that with much conviction. Would you rather be doing something else?"

She smiled at his perception. "No, I do enjoy it. The photography part, but I'm always keeping my options open."

"And the art school?"

"Love it." She finished her wine and started peeling another carrot. She considered telling him what really made her excited. What she really wanted to do. But then, what would be the point if she didn't see him after to-night?

"What did you get your degree in?"

"I didn't."

"But you said you knew Martin through university."

He remembered all that from the—?

Damn.

The vegetable peeler slipped, slicing her forefinger instead of the carrot. She hissed a breath through her teeth as a small bead of blood welled up and dripped onto the counter. Dom was there almost before the stinging pain registered in her brain, grabbing her hand and cupping it gently in his. A strange tingling sensation moved up her arm. The cut wasn't deep enough to be numb, was it?

"Are you all right?" Another drop of blood trickled from her finger, but onto his hand this time.

She pulled away quickly. "Oh God, I'm sorry. Do you have a paper towel or something? Here, let me clean this up."

Ignoring her request, he grasped her elbow and swept her around the island to the kitchen faucet. His arms went around her, his muscular biceps encasing her, and he pushed her hand under the stream of water. Every inch of her back, from her shoulders to her buttocks, was pressed to the muscular plane of his warm torso and she felt his warm breath in her hair.

"Hold your finger under the cold water. Yes, like that. I'll get a bandage from—"

"No, really. I'm fine." She put her finger in her mouth and cranked her head up to look at him. In this light, the blue of his eyes looked a little darker. "See? It's no big deal." But when she pulled it out, the blood oozed again.

In less than a heartbeat, he sucked her finger between his lips, and the breath stalled in her throat. *Oh my Lord.* His mouth was hot and when his tongue slid against the pad of her finger, she shivered, a delicious heat pooling low in her belly. Teeth grazed against—

Suddenly he pulled away from her and strode out of

the kitchen. "It needs a bandage," he called gruffly over his shoulder, his steps heavy on the wood floor as if he were eager to get away.

Out of breath, she held her hand to her chest, her finger still moist from his mouth. She heard a door slam shut somewhere down the hallway. Leaning against the counter, she closed her eyes. *What just happened?*

"Better?"

She jumped, hadn't heard him return. "Um, yeah. It doesn't sting any longer and it's…a…a… I can't even see it."

"Let me put a bandage on it just to be safe." He took her back to her seat and a piece of damp hair hung in his face as he concentrated on her finger. Sweat? She looked at him more closely. No, she didn't think so. Water, maybe.

"So where were we?" He returned to the other side of the island, refilled her wineglass, and began sautéing the onions. "Oh yes, you were just about to tell me why you didn't get your degree."

It took her a few moments to collect her thoughts. Her need to keep things shallow and less emotional didn't seem to be as important as it usually was.

"My mother was diagnosed with Alzheimer's when I was in college and she had to be moved into a special facility. I quit school to care for my brother, who was still in high school, and because the money earmarked for college was needed for Mom now."

"How was there money for him to go to college and not you?"

Okay, he's much too perceptive. She wasn't ready for this. But how would he understand? How could anyone really understand? She let out a long slow breath and stared into her glass. Holding it by the stem, she tilted it slightly and watched as the wine clung to the inside, seeping back down in narrow rivulets. "It's sort of complicated and a really long story."

"I'm in no hurry."

"It probably won't make sense to you."

"I'm also fairly intelligent. Sorry if you hadn't noticed." One side of his mouth turned up as if to encourage her.

"Well, then you really won't understand. All the academic types think it's nonsense."

"I didn't say I was an academic type."

She shuffled through her thoughts, a little muddled from the wine, searching for that little nugget to satisfy his curiosity in order for them to move on to something else. Anything else. This just wasn't the topic of conversation for a first date. And way too deep for a one-nighter.

She took a bigger sip this time. The wine warmed the back of her tongue and slid down her throat. "My family—" *oh, what the hell* "—I told you my father died, right? Well, he went out one evening and never came back. I was ten years old at the time."

"He ran out on you?" Dom looked up from the stove.

"No. That's what everyone thinks, including the police. But they found his wallet, his car, his credit cards, his money. The only thing missing was his driver's license. He just disappeared that day. Never came home."

Dom was quiet for a moment, probably wishing he'd never asked about all this in the first place. It made most people uncomfortable. She knew that. That's why she hardly ever spoke about it. So why were they talking about it now?

"How long have you—" She tried to change the subject, to save him the trouble, but he interrupted with more questions.

"So what does that have to do with you having to quit school when there's money for your brother to attend?"

"That's where it gets really complicated. Why don't we talk about something simple and non-depressing, like what you're fixing for dinner."

"Salmon. Now please continue. I'd like to hear more."

He reached a hand out and touched hers. His eyes, though piercing, had a kindness behind them, prompting her to say more than she might have otherwise.

"My father's disappearance is just one of many in my family. It's happened in each generation for as long as we've been keeping track…hundreds of years. My cousin was the latest to disappear last year."

"What do you think is going on?" He returned to the stove, his voice stilted, almost robotic. Way too much information. She needed to back it down.

"I don't know." She studied his profile and watched as his jaw muscle flexed over and over, as if he were chewing on his thoughts, and he twisted one of his thumb rings with a forefinger. Why had she felt compelled to tell him? He was clearly uncomfortable.

"I'm sorry. I should never have shared all this with you. Maybe I should just—"

"No." He said it with such force that it jerked her head up. "I really want to know more. You think your father's fate awaits you, don't you? And that's why you really quit school."

Oh God. He got it. He really understood.

He gave her the kind of smile that made her ache

inside. "I...I suppose so. Why waste the money? College represents the future, so with Mom's illness and Stacy going missing, I decided to stop fooling myself and get realistic. I know that must sound terribly pessimistic to you."

"Not at all. You're just living the best way you know how within the framework you were given. But your brother obviously doesn't feel the same way."

"My brother? Corey is one of those people who doesn't worry about much. All the weed, I guess."

"Maybe he smokes to drown out the worry."

"Could be."

"And your mother. She's been through a lot, too, hasn't she?"

"Yeah, she sure has. My whole life she's been a worrier. She let her guard down, thinking my father had escaped the curse when he reached his forties, and finally agreed to his job transfer to San Diego. Six months later he disappeared."

"And your mother determined it was the move to the big city, right?" His voice was faraway, distant.

It was like they really were on the same wavelength or something.

He stared out over her shoulder, his eyes dark and unfocused now, and a spot at the base of his jaw pulsed. A strange rush of heat, starting at her toes, ran up the length of her body.

She felt as if she wanted to punch something. She was pissed off. No. More than that. It was fury she was feeling.

What the hell? And then just as quickly, the feeling faded away.

"Yeah," she said. "Got complacent, my mother said.

She took paranoia to the nth degree after that because she worried that the same thing could happen to Corey or me. We moved around to many small towns in Washington and Oregon. We were in the Seattle area when Mom got her diagnosis, so we decided to settle here."

He assembled everything on a large wooden tray, then reached for her hand. "How's your finger? Let me see it."

"It's fine." She kept it in her lap. "Did you know I don't like it when people fuss over me?"

"Yes, I assumed that."

"So why all the fuss?"

He stared at her, unblinking. "When you are here, I take care of you."

To be taken care of by anyone was such a foreign concept. "I don't need anyone's help doing anything, you know, but I appreciate the concern." The words came out quiet and half-hearted even though it had been her motto for as long as she could remember. The ache beneath her ribs widened. Being here with Dom overemphasized what she'd never have in her life.

Enough.

She flipped that familiar mental switch and smiled. "I know you can't say much, but whereabouts are your offices in Canada located? You said British Columbia. Vancouver? Victoria?"

Not answering right away, he sprinkled some nuts into a skillet and flicked them into the air with a turn of his wrist. Yeah, he was the kind of cook who liked an audience. And she was the kind of person who loved to watch. After drizzling some olive oil into a shallow wooden salad bowl, he poured in a small amount of dark liquid from a small bottle with foreign writing and began to whisk the contents together.

"Our region headquarters are in the Horseshoe Bay area. Do you know where that is?"

Her hands flew to her throat. Did she know where that was? "Oh my God, yes. On the way to Whistler Mountain, right? The Ski-to-Sky Highway? Wait. Sky-to-Ski."

"It's the Sea-to-Sky Highway from Vancouver to Whistler, winding along Horseshoe Bay and Howe Sound."

"That drive is breathtaking."

"So you've been there?"

"A few times. But it's been ages. It's one of those places that's so stunning—" she put a hand over her heart "—so moving, you have to pinch yourself to believe that it's real. That your eyes are actually taking in something *so incredible*."

When she looked up, he had set the bowl down and was staring at her. Oh, great. Why was she always doing this around him? Giving him a dramatic play-by-play of how she saw things. He had to think she was much too emotional. Too sensitive. What was it about him that loosened the tight strings holding her together? Normally, she had better control than this.

"Sorry, I'm not usually this expressive."

When he spoke, his voice was hoarse. "Never be ashamed of your emotions around me. I'll have to take you up there sometime. I know of places you've probably never seen before."

"Oh. I'd love that." Something gripped her heart and squeezed. *Do not get attached to him*.

She sat taller on the stool and flicked her hair behind her shoulder. A current of something tangible shimmered in the air around them. Like she could reach forward and strum it with her fingers.

She only spoke again when she thought she could trust her voice. "So, what's the nature of your work?"

"About all I can say is that it's in the law enforcement field."

"That's a pretty broad brushstroke. Is it dangerous?"

"Yes."

"Why do you do it?"

"Some risks are worth taking."

DOM OPENED THE first door in the hallway and mounted the stairs two at a time, his hand at her back.

This is what it feels like when a human man escorts his woman to dinner. Even with everything stripped away, when they were ordinary, they seemed to fit together. He pushed open the heavy steel door at the top and they stepped out onto the rooftop garden. She gasped and her eyes widened as she craned her neck to see everything.

"Oh my gosh, Dom. It's…amazing."

Candlelight from the chandelier hanging beneath the trellis danced in her eyes. If he hadn't made that regrettable promise to her back at the art studio, he'd have pulled her into his arms right now. Instead, he turned to get the salads, but she stopped him with a light hand on his wrist.

"Thank you." She lifted her chin to him, her green eyes fiery in the warm glow from the chandelier. Were his mirroring the same passion?

"For what? You haven't even tried the food yet."

"For everything. Just in case I forget to tell you later."

He swept four fingers under her jawline. She was

delicate, yet so strong. Oh, how he wanted to place his lips there.

His erection surged, straining against the seam of his jeans, and his palate throbbed as the tips of his fangs began to protrude. He quickly turned away and stepped behind her. Grabbing at the leather band around his wrist, he grimaced as he cranked the buckle tighter, the metal barbs of the cilice digging farther into his skin.

Holy shit. Chuck hadn't been kidding when he'd said this thing stung like a sonofabitch.

Sweat beaded on his upper lip as his body acclimated to the higher level of pain. He took a few halting steps toward the outdoor kitchen, grabbed a towel and dabbed at the thin trickle of blood running down his forearm. Chuck had told him he used one of these ancient self-torture devices to control his own feeding urges when he'd first married Shirl and met her large family. The pain it caused diverted his attention away from the blood desire. He ran his tongue over the roof of his mouth. Smooth again. He managed to set a couple of salmon steaks on the hot grill and returned to the table with the salads.

Mackenzie's eyes narrowed to slits. She sensed his pain. Of course she did. But he couldn't take the damn thing off, that was for sure. He wouldn't dare take that chance. He flashed what he hoped was a distracting smile and sat down.

"How about you tell me your happiest memory?" Now it was time to keep himself diverted.

"Only if you will, too."

He nodded.

"Okay, let me think." She speared a large bite of salad and chewed. He liked that she not only ate—he'd been with plenty of women who didn't—but that she did so with gusto. She put a finger up to indicate she must have come up with a story. Before she finished chewing, she began to speak, as if she didn't start now, she'd forget what she was going to say.

As she recalled a visit to an amusement park, her eyes flashed with excitement. "My dad carried me around on his shoulders all day, hunting down every storybook character for my autograph book."

God, he loved the musical quality of her voice and her enthusiasm for just about anything. He could listen to her forever as she talked about purple toucans, fairy princesses, hot buttery corn and caramel apples.

"Do you still have it? The autograph book?"

The night turned suddenly quiet and she picked at her salad. "Yeah, I do," she said softly.

What had just happened? Why was she sad? "I'm sorry. Seems I have a knack for asking tough questions."

"No, not at all. It's just that I made my dad sign the last page before we left the park. Several days later was when he disappeared. That autograph book is kind of special, that's all." For several beats of her heart, her eyes had a melancholy, faraway look, but when she lifted her chin a moment later and smiled at him, her expression was warm and inviting again. "I guess I've had a bit of sadness in my life. I just hope I don't come across as depressing or morbid. I try not to think about the past too much and dwell on things I have no control over."

"You couldn't be morbid or depressing if you tried." He stared at her for a moment longer, wanted to comfort her, to draw her into his arms, but he didn't because of that damn promise. Instead, he rose from the table and returned with their dinner plates.

"Okay, your turn," she said as she flaked off a piece of fish.

He shoved the food around on his plate. She never thought about the past and that's all he could think about. "Mine involves my family, too. My mother."

Mackenzie angled toward him on the settee and he felt himself moving slightly toward her, as well. Her knee brushed his leg and she left it there. He was careful not to move and break the contact when he began to speak.

"I grew up in Europe and we traveled a lot, as well, given my father's occupation. He was a politician of sorts. One night—day, I mean, when the Council was in session, my mother took us to a small art gallery in the plaza. Many artists had taken up residence in Paris at the time."

"Oh, like who?"

Shit. Of course she knows art history. He couldn't very well name any of the 19th-century artists his mother knew, some of whom Mackenzie most certainly would be familiar with.

"Nobody famous. She, like you, loved the whole atmosphere of creativity, although she didn't have artistic talent as you do. When we went into the gallery, an old man with a terribly crooked spine swept my mother into his arms and twirled her around the room. He was so fragile-looking, I wouldn't have believed he could move that way. My mother laughed and I can remember dancing around the room with them. Turns out she had posed for him and the painting sold for quite a large sum of money. It was a nude." He ran the backs of his fingers over her arm and thought he felt her tremble.

"And your father…he was all right with your mother posing nude for someone?"

"Yes. Although my father was a very jealous man, the old man was a dear family friend, very talented, but very poor. He refused to take any monetary help from my father. So he and my mother came up with the idea of her posing for him. He was known for— He made enough money to barely scrape by with his paintings at the time, but at least my parents felt they were helping."

"You said 'we.' Do you have brothers or sisters?"

"I have a sister who lives in the UK. But it was my brother who was with me at the gallery."

"And where does he live?"

"I don't know. We are not…close."

"I'm sorry. When did you last see him?"

His chest tightened, an iron fist squeezed his heart into a ball. "Many, many years ago."

She clasped both of his hands and brought his fingers to her lips as if she were trying to take away his pain. "And your parents? Where are they?"

He took a deep breath and let it out slowly. "They died a long time ago."

A gentle caressing of energy passed from her hands to his and the knot in his chest, which bunched up whenever he thought about his parents, actually loosened a bit. When he looked down into her eyes, it wasn't pity he saw, but understanding.

Her thoughts whispered inside his head as she wrapped her arms around him, soaking up his sorrow with every whirling stroke of her hand against his back. He held on to her, burying his nose in her hair, breathing the coconut smell of her shampoo. Unlike him, with his probing questions, she said nothing, and he felt like a lumbering bastard.

In a span of time that seemed to pass as quickly as a

dozen human heartbeats, powerful in its simplicity, yet way too fleeting, they finished their dinners and started in on a second bottle of Voignier. If her empty plate was any indication, Mackenzie had thoroughly enjoyed what Dom prepared for her. He rested his chin in his hand and watched, enthralled, as she took another piece of bread and swept up the remaining sauce from her plate. She licked a stray crumb from her lips and her eyelids fluttered shut while she slowly chewed, as if she were committing the taste to memory.

"I hope you're not too full for dessert," he said.

"Never. I always have room for something sweet." Her eyes held his for a moment before her cheeks colored that enchanting shade again and she looked away.

He returned a moment later with one plate and an enormous piece of coconut cream pie.

"No, you didn't," she gasped. Was she surprised he'd heard her say she loved coconut? Or that he remembered? "I must be in heaven. Did you make it?"

"I picked it up from Tom Douglas's restaurant."

"This is his triple coconut cream pie? I've heard how good it is, but I've never actually had it myself." She dug into the thick cream and moaned when she pulled the empty tines from her lips. The sound she'd made was almost identical to the one she made when she came against his fingers that night at the auction. Dom shifted in his seat to make a little more room in his jeans.

"Are you not having any?" Whipped cream lingered on her lips.

"No, I don't do sweet. Not usually."

"You mean you got this just for me?"

He nodded.

"Oh, but you have to just try it."

He hated coconut. Always had, or at least he'd thought he did until tonight. Taking the same fork, she sectioned off a huge piece and lifted it to his lips.

"Holy Christ, that's way too big."

"Just wait. You'll love it. Trust me."

When he opened his mouth, she opened hers, mirroring his actions as though she were experiencing the bite along with him. He closed his lips over the creamy filling and she slowly pulled out the fork.

Candlelight sparkled in her widened eyes as she leaned in close for his reaction, probably oblivious to the fact that her breast pressed against his arm. "Amazing, am I right? I am, aren't I?"

The filling was rich and the crust was flaky, tinged with coconut, as well. He mumbled his agreement and had to admit it was pretty good. For a diehard aficionado, this pie must be the pinnacle. When she offered him another bite, he started to lift a hand in protest, but she got so much enjoyment feeding him, he wanted to continue to be a part of it. No, it was more than that. He wanted to be the cause.

He wasn't expecting her kiss. She leaned over so quickly, he had no time to prepare himself, no time to double-check that his deadly instincts were still safely tucked away. With his mouth clamped shut, he ran his tongue over his palette. Nothing. So he softened his lips and kissed her back.

"Thank you for this." Her words rumbled against him. He wasn't sure if she meant the dessert or the kiss. "You taste delicious."

All day, all evening, he'd been hoping she'd touch him first, kiss him first. He wanted any contact to be on her terms, and now they were. He cradled the back of her head in the palm of his hand, held her lips close to his, her tongue sticky and sweet.

When she sidled closer and a tiny moan from her throat vibrated against his lips, it was the only encouragement he needed. In one swift movement, he pulled her on top of his lap and kicked the settee backwards. Dishes clattered as her behind clipped the edge of the table. He didn't care that glasses were broken, that wine was spilled.

From her gasp, he knew he had startled her, but she slipped her hands up over his chest and twirled a length of hair loosened from his ponytail, her breath warm against his cheek. With every ounce of willpower, he waited until she dipped her head to his again. He didn't want her to regret any of what was going to happen. He wanted— no—needed for her to come to him willingly, of her own accord. His mouth hungrily met hers as she tugged at the thin leather tie at his nape, spilling his hair to his shoulders.

"I've been wanting to do this all night." Her fingers dug into his hair.

And the beast inside him roared.

He cupped her bottom, yanked her hips forward against the stiffened erection straining beneath the fabric of his jeans and moved against her core. She arched her back and pressed her breasts to him. When he grasped the zipper at the back of her dress, he paused one last time which surprised him. Normally at this point, it would be all about fucking, pushing himself into the female fast and hard. The fact that he hesitated shocked the hell out of him. He cared about Mackenzie, what she thought now, whether she was completely ready for this, and he cared about what she'd think tomorrow and next week.

Her half-closed eyes were heavy with passion and she

clutched at his shirt, maybe a little desperately. Oh God, he hoped so, because he was certainly desperate for her. He pulled the zipper down slowly, giving her the chance to stop him, but she didn't. It slid past her shoulder blades, the curve of her spine, down to her waist, where it stopped at the small of her back. The straps fell of their own accord, baring her skin to him, and he ran a thumb over her delicate collarbone. Her pulse vibrated at the base of her neck and called out a sweet invitation just inches from his deadly smile.

No, I will take her as a man only.

With a flick of his wrist, her dress was gone and she shimmied out of her tights. Glorious, she straddled his lap, naked except for the thin meaningless triangle of her thong. Although he'd seen her without clothes before, this time was different. This time she was naked for him.

"God, you are so beautiful, Mackenzie. So very perfect." Her breasts sat in his hands, neither too large nor too small, and he marveled at the softness of her porcelain skin as she trembled beneath his touch.

"I'll bet you say that to all your honeys. Wait. Don't tell me. I don't want to know."

"I have never told that to another woman." When she lifted her eyebrow he added, "I speak the truth, whether you believe me or not. I do not lie." *About that.*

His palate ached, his canines threatened to elongate, but he was ready for his body's automatic reaction. He ran a precautionary hand around the leather band at his wrist. Although the barbs had poked into his skin all evening, the movement jostled and reopened the tiny wounds. He stifled a hiss and his primitive instincts were again consumed and dulled by the searing pain rather than by taking her blood.

She cocked her head and narrowed her eyes as she scrutinized his face, no doubt trying to figure out what just happened. Of course she sensed what he was feeling, although she couldn't have known how or why. "Is something wrong? I...I... Are you okay? I've got the strangest sensation that you..." She had been unbuttoning his shirt but stopped.

"Shhh. Don't worry. I am more than fine. Much more."

When he took her nipple into his mouth and ran a thumb over the other one, he heard the ragged hitch of her breath. He circled his tongue against the delicate flesh already peaked from the cool night air and coaxed them both to even greater stiffness.

It was too cold for her to be unclothed like this, and his impatient sex would stay imprisoned no longer. With a grunt, he stood up, her legs clutched around his waist, and he carried her to the large canopied lounge and covered them with a down blanket.

He smelled her desire, stunned by its sweetness. It seemed to wrap around him, drawing him closer, pulling him in. Although he was familiar with women's passions, this was much different, deeper, as if she called to him on another dimension.

He wedged a knee between her thighs and shoved them open. As he went to push the fabric of her thong aside, she grabbed his wrist.

"Wait. This has been all about me. Now and at the auction. It's your turn. I want you. To feel you in my mouth, to know your taste."

Sweet Jesus. Only a fool would turn down such an offer, but he honestly didn't know what he wanted to feel more—her lips or her body molding around him.

She pushed him onto his back and he watched as she unbuttoned his jeans and pulled them over his hips. When she reached for his shirt, he shrugged her away and tore it off himself.

Her hands splayed over his pecs, her soft curls swept his chest as she inched lower and lower. He strained against the powerful urge to take control. God, how he wanted her. Needed her. And like hell he was going to wait—

He raised his head from the cushion, made a move to roll her over, but she flashed him a dark look.

"Down," she ordered.

A moan—almost a growl—started deep inside and rumbled in his chest. He wasn't used to waiting for what he wanted. She continued to glare, daring him to move again, before she settled herself between his legs. Her fingers trailed up and down his belly, teasing him, tormenting him, her touch so light that it numbed his skin.

He balled up bunches of the blanket in each fist in an attempt to anchor himself to the lounge. Would she at least let him watch her lips stretch over his sex as she took him in? He propped himself up on one elbow, but she gave him that warning look again.

"All right," he laughed. "I'll be good this time."

"I certainly hope so."

He trained his eyes on the inside of the lounge canopy instead, the city lights, the stars—seeing everything and nothing at the same time. He was powerless against her and shook with anticipation as he waited for her to continue.

She moved lower underneath the down blanket, her lips and hair whispered against his skin until she finally reached him. He expected to feel the warmth of her mouth and nudged his hips to push inside, but again she held him down.

Spreading his thighs a little roughly, she nestled in deeper between his legs, making herself comfortable. A thrill of anticipation shot through him. What a turn-on to have her handle him like this, like she was the one in charge. He tried his best to obey her this time and lay still. But when she suddenly pulled a ball from his loosened sac into her mouth, he couldn't help himself. He arched his back, dug his heels into the mattress.

Oh God, oh God. Every nerve ending crackled and jumped as she sucked. At least she didn't protest when he buried his hands in her hair. He was going to climax and she hadn't even touched his erection yet.

A hot surge of energy, starting at his toes, coursed through his body as she released his balls and slipped her mouth over the head of his shaft, encasing him in warmth and wetness.

He wasn't going to be able to stop and didn't give a damn if people milling the streets in the city below could hear him. And they probably could.

HIS HANDS WARMED her cheeks and ears as he gently pulled her up. His enormous erection hit his belly with a slap as it fell from her mouth and her lips throbbed in the rhythm of her heartbeat.

"I need me in you. Now." His voice was husky as he reached for his jeans.

"Don't bother. I can't get pregnant. Unless you're worried about—"

"You don't worry me. I was only thinking of you. You are safe with me."

His hands were urgent and she let him roll her over.

With the cushion warmed from his body, she settled against the pillows, and her heart pounded a symphony in her head. He climbed into the eager triangle of her legs and draped his large body over hers.

She had just dominated him, taken what she wanted, toyed with him like a brush against a canvas, and now it was his turn. She ran her hands over the bunching muscles of his shoulders and delighted in the musky fragrance of his skin. As if on cue, she felt another silky rush of pleasure to ease his entry.

Something nagged at the back of her mind. Her daydream. This was just like her daydream. His arms, his shoulders, her body's response. Could it have been some sort of premonition? Before she could consider that further, his mouth came down hard over hers, stealing the breath from her lungs and any other thoughts from her mind.

"I love the taste of me on your tongue," he said.

She held her breath as best she could, focused on the tip of his erection hovering at her center. She wanted to remember every sensation, every sound, every smell.

His hips flexed back to drive himself inside but before she could reach between them to move the thong aside and guide him in, his tip poked against the fabric and denied him access. With a grunt of frustration, he slid down her belly, grabbed the thong between his teeth, and ripped. But instead of coming back up to continue where he left off, he drew her knee over his shoulder, dipped his head to claim her.

Panting, shaking, she ran her fingers over his scalp, grabbed a fistful of dark strands and held on for support. His hair teased the inner skin of her thighs and his breath was hot as he buried his face in her tender folds.

He slipped two fingers inside and moved them in the rhythm of his tongue.

Her release rushed to the surface, as if it had been waiting all night, which it had been, every muscle in her body clenched around the apex of his fingers. And for that moment, that splendid, celestial moment, it was the center of her universe.

When she was done, he pulled his face away, lips moist, eyes smoldering with desire. "You are like honey and now you're ready for me."

She could hardly keep from shaking. This was just the beginning. She gripped his powerful triceps, felt them flex as he reached a hand down to the junction between his legs. He palmed himself, rocked back, and his erection slid downward along her belly, searching for her. She waited, hardly able to breathe, as her folds surrounded the tip of his shaft, beckoning him inside. When he dropped his eyes to hers, she saw the desire in his face and knew it mirrored her own, but she saw something else, as well. Tiny lines creased his forehead, lines she hadn't noticed before.

He was worried? About what? She responded by circling his legs with hers. Now was not the time for thinking; there'd be a time for that later. Now was only about this very moment, and this very moment she needed him.

Carefully and agonizingly slow, he pushed himself inside, sliding in through her body's silky welcome. Oh dear God, he drove deeper and deeper until finally the hilt ground against her opening. Every pore flushed hot and the beautiful humming sound in her head lapped invisibly on the backs of her eyelids. Her climax rose without movement or friction, just from the feel of his overwhelming presence in her mind and body. Cleaving her in half, he stilled and she clung to him, wanting this to go on forever.

He looked down at her, his eyes wide with surprise. "Is this okay? Are you okay?"

"God, yes." She could hardly get the words out as her body adjusted to his girth, stretching and expanding around him.

There was an intensity in his expression, almost disbelief. With his eyes riveted to hers, she saw that his irises were completely black. She wasn't frightened of him, though; she never had been, and now she understood. It was the look of longing, the ache of a hungry man. She wanted to be what he was searching for, whether it made sense or not.

He hooked an arm under her thigh and pressed himself a notch deeper. "And this? This is fine?"

"I'd say it's more than a little fine."

He made a few tentative thrusts. "This doesn't hurt? You're so...damn tight...around me. I've never—"

She dug her nails into the flesh of his backside, rolled her hips. "Oh God, Dom, I'm not going to break."

That must've been the reaction he wanted because he slid himself outward, almost to the point of breaking their connection, the ridge of his sex rubbing against her now ultra-sensitive center. Her shallow breath zigzagged in her chest a few times before it lodged in her throat and waited.

Finally, with the corded muscles of his neck straining, he drove in hard and she cried out in blissful ecstasy. The friction. His thickness. His smell. Everything.

Over and over he pounded into her until the dark margins of her vision threatened to expand. It was as if her spirit soared in the updrafts of a wondrous wind, spiraling to the heavens with this man inside her body.

And then, on the verge of another orgasm, when all of her muscles began to convulse, he pushed impossibly deeper in one final powerful surge and the ridge of his tip locked into something at the very heart of her core. Into something she hadn't known existed.

Her body clamped onto him like a vise and wouldn't let go. Rearing his head to the night sky, Dom's roar echoed through her body as if it was centered inside her. The scent of their lovemaking filled every fiber, every cell of her being. She wanted to swallow him up and never let go. In a blinding fury, his seed spilled into her, pulse after pulse, and shot them both into orbit.

DOM HELD MACKENZIE in his arms, stroking her hair, as she slept in his bed. With every breath she pulled into her lungs, he was lulled by the even rhythm of her chest against his and the sound of the air through her lips.

He was ashamed to admit to himself that before tonight, he had hoped a little fun between the sheets would break him of her, get her out of his system. It had always worked before. A little dinner. A lot of sex. Then goodbye.

His erection stirred again and he reached down to free it from between his legs. Good God, he couldn't seem to get enough of her body. They'd made love several times already.

He should leave her alone, let her sleep, but he couldn't. He slid his hand down the flat plane of her belly into the center of her small strip of curls and her legs opened for him. Heat spread out to his fingers and toes and a growl of pride rumbled in his chest. He loved that his presence affected her that way. That her body responded to him with or without her awareness. He slipped a finger inside her silky folds. Of course she was moist. His essence still lingered within her.

He massaged her flesh with his thumb and forefinger and felt the hum of her pleasure inside his head. With her eyes still closed, she hooked a leg over his and snuggled in close, moving her hips against him, forcing his fingers deeper. He was lost in her sweet smell again, and in the gentle sway of her naked body.

And then fangs broke through his gums.

His body stiffened in horror. How could he have let his guard down like this? He jerked his hand away from her, twisted the thick leather band on his other wrist, and suppressed a hiss. As the protruding spikes jostled the raw skin again and pain shot outward, the holes in his gums closed and his composure returned.

He ran a cautionary tongue over his teeth as the numbness from the cilice spread up his arm. He must never forget what he was capable of doing.

"Mmm, Dom," she whispered against his neck. Did she sense his pain or was she protesting the sudden removal of his fingers?

He kissed the top of her head and she snuggled closer. She felt so perfect against him, so natural. Like a missing part had finally found home. He thought about what Lily had said about *Enlazado por la Sangre*. Could any of that really be true? If so, then he'd be able to transfer his energies to her. Should he try? Mackenzie was tired enough that perhaps she wouldn't even notice anything.

When he sculpted his palm to her cheek and loosened his mind, he felt the familiar electrical flow, but instead of pulling it in, he bore down and pushed it outward.

Suddenly Mackenzie's back arched and her lids flew open. Her gaze locked onto his. The gold flecks in her green eyes sparkled with such depth he imagined he was looking straight into her soul. She grabbed his face and pressed a half-crazed kiss to his lips, her mouth hard and demanding against his.

He cupped her other cheek and she moaned into him. Like the in and out of breathing, their energies mixed, ebbing back and forth between them. She intoxicated not only his body, but his mind and soul, and he had the glorious sensation that he was floating.

In one commanding movement, she climbed on top of him and speared herself with his stiff erection. As she rode him, he had the answer to his unspoken question, but he shoved aside the gnawing ache to address another time.

The scent of sex was heavy in the room when he blinked his eyes in the darkness several hours later. With his nose buried in the crook of his arm, he smelled her musky sweetness in his pores and knew she was gone. A quick glance at the clock made his gut clench. What was wrong with him? How could he have let so much time go by? A couple of hours, maybe, but he'd blown off a whole night and most of the day making love to Mackenzie. No doubt the rest of his team had been on stakeout like he had ordered. He flung off the sheets and stomped to the bathroom. He was a horny-assed selfish bastard who only cared about getting laid.

Just like he had the night his parents were killed.

CHAPTER TWELVE ·

"NERVOUS?" DOM HANDED Lily the projector remote as everyone in the field office's conference room took their seats around the huge mahogany table.

She tried imagining everyone in their underwear, but since she'd seen several of them naked anyway, the trick didn't do much to calm her jittery stomach. Especially considering she was on live with all the other North American Regions, as well.

"A little. I've just never spoken to this many people before." Not everyone knew how she had gotten the job at the Agency, so at least some of them might think she had something worthwhile to tell them. And for those who did know, she just hoped they'd keep their mouths shut and their comments to themselves.

"You'll do great. You're the one with the intel, not them. Everyone listening wants to know what you know. Nice suit." Dom turned to face the group and Lily ran a hand over the light gray wool skirt, the most conservative item of clothing she owned.

"Okay, people. Listen up." At the sound of Dom's commanding voice, the side-chatter ceased and all eyes in the room faced forward. Jackson, who'd been crunching ice from his water, swallowed and pushed his glass away. Cordell, Sadie, Mitchell and a couple of fresh-faced rookies she hadn't met yet—even Santiago—swiveled in their chairs around the large oval table. "Lily, it's all yours."

Her black heels clicked on the wood floor as she walked to the podium. "Thanks, Dom. Good afternoon, everyone." Lifting her chin, she looked into the webcam and knew similar groups all over the country were watching her, as well. "For the next half-hour, I'm going to cover what we know about the current state of Darkblood operations and what we believe to be the direction they're heading."

She pressed a button on the remote to start the Power-point presentation and a map of North America popped up on the screen. "Until now, the Darkblood Alliance has been loosely organized into cells in major cities around the world, with the primary purpose of capturing and subsequently draining-slash-killing humans with Sangre Dulce." She clicked to the next slide.

"The Sweet they collect locally is sold locally. Supply has always been unpredictable and the price high." A few more clicks, a few more slides. Her nervousness faded away as she explained each image. Yes, she did know her stuff and she slipped into a rhythm.

"My sources tell me there has been tremendous pressure within their organization to figure out a way to increase supply. As you all know, several weeks ago, the Seattle field team uncovered data suggesting the Alliance has moved from haphazard blood collection to a capture and release operation. Instead of kidnapping the sweetbloods they stumble upon to drain them of their blood, they're now recording the whereabouts of those with Sangre Dulce. They do a catch, drain, and memory wipe, then return these people to their regular lives to be available for another round of draining later. As you can imagine, it requires a tremendous amount of restraint not to kill them."

While everyone in the room nodded their heads and made sounds of agreement, Dom sat stiff and frozen in his chair, eyes fixed on his clasped hands, probably thinking about how he'd nearly killed Mackenzie. Yeah, he knew from experience it was hard.

"Of course, some may still die in the process, but this new course of action shows their desire to control the flow, pardon my pun, of Sweet." That got a few laughs, none from Dom, and Lily strolled to the other side of the screen.

"How is this change worse for humans?" someone from the Spokane field asked. "They go from draining and killing to just draining. Capture and release—sounds better to me."

Dom banged his hand on the table and everyone in the room jumped. "Because they're still killing. Maybe not the first or second time. But eventually, they'll slip and people will still die." He stormed to the front of the conference room to look into the camera. "For a minute, let's forget about the simple fact that this collection bullshit is wrong, that they're treating these people like a herd of oblivious cattle, that the experience itself must be terrifying. Let's just forget about all that for a moment. By increasing the supply of Sweet, more vampires will have access to the stuff. More will get addicted. The Darkblood Alliance will become more powerful." He pounded his fist again, this time on the podium, and the remote fell to the wood floor with a clatter. "And that is just not acceptable."

"Fair enough," Spokane said.

As Dom strode to the back of the conference room,

Lily picked up the remote, thankful the thing didn't break, and clicked through a few more slides, pointing out trends and patterns in each major U.S. city.

"Here in the Seattle office, we've not noticed a spike in the supply levels yet due to this new program of theirs. In fact, it's decreased and we're not sure why. But it's just a matter of time until there's more Sweet on the streets. If they're doing this here, they're most likely doing it in your areas. But word has it that this is just the tip of the iceberg." Although everyone in the local office was quiet, Lily heard mumbling from the other offices through the audio feed. "My source tells me the Alliance is planning something big. Their researchers apparently are looking for a genetic link or marker among known Sangre Dulce."

"What for?" someone else asked. "You don't need a test to tell if someone is sweet."

"We're not sure," she answered. "All we know at this point is they're telling their people to get ready for large influxes of Sweet to hit the market over the next few years."

"What do *you* think is going on?" San Diego this time. "With your ears on the inside, you must have some sort of idea."

Leaning against the edge of the table, she crossed her legs and picked off a piece of imaginary lint from her slim skirt as she collected her thoughts. When she lifted her head to look directly into the camera, in her peripheral vision she saw Dom pacing in the back of the room. This was eating him up.

"Well, although this is purely speculative, my source tells me they want to move from harvesting to creation."

As voices erupted in the room and over the speakers, Lily's eyes met Dom's hardened gaze.

A woman's clear, crisp voice sounded over the video feed and everyone hushed. "Do you suspect they're developing a synthetically created Sweet product or are you talking cloning?"

Oh my God, was that Roxanne Reynolds? She was the lead scent-tracker instructor for North America.

Lily looked directly into the small camera. "I'm not sure yet, ma'am. Perhaps, but I'm waiting to hear more details from my contact." She paused to give Ms. Reynolds a chance to reply, but when the woman said nothing more, Lily cleared her throat and continued. "Until then, we need all of you to keep your eyes and ears open. We don't know where their research facility is located, but we need to find it soon. My source tells me they're going online within the next few weeks."

"So your *source* claims to know the Alliance is conducting some sort of testing but doesn't know where?" It was the San Diego field office again, but this time she recognized the skeptical voice.

Her euphoria from having Ms. Reynolds ask a question of her evaporated into irritation. "They're being tight-lipped within their organization. Apparently only the researchers and Pavlos know the whereabouts. It could be anywhere."

"How do we know you're getting accurate information?" the same voice asked. "Maybe they're trying to distract us from what Serrano uncovered. We're spread thin, Ms. DeGraff, and they know it. If we're out looking for a quote unquote testing facility, they'll be able to conduct their C and R operation with much less interference from us."

It was a fair enough question, but coming from Gibby, she knew he was trying to trump her, to express his doubt in front of everyone. Did she expect anything different from the asshole? No, definitely not.

Santiago cleared his throat. "Ms. DeGraff's source is extremely reliable." He didn't bother to identify himself or move in front of the camera. Everyone knew that gravelly voice. He tossed his pencil onto the tabletop and brought his steepled fingers to rest against his mouth, his tall-backed chair squeaking as he leaned back. He appeared relaxed and in control, but Lily knew he was pissed—she saw a glimpse of his fangs and his brown eyes were almost black. He had an unfailing confidence in her source. "We're not here to question the validity of her intel, Gibson. If you have any issues with that, you take them up with me. Understood?"

Yeah, the guy could be a major dick sometimes, but right now she loved her CO. Knowing the camera still focused on her, she kept her face composed and tried not to let that smug smile play out on her lips as Santiago continued.

"Most likely the tests are being conducted down south, so Serrano is relocating to your area to head up the search teams. Don't worry. Your region won't be thin, ours will."

Dom moved to the front of the room and Lily stepped aside. "Thanks, Lily, for that detailed analysis. In the Seattle field, although we don't believe the facility to be located up here, we're putting the known sweetbloods on our patrol swings in order to catch any Darkbloods who show up. You'll all need to hack into your local Darkblood systems to get their lists of registered sweetbloods. Cordell faxed each field office with instructions. Lily, keep us up-to-date with what your contact tells you and let us know the moment you learn anything new. And when any of you discover any information about the location of their research facility, let us know ASAP. San Diego, I'll be seeing all of you shortly."

Lily cut the live feed and wondered how long ago he'd accepted the transfer.

CHAPTER THIRTEEN

DOM PARKED THE black SUV at the Ocean View Convalescent Center and held the door open for Mackenzie. As she got out, he lifted his face, letting the ultraviolet rays warm his skin. Funny how you could see a contrasting image of the sun on the inside of your eyelids. He'd forgotten what that was like. The pull on his energy levels was much stronger today. This would be his last time to enjoy it, he thought.

"You didn't have to come, you know." Mackenzie tossed her blue scarf over one shoulder, the beaded fringe flashing in the sunlight. She wore jeans, a pair of well-worn black boots, and a T-shirt with long sleeves pulled down so that only her fingers were visible.

"Yeah, but I wanted to."

He thought about how things could never work out long-term between them. Like a match that flares brightly at first, their relationship was intense but doomed. It couldn't last forever. At some point, he'd have to tell her about San Diego and everything would end. It had to. But for now, he wanted to enjoy the time they did have.

"This means a lot to me." She was quiet, almost melancholy.

Her tone of voice didn't surprise him. He'd overheard her trying unsuccessfully to convince her brother to take their mother to see the cherry blossoms. The petals would be dropping soon and her car was still in the shop. If Corey couldn't take their mother through the arboretum, she'd miss the trees blooming this year.

"Will she have any trouble getting into the passenger seat?" Dom asked. "It's a high step. Perhaps I should've brought one of my company's vans instead."

"She'll be okay, but thanks. It's only her mind that's going, not her body. I should warn you before we go in though. Sometimes my mom is totally with it—so much so that you can carry on a normal conversation with her and you'll wonder why she's here. But then, just like that, she'll go back to her dark place where nothing she says will make sense and you just have to go along with it. Are you okay with that? I mean, if you want you can wait here and I'll go see—"

"I'm fine. I can't wait to meet her."

After checking in at the front desk, they rode the elevator up to the Alzheimer's wing. The place smelled of antiseptic and old things as they walked down the hallway and entered her mother's room. A gray-haired woman stood at the wall next to a television. She held a roll of tape in one hand and a piece of paper—a torn page from a magazine—in the other.

"Hi, Mom."

The woman turned. Her jaw was slack, her expression blank.

"Mom, I'd like you to meet someone." Mackenzie crossed the small space and hugged her. "This is a friend of mine. Dominic Serrano."

Her mother handed Mackenzie the tape and paper and faced him squarely. "You may call me Tabitha or Bea, although many people here call me Cathy."

"What name would you prefer, Mrs. Foster-Shaw?" he asked.

She cocked an eyebrow and gave him a confused look. "Why are you calling me by my husband's name? It's his, not mine. You'd need to call him that, except that he's dead."

"Mom, please. Dom didn't know." Turning to Dom, she said, "My father's name was Foster Shaw. I hyphenated it, making it my last name when we moved here and I started college. My mother is Cathy Shaw."

"I'm sorry, Mrs. Shaw." Dom took her hand and bent to kiss it, but, scowling, she pulled away and slapped his fingers.

"Young man, your forward behavior will get you nowhere with me. I'm a married woman and that is just not acceptable."

Dom bit the insides of both cheeks in an attempt to stifle a grin. "Yes, of course. Please forgive me."

"Mom, here." Mackenzie put her arm around the older woman, guiding her to a chair next to the bed, and threw a rueful smile to Dom over her shoulder. "Sorry," she mouthed.

A nurse entered the room as Mackenzie was getting her mother situated in the chair. "Mackenzie, could I see you up at the nurses' station when you get a chance? We need to update some of your mother's paperwork."

"Dom, do you mind sitting with her? I'll be right back." When he nodded, she squatted next to her mother. "Mom, I'll be right back. Do you want Dom to read from some of your journals? He doesn't know about all the travels you and Daddy made. I'm sure he'd love to hear about them."

When her mother stared at her with blank doe-like

eyes, Mackenzie kissed the woman's fingers, then stood up and walked back to Dom. "Over there is a shelf of her travel journals. She'd probably enjoy it if you picked one to read to her. She and my father traveled everywhere— didn't you, Mom—and she journaled the whole time. I won't be long."

"And you would be...?" Her mother had forgotten her already and Mackenzie slipped through the door.

On the shelf beside Mrs. Shaw's chair, stacks of note-books appeared to be organized by color and date. Dom ran a finger over the spines, selected one from the middle, and sat down in the chair across from her. Mrs. Shaw looked at him expectantly. Mackenzie must do this a lot, he imagined. He settled back in the chair, opened the journal and began to read aloud.

March 7, 1985

The weather is beginning to turn warmer. I can't help but think we should load up the trailer and be on the move north again. Old habits die hard, Foster tells me. Says I worry too much. I suppose he's right. Don't know if I'll ever feel at ease stay-ing in one place as summer approaches. Mackenzie Marie threw a tantrum in the grocery store today, right in front of the huge wall of candy at the check-out counter. I tried to look stern and turn my back on her like all the books say to do, but she was just so cute. She's always so cute. Hopefully, she'll grow out of this stage soon. I think the employees cringe whenever they see us come through the door.

Boneless chicken breasts were on sale, so I bought two packages and will try a recipe from the

newspaper yesterday for chicken satay. Made with
peanut butter, of all things. Susan came over—

"That's more of a real journal, Dominic. Boring and
uneventful. I think we were living in a small town in
Idaho at that time. We did most of our traveling before
Mackenzie was born. She was two and a half in the one
you're reading from. The red ones—" she pointed to the
far left of the shelf "—are Foster's. You can read them
if you'd like. If you pull out one of the green ones, May
1980, you can read our account of the eruption of Mt.
St. Helens. Foster and I were living in a small town in
southwest Washington at the time, right in the shadow of
the mountain."

Mrs. Shaw met his gaze with strong clear eyes, her
shoulders now erect, and with her chin lifted, she appeared to be a completely different person. With her surprisingly smooth skin and the change in how she carried
herself, she seemed much younger now. An older version
of Mackenzie. Just as striking. Just as beautiful.

"That must have been quite an experience. Did you
hear the explosion when the mountain blew?" Even
though Dom was working out of the Perdido Bay Region
at the time, it had been all over the news.

"Didn't hear a damned thing. We were in what they
called the quiet zone. The sound waves passed right over
us, I guess."

Again he tried to hide his smile. It was humorous
hearing an old woman swear. She was tougher than she
looked. He asked question after question about the eruption and she answered each one with such detail he had
a hard time believing she had Alzheimer's disease.

"Mrs. Shaw, if you don't mind my asking, why did you worry if you didn't travel north in the summer?"

"Because of the Shaw Curse, of course. Hasn't Mackenzie Marie told you anything? As her husband, you need to know these things. How long have you two been married?"

"Ah, well…" She was slipping back into the same place where she'd been when they arrived.

"I didn't get an invitation and I'd think my own daughter would've invited me to her wedding."

"She wouldn't dream of not including you, Mrs. Shaw."

"As I was saying, Foster's relatives disappeared during the warm months mostly. It's been documented, you know. I cataloged and charted every detail I learned about every disappearance. Dates, locations, weather conditions, things like that. They went missing mostly from the big cities, but not always. You can never be too careful. We lived in small towns, up here, mostly on the coast, where the temperature didn't get much above 70 degrees in the summer. But it's best to not stay put for long, no matter where you are. Better to move around a lot. I fear we've become too complacent lately."

"Why is that, ma'am?" My God, she knew. She'd figured it out on her own.

She shrugged. "Don't know why. We just did. It's somehow safer. Foster said I worried too much, but when I finally let my guard down and we moved to San Diego, look what happened."

"When your husband went missing?"

"Of course. Do you not know anything?"

Mrs. Shaw leaned forward, reaching for his hands, and he set them in her upturned palms. He willed himself not to take in any of her energy, but it was difficult with the palm to palm contact. She gripped with the strength of a much younger woman and stared at him with eyes that reminded him of an eagle. Sharp, observant and extremely intelligent.

"You are her protector, are you not? A guardian? Someone who will look after her?"

"Yes, I am." Good Lord. How perceptive was this woman?

"Well, then, there are some things you need to know."

When she loosened her hold, he quickly pulled his hands away and she recounted many of the same details Mackenzie had told him the other night.

"And when her cousin, Stacy, disappeared last year, well, that's when things really changed for Mackenzie. I'm not sure she took it seriously until then. And Corey still doesn't."

"What do you think is going on?" Dom didn't want to ask a question to which he knew the horrible answer, but he had to.

"We don't know. It's hard to convince doctors that something's going on when you don't have a body to test. They just think the family has a higher than normal count of crazies. And that doesn't even include me." She tapped her temple with a forefinger. "My niece who disappeared last year was convinced it had something to do with alien abductions. Maybe she's right. Who knows?" She played with her bangle bracelets, four or five on each wrist, clanking them up and down her forearms.

"But how can they say it's mental illness? Have they done any sort of testing—genetic, DNA—to pinpoint any odd commonalities?" The strangeness of discussing genetics with a woman who only minutes ago couldn't remember her name hadn't quite escaped him.

"Can't find a thing. So it's easiest for them to say the Shaws have a tendency to walk away from their lives when things get rough. Can you imagine? Desertion as a character trait?"

Dom said nothing, just stared at the pages of the open journal on his lap, twisting one of his thumb rings with his forefinger. What could he say when he knew the answer?

"Mackenzie fears her father's fate awaits her, doesn't she?"

"Of course she does. That's why she broke things off with that fellow last year. I know you're trying to look after her, but I'm not sure why she thinks you're any different." Her clipped, biting tone made him cringe. He was different all right.

"The Curse tends to strike those before the age of thirty, and we thought surely Foster was safe at forty-seven. We didn't think about starting a family until he was well into his thirties, did she tell you that? We thought he'd escaped the Curse, but we were very wrong."

With a thumb and forefinger, Dom rubbed his eyes. Good Lord, how this family had suffered through the years.

"I expect that you will keep her safe since I am no longer able to do so. Keep her out of the big cities and be especially careful in the warmer months. Don't let her out of your sight. I'm counting on you."

Reaching her hands out to him again, she clasped his fingers and batted her lashes. "Shhhh, don't tell my husband I said this, but you have very beautiful eyes. A girl could get lost in them and completely forget her manners."

SEVERAL HOURS LATER Mackenzie jumped up on the park bench outside the front door of the nursing home and walked it like a balance beam, using Dom's shoulder for support. What an amazing day. She wanted to sing, skip and dance in his arms, which made absolutely no sense because of what she needed to do.

Don't think about it. Just live in the moment. Today was wonderful. Who cared about tomorrow? Her heart protested, but what choice did she have? None. Zero. She just hoped she wouldn't hurt him. But it was better this way. No messy goodbyes. No promises of a relationship that had nowhere to go.

"Thank you so much. You don't know how much today meant to me. And to my mom, even if she doesn't realize it." She caressed his cheeks with her thumbs and felt that incredible surge of adrenaline whenever she touched him. In response, he wrapped his arm around her waist, pulled her off the bench and spun her around. She couldn't help but laugh. If only this moment, this time with him, didn't have to end.

"Your mother is fascinating and I had a delightful time escorting both of you," he said.

She intertwined her fingers in his hair and that strange but calming sound filled her ears again. She was going to miss how she felt whenever she was around him. God, she was going to miss everything about him.

"Did you see the starry look in her eyes as we drove through the Arboretum?" Mackenzie asked. "For her, seeing the flowering cherries each spring is like taking a child to Disneyland. It's breathtaking and exciting no matter how many times she experiences it. You'd think she'd never seen them in bloom before and yet, we go every year. Thank you. I wouldn't have been able to take her otherwise."

"It was my pleasure."

Looking into his eyes, she thought she detected a touch of sadness within their depths, but when he blinked, it was gone. No, she was imagining things. She was simply projecting her own feelings onto him.

She winced inside and concentrated on what was making her happy right now. She'd wait to talk to him when he took her home. She could put off the inevitable for a few more hours. Grabbing the back of his hair in her fist, she kissed him hard and tried to stamp the feel of him permanently in her memory.

DOM REACHED FOR the door handle, but Mackenzie put a hand on his forearm and he hesitated. This was it, he thought, and his heart rolled over in his chest.

The emotion in the air had been evident as he drove her home from the convalescent center. Although he hadn't dipped into her thoughts, things had to be weighing heavily on her mind—their relationship, this bonding between the two of them that she undoubtedly felt, the visit to her mother's which brought the Shaw family curse to the forefront again.

He'd known she was planning to break things off between them at some point. In fact, he'd sensed she'd wanted to do it earlier today, but because she wouldn't have been able to take her mother to see the cherry blossoms given her car situation, he'd insisted on driving them. A selfish move on his part—meeting her mother when their relationship was doomed—but he wanted to be introduced to the woman responsible for bringing such a remarkable human being into the world before he had to say goodbye to her.

Dread stabbed at his insides, but this moment was inevitable. Like a train pulling into a station, there was no going back. No stopping. It had to happen. Long-term, he was a liability to her. Today might be fine, but tomorrow—or the next day or the next—the lure of Sweet might be too much. Like hell would he do to her what Alfonso had done to the girl he'd loved once. Those images would never be erased from Dom's mind. No, Mackenzie was definitely much safer without him.

At least she was the one starting this conversation, rather than the other way around. The instigator of a break-up always had the most power and it was important to him that she drew strength from that. Not that it'd be easy for him, but he'd manage.

"I'm glad you read some of my mother's journals. I hope it gave you some additional insight into what our family has gone through."

"Yes, it did. You've all been through quite a lot."

She cleared her throat and tugged one sleeve, then the other, down over her hands. "If I were a regular person with a normal family history, I would not be sitting here like this, getting ready to say what I am now."

And if he weren't who he was, he wouldn't need to leave her in order for her to be safe.

"But you're not."

"Dom, these past few weeks with you have been wonderful—as in amazing." She dropped her hands in her lap and turned her head away.

"But…?"

"That's the problem. It's too good. I feel myself getting too attached. To you, to what we have together. To the promise of a tomorrow. And…and I can't let that happen. I'm binding myself to a future that can never be."

He ground his molars together and stared, unseeing, out the windshield at the solid beige of her garage door. He knew her bike would be parked just on the other side, on the left, with boxes on the workbench and upper shelves filled with unpacked belongings accumulated from a lifetime of frequent moves. He could hear dishes clanking inside—her roommate was home. Good. Mackenzie would have someone to talk to when this was all over.

"I understand."

She snapped her head around. "You do?"

He might as well make this as easy as possible for her and not argue. "And I agree."

Her eyes opened wide in surprise. He reached over and released a strand of hair caught in her earring. His throat tightened to the point that he wasn't sure his voice would work. This would be the last time he'd look into her eyes while she looked into his. Oh sure, maybe after he moved, he'd have occasion to visit the Seattle office again and could drive by her house, potentially see her from afar.

But never again would he see her like this. Smell the fragrance of her hair. Touch her soft skin. Hear her speak his name—either casually, while asking him to pass the salt as they prepared dinner together, or at the height of pleasure, while he made love to her and her body shattered around him.

He missed her already. "Mackenzie?" he whispered.

"Dom?"

There. She'd said his name again.

"It's best this way. I could never be the right man for you."

CHAPTER FOURTEEN

"MACKENZIE, SORRY YOU have to wait with me like this. She'll be here in a few minutes. I'll be fine if you need to go." Abby should've sounded dejected, Mackenzie thought. Or sad maybe, but she didn't. She sounded matter-of-fact and frank, as if she had expected nothing more from her mother.

"Hey, it's no big deal," Mackenzie said. "Don't worry about it. I don't have any plans. Just heading home."

Mackenzie didn't care what time she got home. She dug her fingernails into the soft skin of her forearm and wondered how long the impressions would stay indented in her skin. She kept pressing, feeling nothing, until the inside of her wrist was lined with six rows of the half-moon scallops.

Since she'd broken things off with Dom, nothing felt right. Like a crucial piece inside of her was missing. She almost hoped he'd argue with her, try to talk her out of it, tell her they'd make it work, that he'd help her find the answers, but he didn't.

She opened up her phone and reviewed for the billionth time the text message she'd received from him three days ago.

The time we spent together was more than I could have dreamed of. Thank you. I've accepted a transfer to San Diego and am leaving tomorrow. Stay safe. D.

Reading that made her feel sick all over again. She certainly couldn't have a change of heart now. He was already gone.

"If the bus went past my house, I could rely on that each week instead of my mom," Abby said.

"That's okay, sweetie. I don't mind. I'd offer to take you home, but I just have my motorcycle and one helmet. Your mom would probably flip out if you got a ride home on one. I know mine would have."

"Well, she probably wouldn't care, but I don't want you to give me a ride home. She should be here soon. She texted me a little while ago. I just hope she didn't forget."

All the other kids had been picked up from art class and she and Abby had been waiting outside the studio for over half an hour. She didn't want to look at her watch because she didn't want Abby to feel she was getting impatient, but it had to be almost ten o'clock. Class on First Thursday Art Walk night always got out late and Abby usually stayed around to help her clean up the studio.

The two of them looked up as they heard the screeching tires of a car rounding the corner. As it pulled up to the curb in front of them, it almost clipped a parked car. A thumping beat echoed through the tinted windows.

"Thanks for waiting, Mackenzie." Abby gave her a cheery smile.

"No problem. See you next week."

Music blared loudly from inside the vehicle when Abby opened the door and climbed in. Without looking, her mother pulled the car into a tight U-turn and almost hit an oncoming car. The other driver laid on his horn and Abby's mother gave him the finger. As they sped off, Mackenzie saw her tilt back a can of beer.

Without thinking, Mackenzie jumped on her motor-cycle and followed them. If she had thought it through, maybe she would have called the police to have them handle it. She would've memorized the license plate number, made note of the street and direction they were driving, and called it in as a drunk driver. Then she would have gone home and climbed into bed. Or taken a bath first.

But she didn't, and because of that one decision, everything in her life changed.

Thankfully, Abby's mother was a slow drunk driver. Mackenzie was able to keep up with her and only once, while going over the West Seattle bridge, did she get really worried. The woman never crossed the center line, but she came close. Mackenzie followed them for miles and at every turn, every passing car, she said a silent prayer.

When they pulled into a driveway in a rundown neighborhood, Mackenzie drove by slowly. Thank God they arrived home safely. She knew she'd have to confront the mother at some point, but tonight she just wanted to go home. When Abby climbed out of the car, she waved at Mackenzie.

She knew I was following her. Sweet girl.

Flipping up her helmet's visor, Mackenzie blew her a kiss and drove off.

As she left the neighborhood, she realized she had no idea where she was. She had been so focused on following Abby, she hadn't paid attention to all the streets they had turned down. Now she was in a seedy, dilapidated part of town that she'd never been to, without any sense of how to get back. She had a vague idea where the bridge was from here and headed in that direction.

Junker cars littered the front lawns of many of the unkempt houses. Weeds grew from broken sidewalks, neon lights of adult businesses flashed on almost every block, along with a few used car lots and pawn shops. She made it onto a main thoroughfare and hoped it led back to the bridge.

At the first stoplight, a group of teenage boys loitered on the corner. There must've been about seven or eight of them, she guessed as she came to a halt. At this time of night, they couldn't be trading Pokemon cards.

Keep looking straight ahead. Just ignore them.

"Hey, it's a chick on a bike," she heard one of them call. She felt them all turn to look at her. Someone whistled.

"Wanna ride me, baby?" another one yelled.

"I'll give you something huge to feel between your legs."

Turn green. Turn green. Please turn green.

One of the thugs stepped off the curb and swaggered toward her. He had something in his hand.

Fuck it. Glancing both ways in the intersection, she cranked the throttle and ran the light. Adrenaline coursed through her system as she dragged a foot, fish-tailing the back of her motorcycle before the tire gained traction on the pavement. It lurched forward and she left them in the acrid haze of her smoking tire.

This didn't look right. She worried she was heading the wrong way. The poorly lit roadway was virtually empty so she couldn't gauge where to go based on where other cars were headed. She thought she remembered passing a fast-food restaurant on the way to Abby's house, but unless she counted a 24-hour tattoo parlor that served espresso, there were no food joints anywhere in sight.

The wind blew hard into her face so she dropped the

visor of her helmet. Although it was spring, the air still had a bite to it and her cheeks stung from the cold.

At the next intersection, she had to stop again. Why weren't the lights synchronized to turn green so she wouldn't have to stop at every one? She was getting tired and just wanted to find her way home to bed.

While waiting for the green, the little hairs on the back of her neck stood up. Someone else was looking at her. She could feel it. Craning her neck around, she expected to see another gang of thugs approaching, but she saw no one. She was completely alone on this stretch of road except for a Jeep Wrangler pulling up on the other side of the intersection.

She couldn't shake the feeling and focused on the other car. It was them. They were watching her. Two men inside the open-air vehicle were fixated in her direction. Was there something behind her? She turned around. Nothing. Maybe her bike. Maybe they were looking at her bike. *A woman like you on a Bonnie is hard to forget.* Wasn't that what Dom had said? God, she hoped it was the bike.

Something about the two men scared her more than the rowdy hoodlums a few blocks back. Her scalp began to tingle, almost vibrate. She smacked her helmet with the heel of her hand and tried to clear her head.

When the light turned green, she revved the engine and sped through the intersection. The Jeep remained fixed and the men turned their heads in unison to watch her pass. She got a glimpse of the driver lifting his head as if sniffing the wind.

Moments after passing the Jeep, she saw a flash in her rearview mirror. Glancing over her shoulder, she saw that the Jeep had made a U-turn. Her heart hammered in her ears and the tingling became a rumble.

Oh, shit.

The long hair was a dead giveaway. Why hadn't she tied it up and stuffed it into her helmet? With her all-black outfit, most people would've assumed she was a guy on a bike, not a girl. She was a damn freak magnet tonight.

She hit the throttle and sped up, thinking she'd outrun them and they'd give up, but the Jeep stayed on her tail. She felt bile rising in her throat and she willed herself to stay calm.

Oh my God. Which way?

Nothing looked familiar. Just closed-up businesses with bars on the windows, a storage facility and a bunch of warehouses.

The intersection up ahead looked more substantial than the others she'd passed. Left or right? She had to make it fast. The Jeep was just half a block behind her. Left. She cranked the handlebars and leaned into the turn.

Please be the road to the bridge.

Rows of dark warehouses loomed ahead and she realized she had made a horrible mistake. Fear swelled her throat and she could hardly breathe. This wasn't a major intersection. It was just a stoplight for the warehouse complex. She was now in a dark parking lot. A dark deserted parking lot, and the lights of the Jeep flashed behind her.

She weaved around a few buildings, accelerating when she could, looking for another way out, but everywhere the Jeep was on her tail.

When she turned right, a loading dock loomed straight ahead, blocking her way. A dead end.

Her breath came in shallow bursts, the ringing in her head became a roar. She cranked the bike around, the loading dock behind her. The Jeep stopped about twenty feet ahead of her, its headlights blinding her for a moment.

The wind picked up and she heard one of them, or maybe both, laugh. The high-pitched sound promised nothing but evil and her whole body trembled. For some reason, she cried out silently for Dom. If he was here, he'd know what to do.

The men climbed out of the vehicle simultaneously, and with each step, each swing of their arms, they seemed to be a perfect mirror image of the other. Their toothy smiles reminded her of hyenas eager to attack their prey.

I'm almost there, she imagined Dom saying.

Empowered by the voice in her head, she reached back, unsnapped the top of the saddlebag and fished out her handgun. She could do this. This was why she owned a handgun and spent time at target practice each week. Her instructor drilled it into her head that if you carry a gun, you needed to be prepared to shoot and kill. She had never been more ready in her life.

"Mackenzie. Do exactly as I tell you." It was Dom, as clear as if he were next to her. It gave her strength and she brought the gun up.

"Aim at their torsos and pull the trigger. Fast. Both of them. Hear me?"

"Yes, but—" It sounded like she was talking to herself.

"Now. Do it now." His voice boomed in her ear.

Taking a deep breath, she aimed at the guy on the left and pulled the trigger. He stumbled backward. She hit him directly in the chest. Just as she took aim at the other one and fired another round, she heard Dom's voice screaming in her ear. It was then she saw a glint of metal.

"Duck left. Left."

She barely shifted her weight when something slashed through her jacket sleeve and she felt a slicing pain. But how could he—? How could she be hearing—?

"Go. Go. Go." Dom yelled in her head.

She didn't have time to think about what happened, about the warm wetness flowing down her arm. She jammed the gun into her waistband and hit the throttle. The bike jumped ahead and she surged forward.

"Right past them. Don't slow. Don't look. Just go."

Out of the corner of her eye, she could see one of the men getting up. What the hell? He was the one she'd shot right in the torso. He should be dead, or at least seriously wounded. When he made eye contact with her, she saw what looked like fangs hanging from his mouth.

The panic that had coated her insides was suddenly replaced by a chilling horror. Her hands numbed and her vision blurred.

"Mackenzie, listen. Steady yourself, I'm almost there. Go left at the next building. Hustle."

Dom's voice yanked her out of this strange reality. She cranked the handlebars, dragged a foot and leaned into the turn.

"Good. See the second building on the right? The one with the blue awning?"

"Yes."

"Turn right when you pass it."

She accelerated and as she leaned into the next turn, a flash of light glinted behind her. Headlights.

"Oh God, Dom, they're following. How is that possible? I shot them." She knew she sounded hysterical and tried to push the panic away.

"Love, I'm almost there. I'm coming for you. Just keep going. I can feel you. We're getting close."

Mackenzie saw the main road straight ahead and the headlights of another car approaching. It careened into the parking lot, fishtailed a couple of times, then barreled straight toward her. With a screech and another hard turn, it stopped about fifty feet in front of her.

"Ditch the bike." Dom's voice boomed so forcefully she couldn't be sure if she heard it out loud or in her head.

"But—"

"Goddamn it, now."

Headlights from the Jeep flashed on the open passenger door of Dom's car. Squeezing the hand brakes, she jammed her weight to the side, lifted one leg and laid her beautiful bike into a slide on the pavement. The skidding, scraping and grinding echoed in her ears as she imagined layers of chrome and pearlescent white paint on the pavement.

She tensed her muscles, ready to push her body away, when from out of nowhere strong arms wrenched her off the still-moving bike and shoved her into the car.

The door slammed shut and Dom flattened himself against it, a barrier between her and the Jeep. When the vehicle stopped, Dom pulled something from his waistband and swung his arm around his head. A crack like a whip stung the air, jangling her raw nerves. His arm jerked down and a body flew from the Jeep, landing on the pavement in front of Dom's car.

Like a snake striking, Dom was on the man before her mind even registered that he'd moved from the door.

He stood astride one of her attackers, his heavy boot crushing the man's neck. Flailing and kicking, the man struggled, trying to push Dom's foot away. For the briefest moment the guy managed to turn his head toward Mackenzie and her heart practically stopped. The headlights illuminated him like a spotlight. Fangs hung from his mouth in a wide snarl and his eyes were two black orbs with no whites. Mackenzie's hands flew to her face and she watched through the slats of her fingers.

A long glint of metal caught the light as Dom lifted both arms overhead, his back arching, his strength coiling. The blade flew down in a fierce blow and plunged into the chest of her attacker.

A sob spilled from her throat as the man shuddered and convulsed. She wanted to pinch her eyes shut, to block the horrifying images from her brain, but she couldn't. The man's body folded in on itself, leaving a dark pile of rubble, ashes maybe, because a few small bits floated away, disappearing beyond the headlight beams into the night air.

Oh God, this couldn't be happening. It was just a dream. A damn nightmare.

As Dom holstered the knife somewhere beneath his clothes, he raised his head and his eyes locked onto hers. And that was when she saw them. His fangs.

He was one of them.

DOM TOOK A step toward the driver's side and Mackenzie flung herself over the console, scrambling for the lock. She hit the window button and it rolled down slightly before she found the right one. With a click, the locks engaged.

"Open the door." His mouth was at the crack in the open window.

Stifling a scream, she fumbled with the keys and turned them in the ignition. A harsh sound grated the air. The car was already on. She grabbed at what she thought was the stick shift, but it was the emergency brake and nothing happened.

"Mackenzie, I'm not going to hurt you. Open the damn door. There are others coming and I can't take them all down myself." He rattled the handle and she flew back to her seat, away from the sound of his voice. She grabbed at the passenger door handle, which lifted easily without opening. Locked. A movement outside the window caught her eye. A figure emerged from the Jeep. Blood pounded in her temples. She was trapped.

A weapon. She needed a weapon. She patted her waistband. Nothing. It must've fallen out in the slide.

Oh God, oh God.

"I'm sorry." Dom's voice was low from the driver's window and her head snapped to the left. He stood on the other side of the glass with his dark brows pinched together in an unfathomable expression of worry, the ice blue eyes pleading with hers. He looked almost normal except…

A swirling gray cloud enveloped him and he was gone. She whipped her head around. Where was he? What had happened?

A thick fog spilled in through the crack of the window, cascading into the car like a waterfall. Her screams echoed in her ears and she clawed at the door to get out.

The man from the Jeep was at her window, teeth bared, blood dripping from his temple. With nowhere else to go, she scrunched down into the foot well and covered her head with the collar of her jacket, wishing she could snap her fingers and be gone.

With a jolt, her head bumped the underneath side of the dashboard as the car lurched backwards. Knees and elbows banged against hard surfaces as she was buffeted about like a rag doll.

"Get up." A hand grasped the scruff of her collar and wrenched her up.

As Dom cranked the steering wheel hard to the right onto the roadway, she fell on the center console, almost into his lap. He punched it and the car shot forward. She flew back with what seemed like the G-force of a jet fighter.

"Seat belt. Now."

What did he just say? Her mind was numb as she tried to translate the words into something she understood. Seat belt? She pawed at the side of the bucket seat where the strap originated but her hands fumbled getting the thing over her shoulder. Without taking his eyes from the road, Dom reached across her chest, pulled the belt over her lap and snapped it into place.

The dull throbbing pain in her upper arm pulsed over and over with every bump and turn. Warmth dripped down the inside of her sleeve and she tried stanching the flow with her good hand. *Don't look. It only makes it worse.* She leaned her head against the cool glass of the window, closed her eyes and wished she could sleep, make everything go away. Another jolt knocked her hand free. It was covered in blood.

"Here. Use this." Dom waved a handkerchief. His knuckles were white as they gripped the steering wheel and his hair billowed in the wind from his rolled-down window.

Her mind barely registered the car rounding another sharp corner but the pain in her arm had sharpened even more. Dom grimaced as he looked in the rearview mirror.

He didn't act like one of those monsters, but she knew what she saw.

So when Dom's darkened gaze met hers, the blue of his irises completely gone, she remembered the monsters in the Jeep and everything went dark.

DOM LOOKED IN his rearview mirror. The freak was still on their tail. Must be a fortified engine in that rig. He should've been able to put more distance between them by now. If he couldn't outrun them, he wouldn't be able to head to the loft. He'd have to think of some other way.

The Porsche practically flew over the bridge, catching air a few times, and he banked it sharply to the left into the SoDo district. The sound of his suitcase thumping against the side reminded him he wasn't catching that flight to San Diego tonight after all.

Punching it, he saw he had put some distance between them. With the Jeep's high center of gravity, it wasn't able to make the turn as tightly as the Porsche had. The key to outrunning it would be in the cornering, not the straightaways.

Dom turned up and down various roads heading into downtown. The Jeep still followed and even though it fell farther behind, he didn't dare take a chance and head to the loft. They weren't that far ahead.

As he cranked the vehicle under the Alaskan Way Viaduct, he heard the horn of the ferry up ahead, signaling its departure.

If only...

He slammed on his brakes and veered into the holding area, flashing his pass at the ticket booth. The last vehicle had been loaded, the tie ropes cast off, and a ferry worker reached for the neon orange netting to secure the car deck.

Laying on his horn, he sped down the loading chute. The worker jumped out of the way as the Porsche caught air and flew onboard, skidding to a stop behind a delivery van.

Thank God the terminal was quiet this late at night. Doing a mass mind scrub wasn't an easy task for one.

"What the hell. Are you crazy? You can't do that." The ferry worker ran toward them, grabbing his walkie-talkie from its shoulder holster. Dom jumped out of the car and flashed him his identification.

"You still can't…"

Dom brushed a hand across the man's temples.

"We paid at the gate and were the last car on the ferry before you attached the netting and pulled away from the dock."

The man blinked a few times and said, "You staying on the island or heading to the peninsula?"

"Not sure yet," Dom said and watched the Jeep screech to a stop on the dock as the ferry churned through the water away from the city.

CHAPTER FIFTEEN

"STAY HERE." A door slammed shut. Mackenzie turned her head slowly, as if she were in a dream, and blinked a few times, but all she saw was the empty driver's seat.

Where was she? Who was that? Her eyes couldn't seem to focus as she looked out the window, the muscles in her neck ached, and her arm throbbed. A narrow steel tunnel? She heard the deep low blast of a marine horn and felt a shuddering movement beneath her. She was on a ferry. As the sound faded in her ears, its familiarity contrasted with something she'd heard not long ago. What was it? An unearthly sound. Laughing—oh God, awful, hideous laughing. And the horror of the night imploded on her.

With every last ounce of energy she possessed, she wrenched open the car door and clambered onto the deck. An icy blast of wind whipped her hair around, roaring in her ears, and her knees collapsed to the pavement.

Run, her mind told her. *Run*.

Before she could move, strong arms lifted her from the ground and pinned her tightly to a warm chest. The scent of sandalwood filled her nostrils and a tidal wave of relief washed over her, dissolving her fear.

"They're gone. You're safe with me. I promise." The reassuring rumble of Dom's voice vibrated against her cheek.

Wait. His teeth, his eyes, the strange fog. She should push away from him, but as he stroked her hair, every muscle in her body relaxed. She didn't want to move away from him.

"I wish you hadn't seen what happened back there."

Was this really happening? It didn't make sense. Not the comfort she felt with his arms around her, the way her body automatically melted into his, or the soothing effect his voice had on her heart. Images of the night flashed in her head, but she blinked them away. Why wasn't she scared out of her mind given what she'd seen? Why did his embrace feel perfect, so right? She had a million questions for him, but for now, at this exact moment, all she wanted was for him to hold her.

His arms loosened their grip and for a moment she thought he was going to release her, but he didn't. The harsh overhead lights of the car deck cast angular shadows on his face, but they couldn't mask the concern and worry in his expression. She smiled up at him as if it were the most natural reaction to want to ease the tension she felt in him.

Her good arm slipped inside his hip-length wool peacoat and wrapped around his waist before she knew what she was doing. Like her body was on autopilot or something. He opened his lapels farther and pulled her inside against him. The smell of him calmed her senses as her cheek pressed against the muscular planes of his chest beneath his tight T-shirt. A tiny moan escaped her lips. Oh God, he felt good and she knew she was safe.

The loud drone of the engines made talking impossible. But that was okay. She didn't want to think right now, anyway. He held her for what seemed like hours. Then in one movement, he swept her feet from the ground and set her back inside the Porsche.

"Your arm. Let me take a look at it." His nostrils flared slightly and his mouth pressed into a hard line of concentration. She examined the chiseled lines of the face she hadn't seen in a week—his strong jaw with its slight stubble, the chaotic state of his hair as it hung in pieces over the forehead currently creased in a troubled frown. It was a week that had felt like a lifetime.

"What happened back there, Dom?"

He closed his eyes for a moment and took a deep breath. When he opened them, his expression was hard, like he had a job to do. "Your injury. Let me attend to it first."

She slipped her arm from the sleeve as carefully as she could, but she clenched her teeth together when sharp, searing pain shot from the wound. He scowled but his hands were gentle.

"Is it bad?"

"I've seen worse." Curiously, his pupils expanded, leaving only a ring of the blue iris.

"Why do they do that? Your eyes?"

His jaw muscle tensed, but he didn't answer.

The pulse on the sensitive skin of her arm beat against his caressing fingers and when she saw a similar spot flicker on his neck, for some reason she wondered if they matched. He didn't seem startled when she rubbed her thumb over his pulse; in fact, he leaned almost imperceptibly into her hand. He licked the pad of his thumb then, ran it over her wound. Instantly an effervescent sensation, like the crackling of tiny pop rocks, tickled her skin.

"There. Good as new." Before she could say anything more, he stood and shut the door.

She could hear him talking on the phone as he walked to the driver's side. What the hell had just happened? She looked at her upper arm. Rather than a gaping gash, only a thin pink line remained. And even that seemed to be fading. Just like when she'd cut her finger at his loft.

The car shifted slightly when he climbed in.

"What's going on, Dom? What is all this?"

"It's complicated."

"I'm listening."

He stared straight ahead.

"What if they come back? They probably have my wallet and ID. Don't I need to know if I'm in danger or not? And my arm…" She rubbed it but felt no pain. "How is any of this possible?"

"My associates are taking your motorcycle home and will make sure your belongings are secure. As for the others, I'm taking you to a safe place then I'm going back to hunt them down myself."

"Yourself?" Her stomach tightened with panic. "What about the police? Shouldn't we call them or did you do that already?"

"The police can't handle them."

"And what are you going to do? Maybe you got lucky back there. Please, Dom, don't. I don't want you to go—to get hurt." Her voice caught in her throat. Although she couldn't deny what she saw, Dom was different—much different.

"I'll take care of him like I took care of his partner." His tone was calm, as if he'd done this sort of thing many times before.

The ferry engines quieted for a moment, then groaned loudly in reverse as the vessel glided toward the dock.

Ignitions fired up as people prepared to drive off and soon the line of cars next to them began to move.

What if she jumped out of the car? Walked away and went back to her ordinary life, pretended the events of the night were all part of a strange dream? Would tomorrow be normal? Would her students ask her the normal questions in class?

"Don't even think about it, Mackenzie," he growled as he turned the key and the engine roared to life with a little more gas than she thought was necessary.

"How do you know what I'm—" She gave a sound of exasperation. "Listen. You didn't need to say that. I'm not going anywhere. I was just reviewing my options. But you'd better be ready to start explaining or I will leave. So you think about that."

HE MANEUVERED THE Porsche slowly onto the ramp so it wouldn't bottom out.

As they drove off the ferry, he waved a quick thanks to the dock worker, a nun dressed in a knee-high black skirt, white athletic socks, tennis shoes and an orange reflective vest. She smiled and waved back. The Sisters managed the ferry docks on this side and seeing them here always reminded him that good existed in this world in some very unexpected places.

"You won't like what you hear. You're safe. That's all that matters."

"I've lived under a cloud of uncertainty long enough and I'm tired of it. I know that—" she pointed a thumb over her shoulder in the direction they came from "—is the answer."

He ran a hand over his face. Of course, she was right. He was just delaying the inevitable. She deserved to know, even if he had to wipe it from her memory later. "All right. I can't shield you from the truth, Mackenzie, no matter how much I'd like to. You have seen too much." Taking a deep breath, he jumped in.

"There are things in this world that have only been rumored, whispered about late at night, stories meant to scare the young and titillate the old. Most of those old stories are made up and passed down through generations. Werewolves, alien abductions, the Loch Ness monster, unicorns. But some of them have a basis in reality. They weren't just invented from nothing. They started somewhere. And that somewhere is the reality I'm talking about."

She looked calm enough and he didn't sense any spike of distress. Her eyes met his and she gave him a pursed-lipped smile, not quite bold, but definitely not weak or scared.

"You saw the fangs, the bloodlust, the resistance to bullets, and you saw what I did to that guy. And I can't forget that you saw me *vapor* into the car." Yeah, that surprised the hell out of him, too. *All right. It's now or never.*

"Mackenzie, we are vampires. Different maybe from what you think one is, but that's essentially what we are." He kept his eyes on the road ahead and waited for her reaction. She stayed silent and clutched her arms tighter.

"Are…are you okay?"

Without lifting her head, she nodded, so he continued.

"Many of the myths surrounding us are not true. We're not immortal. We do die, but our lifespan is much longer than a human's. Garlic, crosses, holy water—all myths, although our bodies are highly allergic to silver and we are sensitive to ultraviolet light. We still occasionally drink human blood, but we don't kill. At least most of us don't. I oversee a small team of Guardians here in Seattle. Enforcement agents within the Agency, the legal arm of our Governing Council."

He explained about the Darkbloods and Sangre Dulce. He wanted her to know everything, but why? Why not just give her the bare facts with no details when he was going to wipe her memory anyway? He thought he knew the answer, but didn't dare think further about it.

He wanted to dip into her thoughts, to know how she was processing it all, but he gave her the privacy she deserved. She needed to come to her own conclusions without his interference. The headlights formed a tunnel through the dark trees flanking the road and they drove in silence for a while.

"Is this blood condition, this Sangre Dulce, hereditary?" Her voice was barely audible above the road noise.

"We're not sure, but we suspect it is."

He sensed the tears well up in her eyes before they spilled down her cheeks. And when she turned away from him, a part of him withered. He desperately wanted to comfort her, to pull the car off the road and drag her in his arms, to tell her how much he cared about her and that he would never hurt her. But he and other vampires were the cause of all her grief. The only comfort he could offer her, until he did a memory wipe, was verbal and he didn't know where to begin.

"Mackenzie, I'm so sorry."

"My father," she choked. "My uncle, my great-grandmother, my cousin—countless relatives tracing back

centuries. All of them gone without a trace. And you…
your people were responsible."

Her shoulders rounded with sobs and with each gasp a
piece of his heart chipped off. Mile markers on the side
of the road ticked by as her face stayed pressed against
her knees, long hair cascading everywhere. Nothing he
could say or do could remove the agony he felt rolling
off her body. Several times, he reached over to touch her,
to offer some sort of comfort, but each time he caught
himself and pulled his hand back. His touch would be
the last thing she'd want.

Then, almost imperceptibly, she began rocking. He
could feel her agony as if it were his own. Without really
meaning to do so, he laid his hand on her back and began
rubbing gentle circles with the palm of his hand, wishing
he could absorb her sadness and take it on himself.

Abruptly she sat up and her tear-soaked gaze raked
over his face. Was she examining him as a monster?
When she reached over, he half-expected her to lash out
at him, to take out a lifetime of suffering, but instead she
rested her hand lightly on the forearm of his coat.

"It's all so unbelievable, and yet…"

She slid her palm over the top of his hand, intertwined
her fingers with his, and his heart jumped into his throat.
Could she possibly be accepting the reality of all this?
The tiny ray of hope he'd felt earlier sprang back to life
again.

"It's the only thing that makes sense. Thank you for
saving me from them and for telling me the truth."

She was thanking *him?*

"Can you tell me about your group? The Agency? Is
this the secret government agency you talked about? The
one you'd have to kill me over if you told me about it?"

Her eyes were red and swollen, but she smiled at him through her tears. She had never looked more beautiful.

"I joined the ranks of the Agency as a Guardian over a century ago and now oversee our team here in Seattle. My father, as an Elder on our high Council, spearheaded the efforts to fight the Darkblood Alliance by allocating funds for the Agency's creation. Back then it was called the Society of Guardians, but today we simply refer to it as the Agency. Guess it sounds more modern. We've got a presence in many parts of the world and we work to keep humans safe…when we can."

She chewed on a nail for a moment. "And these Darkbloods want to live like your ancestors did?"

"Yes. There have always been fundamentalist vampires, those who shunned the new ways. In the middle of the last millennium, when my ancestors consumed only human blood, much of Europe's population was stricken by the Great Plague, or Blood Fever, as we refer to it. Not only did it kill millions of people and eradicate our food source, but vampires who fed from a human with Blood Fever died, as well. Although some humans recover after contracting the Fever, vampires never do.

"After generations of seeing our population dwindle even more rapidly than the human population, our ancestors discovered we didn't need to rely solely on human blood for sustenance, that we could simply absorb much of our energy needs through skin-to-skin contact rather than blood consumption. Just like the human diet has changed dramatically over the centuries—vegetables used to be thought of as food primarily for animals and the poor—so has our diet. However, some vampires believe it's our true nature to feed from humans and they shouldn't be denied this right. Unfortunately, there will always be those of my kind who feel this way."

They drove in silence for a few miles as he let her process everything.

"My missing day. We didn't just happen to meet at the auction, did we?"

"No." He took a deep breath and let it out slowly. "I was injured by a silver bullet in a shootout with Darkbloods. I managed to float downstream to the cemetery before I was able to pull myself ashore. You found me at my weakest point and because you are Sangre Dulce, I took too much of your blood and almost killed you."

"You bit me," she said softly, almost to herself, and lifted her hand to rub her neck. Although the interior of the car was warm, his fingers felt suddenly cold. Then she lowered her hand back to his and he was warm again.

"And I absorbed your energies."

She looked confused.

"Here." He turned his hand over. "Slip your palm onto mine."

When she did, his body tingled with her energy and he quickly released her. "Did you feel that?"

"Oh my God, yes."

"Hand-to-hand or hand-to-face is how we absorb most of the energies from…a…you. We're sensitive to the sun's rays, unable to process ultraviolet light into energy. We must obtain it by absorbing it from humans. But too much can make some of us more aggressive. In parts of the world with higher amounts of UV full spectrum light, there are higher concentrations of this energy within the human population. The more aggressive members of our race tend to live in those regions."

"But how can you absorb it without us knowing? I

mean, it's like a jolt of electricity when you touch me. And I find it very…nice." She closed her eyes as if she were savoring the feeling.

"Most people are tired when the energy leaves their bodies," he said. "A little rundown, like you'd feel if you didn't get enough sleep. But it appears you feel what I do. I think you must be taking some of my energies."

"And that's not normal?"

He shook his head.

"And when you took my blood, why didn't I turn into a…and I didn't die."

"Just a bite won't turn a human into a vampire. It takes an almost complete blood draining followed by a blood transfer from several vampires. In fact, it's forbidden unless…well, it's not allowed."

"And why don't I remember any of it?"

"We are able to manipulate a person's recollection of events, suggest a different memory of what happened."

"So that explains my missing day." When she paused, the atmosphere inside the car grew thick with all the questions he knew she had for him. It was just like her to look at things from all angles, as the artist she was, to better understand what stood before her.. "If you're like them, like the ones who have been preying on the Sangre Dulce members of my family, how are you able to control yourself around me? Why didn't I die that day if I'm…if my blood is so…sweet to you?"

"I don't know really. I surprised myself. To stop was one of the hardest things I've ever done. I almost killed you and for that I'll always be horrified."

"You nursed me back to health then, didn't you? I've had such odd recollections of that time that I've not been able to make sense of. Cool damp cloths on my wrists. You brushed my hair over and over, didn't you?"

He nodded.

"And the auction?"

"I followed you there to get the phone back."

"Oh God, that phone." She laughed, but quickly sobered again. "What about the mind-reading? Back at the warehouse." She shivered. "And on the ferry. Is that common? Can you all read minds?"

"No. I've never heard of it happening before." Her shoulders dropped a fraction and he sensed her tension dissipating. Her questions. All her wonderful questions. She wasn't shutting herself from him. The beginnings of a smile wanted to seep onto his face, but he made himself concentrate on the road ahead.

"So if you took my blood and can now hear my thoughts, why can I hear your words in my head?"

"I had to give you a little of my blood. I thought you were dying. I was sick with guilt for what I had done, so I was forced to share a small amount of my blood with you and now it seems…we are blood bonded. *Enlazado por la Sangre.*"

"Bonded by blood. Is that why it's forbidden?"

"No. The blood bond is a completely separate issue. It's always forbidden to share blood with a human. Vampires share blood with each other when we—" He caught himself. She didn't need to know that vampires shared blood during sex. "Blood sharing is common, but blood bonding is not. Before you and me, I thought it was just a myth."

"So, you broke your laws when you gave me your blood? To save my life?"

"Yes."

"That's twice now, you know…that you saved me." Her words trickled off until they were mostly air.

Saved her? Good Lord. "You also almost died because of me."

"How are you able to control yourself around me now? Especially with my arm like this? Is that why your eyes go black?"

"Yes, I'm afraid so."

Tiny lines stacked between her brows and around her eyes, punctuating her apparent confusion. "So your eyes darken because you want me. My blood?" Her voice was low and unmistakably husky. Why wasn't she frightened? "I saw it happen the first time at the auction. Is the urge hard to control?"

He kept his eyes on the road as the Porsche's headlights tunneled through the night. "Yes, incredibly hard. You had no idea that night what your innocent and unexpected touch did to me. Your hand upon my face. But it's the hardest to control when I make love to you." The sound of her elevated heart rate reverberated in his head and stoked the embers of his memory. "It's during lovemaking that couples regularly share blood. The urge to take yours is almost beyond my comprehension."

His cock hardened at the thought and he hoped she didn't see the bulge in his pants. He shifted slightly in his seat. There would be none of that, he thought, as his fingers rubbed anxiously over his naked wrist and what was noticeably missing.

"What would happen if you took my blood again?"

"I would not be able to stop. I would kill you."

A COUPLE WITH salt and pepper hair—his short, hers pulled to the top of her head in a Gibson-girl style—stood on the well-lit veranda of a huge house. Dom maneuvered the car around the circular driveway and came to a stop under a porte cochere and a wagon wheel chandelier dangling from the center support. With all the river rock and the massive wood support beams, Mackenzie knew this place couldn't be just a house. It had to be a small hotel or resort.

After climbing out of the car, he said something to the couple as he jogged around the front of the hood to help her out. When their gaze met through the windshield, an odd expression passed across his face before he scowled and turned away.

Mackenzie opened the door.

"Stay right there. Don't get out." What? Why? His bossy tone prickled irritatingly under her skin, so she ignored him. Her cramped legs needed stretching.

The woman clambered down the steps with an ambling but efficient gait, bypassing Dom, and stretched out her arms when she reached Mackenzie.

"Mackenzie, this is Shirley Cartwright and that's her husband, Chuck."

"Please call me Shirl." The full-bodied woman gave Mackenzie a tight hug, crushing her against an ample bosom. Mackenzie winced, preparing to feel the stinging pain of her wound, but then she remembered. Dom had healed it.

"Don't mind Chuck." Shirl inclined her head toward the house. "He'd hug you, too, if he could, but Dom didn't want him to get too close. At least, not yet."

Mackenzie looked over and Chuck lifted a stoic hand to her as Dom took the porch steps two at a time.

"Dom didn't give me much notice, so I hope I've got everything you need down there." Shirl looked Mackenzie up and down and clucked. "He described you perfectly. Let's hope the things I picked out from the gift shop will fit. If not, you come up tomorrow and we'll get you situated."

"Uh, thank you, but I'd imagine we'll be leaving by tomorrow."

Shirl patted Mackenzie's hand and the lines around the woman's eyes deepened as she smiled knowingly. "You've got that deer-in-the-headlights look. I think I might be able to give you some insight into all this craziness." Mackenzie raised her eyebrows. Was it that obvious? "We'll talk tomorrow. Go. Get some rest. You must be exhausted after what you've been through. Dom's a good man, dear. But then you knew that, didn't you?"

Dom returned and with his hand at the small of her back, he guided her across what appeared to be an expansive lawn, though she couldn't be sure in the dark. Strings of draped twinkly lights illuminated the oyster-shell pathway and, as their feet crunched on the packed surface, the sound of the nearby surf intensified.

Before she could protest, Dom stooped in front of her and hoisted her up, piggyback style. A surprised squeak escaped her lips and with one little hop, her arms and legs wrapped comfortably around him as though she belonged exactly here.

When they reached the edge of the bluff, waves hit the beach in the darkness and she saw just the hint of white crests before they faded to black. If she focused on a point slightly away from the waves, didn't look at them directly, she could see them better.

After passing three other cabins, Dom bounded up the steps of the last one. The interior was airy and clean with a wall of windows marking the view, framed by an automatic blind system similar to the one in his loft. The living room functioned as a great room, with the kitchen in the back and a small dining table off to the side. A short hallway ran next to the kitchen and two doors led to what were probably the bathroom and a bedroom.

"Why don't you freshen up? It'll do you good to wash away the night. I'll see what there is for you to eat before I leave."

"You're leaving?" An invisible hand wrung out her insides.

And then he was there, wrapping his arms around her. His fingers slipped up into her hair, running across her scalp before he grabbed a handful and pulled her head back. Her parted lips tingled in anticipation of his kiss.

He abruptly dropped his hands and stepped away. "We'll talk about this after you eat. Now go."

Disappointed, she shuffled toward the bathroom. A shower did sound fabulous, but once inside, when she saw the large soaking tub, she opted for a bath instead. She turned on the hot water and peeled off her clothes. After dumping a few capfuls of bath salts, she climbed in and moaned with contentment. The heat melted away any remaining tension as the scent of lavender wafted up and she slid down deep.

Her mind was a jumble as she tried to sort through everything that happened to turn her world upside down in a matter of hours. Vampires? How completely crazy was that? She'd never have believed it if she hadn't seen it herself. She had so many questions. But what she kept coming back to was that Dom had saved her life and had given her answers.

Leaning back, she closed her eyes. Only just for a minute. God, the water felt good. When had she ever felt this calm? So completely at peace? Hearing the clink of silverware from the kitchen, she knew it was because she was here with him.

She awoke with a start to hear a light tapping on the door. The water was tepid.

"You all right in there?"

"Yeah," she called. "I must've dozed off. I'll be right out."

After drying off and finger-combing her hair, she realized she didn't have a change of clothes to put on, so she donned one of the robes hanging from a peg behind the door and walked out.

The smell of tomatoes and spices made her mouth water. She didn't realize how hungry she was. "Smells wonderful. Spaghetti?" she asked as she padded barefoot into the kitchen.

He glanced at her over his shoulder and paused. His eyes went dark for a moment and a little thrill tickled at her insides. She loved that his desire for her was so obvious and knew it was more than just her blood. "It's nothing fancy. Jars and bags. Hungry?"

"Famished."

Seeing a bag of prepared lettuce sitting next to a bowl, she tore it open along with the dressing pouch and tossed it all together with the tongs.

"So…a… You eat food, obviously, but do you still… I mean, how often…"

"What exactly are our dietary requirements?"

She nodded, making sure every piece of lettuce was evenly coated.

"Most of us feed from a live source once every few weeks. It may be a donor—yes, there are a few humans who know about us—or we may take it from someone whom we've put into a light hypnotic trance so as not to frighten or scare them. We don't need much and we leave no trace. But we do require human energy on a fairly regular basis."

Human donors? She rubbed her neck. What would that be like? she wondered. After finding the silverware drawer and grabbing two forks, she carried the salad to the small dining table, lit with several votive candles, and sat down.

He thinks of everything.

Her head hummed and she looked up to see him smiling as he set the pasta on the table and pulled out a chair.

"You're listening to me, aren't you?"

"I try not to, but sometimes I can't help myself."

His dark hair fell forward as he took his seat. Would it brush her cheeks if she kissed him?

"I'd say you had an unfair advantage since I just found out about this tonight. You've been able to read my mind all this time." Her face heated as she thought of the times they'd been together. When he—and she—

He nodded and dished out their meals. "It is rather an invasion of your privacy so I try not to do it too much, although sometimes I find I can't help myself." She saw a hint of a smile.

"You can't help yourself?" *As if he's so innocent.* "I'll bet you knew I wasn't wearing panties at the auction. Is that why you took advantage of me on the roof deck?"

"I seem to recall that you jumped me first. I would've let you walk away."

"Walk away? You are such a—" She threw a crouton at him, but he dipped his head and caught it in his mouth.

* * *

"I trust you, you know," Mackenzie said. "I know you won't hurt me. It's not in your nature."

Even through the pungent smoke of the bonfire, he smelled the sweet scent of her desire rolling off her skin and his cock grew stiffer. How had he let her talk him into this? She should be in bed and he should be on his way back to Seattle to fry that bastard, but here he was on the beach in the middle of the night with the most beautiful woman in the world. Well, maybe it wasn't so hard to imagine after all.

"That's a pretty bold statement. Rather naïve actually, considering everything you've seen. I wouldn't dare try— ever—because I wouldn't know if I'd be able to stop."

"This thing isn't one-sided, Dom. I can feel you in my blood, too. It all makes sense now. You're not capable of hurting me. All you've done is healed me."

He rubbed his bare wrists and wished he were that confident. Not expecting ever to see her again, he had packed away the cilice. God, he wished he had it with him now. She snuggled into the crook of his arm and he pulled the blanket up higher on her shoulders.

"How did you find me tonight?" The glow from the fire flickered over her slightly upturned nose and the small mole above her lip that moved as she spoke.

"Because I've had so much of your blood, I can not only hear you, but I learned if I really concentrate, I can see your surroundings with my mind's eye. I am highly aware of your energy trail—the energy of your life force. When it's disrupted or disturbed, it ripples inside me and that's how I knew something was wrong. I tuned into you immediately when I felt your worry. I recognized the part of town you were in and raced to find you. My God, I can't believe how close—"

"Shhhh. My energy trail? My life force?" She snuggled in closer. "It sounds so science fictionish. But I like it. I want our life forces to get together again. The feeling is out of this world."

He threw his head back and laughed. Her spunk, her sassiness and her comfort with him lifted the heaviness anchoring him down.

"If I had more of your blood, would I be able to hear and feel you better?"

"I'd imagine you would."

"I'd like that."

Was she crazy? She turned her face up to his. Her eyes burned with an intensity hotter than the embers at the base of their driftwood fire. Being with her felt so natural, so easy. He had a plan for his life and love had never been a part of it before. As he leaned in to kiss her, the flickering light glinted on her earrings and he pulled away.

"What?"

"Your earrings. They're silver."

With a few flicks of her fingers, they were gone. "Better?"

"For me, but maybe not for you. You probably should have kept them on."

"Stop worrying. Does your head vibrate a little when you hear my thoughts?" she whispered as his lips hungrily sought out hers.

"Yes, and when you're nearby." Her kiss was warm and spicy, tasting faintly of oregano.

"Mmm. Me, too. And do you hear two heartbeats until we're closer?" she asked.

He slipped the robe off one shoulder. When he ran his

fingertips under her breast and caressed a thumb over her stiffened nipple, a moan of pleasure escaped her lips. "They mesh into one sound when our air mingles. And your heart becomes mine when I'm in you." She sighed heavily and he breathed her air into his lungs.

Without a word, she slid a hand to his face and stroked her thumb over his temple. The vibration in his head as their energies mingled swept him into another dimension. Over the sound of the waves lapping and retreating on the rocky beach, nothing existed any longer except the two of them. *I want you like I've never wanted anything else before.* Her words. Blood pounded between his legs when he heard them in his mind and he took her mouth with a fervor that surprised him.

Pushing her down on the blanket-covered sand, he peeled off his jeans and his erection sprang free.

She held her arms out to him and opened her legs. *My proud, beautiful savior.* He groaned when he heard her words and enveloped her body with his.

MACKENZIE LET DOM spread her knees apart with his thick thighs as he settled his body over her. His erection probed her hip and inner leg searching out her entrance. She arched herself to help him. Waiting for his thrust, she was surprised when he pushed up on his forearms and looked into her face. His hair hung over his forehead and his eyes were dark in the flickering glow from the fire.

"What?" she whispered. "Don't stop. Not now. I need you now, Dom." With secrets gone and questions answered, she wanted to feel the truth of him.

"I love how my name sounds on your lips," he said as he kissed her. His erection stood poised, ready to enter her.

Did his teeth just graze her neck? She wanted him so

badly that a little part of her died each moment he wasn't inside her. She wrapped her legs around his hips, forcing his tip inside. But still he didn't rock forward. She impatiently slid her hands to his buttocks, digging her nails in deep, but he didn't go in.

"Please. I'm dying here."

His laughter vibrated against her chest. "Are you always so impatient? Maybe I want to just lie here and look at you for a moment. To sear your face into my memory and compare it to how it looks after I leave a bit of myself inside of you." His large palm slid down to massage her hip, as if he were getting ready to take hold, and her breath stopped halfway in her throat.

"Stop testing your willpower. It's much stronger than mine." She needed him. She needed this. She was suffocating without him.

In the firelight his pupils expanded, leaving a ring of crystal blue and the muscles in his face relaxed. She kept her eyes pinned to his as he thrust his hips forward, sheathing himself inside.

"Dom." She breathed out his name as the sound of his heart filled her body. His eyes danced with excitement as he flexed his buttocks and drove deeper. She was so ready that she came hard and fast around him almost instantly.

"Oh, darling," he murmured into her hair. "You are so sweet to my body. *Amada mia.*"

He pulled out of her then and she let out a little cry of protest. "Shhh. I can go deeper this way." His sex glistened in the glow of the bonfire as he urged her to roll over. The breath caught in her throat. He was utterly magnificent. Powerful, commanding. She needed that strength filling her from the inside. On her hands and knees, his body warmed her back as he searched her out again. She rocked back and took him inside.

Grabbing her hipbones, he pulled her toward him as he thrust hard. The sound of the sea muffled her moan. He pushed even deeper until finally she felt him graze that swollen bud at the end of her channel. Coaxing and prodding, he moved inside her until she began to climax again. His sex quivered and her body fully welcomed him inside with a glorious hitch.

As the world faded away, revolving only on the axis of their joining, a strong urge clamored in her head. She wanted to give all of herself to him, to please him in every way she could. She needed to be his everything.

He wanted to drink from her, she could sense it. Flipping her hair away from her shoulder, she exposed her neck to him and reached back to pull his head down.

She felt his warm lips against her skin just as she reached the crushing peak of her orgasm.

As HIS FANGS elongated from his gums, he stared at the graceful arch of her neck. He lifted her off her hands. Back to front, he fit the contours of her body to his. With his fingers, he sought out the precise location of her artery. It fluttered as if it was calling to him and his mouth watered. Perfect. So beautiful. He wanted to feel her nectar slip down his throat as his seed spilled into her. As she climaxed around him, he reared back to bite.

He brushed her mind, but sensed no thoughts about pain or danger, just her eagerness to give herself to him. Oh God, she trusted him in a way he didn't deserve.

Bastard. What the hell was he thinking? He'd drain her dry without the distraction of the cilice. Of course he would. He wouldn't be able to stop and she'd die.

His whole body stiffened then, his arms going rigid. Cursing, he tried to pull out of her, but her internal muscles held him tight. Her body refused to release him until he climaxed. He cried out in agony. This couldn't be happening.

Pushing her down on all fours again, he arched his head to the darkened sky, trying to put what little distance he could between them, but he salivated with anticipation.

Take her. Do it now. Look how beautiful she is, and she is yours. Remember the rush of her sweet taste in your mouth. The invincibility it gives you. For God's sake, you can even vapor. *Drink from her and use that strength to finally kill Pavlos and avenge your parents' deaths. That's what you want, isn't it? You've waited a lifetime for this opportunity. Don't waste it. Take her now.*

"No. No," he cried as he released into her and plunged his teeth into the skin of his forearm. Her body loosened its hold when it received what it needed from him and he pulled himself out.

"What is it? What's wrong?"

"Get away. Get the hell away." He scrambled to the far side of the dwindling bonfire. *It's not too late. Look at her. She wants to give herself to you. She wants you to take her blood again. To sacrifice herself for your cause. She was made for you, don't you agree? And you were meant to defeat Pavlos. So take what you deserve in order to kill him. Do it now.*

"Oh God, I'm sorry. Are you okay? What happened? Dom, please."

She was concerned for him when she was the one in danger. That floored him. What had he been thinking, bringing her here like this, cooking for her like they were mated, pretending he could make a normal life with her? *What an idiot.*

He crouched in the sand like an animal, ready to attack. Through the hanks of hair covering his face, he watched as she stood and wrapped herself with her robe.

"I know you won't hurt me, that you won't go too far. I feel it, Dom. You'll stop when you need to. You're not a monster. You're a good man and…and I love you."

Dios mio. She loved him? Like this? Anguish tore his heart open and he became suddenly light-headed, as if the oxygen molecules in the air around him had been sucked away.

Was she insane? Did she not know what he was capable of? What he truly wanted? What had he done to deserve an angel like her? With her hair tousled and her skin flushed from their lovemaking, she was way too perfect for him. She reached out to take his hand and he felt his foot dig into the sand, compressing it like a starting block, his body ready to spring.

When she didn't move right away, he bared his teeth to her. Her eyes widened and she took a step back. With the firelight playing off his fully extended fangs, which dripped with coppery blood from where he'd bitten himself, he knew she saw the nightmare he truly was. "You think you want this? Run to the cabin and lock yourself in the bathroom. Pray I don't break down the door or *vapor* through the cracks. Go. Go now."

CHAPTER SIXTEEN

"Sir, a new capture team in Seattle is on to something."

A tall, slender man floated over to the monitor, his feet barely touching the floor, and he placed a bejeweled hand on the computer programmer's shoulder. It lingered a moment longer than necessary as he bent down until he was eye-level with the screen. Maurice tried to keep from shivering but wasn't having much luck. The Overlord's breath reeked with the stench of his all-blood diet. Maurice hadn't completely reverted to the old ways. He still enjoyed fast food. Maybe all those French fries would keep him from smelling this bad.

"What did they discover?" the Overlord asked.

"We've been checking and cross-checking our Sangre Dulce database against census reports and internet search engines, trying to track down other family members of known sweetbloods. The researchers think some families may carry the recessive gene that they can isolate in the lab."

"I'm liking the sounds of this already." The vampire's thick, yellowed nails dug into Maurice's shoulder. "So instead of mating two sweetbloods, they may be able to mate two non-sweetbloods who have the recessive trait and still get Sangre Dulce offspring? Is that what you're saying?"

Maurice nodded, but he doubted the Overlord would like what he was going to hear next.

"So what has that Seattle cell discovered?"

"Remember that prolific family, the Shaws from Southern California, the one that produces several sweetbloods each generation?" He pushed his glasses up higher. They slipped down his nose when he sweated. And he always sweated when the Overlord was this close.

"Yes. I know them very well indeed. Let's just say I've had a personal relationship with quite a few of them over the years."

"Our boys were playing around on their new computer and accessed our database. Seems one of them has some internet sleuthing abilities, as he traced a Shaw female to the Seattle area. She had hyphenated her last name so she wasn't flagged by our system."

"A Shaw female there? Two *new* team members found a human with one of the most sought-out bloodlines? I'd call that an egregious oversight."

"Yes, I agree, sir. We've put a patch into the code so our spiderbots are looking for hyphenated names, as well."

"How did they find her?"

"She recently set up a website and her About Me page mentions San Diego. We would have found her eventually, sir. We did locate her brother—he doesn't have a hyphenated last name and he's not Sangre Dulce."

The Overlord cursed quietly under his breath, halting the movement of air in Maurice's lungs. "And you're just figuring out now he has a sister? Do we know if she's Sangre Dulce yet?"

"Yes, she is. They believe she has the sweetblood." Maurice took off his glasses and mopped his forehead with a tissue.

"You *believe?*" The stench rose off the Overlord like a mist.

"She actually hasn't been captured yet. The team had her cornered, but somehow before they could bring her in, one of them was staked and the other one ran."

The pungent smell intensified and bile bubbled into Maurice's esophagus, burning away at the lining. He could hardly keep his glasses perched on his nose.

"Who staked them and where is the female?"

"Agency operatives, sir, and we think one of them has her."

The sound Maurice heard next surprised him a little. He'd figured death would hurt, but he hadn't expected it to have a sound. It was rather like a juicy thud, a watermelon sliced in half with a sharp blade.

EVERY NERVE IN his body had frayed like ends of an unraveled rope by the time Dom pulled into the parking garage. If it hadn't been dawn, he'd have walked the streets of Seattle looking for a fight. Any fight. It wouldn't have mattered whether he ran into a Darkblood or not, as any confrontational being would've served the same purpose. His body itched with aggressive energy and he needed to unload it somehow.

A short time ago a willing female would've provided the necessary outlet for his pent-up aggressions. But it didn't hold much appeal now since all he could think about was Mackenzie. He would not lie with another woman. If he were to be with someone else, he had to assume she'd do the same. And the thought of Mackenzie underneath another man, those emerald eyes looking up into a face other than his own, her lips swollen from another man's kisses, another man's name on her tongue, made him seethe with anger.

Should he call her? It was still early and he hoped she was sleeping back at Chuck and Shirl's. He pulled out his cell phone, punched in her number. His thumb hovered over the Send button for a moment before he flipped the phone shut. He ached to hear her voice again but didn't know what he would say. "I love you but I want to kill you. I want to be with you but I have no life to offer you." What a fucking catch he was.

He pressed Send anyway and clicked his earpiece. He had to hear the spirited lilt of her voice again, even if she was frightened of him. Or angry with him. He wiped his sweaty palms on his jeans and clicked the wireless earpiece. It rang once and his heart tumbled in his rib cage. Twice and his scalp prickled with sweat. Three times and it went to voice mail. He listened to her whole message, letting the sound of her voice echo inside him, then hung up without leaving one of his own.

She deserved far better than anything he had to offer. He was an idiot to even contemplate a future.

After going through security, he took the stairs down to the field office two at a time. Changing out of his street clothes, he slipped on his favorite set of gloves and pummeled a punching bag until rivulets of sweat stung his eyes and blurred his vision. After a quick swipe with a towel, he grabbed a pair of wooden knives and worked the knife dummy, thrusting and twisting until his muscles screamed in protest. And then he did it all over again.

LILY HAD BEEN Looking forward to her daily run on the treadmill before turning in for the day, but when she pushed open the double doors to the gym and heard familiar, yet very irritating music screeching through the speakers, she knew her mindless 5K probably wasn't going to happen. It had to be Dom. Why was he back so soon? She'd figured he'd be gone for another day or two—even if he had received her text message about what they'd found at the Darkblood den. Must not have gone well with the woman last night.

On the far side of the boxing ring, amidst a row of speed bags and heavy bags, she saw him. He was beating the crap out of a punching bag like an experienced fighter—an experienced, pissed-off fighter—dipping his head to avoid invisible fists as the balls of his feet danced on the mats. Faster, much faster than the tempo of his horrible music. His pace picked up as she approached, as if he were telling her to stay away and didn't want to talk.

She scrutinized his hooded eyes and saw that his olive complexion looked even darker with the stubble on his chin. Holy shit. Had he drained the woman? Lifting her nose in the air, Lily casually sniffed. Just the same hint of Sweet she'd smelled back at the bar, maybe a tiny bit more, but definitely not a killing amount—thank goodness.

"I'm surprised to see you here, but then who else could be playing this kind of garbage?" She waited but got no response. She'd have to try something else. "In the mood to grapple, love?"

Wiping the sweat from his face with his shoulder, he grunted something and continued punching.

"I was going to log a few kilometers on the treadmill before calling it a day, but it looks like you could use some horizontal work on the mats. A little BJJ then a BJ?"

"Brazilian Jiu Jitsu and a blow job? Shit, Lily, go away."

Didn't that at least warrant a smile from him? Guess not. "Where's, uh…Mackenzie. Everything okay?"

"On the island."

Chuck and Shirl's. Good. She'd be safe there, Chuck would see to that. He may be retired from the Agency, but he was still more than capable.

Dom grabbed a pair of wooden knives and the dizzying sound of repetitive clattering echoed above the music. Given what had happened last night with those two Darkbloods, the woman was probably safer on the island right now than she'd be in the Seattle area anyway.

Lily climbed onto her favorite treadmill and put in her ear buds as the belt slowly gained speed. What music could she play to drown out this crap? Before she could select a playlist, she heard a crash, then saw the wooden dummy fly across the room. Whoa. She grabbed at the handrails to regain her balance. He'd kicked the whole thing off its support posts. Was he jacked up or what?

After mopping his face with a white gym towel, he sat—no, collapsed—on a nearby bench. Interesting. There were many other places to sit, yet he chose this one. And he faced her. She draped the cord of her headphones around her neck and eased into a slow, non-confrontational jog.

"Feel like talking?" Lily asked.

He flashed her a look that said no. As in, hell no, but he couldn't fool her. She didn't have to wait long. "About BJJ and BJs? Thought you had a regular hook-up anyway," he said.

"Maybe. Maybe not." Had Santiago said anything? Surely he wouldn't without consulting her first.

"Don't want to make you tap out if you have a boy-friend. I'll leave that for him to do."

Figured he'd come out of his funk to torment her. "Me? Tap out? The only way you could do that is if I let you. You okay, love?"

"So you admit it. There is a guy." He ignored her question. That was okay. He didn't want to talk about it. At least she'd addressed it with him and he knew she cared.

"Who said anything about a guy? Maybe I've come to like my bread buttered on the other side, eh?" Lily said.

He picked at the white tape around his wrists and hands and said nothing more. After punching a few buttons on the control panel, she began running at her normal pace.

"How's Zoe?" he asked. No matter what was going on, he always had a soft spot in his heart for her daughter.

"Great. She loved the latest Hello Kitty stuff you got her. Carried around that little purse all week. Today when I called to give her a long-distance good-morning kiss, Mother said she's been sleeping with it, too."

That got a smile. Finally. She hit the stop button on the treadmill and walked over to the bench. "Feel like talking?" His shoulders relaxed a notch, but he shook his head. "You don't have to tell me what caused you to come back. To be separated from her must be difficult. But if there's something else…"

For several moments, he sat with the towel over his head before he cleared his throat. "It's the weirdest thing, Lil. I…a…discovered I'm able to *vapor*."

Holy hell. "No way. You mean like our ancestors were supposedly able to do?"

"Yes. That's it exactly. When Mackenzie was threatened by the remaining Darkblood, I *vapored* into the car through the crack in the window to get her to safety. I suppose I could've fought the bastard like I did with his partner, but I was overcome by the desire to get her away from him. My solid form just sort of disintegrated and flowed into where I wanted to be. I wasn't consciously aware of it until I was sitting in the driver's seat."

"My God, Dom. How can that even be possible?"

"I have absolutely no idea. But I have a feeling it's because of the way Mackenzie's blood reacts with mine. She's the source of my power."

The double doors to the gym burst open and Jackson strode in, cell phone glued to his face. Dom stood from the bench, his eyes flat and dull.

"Not a word, Lil." He turned and headed toward the locker room. She'd never seen him like this. He was a friggin' mess. But could you blame him?

"Hey, did you hear what we found out about the guy you stiffed last night?" she called after him. "I sent you a text, but maybe you didn't get it."

Dom stopped, but didn't turn around.

"We tracked his buddies to a shithole of a house on the Eastside. I thought it was all McMansions over there in software land, but this guy lived in a pigsty. It's a wonder the neighbors didn't call the cops because of the stench. I nearly lost my midnight snack when I smelled it. Jackson said you'd want to take care of the dude yourself, but I didn't want to risk losing him—" well, that and she wasn't sure what his San Diego plans were "—so I wasted the asshole." She climbed back on the treadmill. "We searched the place, not expecting to turn up much, but we came up with some stuff that was off the hook."

Jackson snapped the phone shut as Dom finally turned. "You got that right." He pulled out a triangular sandwich half from somewhere. Wearing a black Extreme Couture ball cap, a ripped gym T-shirt, and a pair of black sweat-pants rolled down at the waist, he adjusted his crotch and sauntered over. Streaks of pale gold and light brown highlights mingled with his natural brown hair, which curled onto his shoulders. For a gym rat, he sure spent a lot of time on his hair. When he turned, a flash of color on his arm caught her attention.

"Nice ink."

Jackson's muscular biceps were the size of a human male's quads and one sported a colorful new snake design that began on his forearm, wrapped around the inside of his elbow and ended with the head strategically placed on the largest part of his guns. Hell, he was looking pretty fine. Too bad he had the attention span of a gnat when it came to anything that didn't involve sex. She loved the guy like a brother—well, not really. Maybe more like a friend with occasional benefits when neither of them had regular hook-ups.

"You like it?" Jackson said.

"Flex those bad boys on over here."

He made a show of it, grabbing his wrist and tucking his arm in tight like a bodybuilder. The snake's head appeared to strike as he pumped his muscle, but the stupid sandwich in his other hand sort of detracted from the picture.

"Nice, Jacks. Verra nice."

"Thanks. You're looking good, too." He raked his eyes over her body and she noticed his gaze resting for a moment longer on her ass. She sucked in her stomach a little farther and knew she looked pretty damn good in these boy shorts.

"Hey, Dom, how's it going, man?"

Dom raised a hand but didn't look up. "Thanks for last night."

"With that chick's bike? No problem." Jackson patted his chest as if he had pockets there, then his hips. "I've got her keys somewhere."

Lily cleared her throat, pretending to be offended that Dom hadn't thanked her, as well.

"You, too, Lil. Had me confused with all that talk about BJs…and stuff." He took the keys from Jackson and gave them a long look.

"BJs? What did I miss?" Jackson stuffed the sandwich into his mouth in one bite.

"That's the problem, Jacks. Not a damn thing." She lengthened her stride slightly as she got into sync. Man, she wished someone would turn that music down, but Dom was understandably operating on a hair trigger this morning and she didn't feel like pushing it. What was it about men and 80s music these past couple decades? She just didn't get the allure.

"You know I'm always game." Jackson flashed her a smile that would give an orthodontist a hard-on, then he turned back to Dom. "Hey, I thought you'd be in San Diego by now."

When Dom didn't answer, Lily wanted to speak up quietly, but the music was so damn loud she practically had to yell. "He was heading to the airport when he got word Mackenzie was in trouble."

"Bummer, dude. How's Miss Hello Kitty doing anyway?" Jackson turned sideways to admire himself in the full-length gym mirrors and took hold of his crotch as if checking out the profile of his package. He didn't see Dom's narrowed eyes or slightly flared nostrils, and certainly not his balled fists. "Got her holed up and satisfied? I figured you'd be gone another couple nights with the likes of her, since you missed your flight. Why aren't you with her? What's up with that?" Jackson's hand lingered on his junk a moment too long.

Lily gave Jackson a throat-choking sign, but he didn't look over. This wasn't going to be pretty if he kept flapping his gums.

"Not as daring in the sack as she is on that bike, huh?"

Oh, hell. Jackson could be so stupid sometimes.

Before Lily could step in to prevent what she knew was coming, Dom had Jackson flat on the ground, standing over him with a foot on his neck. "You better shut that goddamn hole in your head."

Jackson choked, gripped Dom's shoe and tried to pry it off his throat. "Jesus, Dom."

Lily slowed the treadmill to a jog as Dom's face twisted with fury. Usually, he didn't give a rat's ass about anything, just did his job like a robot—a friggin' intense robot—biding his time until he could transfer out of here. But now that his long-awaited transfer had finally gone through, he didn't seem eager to leave. How interesting.

"If you say another disrespectful word about her or if I even sense you're thinking of her in a way that's a fraction less than honorable, I'll have you regretting you were born male. You got it?"

Jackson gave him the thumbs-up sign and Dom stepped away. Coughing, Jackson rolled onto his hands and knees, hanging his head between his shoulder blades for a moment before he pushed himself up, the snake bulging on his biceps. "Sorry, man. I forgot how sensitive you are about her. I was just messin' with you." He repositioned the cocky tilt of his hat and rubbed his throat.

Lily slowed the treadmill to a walk. "Jacks, those loose lips are gonna cost you one of these days. That, and your dick."

"Yeah, thanks. It is lethal."

Lily patted her hips, her midsection and her arms, as if looking for something. Then, with her mouth ajar, she gave him a look of mock surprise. "Wow, that's strange. I'm still alive."

He flipped her a one-fingered salute as he stumbled to the watercooler.

"Lil, you said something was off the hook at that Dark-blood den. What'd you find?" Dom asked.

She punched the up arrow and broke into a run again. "Jackson, you tell him. I'm in the zone here."

Jackson filled a pointed paper cup from the water dispenser jug and walked it over to Lily. Yeah, he wasn't as self-absorbed as he appeared. Pouring one for himself, he cleared his throat.

"Well, the place was a pit, a regular science experiment on every hard surface, so we didn't expect to find much. Figured they were a couple of routine ferals and not part of the organized Alliance. We found some crazy shit in the basement though. Curdled my blood, and that's hard to do." Jackson rubbed his neck again.

"Crazy? As in how?" Dom asked.

"Torture and experiment crap. Chains, surgical instruments, leather straps, a couple of metal gurneys, needles, IV bags. Really creepy shit."

"Yeah, real creepy," Lily said. "Like horror movie creepy. We located their hard drive and Cordell is hacking into it right now. But I've got a bad feeling about this. If fuck-ups like those two guys have an operation like that, what the hell is going on? They couldn't have their—"

"You're sure it's Alliance?" Dom paced back and forth next to the boxing ring.

"It was too ritualistic down there for the likes of those two." God, that music. Like a hangnail on a fresh manicure. She simply couldn't stand it any longer and turned to Jackson. "Can you turn that crap off, or at least down? It's giving me a flipping aneurism." She slowed the treadmill once more as Jackson twisted the volume knob and the sound of a screeching guitar died into background noise. Much better. She could think again. "As I was saying, everything was too neat and tidy. Things were arranged neatly on a pegboard and labeled, like a retired engineer's workbench, if that retired engineer planned on doing medical experiments and torture in his basement. It was as if the whole place was set up according to some master plan. We even found a couple of planograms."

Dom kept pacing but scrunched up his forehead.

"You know, retail stores have POGs from their home office telling them how to display all their shit. Put this here, hang this over there, so that every store is set up the same way. There's no way the losers who lived upstairs could have organized that basement without any outside help. And that kind of organization screams long-term, not just 'hey, in case we run into a sweetblood or two.' You know what I mean?"

Dom stopped and his eyes met Lily's as the realization of their findings evidently sunk in. Experiments conducted on sweetbloods. Here. In Seattle. "Was it just the two of them living there?" His voice, though quiet, seethed with rage. She could almost smell it in the air.

"Yeah, just two bedrooms with blackened windows and a coffin in each." After glancing at the treadmill panel, Lily stepped off and snatched a clean towel from the stack near the watercooler. She guessed 2K was better than no K.

"I even peeked inside. They've got goddamn dirt lining the bottoms. That is just so wrong." Jackson stuffed another sandwich half into his mouth. His jaw popped as he struggled to chew the large mouthful, which would've taken her six or seven bites to get through. At least. The guy burned food like a coal furnace.

"Cordell. Where is he?" Dom strode across the mats and kicked the doors open.

"Computer lab," Lily said, trotting after him.

"Wait up, guys. I'm coming with," Jackson said, his voice muffled through the bread.

MACKENZIE PACED AROUND the living room a few times before she found the nerve to call Martin. Stuck somewhere in the San Juan Islands—she wasn't sure which one—she didn't think she'd be back in time to teach her class tonight. She never backed away from her commitments and didn't feel comfortable putting her class in the hands of one of his grad students. But she saw no other option at this point since she was stranded so far away from home. Thank God she'd emailed Steve her latest photos yesterday and didn't expect to be sent out anywhere for a location shoot for the next few days.

"The islands, huh? Staying in a romantic bed and breakfast with him?" Martin asked.

"Him who?"

"Hello? Don't play dumb with me. I know I didn't fail

at my little matchmaking attempt the other day, regardless of what you say. Having a nice time with Dom?"

"He's actually not here. He was, but not now." She wanted to add that she didn't know if he was coming back and that she had to figure out how to get home, but she didn't.

"Honey, what happened? Are you okay?"

"I'm fine." She tried to give her voice a casual lilt. "He had to leave suddenly. I just wasn't sure I'd make it home in time to teach my class tonight."

"Don't pull that nonsense on me, babe. I can tell you're upset. What's wrong? What happened?" Martin asked.

"Nothing happened. I'm fine."

"Well, you don't sound fine. How are you getting home? Do you need a pick-up? I've got a full class load today but I can come later on tonight or first thing tomorrow morning. I must've been all wrong about him, Kenz. I'm sorry. I pegged him as a good guy. What did he do? He didn't hurt you, did he?" Martin's concern was touching.

"God, no. He's a wonderful man." As tears formed on the backs of her eyes, she took a deep breath and hoped her voice sounded strong. "An emergency came up that he hadn't expected and he had to leave. I'm sure I'll be hearing from him soon, but I just wanted to make sure my bases were covered for tonight. No big deal. Really."

Why did she feel she had to gloss over the ugly details? Of course she couldn't tell him the whole truth about Dom, but she didn't feel compelled to tell him that Dom had abandoned her, either. What did it matter if Martin knew she was stranded with no means to get home? Why did she care if Martin detested Dom or not?

"Are you sure?"

"Absolutely. He'll be back soon, I'm sure." She forced herself to sound chipper as she changed the subject. *Divert and distract.* "Oh, you should see it here, Martin. It's gorgeous. I can't wait to head out to the beach. I just wish I'd thought to bring along my sketch pad."

"I can't wait to see your pictures."

She didn't tell him she didn't have her camera, either.

"Listen," he continued. "I'm glad you called. Have you talked to Mary yet?"

"The department secretary? No. Why?"

"It's probably not anything to get worked up about, but two odd fellows came to the university the other evening asking about you. They were quite the duo, both tall and skinny, and shabbily dressed."

The room started to spin and she willed herself to breathe.

"Mary called me wanting to know if she should give out your contact information. Evidently they inquired about a Mackenzie Shaw, not Foster-Shaw, so she wasn't sure if it was you or not. I told her not to tell them anything, so they insisted on speaking to me."

She felt as if she'd been punched in the stomach with a baseball bat. The attack on her had been premeditated. She hadn't just been in the wrong place at the wrong time. Those monsters had sought her out. She grabbed the edge of the counter for support.

The day her father hadn't come home, had this happened to him? Her mother had prepared his after-work snack like she always did. Sliced dill pickles and black olives on the same yellow plate with a chip on the edge. It sat untouched on the coffee table for three days. The police officer who came to talk to her mother ate all the dried out, three-day-old olives. She had laughed about it later to her mother and couldn't figure out why her mother cried. What was so sad about eating old olives? she remembered thinking. Funny what a kid remembers.

Did two Darkbloods follow her father around all those years ago? Had they waited for the right opportunity to attack him? Had her father been as terrified as she had been? And how about Stacy? Had her cousin known what was happening to her?

She didn't trust the ligaments in her legs to support her weight any longer, so she sank to the kitchen floor.

"Do you know what they wanted?" she managed to ask.

"Just that they needed to speak to you about some matter from long ago. You're not in the witness protection program, are you?" He laughed.

She forced herself to join in, but didn't trust herself to speak. If only he knew what was really going on.

"I don't know if they'll come around again—they didn't leave any contact information—but I thought I'd give you the heads-up."

She fought to keep her voice from cracking, but her hands shook violently and the phone almost fell from her grasp. "Thanks for looking out for me, Martin. I wonder who they are." She had a glimpse of Dom raising a stake above his head and pounding it into that guy in the dark warehouse parking lot. "Must be someone else they're looking for, but thanks for letting me know."

As he walked down the labyrinthlike hallway toward the computer lab with Lily and Jackson, Dom felt as if someone had reached into his chest with a knife and sliced his heart in half. *Mackenzie!* Something was wrong.

"Go," he told the others. "I'll be there in a minute."

He fumbled with the cell phone and dialed her number. Two rings, then her voice. For real. He leaned a shoulder unevenly against the wall.

"Mackenzie, are you okay?"

She didn't answer him right away, but he could hear her breathing. "Yes." Her voice was thin, barely audible.

Dios mio.

She had been worried or scared a moment ago, but now she just seemed angry. He slid down the wall and sat on the floor of the sterile hallway, cell phone cradled against his ear.

"What's wrong? What just happened?" Dom asked.

"Other than you leaving me last night?"

"Mackenzie, I'm sorry. I wanted to stay, but you saw what I was capable of."

"I saw a warrior last night, Dom. A man who was willing to fight for me, even to die for me. And yet—"

"Die for you? I practically killed you," Dom said.

"Why do you not see yourself as I do?" She gave a sigh of exasperation and her voice had a sudden, cool edge. She was distancing herself from him, and that imaginary knife continued its sawing motion. "I have nothing here. No credit cards, no transportation, and my effin' phone battery is almost dead. I'm fine, really. Maybe I'll just walk home."

"I said I'd be back and I meant it. What happened last night—"

"What happened last night was a nightmare. I just want to get the hell out of here and go home."

He heard a click in his ear as she ended the call. He flew to his feet and pounded a fist against the wall, so hard that cement dust covered his boots.

She was mad at him now, but what had frightened her a moment ago?

CHAPTER SEVENTEEN

MACKENZIE HEARD A light tapping on the cabin door.

"Good morning. Or should I say, good afternoon." Shirl stood on the top stair dressed in army green hip-wader boots. She held two empty buckets in one hand, two rakes pinched under her arm, and a to-go mug in the other, which she held out to Mackenzie. "It's a two-percent mocha with extra whip. Sorry, it's not nonfat. We don't do skinny around here." She laughed. "Thought maybe you could use some company, since I heard Dom freaked out and split."

"Thanks. He called you?" Mackenzie pulled the lid off to dip her finger into the whipped cream. Dom must've told Shirl how she liked her espresso drinks. She would've been touched by his thoughtfulness if she hadn't been so pissed off.

"Yeah, I can't believe he left. He knows he could've come up to the main house and we'd have gotten him another room if he was so worried about hurting you. Hey, open the hall closet there and grab a pair of boots, will ya? I'm taking you clamming. It's a minus tide and the water will be out at its farthest point soon."

"I'm not really—"

"Nonsense," Shirl said. "Let's get going. The tide's only out for another half hour or so. It's not often we get such a low tide during the daylight hours, so we gotta take advantage of it. It's usually in the middle of the night, so I send Chuck."

One mocha and ten minutes later, they were raking the rocky beach for butter clams.

"I was so mad at Chuck when he came to bed this morning. He and Dom had a long talk before Dom left for Seattle. For Pete's sake, if I had known he was leaving, I'd have gone out there and talked him out of it."

"Chuck is a…" Mackenzie still couldn't say the word.

"Vampire, dear? Yes, he is. That's why he didn't come down to the car to greet you last night, being that you're of the sweetblood. He's actually very charming. He and Dom are very close, almost like father and son, and he wanted to meet the girl who swept Dom off his feet. I sort of think that's why Dom brought you all the way here."

Even in the chill of the sea air, Mackenzie's cheeks flared hot as she plucked several pale gray clams from the overturned sand and placed them in her bucket. "You're obviously not a…a vampire. How…"

"How did that happen? How do we make it work?"

Mackenzie nodded. She told herself she was curious just for the sake of being curious. Like a detached reporter interviewing a witness, gathering information for a story.

"We met and fell in love. Just like two regular humans do. We talked about having me go through the change. You know, to convert me over to a vampire? We got married and even obtained Council permission. But when it came to the commitment ceremony a year later, I still couldn't do it. I've got this huge blood phobia. As in psychiatrist-and-support-group phobia, and I couldn't do it. The conversion process involves…"

Shirl stopped and wiped her forehead with the back of her hand. "Well, let's just say I couldn't bear to go through it. But boy, did I consider it. A vamp and a human can't conceive, but a vamp and a changeling can. I'd always seen myself with a whole brood...but I guess it wasn't in the cards for me. God sure does have a sense of humor. Me with my blood phobia, falling in love with a vampire? Go figure."

Mackenzie stooped down to turn over a rock and watched as a few tiny crabs skittered away to find another hiding place. *A sense of humor? Like me being a sweetblood and Dom being a vampire?*

The older woman meandered across the beach, which was sandier at the low tide mark than up at the top, her eyes glued to her shuffling feet. Mackenzie followed. They walked toward a large gathering of seagulls that flew off in unison, cawing their irritation into the wind. Evidently finding what she had been searching for, Shirl began raking the sand again.

"Is it hard for you and Chuck to think about? I mean, that you'll...I mean...he'll live so much longer..."

"That I'll kick the bucket before he does? That I'll age while he stays young?" Shirl held her hand up to her mouth as if she were going to tell a secret. "Thank God, I fell in love with an older man. Much older. Way older." She snorted and slapped her thigh. "Can't imagine what we'd have done if he were younger when we met."

"If you were to do it all over again, would you still choose not to convert?"

"I don't know, honey, but all I can say is that if I wasn't so averse to blood, I'd be a grandmother by now."

"WHAT HAVE YOU found?" Dom watched as Cordell's dark, slender fingers flew across the dual keyboards and his head cranked left and right, scanning the huge monitor. He was vaguely aware that Lily had just entered the room behind him.

"I haven't been able to hack into their main site. Their security is pretty tight. But from what I can tell, they're stepping up their capture efforts. Look here. They've got several laboratories here in the States. Atlanta, Dallas, Orlando."

Jackson elbowed Dom in the ribs. "Your buddies in the Orlando field office will be thrilled to hear this from you. Are you still not speaking?"

"Shut up, Jacks," Lily said, as she came up behind him, a little out of breath. "Dom, I just got off the phone with my contact."

"And?"

"It's a breeding operation. Darkbloods are setting up a goddamn breeding operation."

He felt his pupils dilate and the blood pounded between his ears. "With sweetbloods?"

"Yes, they're capturing them to breed them. They're keeping them alive, hoping they can successfully mate two sweetbloods to create more."

"That's whacked," said Jackson. "I knew they were a bunch of freaks, but that's just twisted."

"And it's set to commence soon," Dom reminded them. "We need to find these facilities—as in yesterday. Cordell, you said you couldn't hack into their system. How do you know the labs are in those cities?"

"Those losers must've copied these reports from the main Darkblood site that we can't break into." Cordell paged down to the next screen. "Phoenix, San Diego." He craned his neck around and looked at Dom. "And Seattle. They've got one clear up here."

Panic knotted his gut as an overwhelming sense of protectiveness came over him. *Mackenzie. Dios mio.* He took a half-step backwards and grabbed the edge of a table. A piece of it crumbled under his fingers.

She wasn't on their database up here, though, he told himself. They didn't know about her—the information he'd downloaded to his phone proved that. But then what about last night? Those DBs sure as hell knew about her. Could they have run across her by chance?

Cordell's fingers flew across the keys. "I can't find exact locations for any of the facilities."

"Send out an alert to all the regions letting them know about Lily's new information and what you've discovered. Maybe someone's turned up something that can help us locate the sites." Dom twisted his thumb rings as he paced.

"Look," Lily said, pointing to the screen. "There's a spreadsheet of names of the family lines they're seeking. Can you pull up that document?"

"Sure." Cordell clicked open the file. They all leaned over his chair as a detailed chart popped up on the screen.

"Holy shit," Lily said. "Looks like they've captured a few of them already."

Dom cursed under his breath and began pacing again, unable to get it out of his head that Mackenzie was on the island and not under his immediate protection.

"We've got to change our focus from tracking DBs to locating this facility," Jackson said. "If we find that, we hamstring their whole operation."

"I agree," Dom said. They needed manpower for a widespread search, but with Stryker still not a hundred percent, they were seriously short-staffed. "Cordell, contact Portland and Vancouver. See if they can spare any Guardians. Lily, we'll need a few more Class-A scent-trackers. Can you—"

"I'm on it," she said.

Good. They'd mobilize as many—

"Um, Dom?"

He stopped pacing and turned around. Lily was pointing to the screen. "What's Mackenzie's last name?"

His blood turned icy in his veins. "Foster-Shaw."

"According to this spreadsheet, those guys who were after her were looking for a Mackenzie Shaw."

The vise around his internal organs tightened further. *They didn't just happen upon her last night? They've been looking for her?* "But the database I downloaded onto my phone showed no Fosters or Shaws."

"Dunno, love. That was a couple weeks ago. The name's there now," Lily said.

"Lemme see," Cordell said. "Maybe it's not the same person."

"Yeah, what are the chances of that?" Jackson said.

The tech lab felt eerily quiet except for the clicking of the keyboard. While Dom paced, the seconds slipped by as if they were large grains of sand in a too-small hourglass.

Finally Cordell spoke. "Does she have something to do with the University of Washington? Wait. Is this her website?"

Dom snapped his head around to see an artist's website pop up on the screen and Mackenzie's picture smiling back at him.

The sudden roar in his ears numbed his whole body and he stumbled backwards. *They know about her. Darkbloods know about Mackenzie.* What in hell was he thinking leaving her on the island? How could she possibly be safe without him?

"Jackson, Lily, I want you each to lead a search unit," he yelled as he ran for the door. "Cordell, you coordinate things from here. Put together a list of the most probable places for them to locate such a facility. I'll contact Santiago. Have him send as many Guardians as the other field teams can spare, using Daytrans vehicles if necessary. We'll have a tactical at 2:00 p.m. tomorrow and be ready to hit the streets by nightfall."

He glanced at his watch. He could make it to the resort by late afternoon. "I'll be back as soon as I can."

CHAPTER EIGHTEEN

DOM KNEW THAT to anyone watching, he must look like a drunk as he ran down the oyster-shell path to the cabin—his knees buckling every few steps, his arms stretched out for balance. It was midafternoon when he'd pulled into the resort a few minutes ago. Even with the tinted windows of the Porsche, dark sunglasses, a hoodie and a ball cap, the sunlight had sapped much of his energy—too much to allow him to *vapor* to the island. Although exhausted, he needed to see to Mackenzie's safety himself. Chuck had assured him she was fine, but that wasn't enough. Knowing she was on the DB list, he couldn't rest until he was with her.

He clung to the railing, stumbled down the stairs, but on the last step, he tripped and sprawled on the pathway. As if a flimsy curtain was lifted, the unyielding sun pelted his face and eyelids with searing heat. His sunglasses and cap were gone—lost in the fall. He crawled on his hands and knees, and somehow made it to the cabin before he collapsed.

Her scent filled his nostrils but he didn't feel her presence inside. He didn't need to search the rooms to know she wasn't here. The entry mat just inside the door felt bristly against the back of his head. He focused inward, concentrated, and picked up her latent energy trail. She was somewhere nearby.

He pushed himself up and made his way to the windows. Thank God the automatic blinds had been deactivated. He didn't know if he had the strength to find the switch if he had needed to open them.

He spotted her immediately, walking alone on the rocky beach, wearing some crazy red boots.

How could he have left her, like he had his parents, when he knew the danger she faced? What a goddamn fool not to admit to himself what she meant to him. To assume she'd be fine without him.

He watched as she pulled her hair forward and over one shoulder, then she stooped to turn over a rock. His heart slammed in his chest and his throat was thick and swollen as he remembered that afternoon in the cemetery. Her hair, her graceful movements, her long legs. She entranced him now just as she had then.

Mackenzie. My beautiful Mackenzie. She turned then, stared up at him. Of course she could feel him.

A hidden reserve of energy surged through his veins. He made it out the door and down the three steps to the beach. When he saw her running toward him as well, his heart surged. She wasn't still angry with him for last night. It was a sheer miracle he didn't fall backwards when she jumped into his arms and wrapped her legs around his waist. He hadn't realized how empty he had felt until he was holding her again. His knees gave way and they sank to the ground.

"I'm sorry I left you."

His fingers gripped her hair and he pulled her lips to his. Greedily, he kissed her cheeks, her eyelids, her neck, her earlobes. He couldn't get enough. Oh God, he needed to make love to her, to have nothing separating them but skin. Share energies and—

If it were dark, he'd take her right on the beach, like he had last night. How had he ever thought he could leave her?

I love you. The words, his words, tumbled unbidden in his thoughts.

"I love you, too," she said huskily as she pulled back to look at him. Her hair cascaded around them, shielding them from the outside world. Her eyes were heavy with passion.

He hardly heard the dull roar of the waves or the seagulls screeching in the wind as he pushed himself up and swept her into his arms. Rejuvenated by her energies, he carried her back to the cabin.

Not stopping to close the blinds, he slammed the door shut with his foot. His boots pounded on the floor as he strode into the bedroom. All that mattered was what he was going to do to her in about ten seconds. He needed her in a way that defied all logic. Given how her nails dug into his shoulders and her heart banged in his head, she clearly felt the same. He didn't need to get into her mind to know that—her body language didn't need translating.

He tossed her on the bed, kicked off his boots, and unzipped his fly. It was the only undressing he did. She shimmied her jeans around her ankles and wrenched one leg free. He was on her in an instant. With an other-worldly cry he'd never uttered before, he plunged himself inside.

"DARLING, I WANT you to know that when you're ready, if you ever are, I'm ready." She could see the doubt in his eyes. He obviously didn't think he was strong enough, but she knew otherwise. She was sure of it. "I trust you completely. I won't push you, but please know it's important to me to give all of myself to you." Her voice caught on the lump in her throat. She knew she'd break in half eventually if he didn't drink from her. It was that vital, that important. "I want to be everything you need."

His eyes clouded. "You are, Kenz. My God, you are, but—" He started to say something else, probably a protest about it not being safe. Some nonsense about him hurting her, but she shushed him with her lips.

"No talking. Just know that I want that someday. For now, I need you to love me."

The rumble in his chest echoed inside her as his hands grazed lightly down her sides. Obviously, it was going to be slower this time. Slow and meaningful. Although hard and crazy was good, too. Sex with him was a drug—she was an addict who constantly needed more. She wanted to breathe in his essence and bottle him up inside to save him for later.

He cupped her bottom and lifted her onto his erection with an ease that made her feel weightless. He obviously hadn't softened from what she could tell, and he slid in effortlessly again. They moved together as one, a choreographed dance both of them knew by heart. She was in a dream that she never wanted to end. If she could feel him like this every day for the rest of her life, she'd know the meaning of heaven on earth.

His lips caressed one nipple as his thumb rubbed across the other. She arched her back and moaned his name.

"I love how my name sounds on your lips," he said, speeding up the pace of his thrusts. "I want to hear it from you again, when I lock myself inside you."

Every nerve ending sizzled with anticipation as his large hands gripped her hip bones like handles and pushed her down farther. There was that hitch again and her body welcomed him home.

"Oh God, Dom," she heard herself cry, not consciously forming the words, but nonetheless uttering them as he had wanted. Her body clearly responded to him with an awareness all its own.

With his warm hands spread wide on her thighs, he kept her clamped tightly against him. No thrusting, just gentle rocking back and forth. He seemed hypnotized by the swaying of her breasts, watching them through half-closed lids, almost as if he were waiting for the snap of a finger to spur him to action. The tip of his tongue darted out for a moment.

Seeing his desire for her lifted her to new heights. And just like that, he lifted forward and took a nipple into his mouth.

Oh God. She tried to wait, to savor the glorious sensations, to revel in the beauty of his chiseled body beneath her, but it was no use. Her muscles quivered as the pressure cranked to an almost mind-numbing pinnacle in an instant. With her fingers against the damp skin of his chest, the cords of his neck strained and he shuddered between her legs. When his sex pulsed inside, she crashed around him yet again.

MARTIN WAS PUTTING away the last of the art supplies when the front door buzzer sounded from downstairs. One of the kids must've left something. A quick examination of the art room didn't reveal a stray backpack or anything else that looked out of place. Mackenzie ran a tight ship; the place was immaculate.

He glanced at the clock. Nine-thirty. Dinner reservations weren't for another half hour. Maybe Paul had decided to pick him up here, but surely he'd have called first. It was probably just the night janitor.

He rummaged around in a few cabinets looking for the cleaning spray and rag. All he had left to do was wipe down the tables and lock up. The classroom door clicked open, but his head was buried in a lower cabinet so he didn't get up. "Did you leave something?" he called.

"Where is she?"

The man's raspy I've-just-smoked-two-packs-of-cigarettes voice startled Martin. He bumped his head and turned around to see two men saunter into the room, their arms and legs moving in unison. With long black trench coats, combat boots and sunglasses, they looked like they'd just stepped out of *The Matrix*.

"Pardon me? Can I help you?" There was something familiar about them, although he couldn't place their faces. Sweat broke out on his upper lip.

The shorter one yanked open a closet door. "'Pardon me. Can I help you?'" he mimicked in a high-pitched voice.

What the...

"The woman. Mackenzie Shaw." The other one took off his sunglasses and even from across the room, Martin could tell something was terribly wrong.

His heart beat like a bass drum behind his eardrums as he saw the whites of the man's eyes were actually gray.

Oh, help me, Lord. "I...I don't know who you're talking about."

"Don't fuck with us. We can smell her all over this place. Where is she?"

Smell? What the hell?

"There is no Mackenzie Shaw here." What did they want with her? Although they weren't the same two men who showed up at the University the other day, their mannerisms were exactly the same. They definitely were affiliated.

"I didn't ask if she was here. I asked where she was. Big difference."

Martin glanced around the room. The one doing most of the talking blocked the door to the hallway. The other one stood on the far side of the room. With the student tables between them, if he ran, he might be able to reach the door behind him that led to the adjoining classroom. Could he make it?

"Either you tell us where she is and we'll show you mercy, or you keep quiet and we won't. It's really that simple." The boss reached out his clasped hands and cracked his knuckles. "Now, I'm going to ask you again. Where the fuck is Mackenzie Shaw?"

"Okay." Martin took a step forward as if he were going to cooperate, then in a flash, he jumped backward and ran through the adjoining door into the other classroom. He could hear tables crashing as the men gave chase. He made it to the exit and yanked it open.

As he ran down the stairs two at a time, he pulled his cell phone from his pocket and speed dialed her number. Damn. Straight to voice mail. They were at the top of the stairs now, barreling down.

"Two men. After you." He could hardly get the words out. They were right behind him. The short one was laughing again as if he were enjoying himself.

Something heavy hit him square in the back and he fell forward on the last stair and slid across the tile floor of the lobby, his chin acting as a rudder. The phone flew from his hand and shattered against the receptionist's booth.

Strong hands grabbed him by the scruff of his neck and flung him through the air. He heard a high-pitched screeching again and thought at first it was the short man until he realized the sound had come from his own lips. It was his own screams he heard as his body smashed against the far wall of the lobby and he fell to the ground like a rag doll.

CHAPTER NINETEEN

"I DON'T UNDERSTAND how one minute you can be in complete control and the next you feel as though you aren't."

She had a damn good point and Dom wished he had an answer. "Yes, I know. It's like a switch. But one thing's for sure, I won't risk hurting you."

"So you could just leave me again? Is that what you're saying?" she asked.

"I may have to physically leave, but I won't desert you. That was wrong of me."

Hurt simmered in her eyes. She stood up to carry their plates to the sink but he grabbed her wrist and pushed a little of his energies to her. Her lashes fluttered for a moment. "As long as you'll have me, you'll never be alone. We may not be standing side-by-side, but you'll always be here." He placed her open palm on his chest and watched her face soften. "And I pray you'll forever let me be here," he said as he lay her small hand over her own heart and covered it with his.

He closed his eyes, concentrating on the gentle hum of her prana and the beat of her heart in rhythm with his. *As long as she'll have me.* He hoped it'd be forever. Seconds, minutes, maybe hours ticked by as he held his hand over hers. Her warm energies swirled inside him and he pushed to her an equal amount of his. He felt as if he could soar off the highest peak and float to the heavens with her and wondered if she felt the same.

Her voice was soft when she finally spoke and looked down into his face. With her dewy eyes heavy with emotion, her full, slightly swollen lips, she was more beautiful to him than she had ever been before. "As far-fetched as all this is, this whole bizarre world of yours, it's the missing piece of my life. It explains everything. So last night, as crazy as it may seem, I had a glimpse that maybe I did have a future." He shivered when she ran a light fingertip along his temple, and pulled her onto his lap.

"Knowing why my family has experienced all these tragedies is very empowering. I couldn't fight an unknown enemy, so I gave up and refused to think of my future no matter how much I wanted someone to…to love and love me back." Her voice wavered. "But I can fight a known enemy and for the first time in my life, I felt there might be a future for me. One with you in it. That's why when you left it hurt so much."

He buried his face in her soft hair, letting it pool around him, and prayed Chuck had found some answers. And if he hadn't, well, Dom would figure something out, because he couldn't imagine life without her.

"I'm sorry. The thought of…of tasting you again that way is overwhelming. God knows I've wanted to." He inhaled the natural fragrance in the fragile hollow of her neck. Oh, to taste her sweetness again. Maybe he—

No, he couldn't.

Instead, he flicked his tongue against her skin and she melted in closer. It was clear to him she wanted him to do it almost as badly as he did. "I don't know that I could ever try it without the fear I'd kill you. Wearing this cilice helps, but it's certainly no guarantee."

She pushed back and looked at him. "What are you talking about? A cilice?"

He lifted his wrist, indicating the leather band. "It's a constant reminder to keep myself in check around you." She looked confused. He'd have to show her. Would she freak out when she saw it? It was bound to look messed up.

Resting his elbow on the table, he carefully unbuckled the clasp and eased the strap away from his wrist. One by one, like the teeth of a zipper, a few of the steel studs released their hold. She gasped when a tiny trickle of blood dripped from a puncture hole in the tender skin of his inner wrist.

"What the hell are you doing to yourself?" Before he knew it, she'd touched a finger to his blood and put it to her lips. Instantly, the vibration in his head got stronger.

"Oh my— That is— Wow." She shook her head as if to clear her thoughts. When she opened her eyes, the golden highlights in her green irises seemed to have deepened in color. "My God, Dom. I thought it was just a leather band you wore. But it's cutting you. Why?"

"It's nothing. Really. The small amount of constant pain deflects my focus if things should get out of hand with you. I seem to do better at controlling my urges when I have it on. When I don't—well, that's what happened last night. Last night I was out of control."

"You've got to take it off. I don't want you to hurt yourself to be with me. I had no idea. It looks so painful." Her fingertips were like the brush of a feather against the torn skin and she kissed his palm. With her lips just inches from his blood, he pulled his hand away, but he couldn't help wondering what it'd be like if she had more.

"Trust me, I'm fine." It hurt like a mother, but hell if he'd admit it.

"I hate that I'm so hard for you and your people to be around. Please, Dom. Take it off." Her fingers raked at her hair, taking several tries to get it behind her ear. She was shaken at the sight of his mangled skin.

"It takes the edge off. I'm like a pitbull with a barbed collar—manageable until the thing comes off. I'll remove it…for now." As he pulled the strap away from his skin, he sucked in a hiss of air through his teeth. Blood had dried around each spike and now acted like glue. Plastering on a fake smile, he ripped it off in one single movement. *Dios mio.*

Her face screwed up in knots and she jumped as she sensed his pain. Great. Now she was going to be acutely aware of the thing when he put it on again. He tossed it onto the table and, gripping her shoulders, he turned her away so she couldn't see it, but he couldn't sway her that easily.

"You're hurting. Don't give me that look. All this prana and mind-reading business isn't one-sided, you know. I can feel how it hurts you almost as if I had it on myself. Let me get some salve and bandage it up. Shirl's got to have a first-aid kit around her somewhere. "

"Not necessary. I heal fast. It's feeling better already."

She gave him a lopsided scowl and climbed off his lap. Nope, she wasn't buying it. He heard her rummaging through the bathroom drawers, and a few minutes later she returned with a tube of ointment and a box of bandages.

"You may heal faster than I would, but I still know a

nasty wound when I see one. You're not putting that damn thing on again. Gimme your hand."

Too bad. As long as she was around him, the device wouldn't be far away.

He watched as she squeezed a small amount of ointment onto her pinkie finger. Cradling his forearm gently in her hands, she seemed to be examining the wounds for an extraordinarily long length of time. In his head he felt the beating of her heart increase its tempo and he ground his teeth together. No, he couldn't let her go there. Making love to her was one thing, but if she took any more of his blood, he knew his willpower would be gone. Shredded. Zilch. Cilice or no cilice. Like committed couples who shared blood, his body would need that from her. It wasn't a one-sided thing. If she fed directly from him, he would need to feed directly from her. But that would have disastrous results. He pulled away.

She scowled and grabbed his hand again. "Hold still, will you?" Then she gently touched her finger to each puncture wound.

"You were saying something about biting and making love. What do you mean? Is biting like a sexual thing?"

"Sometimes. Blood sharing is a common practice when we make love. Not necessarily when having sex just for the hell of it, but when there's a deep emotional connection between committed couples, some feel the urge to share blood. Or so I'm told."

She applied the last bandage and his eyes met hers. Yes, she felt the same urge. The urge to share blood. She wanted his, too.

"Committed couples? Have you ever shared blood with anyone?"

"No. Never had the desire till now and I've, uh. . ."

He coughed. How could he word it so she didn't think he was some easy man-whore? Hell, most unmated vampires were. Who was he fooling? He was no different. Before he'd met her, there weren't many weeks that passed without several hook-ups. Casual sex to the extent his kind engaged in wasn't as accepted a practice among humans. But it was a healthier, more acceptable way to deal with their aggressive natures. "I've had lots of experiences and… Well, it's just never happened to me before. I wasn't expecting it."

"And it's not something related to my being Sangre Dulce?"

"The bloodlust—yes. But the emotional connection, the need to drink from you—no. And you know your desire for me to take more of your blood?" He waited for her to nod her head. "I've got the same feeling, too. Like a drumbeat in my head. I want you to have some of mine again." He'd hardly realized that was what the need had been, but seeing her taste the drop of his blood clarified what he hadn't been able to define.

She was quiet. He'd have to tell her it was against Council rules to share with a human. Unless they had gone through the mating ritual.

"Mackenzie…I—" His lips went suddenly dry. "Given my family history, I freaked out."

"What do you mean? What happened?"

Why the hell had he even brought it up? Things had been going along perfectly fine without mentioning *that*. Just thinking about it made him feel sick. But there was something about the strength behind her eyes that made him want to tell her things he'd never felt comfortable sharing before. He wasn't sure he could get the words out.

Running his fingers through his hair, he got up and walked to the window. The sun had dipped behind the distant horizon of the peninsula and washed the sky in enchanting shades of pinks and oranges. His heart banged against his ribs and when he felt an unfamiliar welling of emotion, he realized he was looking at the sunset as Mackenzie would.

"Is it dark enough for you to comfortably go outside?" she asked, as she gathered the dishes from the table. "Want to take a walk? I promise not to push you in. I might even let you give me a piggyback ride."

The fresh air sounded good. He needed to clear his head. "Sure. But you couldn't push me in even if you wanted to."

"We'll see."

Her concern for his comfort outside suddenly registered. Could she even fathom what she did to him? That a simple thought or word from her was all it took for him to grovel at her feet? How just watching her made him forget an outside world even existed?

"Love those boots," he said, as he watched her pull on the bright red galoshes he'd seen her wear earlier. If they weren't obviously an adult size, he'd have sworn they belonged to a seven-year-old.

"Next time, I'll have to bring my own. You'll love them. They're pink Hello Kitty ones."

CHAPTER TWENTY

"WATER BREAK. Catch you in five." Lily left her class on the mats and walked down the hallway of the mixed martial arts studio.

She dialed the field office number. Was Dom back yet? She had assembled her team earlier and they'd be ready for orders as soon as he arrived. With nothing to do but wait, she headed to the Krav Maga center where she sometimes subbed as a martial arts instructor.

"You're an angel, Lil," Johnny Sinclair had said when she told him she'd be happy to take over his zero-dark-thirty class. "I'm working swing today at the precinct and have a full load of classes here this morning. Didn't have time for coffee or breakfast. Back in thirty."

If Dom didn't arrive soon, it meant he probably wouldn't be coming until this evening. She doubted his lack of UV sensitivity could last two full days in the sunlight. Was it a good sign that he didn't come back right away? Maybe, maybe not.

As she rounded the corner, a strong pair of hands grabbed her waist, pushing her against the dark wall. Greedy lips met hers as her sports bra was shoved up over her breasts. Dipping his head, her visitor sucked roughly at her nipples.

"I love it when you surprise me like this. I only have a minute. Think you can be fast?"

The zip of his fly was his answer and she dropped her workout shorts to her ankles. Turning around, she splayed her hands on the wall and arched her back.

Without any fanfare, he entered her hard and her breath caught in her throat as he growled. His fingers moved her hair aside and she felt his mouth against her neck. She had to bite her lip to keep from making a noise with her students just around the corner. Once, twice, three times and, as his fangs pierced her skin, she climaxed along with him. A moment later he sealed the twin puncture marks and withdrew. She pulled her shorts back up and straightened her sports bra as he zipped up his jeans.

"What a nice treat." She kissed him long and slow as she ran her tongue along the tips of his fangs. He tasted warm and spicy. "But what the hell are you doing here? You know it's not safe."

"I have more information for you. The operation is going online within the week. Two females are set to ovulate and the males are ready to go. Several other capture orders are being undertaken as we speak. They hope to have five or six breeding pairs over the next few weeks."

"Any closer to finding the location?"

"Unfortunately, no. It's cloaked and they're keeping it top secret. Just the researchers and the Overlord—I mean Pavlos—know where it's at. Everyone else is on a need-to-know basis. All I've been able to determine is that it's located somewhere west of the Cascade Mountains within about three hours of the city."

"Baby, you're good like that." She grabbed his ass and yanked him close. "Now be careful."

He wrapped his arms around her. "Always."

And with that, he released her and was gone.

* * *

Dom leaned against the cabin's deck rail, the cup of tea now lukewarm in his hand, and stared into the darkness.

"My brother, Alfonso." A bitter taste filled his mouth. He could hardly stand to form that name on his tongue, but the need to open up to Mackenzie was something he couldn't fight any longer. "He used to date a woman with Sangre Dulce. He ended up draining her dry one night and left her for dead. I discovered the body and had to cover up the whole goddamn thing from the human authorities. It was difficult—her family was very influential. The Agency tried to locate Alfonso, but he was never caught."

"Were they bonded like we are?"

"I don't know anyone who is."

"Have you talked with him since?"

"No. A long time ago, he betrayed our parents to Pavlos and joined the Alliance. Or maybe it was the other way around. In any event, all he cared about was himself and getting his hands on more Sweet."

Mackenzie set his cup on the table behind them and took his hand. "So why do you blame yourself for your parents' deaths?"

"I knew about the threat, but I left them unprotected anyway." Her calm energies soothed him and the familiar angry knots that balled up in his shoulders whenever he thought about his family didn't feel quite so solid.

"You said your father was on the Council. Did he not know about the threat?"

"He actually knew about it before I told him. All Council families were in danger and I urged him to take

Mother to London, far away from Madrid, until we got a handle on things there."

Mackenzie pursed her lips, lost in thought for a moment. "Did you have extra knowledge that you didn't act on?"

"No."

"Did your father not believe the threat was real?"

"He knew it was real, but I'm not sure he thought it was imminent. He planned to take my mother to *Casa en las Colinas*, our family's estate overlooking the Cantabrian Sea, but Alfonso brought Pavlos the night before they were to leave."

She gasped. "Your brother?"

"He waited out in the coach while Pavlos, the Darkblood Overlord, slaughtered our parents. The guards only let the coach through the gates because my brother was inside."

TIRED FROM THE late night, she awoke midmorning, wrapped in the protective cocoon of his arms. During the night, she'd awakened occasionally to find him caressing or lightly kissing her hair. She had hoped to roll over just once and hear the sound of deep, sleep-induced breathing, but she never did.

"What's bothering you?" Her hand ran absently over his chest.

"Darkblood concerns. Nothing for you to worry about, but we do need to go soon."

She stiffened. "Didn't you find that other guy?"

"Lily did. She took care of him."

Thank God. Her muscles loosened again and she nestled deeper into his arms. "Then what's wrong?"

"We've uncovered a new Darkblood plot."

She propped herself up on one elbow to find him staring at the ceiling, his thoughts clearly focused elsewhere. "Do we need to get going so you can get back to work?"

"We're waiting for other Guardian teams to arrive later this afternoon."

That explained the faraway look, but why was she picking up his reluctance to say more? Did it somehow involve her? Was that it? She couldn't imagine how things could get any worse than having two vampires hunt and almost kill her. But those two were gone. Dead. So why was he worried?

Like a slap, the realization hit her. The threat wasn't gone after all.

"Tell me," she said. "I deserve to know."

The small muscle at the base of his jaw tensed. "I suppose it's only fair you know, but I don't want to frighten you further."

"Well, if it helps, I've never been more unfrightened— is that a word?—than I am when I'm with you." She felt him relax, sensed some of the tension seep from his shoulders. "Tell me," she repeated.

He pinched the bridge of his nose and sighed. "We've discovered the Alliance has created a genetic breeding facility and they're searching for Sangre Dulce humans to be their test subjects."

"A breeding facility? Why?"

"To harvest sweetblood. They want to create a group of selectively bred Sangre Dulce humans to produce unlimited supplies of the blood. More Sweet means more power."

Humans as breeding stock? Like animals? The...the babies?

Her legs were rubber bands as she jumped from the bed and ran to the bathroom. Dom was there, his strong arms supporting her as if she were a small, sick child. He held her hair away from her face, gently stroking her back as she retched. When she was finished, he gave her a damp cloth and wrapped his arms around her.

"I'm here, love. You're safe with me. You're okay."

"It's just…so…awful." She could barely wrap her mind around it. The cruelty was impossible to comprehend.

His shushing in her ear soothed the gnawing ache in her belly, and she melted into his embrace. She didn't know how long it took to finally calm down, but he held her the whole time.

"Thank you," she whispered as she pulled away. "I'm okay now. But you really must get back. Your work is out there—not here with me."

He wanted to catch the next ferry, so she didn't have time for a shower. After brushing her teeth and splashing her face with water, she pulled on some of the clothes Shirl had bought for her. Black leggings and a Washington State University Cougars sweatshirt. Great. It killed her to put it on, but her only other set of clothes was damp and caked with sand from clam digging.

When she exited the bathroom, she heard the washing machine running. Dom had pulled the linens off the bed and started the laundry so there'd be less cleanup for Shirl.

When they got to the main house, Shirl stood up from a flower bed where she'd been tending to the rosebushes. Taking one look at Dom, she said, "Chuck's in the kitchen."

"Wait here," Dom told Mackenzie, and he disappeared inside.

"Told you he'd come back. To travel all this way in the bright sun…" Shirl shook her head and whistled. "That man is über-crazy about you."

Before she could respond, she heard footsteps on the porch behind her.

"Hello, Mackenzie," Chuck said, giving her a brief nod. Dom was right beside him. This was the closest she'd come to the older man.

"Kenz, walk to the bottom of the steps," Dom said. "Okay, now turn around a few times."

"What for?" She felt like a ballerina as she twirled for them.

Dom kept himself between her and Chuck. "Good. Now slowly come up to the top step and stop." His eyes were glued to the man as she complied. "Chuck?"

"I can tell, but it's not as distinct," he said, sniffing the air.

"Hmm. Interesting," Dom said.

They murmured a few words she couldn't hear, then Chuck laughed—guffawed, actually. As Dom turned around, he held his chin a bit higher, a cocky grin plastered on his face.

"Okay, what's going on? Is this some sort of joke?" Both men laughed this time. "Guess so," she muttered to Shirl.

The woman responded by rolling her eyes. "Men."

"Thanks for everything," Dom said to Chuck. "We'll be in touch."

Shirl grabbed Mackenzie in a bear hug, then led her to the car. "Everything will work out, honey. Just you wait and see. It's like you're the spark that lit Dom's world on fire." The woman gave Mackenzie one last squeeze and released her. "Nice sweatshirt, by the way. It looks good on you."

"Thanks for everything, Shirl. But did you know I'm a Husky?"

"Yes, I did. Rawr." She clawed the air with her fingernails, and it was her turn to laugh as Mackenzie climbed into the car.

CHAPTER TWENTY-ONE

DOM SHADOWED MACKENZIE the whole time they were at her house, not letting her out of his sight. If he'd had his way, she knew he would have come for her things himself.

"Let's go." He barked out the words as if she worked for him.

She glared at him. "Hold on. Just let me grab my phone charger and water my plants. Orchids are delicate and require a lot of care."

"Bring the damn thing with you then and let's get going. We don't have time for all your obsessive chores."

"Do you have my laptop and camera?"

"Yes." He paced back and forth in the dining room with such a heavy step the china in her mother's hutch rattled.

"What about my mail and newspaper?"

He let out a sound of frustration. "Can't your roommate do that for you?"

"She's hardly ever—"

As if to make a mockery of her words, headlights flashed in the window and a moment later Sam burst through the front door in tears.

"What's wrong? What happened to you?" Mackenzie took Sam by the shoulders and tried looking into her eyes, but Sam didn't answer, crying into her hands instead.

"Where is he? Your boyfriend?" Dom asked.

Before Mackenzie had time to wonder why Dom would ask, Sam responded. "He dropped me off. He's probably down the block by now."

"Stay here," he ordered and ran out the door.

Mackenzie had just finished making Sam a cup of tea when Dom returned. "He won't be pulling that bullshit on you again," Dom said to Sam. He grabbed one of Mackenzie's bags and slung it over his shoulder. "You ready?"

"I don't feel comfortable leaving Sam. Can we stay here and—"

"I'm fine. Really. My mother's been after me to visit her. I haven't been as good a daughter as you. It's been a couple of months since I've seen her."

"And you're sure she's home?"

"Yeah, tonight's a big television night for her. She DVRs her favorite soaps and watches them all at once."

Dom loaded the Porsche with Mackenzie's things as they waited for Sam to pack her bags, and when she pulled her car out of the garage, they were right behind her.

"What was that all about?" Mackenzie asked. "With her boyfriend."

"Sam is a massage therapist, right?"

"Yes. She works for one of the boutique hotels downtown."

"She doesn't realize it, but her boyfriend is a vampire. I only had to look at her to realize it. He's been taking too much of her energies through her massages and other touches, which has made him a little too aggressive. That happens sometimes, but it's more common in the South."

That explained why her roommate had been looking so tired lately. "What did you say to him?"

"I didn't do a lot of talking."

BACK AT THE loft, after Dom left for the field office, Mackenzie took her mocha, her laptop and her recharged cell phone up to the rooftop terrace.

She had a few voice mail messages, but she decided to call Corey first. Dom wanted to meet him as soon as possible to see if he was Sangre Dulce. If so, he was in danger and they needed to figure out how to get him either here or to another safe house. But what were the odds both of them having this type of blood? Not high, Dom had told her. He'd also said Corey hadn't been on the list of known Sweetbloods, but still, they couldn't take any chances. She wouldn't be able to relax until she knew for certain Corey didn't have the same blood characteristics she had.

"Hey, Kenzie, what's happening?"

"Are you free for dinner tonight? I've got someone I want to introduce you to." She didn't know that she was quite ready to start introducing Dom as her…what…boyfriend? What an inadequate description. But it made for a good excuse to get together with Corey.

"I'll have to talk to Vanessa first. She hates it when I make plans without consulting her."

"Talk to her and let me know as soon as possible, all right?"

"Does it have to be tonight? I'll have a better chance of talking her into it if we schedule something in advance."

"No," she said quickly. Realizing she sounded a little desperate, she cleared her throat to give her a moment to collect herself. "It's just that this guy means a lot to me and I really want you to meet him."

"Okay, what's going on? You're not planning a trip to Vegas anytime soon, are you?"

She didn't argue. Might as well let him think what he wanted if it got him to agree to dinner this evening.

After she hung up with Corey, she looked out over Elliott Bay and knew she could never tire of this ever-changing yet constant view. Today the sky was completely gray with clouds and the water looked cold and ominous. She hoped Sam was doing better.

Okay. Email or voice mail?

Remembering she hadn't checked the email for her new business in a few days, she settled back on the canopied lounge, tucked the blankets around her legs and grabbed her laptop. Cool. A friend from college she hadn't seen in a couple of years had found her website and contacted her. Mackenzie fired back a quick hello and suggested they meet for coffee sometime. Oh, and someone from a small farming town near the Canadian border was interested in having her do a commissioned piece of one of her whimsical landscapes. Wanted to send her a few pictures or drawings—weird—of his childhood home in Europe. Oh well, should be fun.

After finishing her email, she speed-dialed her voice mail. Five new messages had come in while her phone's battery was dead. Steve needed some pictures of a small marina in the evening. If Corey could meet tonight, maybe she could drag Dom to the one in Des Moines. That way she could take a few pictures while they were down there as she didn't know when she'd be able to go out again. Dom certainly wasn't about to let her go out on her own anytime soon.

Three messages from Dom. She listened to them next. Closing her eyes, she pressed replay a few times just to hear the timbre of his voice. He sounded heartbroken. She felt a little guilty that she enjoyed hearing just how torn up he had been about leaving.

When she played the final message, her blood ran cold and she nearly dropped the phone.

"Oh my God. Martin."

She dialed his number but it went right to voice mail. She checked the call history to see what time he'd left the message. When she rang his condo and he didn't pick up, she called Dom.

"Everything all right, Kenz? I'm sensing—"

"Martin, they have Martin." She relayed the contents of the brief message to Dom. "That was the class I was supposed to teach last night."

"I'll head over to the art school at dusk to check it out."

"We can't wait that long. That's in six hours. I'm going now." She rushed down the stairs from the terrace and burst through the door into the hallway of the loft.

"No, you're not," Dom yelled at her through the phone. "You're staying right there. It's not safe for you to be out alone."

"I can't just sit here. You can't go out and neither can any of your people. That leaves me. Since the Darkbloods won't be out, either, I'll be fine."

"Goddamn it, Kenz. You're not going anywhere." The line went dead.

She didn't know how far away the field office was, but she was determined to be gone before he arrived. She grabbed her purse and hoped she'd be able to quickly find a taxi. After waiting a moment for the slowest elevator in the world to reach her floor, she decided to take the stairs. She'd only made it down one flight when a deep voice boomed from above.

"Where in the hell are you going?"

She let out a little yelp and kept going. "Don't try to stop me," she called over her shoulder. "Martin needs—" She smacked into Dom's chest at the next landing. She would've fallen to her knees if he hadn't caught her. "How the hell—" He grabbed her wrist and started to yank her up the stairs. "Let me go." She dug her heels in and leaned back with all her weight, struggling to break free. When Dom kept hauling her up the stairs as if she were a naughty child, she kicked at his shins.

Without a word, he hoisted her up and slung her over his shoulder. She tried to kick, but he held her legs tight at the ankles, so she pummeled his back with her fists. "Goddamn it, Dom." She was sobbing now. "I've got to get to Martin."

He kicked open the steel door of the loft and stomped down the hallway to his bedroom. With another hard kick of his boot, he slammed the door shut behind them and flung her onto the bed.

His eyes narrowed and the muscles in his jaw flexed as he ground his teeth together. She wasn't surprised to see the tips of his fangs. With the exception of that night in the cabin when he'd left, she'd never seen him so angry, but she was determined to stand against him this time.

"I told you to stay put and I meant it." His words sounded different with that mouthful of teeth.

They probably weren't conducive to speaking. *Well, screw that.*

She jumped to her feet on the bed, empowered by the vantage point of looking down on him. Seeing his teeth should've frightened her, but all she felt was pissed off and frustrated at being forced into his room like this. Fangs or no fangs—no one ordered her around like this. She poked her forefinger solidly into his chest.

"How dare you tell me what I can and cannot do? Martin is a dear friend. Something happened to him because of me. You sure as hell can't do a fucking thing about it at this time of day, but I can. So get out of my goddamned way."

"You don't go anywhere without me or my approval." He spun on his heel and strode out the door before she could jump from the bed. When she heard the sound of a deadbolt sliding into place, she grabbed the lamp off the nightstand and swung it at the door like a baseball bat. It shattered into a million pieces and she sank to the floor.

CHAPTER TWENTY-TWO

A THICK, OPPRESSIVE blanket of clouds covered the sun, reducing the UV output dramatically. With a skull cap, long sleeves and his collar pulled up, Dom hoped he'd be able to withstand the daylight for a short while before noticing an energy drain.

He arrived at the art school just as his buddy on the Seattle Police Department, Johnny Sinclair, pulled up in an unmarked vehicle. They'd first met when Johnny was in Special Forces and Dom was an expert they'd brought in to teach knife-fighting skills. The two men had stayed in touch over the years. When Johnny joined the SPD and Dom was transferred here by the Agency, they occasionally helped each other out. Johnny was one of a few select humans who knew about his world.

"Anything?"

"A man named Paul Cook called in a missing person's report this morning on a Martin Johanovich. They were supposed to meet last night for dinner but the guy never showed. He was also a no-show at work. He own this art school, too?"

"Yes. He was teaching a class that my...that someone very special to me was supposed to teach. He left a message on her voice mail at 9:43 p.m. saying two men were after her. He sounded scared and out of breath, like he had been running. We believe this is connected to something that happened to her two nights ago. She was chased by a couple of Darkbloods but she got away."

"Think it could be the same guys?"

"Uh, no. We took care of the first two assholes. These two must be their replacements."

"Wow, someone wants her in a bad way. Any idea why?"

"Because she's Sangre Dulce."

"Shit, man. And she's your woman?" Johnny let out a low whistle when Dom nodded. "Let's go in and see if we can find out what happened to Mr. Johanovich."

Johnny barely had the door open when an undeniable stench filled Dom's nostrils.

"Fuck. Darkbloods."

"Look at the blood over there. We got us a crime scene. Gotta step outside and call this one in."

On the sidewalk, Johnny pulled a cigarette from behind his ear, closed his eyes and sniffed it.

"I thought you quit that," Dom said as he stepped under an awning, attempting to shield himself further from the light.

"I did. I just like the smell of 'em from time to time. Makes me feel more in control that way. Like I could light it but choose not to. Stupid, I know." He rubbed a hand over his short-cropped dark hair. "So, tell me about your woman. Must be serious if you're going out during the daytime for her. Can't remember if I've ever even seen you before sundown. Thought you didn't have time for anyone if it lasted past breakfast."

Dom shrugged. "I'm going to check around back in the alley."

Johnny chuckled at the brush-off. "Well then, let me know if you find anything."

Dom rounded the corner to the alley and there it was again. Although the smell had faded, he was positive the Darkbloods had come out this way. He detected the same blood scent from inside, but it was much more potent out here. With every step, it got stronger until he followed it to a nearby rusted-out green Dumpster.

"Ah, hell."

A SHORT TIME later, Dom entered the loft and burst through the doors of the bedroom. Mackenzie looked up from her laptop, eyes wide. She'd pulled his overstuffed chair to the window where she sat with her feet tucked beneath her.

He barely paused to hit the controls closing the automatic blinds and with three giant strides he was at her side, pulling her into his arms. With his nose buried in her hair, he held her tight, almost too tight, but he couldn't help himself. He had to feel her close, to reassure himself she was all right. She was their intended target. It could've been her that he found, not Martin.

"Dom, what is it? Where's Martin? I've been trying to call him but—"

He struggled to speak, his throat tight with the magnitude of what he had to tell her.

"What happened? Where is he?"

"He's dead, Kenz. Attacked by Darkbloods at the art school."

She staggered and he held her close. "How do you know? Are you sure?"

"Kenz, I was the one who found him."

Her legs went limp and he sank to the floor with her, wishing he could wash away her pain.

* * *

"So what are you going to do? Meet Corey at the restaurant and say, 'oh, by the way, your sister couldn't come
but it's real nice to meet you?'" With her hands on her
hips, Mackenzie stood in the foyer of the loft. Despite the
fact that her whole body ached from all the crying, she
was pissed at the stupid idea.

"Things are way too dangerous for you to be out," Dom
said as he snapped the strap of his knife holster, securing
a big-ass weapon to his torso, and shrugged into his wool
peacoat. With two handguns strapped to his back that she
did see—one of them she was pretty sure wasn't even
legal—how many other weapons did he have on him that
she didn't see? The man was a walking arsenal. "I'll go
to his house and check him out. I should be able to detect
from outside if he's got the sweetblood or not."

"Well, that's just crazy." She wiped the heel of her hand
across her swollen eyes. "What if he is Sangre Dulce?
What then? Are you going to knock on the door and make
him come with you when you've never even met? That's
so not going to fly."

And like hell was she going to sit back in the loft and
wait again. She was tired of all the waiting, of letting
things happen around her—she'd been doing it all her
life, waiting for the inevitable. Waiting for a hammer to
fall.

"I don't care if you can massage his memory. I don't
want that done to my brother. I need to be there, whether
you like it or not."

Dom pulled his pant leg down over his boot holster,
which held another knife, and when he straightened, he
leveled her with a hard stare.

There was no way she was letting him leave without

her. She grabbed his arms and wrapped them around her, pinning his wrists against the small of her back.

"What do you think you're doing?" he asked.

"It's not as if I'm going out alone. You'll be there. I'm safe with you."

His nostrils flared slightly, that tiny muscle in his jaw flexing. "Get your things," he said finally. "We're late."

The restaurant parking lot was half full when Mackenzie and Dom arrived an hour later. Through the large picture windows, the sun was still setting over Vashon Island, but she felt so numb she hardly noticed.

"How are you holding up?" Dom asked, his arm cast protectively around her shoulders as they made their way to an empty table in the bar.

"Barely." Martin's terrified voice kept replaying over and over in her mind. "But I can't possibly wait to find out about Corey."

"You look as though you've been crying. What will you say to him?"

She rolled her eyes. "Trust me. He won't notice. Besides, it's dark enough in here that even if he wasn't perpetually stoned, he still wouldn't notice."

"He's that much of a pothead?"

"Family curses aside, you'd be a stoner, too, if you lived with someone like Vanessa. There he is now." She waved him over. *Please don't let him be like me,* she prayed silently. Perched on the edge of her chair, hardly daring to breathe, she chewed on the inside of her lip as her brother zigzagged through the tables.

In true skater-boy fashion, his longish sandy-blond hair curled into his eyes and resembled a wild mop on the top of his head. He wore a gray T-shirt that was actually vintage—Mackenzie recognized it from his high school years and knew it probably still had that small hole under one of the arms—emo-tight jeans that hung from his lanky hips, and turquoise skater shoes that were unlaced. She managed to smile. He'd been dressed exactly the same the last time she'd seen him, down to the black shark's tooth and small macramé cross worn on leather cords around his neck.

She stood to hug him and noticed a raspberry scrape alongside his face, as well as an acrid smell like burning leaves on his clothes. He'd probably smoked out in the parking lot. Either that or he hadn't washed this shirt since the last time he'd gotten high.

"Kenzie!" Corey gave her a brotherly hug, almost yanking her off her feet, and when he clapped her on the back, her molars rattled. He held a hand out to Dom across the table. "Hey, I'm Corey."

Mackenzie kept her eyes on Dom as she introduced them. When Dom gave her an almost imperceptible shake of his head, a huge weight lifted from her shoulders. *He's safe, thank God.* "I'm sorry Vanessa couldn't come. I hope that didn't cause any trouble between you guys."

"Nah, I love last-minute stuff. Vanessa—not so much."

They ordered a round of drinks and appetizers, and as they waited for their food, Corey talked about school, Dom told him the abbreviated version of what he did for a living, and Mackenzie filled him in on her website, trying to act excited. She decided not to tell Corey about Martin—at least not right now, not while the pain of losing him was so fresh. The server returned a few minutes later with a pitcher of Hefeweizen, teriyaki beef skewers and a huge plate of nachos for Corey, along with his always necessary side of Thousand Island dressing.

"So how did you get that nasty-looking raspberry? Looks like it hurt."

"Skateboarding. Don't worry." He held up his hands, a chip clutched between his finger and thumb as he made a goofy okay sign. "Had a helmet on, so chill. A buddy opened up a new indoor skate facility in South Tacoma. One of the rails was slicker than I expected, and bam."

Dom gave her a dry look and she lifted one eyebrow in a silent question. With the hint of a smile, he shook his head and grabbed another skewer.

"What else have you been up to?" Mackenzie asked as she ran a finger around the thick rim of her beer glass. Dom put a beef skewer on her plate, but she knew it'd sit there untouched. She wasn't hungry. "Did you get that money I deposited in your account for books?"

"Yeah, thanks." Corey dipped a cheese- and jalapeño-laden chip into the Thousand, crammed the whole thing into his mouth and started talking. "Visited Mom the other day and she looked pretty good. Said you and your—" Corey swallowed and laughed, took a swig of his beer. "Sorry, Mom thinks you guys are married."

Mackenzie glanced at Dom and saw the corner of his mouth twitch.

"What's Vanessa been up to?" Mackenzie asked, changing the subject. "I'm sorry she couldn't make it tonight." Not really, but she felt it was her duty to at least ask about his live-in girlfriend of the past year.

"Same old. Her Seasonal Affective Disorder is giving her a lot of trouble 'cuz of the dark winter and dreary spring. Even with one of those light boxes, she says she's not getting enough UVA or UVB. All she wants to do is lie around and watch TV."

Somehow, Mackenzie doubted Vanessa's bad attitude could be blamed entirely on SAD. She was bitchy in the summer months, too.

CHAPTER TWENTY-THREE

PAVLOS SNAPPED HIS cell phone shut and glided to the two-way mirror on the far side of the small room. One of his most capable lieutenants was preparing for an important pickup. He was to report back as soon as he made the capture, hopefully in the next few days.

He watched through the glass as two Darkblood doctors, outfitted with personal oxygen masks, strapped a struggling woman to a laboratory table. Too bad she couldn't be tranquilized for the tests, as he'd like to be in the room and personally oversee the whole procedure. But he just couldn't tolerate a screaming human unless he had his teeth embedded in soft flesh, and then it would be sweet music when the sound vibrated against his lips. Without the vein, it was fingernails on a chalkboard.

Considering her dyed hair and the faint wrinkles around her eyes, he guessed her age to be around forty-five. Rather remarkable she'd lived this long, he thought as her legs went into the stirrups. Sweetblood was compelling to all vampires, and even neophytes made mistakes.

With a ring-laden hand, he wiped the corner of his mouth as he watched the action unfold. It had been at least three weeks since he'd drunk off the hoof from a sweetblood and he was so damned thirsty. And the weak energies in this god-awful place weren't helping, either. Why the hell did any vampire choose to live up here?

Although he couldn't wait to get back home, he had been dreaming of this day forever. The day all vampires would look back on and recognize as a defining moment in their history. A history that he'd shaped and created. Would he have a day named in his honor? A statue erected? Euphoria lifted him off his feet and he ghosted closer to the window.

Soon everyone would see him as the reformer he was, bringing glory back to their kind, elevating them to the top of the food chain again, where they rightly belonged. All those doubters, those weak Council followers, would bow down before him.

He wiped his dripping hands on the folds of his black robe. Yes. Those who'd laughed him off as a feeble, ineffectual youthling would be forced to admit he was right. That their kind did become stronger on a diet consisting strictly of human blood.

A heady scent poured off his skin and he inhaled. It was the scent of a leader.

If things went as planned, in less than a year, when the first batch of sweetbloods was born, the lucky souls who chose to follow him would be granted unlimited Sweet. How much blood could they take from a human infant without killing it? They'd soon find out. If things progressed well up here, the other labs around the country were set to go online shortly, and then they'd have a plethora of test subjects. Many of his kind had never even tasted Sweet before and when they did, he had no doubt he'd have throngs of eager followers. No, he wasn't about to let the momentous events of the next few days pass without witnessing every last detail himself.

He tilted his head as the woman screamed, but he didn't hear a thing. Thank God for soundproof glass. Maybe she wouldn't pass the tests. Sweet from a vial didn't compare to the energies one could get straight from the source. Forty-five was a bit old to bear children, so it was a definite possibility she'd fail to qualify for their little project. If so, he'd have her brought around to his quarters for disposal.

One of the doctors, holding a metal instrument, stepped between her spread legs. The woman twisted, tried to buck her hips up from the gurney. Was that glitter polish on her toenails? With narrowed eyes, the Overlord noticed her white-tipped fingernails, too. She was a woman who took care of herself.

He pressed the intercom button. "Remove the sheet."

The woman's head cranked around in the direction of the speaker and someone whipped off the hospital-blue cloth.

As the Overlord eyeballed her heavy breasts, curvy hips, and shapely calves, his erection tented the fabric of his robe. On second thought, maybe he'd have a little fun first. Licking his lips, he watched as the testing began.

"So what did you need this for again?" Mackenzie put her driver's license back into the slot in her wallet.

"I want to be able to take you into the field office and you needed clearance. Here's your key card."

She slung the lanyard around her neck and followed Dom out the door of the loft. "I'm a little nervous. Won't they all want to…ah, you know. Bite me?"

"As a Guardian, part of our training involves becoming desensitized to attractive nuisances. You should be fine, although you shouldn't sneak up behind someone. In fact, that cat bell idea you joked about earlier isn't a half-bad idea." She glared at him as he pressed the elevator button. "I wish I were kidding, but I'm not. Chuck has a theory that— Never mind. I'll be with you at all times. I'll never let you out of my sight when we're around other vampires. Except for Lily. You'll be safe with her. And Cordell. Changelings don't seem to be as affected by Sweet as the rest of us."

"Why is Lily okay?"

"She's been around several sweetbloods. I think one of her last human boyfriends was Sangre Dulce. Oh, and Kenz, just so you don't think I'm keeping secrets from you, she and I have slept together."

Mackenzie bristled. "Were you in love with her?"

"Hell, no. And she doesn't and hasn't ever loved me. She's just a very dear friend. Remember when I told you about our sexual drives? For us, it's a relatively common occurrence among unmated couples. It really was quite casual, but I know it must be hard to comprehend." He gave a reassuring squeeze of her shoulder. "But in a committed relationship, we're completely monogamous. Much more so than most humans are."

Mackenzie relaxed somewhat, although she was prepared to hate this Lily chick. "What is Chuck's theory?"

The elevator doors opened and they stepped inside. Dom flashed her a naughty smile—the same smile he'd given her back at the resort—inserted his I.D. card in a slot on the panel and pressed the button for the lower level.

"He thinks that when we're together—when we've made love—it alters your scent slightly to make you less…how shall I put it? Less potent-smelling to other vampires."

She almost choked. "You mean the more sex we have, the safer I am around them?"

"I think so. Chuck said it was…ah…very obvious when we left."

With a clunk, the elevator stopped and the doors slid open. She followed Dom into a dimly lit corridor. The lights must've been on a motion sensor because every time they were about to step out of the ring illuminated on the cobblestone floor, the next overhead bulb clicked on. Good thing she wasn't claustrophobic as the tunnel seemed to stretch out endlessly in the dark. The air had a stale, dry smell to it, as if it didn't get aerated much.

Ten minutes later, Dom inserted his key card into a slot near another heavy door. It slid open and they stepped into a gold-carpeted foyer. A huge bouquet of fresh flowers stood on an ornately carved Queen Anne table between two elevator doors.

"Geez, with all this walking, a girl wouldn't need to work out."

Another hallway, another door. When Dom grabbed the handles and pulled the door open, she heard the sound of country music coming from inside. She followed him into a mammoth workout facility. A gym at the field office? The high, open-beam ceilings had to stretch at least three stories tall. State-of-the-art cardio equipment was clustered together on the right side of the room, while free weights and weight machines were on the other side. Just beyond what she thought was a juice bar, a boxing ring sat in one far corner, a fenced-off trampoline in another, and thick mats lined the floors. She smelled chlorine. There must be a pool somewhere down here, too.

A blonde with a face that belonged on a skincare commercial approached them. Barefoot, she wore baggy pajama bottoms rolled down at the waist, a glittery something in her belly button and a cutoff shirt that barely covered the underside of her breasts. When she yawned and stretched her arms up, Mackenzie averted her eyes in case a boob popped out. Dom introduced the woman as Lily, the only Class-A scent-tracker assigned to Seattle.

Great, just great. Dom's ex is a cover-model.

With wide-set, Bambi eyes, Lily looked at Mackenzie's outstretched hand and shook her head. "Don't want to slog any of your energies, love. I'll leave that for Dom, eh?" Even the woman's voice, with its subtle accent, was sexy. Canadian, maybe? Lily closed her eyes, lifted her nose and smiled. "Good God, you smell fab, though." Then she gave a slight nod and Dom visibly relaxed.

Damn. Did everyone know about Chuck's theory? Mackenzie might as well wear a sign announcing that yes, they'd had a lot of sex, and save everyone the trouble.

"Nice to see you dressed up," Dom said to Lily.

"Hey, fu— Bite me. Sorry, Mackenzie. I ended up crashing here and didn't get to bed till way after dawn. Didn't know you were coming this early or I'd have gone back to my place and changed. Usually I don't look this horrid." She fluffed her hair and there was that boob again. "Oh, here's Jackson," she said, looking over Mackenzie's shoulder. "This ought to be interesting."

Mackenzie turned to see a bare-chested, muscular man stumble through one of the doors off the main room. He had light brown hair that might be long enough to touch his shoulders if it weren't sticking up everywhere. One hand was inside his sweatpants, stretching the waistband precariously low, and the other held an apple. Dom's hand on her shoulder suddenly felt even more protective.

"Oh for chrissake. If it's not you," Dom said to Lily, "it's him."

"Dom. Lil. Hey, Mackenzie," Jackson said. "We've never really met, but I know you." He pulled his hand from his crotch and extended it to shake hers.

"For God's sake, Jackson." Dom knocked his hand away.

"I was just scratching an itch. Sorry."

Mackenzie stifled a smile. That'd be something Corey would do. She cocked her head, trying to place him. "Sorry. Mind-scrub." She tapped her forehead. "I seem to have forgotten you."

Jackson threw his head back and laughed. "I was the one who— Mind if I tell her, Dom?"

"Whatever."

"I was the one who set up the road blocks after you went back to the cemetery. So I definitely remember you, but you never saw me. I watched you, silently laughing my ass off."

"Come to think of it, you do look like a bastard."

Both Dom and Lily laughed.

"Hey, blame him. I was just following orders." Jackson walked a wide circle around her, and he, too, sniffed the air. "Are you sure she's sweet— Oh, yeah, now I smell it. Subtle though. Way to go, stud."

He knows, too? She glared at Dom. Was that what all vampires did—talk about their sexual exploits as you'd go over a football game? "Do all of you live here?" Mackenzie asked, changing the subject. They must, because they both looked like they just rolled out of bed.

"Some of us do," Lily said. "Dom's place is roughly up

over there." She pointed behind Mackenzie's right shoulder. "My condo, when I'm here, is a couple of blocks over there." She stuck a thumb out behind her. Seeing the confused look on Mackenzie's face she added, "The whole area around Pioneer Square is joined using the tunnels our builders constructed many years ago in Underground Seattle. Only a small portion of the Underground is open to the public and our tunnels make use of some of the vast unused space which sits below the city. It's pretty handy actually. And thank God. Otherwise, when we're on rotation, we'd be forced to live together in one facility like they do in most of the other field offices, with bunkrooms and shit."

"What's so bad about that?" Jackson said. "Talk about convenient."

Lily rolled her eyes. "A couple of the changelings live on the other side of Lake Washington since the sun doesn't affect their energy levels as much. Our Region Commander has an apartment over there that he uses when he's in town. And Jackson, well, he's sort of homeless right now. Aren't you, love?"

It was clear that Lily liked to talk, but oddly enough Mackenzie wasn't put off by her as she thought she'd be.

Jackson scowled at Lily and rubbed his apple on his sweatpants.

"He's been sleeping in the media room the last few nights," Lily explained.

"What happened?" Dom asked. "I thought you were serious with someone."

Jackson opened his mouth to answer, but Lily interrupted him. "He was dating her for a couple of months before he screwed up. That's about as serious as it gets in his world."

"Very funny," Jackson said. "It wasn't working anymore, that's all. She doesn't understand me."

Lily barked out a laugh. "Yeah, it was working until she caught him banging some redheaded human chick he met at The Pink Salon."

"I hadn't fed in weeks and my willpower was shot. Got a little carried away with this really gorgeous woman I met at the club. One thing then led to another and well—" He glanced up, looking for sympathy or something. "Aw, fuck," he said and sunk his teeth into the apple.

"Yeah, that's what it's called, eh?" Lily said. "I kinda liked Sandra, too. We used to swap books. I'm going to miss her."

Mackenzie pressed herself a little more closely to Dom. "What happened to her? The woman from the club? Did you…did she die?"

"Hell, no. It was the next night, when we hooked up again at The Pink Salon, that I got busted."

Mackenzie relaxed.

"Poor Sandra," Lily said. "She thought you guys had something special, but obviously not."

Jackson wiped the apple juice off his chin with the back of his hand. "I don't need this shit from you. Gonna do some serious grubbing in the kitchen. I'm starving. Nice meeting you, Mackenzie." He lobbed the core into a garbage can with a fancy flick of his wrist. When it swished inside, he slapped his butt and mumbled something she couldn't quite make out. Lily evidently heard him because she snickered and rolled her eyes. "What time are we meeting, Dom?" Jackson asked as he pushed through the double doors.

"At two. In Classroom B to discuss logistics. Need to be ready to go at sunset."

Mackenzie turned back to Lily. "Dom tells me you have a daughter, Zoe?"

Lily's eyes brightened. "Yes. Seven years old and the light of my life. She stays up in Horseshoe Bay with my parents when I'm on rotation. With things as crazy as they've been lately, I haven't been able to get away much. But I'm hoping to fly up there a few nights from now. I've got some time off coming up. Right, Dom?"

"Tentatively. Depends on whether or not we get a line on where the Darkblood testing lab is located."

"That's fair. I wouldn't want to leave if we did. Mackenzie, let me show you around. I've got a picture of Zoe in my gym locker." Lily offered her elbow and Mackenzie reluctantly hooked her arm through.

"Dom's probably dying to take you into the women's locker room just as an excuse to see it," Lily called over her shoulder to make sure he was listening, then she turned back to Mackenzie. "But we females won't allow the boys in, no matter how much they want to or how they try to tempt us. They can eff up their own locker room all they want with their wet towels and half-eaten food. They don't need to do that to ours. Besides, we've got private lounges set up out here for any fu—for any horsing around. Come on."

"You don't have to edit yourself on my account," Mackenzie said as they made their way around the juice bar. "It's not like I'm a prude or anything."

"I have to watch my language around Zoe, so it's good practice. I really only cuss around these ass— guys. My mother nearly had a heart attack when I let the f-bomb slip last time I was up. Said talk like that is too rough for someone like me—imagine that. Promised her I'd work on it for next time."

When Lily unlocked the door to the women's locker room and it swung open, Mackenzie felt as if she'd just stepped into a fancy spa. A dark wood shelf, probably mahogany, with diamond-shaped compartments holding rolls of white towels, lined the back wall of the handsome foyer. On a cocktail table several glass pitchers of ice water with floating slices of cucumber and lemon sat alongside a heaping bowl of fresh fruit. Mackenzie half expected an attendant with a tip jar to offer her a fluffy white robe and assign her a locker.

"You must have employees who keep this place up. But is it difficult with the daylight restrictions?" Mackenzie asked.

"We employ a few changelings as well as humans who are aware of the vampire race and have proven themselves to be very loyal. They even serve as donors from time to time. I'll introduce you to Xian. I think you'll find his family history very similar to your own."

Lily stretched out her free arm in a perfect Vanna White impression. "Back around here are the private changing rooms and showers. We girls like a little more privacy than the boys. They don't mind their business hanging out for all to see, but some of us are a little more modest." She scratched her flat belly and the crystal in her piercing flashed. "Well, some of us, that is."

"How many female agents work here?"

"Right now, there are only three of us on rotation. One is out on maternity leave, but she might not be back. She's into the mom thing right now."

"Were you working here when Zoe was born?" Being a Guardian seemed like a difficult job for someone with children. She wondered if any of them had serious relationships.

"Yeah, off and on between a few different field offices. As a scent-tracker, my schedule is project-based most of the time." Lily led Mackenzie to the sauna and steam rooms. "Hopefully we'll get a few more female agents soon. It gets pretty testosterone-laden around here. We also have a co-ed whirlpool tub through those doors. It's quite the hot spot. Gets a lot of action, as you can imagine."

Yeah, she could. With each step she took, the razor burn from Dom's stubble on the tender skin between her legs reminded her of how she'd spent her last twenty-four hours. He'd explained about vampires' ramped-up sex drives compared to humans, but she wanted to hear a woman's perspective. "Tell me about that. You all seem... much more sexual. Am I right?"

"You're absolutely right. Not only does sex help curb our naturally aggressive tendencies, it's a survival thing, almost as necessary as eating or breathing. Centuries ago, our race nearly went extinct and, since then, infighting among our people has kept our numbers low. Plus, because of the increased energy requirements, not all of us are capable of bearing children. I was a lucky one."

Recalling what the doctor had told her about not being able to bear children, Mackenzie realized that her situation wasn't unique. At least they had that in common.

"Speaking of sex, Dom's told you we've shagged, right?"

Mackenzie nodded, tried not to look surprised. God, they were blunt about their sexual habits.

"Good. I'd hate for there to be any weird secrets." Lily smiled. "Don't worry, love. We've not slept together in

years. I've been in a committed relationship for a while.
Don't tell anyone else, though—I'd like to keep it a secret
for now. Just between us girls, okay? Here, let me show
you how these massage chairs work."

On the surface, this woman would be easy to hate,
but the more they talked, the more at ease Mackenzie
became. Although Lily was model-gorgeous and somewhat brash, Mackenzie liked her, found her demeanor
warm and welcoming. She climbed onto the leather re-
cliner and Lily explained how all the controls worked.
As her chair hummed and the massaging action began,
Lily sat in the next one over and programmed her own
controls.

"How are you able to be around me?" Mackenzie
asked, her voice a little shaky from the vibration of the
chair. "Isn't it hard?"

"You do smell fantastic, that's for sure. I used to live
with a human guy, a sweetblood, many years ago, so I got
pretty used to it. It's really not hard when you set your
mind to it. Dom's doing well, I see."

"I think so, but he'd disagree. What happened to him?
Your boyfriend. Did you guys break up?"

"Darkbloods got Keith during the damn day. I think he
stumbled into their den somehow. Sorry. Don't mean to
freak you out, but that's one reason Dom is so paranoid
about you. He knows what they're capable of."

"I'm so sorry."

"Thanks. Fifty years ago, and I remember it sometimes
as if it were yesterday."

Mackenzie closed her eyes as the chair kneaded the
back of her calves. "Can I ask you a personal question?"

"Sure."

"Did you two…you and Keith…take each other's blood?"

"He didn't know I was a vampire."

How was that even possible? Mackenzie was attracted to everything that made Dom who he was—including his being a vampire. "Was it difficult to keep secret from him?"

"I drank from him only once and did manage to stop, but I was afraid of taking too much the next time, so I never did it again. I wasn't really in love with him, eh? So it was no big deal." Lily reached over and patted Mackenzie's hand on the armrest.

"WE'RE AT A critical juncture, everyone," Dom said. "The Darkblood lab is set to go online in two weeks, with several breeding pairs already lined up. Lily's source tells us they are searching for a few more pairs. Their prisoners are undoubtedly being subjected to some of the most horrible testing procedures, let alone acting as forced donors, even though the operation isn't in full swing yet."

"Any idea where the facility is located?" someone asked.

"Just that its exact location is top secret," Dom said. "Only those directly involved know where it's at—not even the DB power structure has that information. All we know is that it's somewhere west of the Cascades within three hours of Seattle. That's a big area stretching north to the Canadian border, down to Southwest Washington and west to the Kitsap peninsula and San Juan Islands. We'll have to take into consideration the ferry times as well as how long it takes to drive over the Narrows Bridge to Gig Harbor and up north over Deception Pass and onto Whidbey Island. Lily, you and your team have the southwest. Jackson, your team has the northwest. I'll take a unit west to the peninsula."

"How are we going to find the place if it's cloaked?" asked Mitchell. He paced near the door like a caged tiger, clearly excited about going out into the field again.

"I've assigned each unit several Class-A scent-trackers. We've got a few of these individuals coming from the Horseshoe Bay office and Portland on day-transport vehicles. They should all be here by tonight. Additionally, Cordell has run a few search algorithms pointing out the most likely areas for such a facility to be located in each of the sectors you've been assigned to. This will be like a search and rescue mission, where you set up your perimeters and methodically cover the ground within. If nothing turns up, then you move to the next sector. We need to be methodical and quick, people. We've got lives at stake."

"How long do you think you'll be gone?" Mackenzie sat on the bathroom counter, eating a handful of peanut M&M's as Dom zipped up a small duffel bag.

"I don't know. Maybe we'll get lucky and find the facility soon." He stepped between her knees, scooted her hips closer, and pressed a long kiss to her lips. His hand went automatically to her breast, stroking her nipple from the outside. God, it gave her a thrill to have him take what he wanted from her like this, whenever he felt like taking it.

"I'll check in with you when I can," he continued. "But you must promise me—" he leaned back and looked her square in the eye "—not to leave the loft under any circumstances unless you go into the field office. You know Cordell. He'll be manning the command center and you are to go to him with any questions. If you need anything else, food or various sundries, call Xian and he'll get what you need. The peninsula often has spotty cell phone coverage, so you may not be able to get ahold of me right away. Here, come with me." He pulled her off the counter. "I want to show you something."

Back at the field office, they took an elevator to a lower level. It opened up into an underground five-lane shooting range that lit up automatically when they walked through the heavy soundproof door. A glass case to the right of the door held rows and rows of semi-automatic and automatic rifles. She didn't know much about them, just that they looked rather ominous. To the left of the door, floor-to-ceiling cabinets and drawers lined the wall, probably housing all sorts of weapons. Dom reached into one of the drawers, ran his finger over the contents inside, then, evidently finding what he was searching for, he pulled out a small yellow ammunition box.

She was just about to say that she didn't have her little Ruger, having lost it after shooting the two Darkbloods, when Dom magically produced it and handed it to her. "Come on. I want to see what you're made of."

After donning eye and ear protection, she situated herself in lane two, the one she always chose regardless of the gun range. With a full magazine and the target in her sight, she kept her knees loose and stilled her breath, but no matter how hard she tried, she couldn't seem to focus on the human-shaped target. Dom was too close. He disrupted her concentration. "Do you mind?" She jerked her head to the side. He complied, shaking his head in amusement.

Aware that he was watching her, she squeezed off rounds, hitting the head of almost every target.

"I'm impressed," he said a short time later when several magazines had been spent. He handed her another. "Let's see how you do when they move." He pressed something on a side wall and a row of square targets sprang up along the back of the range. They moved side to side and up and down like a carnival game. She shot one round after another, pausing only to load the other magazine until her arms felt as if they would fall off and her dominant eye began to see double.

"That's not really a target pistol, but you're a hell of a shot."

"Thanks."

"Here. Come sit with me."

After visually checking the gun for rounds, she set it down, peeled off her gear and walked over to him. He pulled her onto his lap. "It makes me hot to see you shoot like that."

"Everything makes you hot."

"True." He pointed to a small metal ammo box. "Listen, I want you to use those when I'm gone."

"What is it?" she asked as she lifted the lid. Just a bunch of normal-looking bullets.

"They're silver hollow points. I want you to have both magazines loaded with these bad boys."

Did he think she was in danger here? "But—"

"Just as a precaution. As a sweetblood, your gun should always be loaded with them. But you and I both know you are not to leave the loft, right? Here. I can't load them myself without gloves. You do it."

CHAPTER TWENTY-FOUR

MACKENZIE PADDED DOWN the hallway of the loft in bare feet and stepped into the kitchen. She had tried to sleep, but Dom's bed seemed so big and empty without him. Maybe a cup of tea would help. She put on a pot of water and rummaged through a few drawers until she found an impressive stash of teabags. Yes, chamomile.

After pouring the boiling water into a mug and adding the teabag and some weird natural sweetener she found in a cupboard, she walked back to the bedroom and noticed her phone was vibrating with a text message. She picked it up. Corey.

Fun last night. Do it again soon.

She punched in his number and smiled when she heard his voice. "Hey, Corey. Just got your message. You're up late."

"Yeah, well, Vanessa wanted some ice cream. And you know me—I live to serve."

She laughed and took a sip of the still-too-hot tea. "I could tell you were going somewhere. Hey, thanks for having dinner last night on such short notice. It, ah… meant a lot to me."

"No prob. It was fun. You guys seemed pretty into each other. That doesn't mean you're planning on dumping him soon, does it? Oh, that's weird…" His voice trailed off as if he was focused on something else.

"What?"

"Oh, nothing. Just some idiot behind me. He pulled a U-turn after he passed me and now he's tailgating me. Like, big-time. So you're not going to pull another family curse excuse and break up with this guy soon, are you? What the—" He swore under his breath. "What an idiot."

"Who? What are you talking about?"

"The guy behind me. He can't be more than a foot or two off my back bumper."

Mackenzie's stomach seized up. "What kind of car? Can you see the driver? What's he look like?"

"Hold on. We're coming to an intersection. Lemme see if I can tell." Corey paused for a moment before he continued. "Two dudes wearing sunglasses. They're in a Jeep—the kind with no doors. What freaks. It's gotta be like forty degrees out."

It's them. But he's not Sangre Dulce. This can't be happening.

With the phone cradled against her shoulder, she yanked on her jeans and stuffed her feet into a pair of sneakers. "Corey, don't ask me why, but you have to get out of there. Keep driving, stay on the main roads and for God's sake, don't go home or stop anywhere."

"What the hell? What's going on, Kenzie?"

"I'm not sure. But I had a similar thing happen to me the other night. Trust me, Corey, you've got to lose them. Hold on a sec."

She threw the phone on the bed, heard the tinny sound of Corey yelling at her through the small speaker, and grabbed the loft phone. She stabbed out Dom's cell number, but it went straight to voice mail.

Damn.

"Corey, what's going on now?" she said as she jammed her arms into the sleeves of her leather coat.

"Oh, shit. One guy is getting out."

"You're not still stopped, are you? I told you to drive. Drive. Get away from that intersection and don't stop at any others."

"Kenzie, what the hell's going on?"

"Listen to me. They…they want to kill you, all right? You've got to get away from them."

"Kill? What are you talking about?"

"Just fucking go!"

He gunned the motor—finally.

"Surprised 'em, Kenzie. They weren't expecting that. Oh, man, he jumped back in. They're following me again."

"I want you to get onto I-5 North toward Seattle. Don't go home. That will give me a chance to figure out something. Please tell me you have a full tank of gas."

"I've got a quarter-tank."

"Damn. How close are you to getting on the freeway?"

"I'm taking it now."

"Good. Just keep driving. No stopping no matter what, okay? I'll call you back in a minute."

She picked up the loft phone again, but this time pressed the button that connected to the field office.

Please, Cordell, pick up. She knew he was over there but she didn't want to take the time to run all that way. *Goddamn it, pick up.*

"Mackenzie?"

Thank God. "Cordell, I can't get ahold of Dom. Two Darkbloods are chasing my brother Corey. He's not Sangre Dulce, so I don't know what the hell is going on.

He's north of Tacoma heading this way on I-5. We've got twenty or thirty minutes tops before he gets up here unless they take him out on the freeway."

"Holy mackerel, they're usually not that bold." She heard his fingers clicking away on a keyboard. "They prefer to work in the shadows. Your brother should be safe enough if he stays on the freeway. Here, lemme send Dom an emergency text message. Oh, great."

"What?"

"Right now Dom's on Bainbridge Island in a small pocket with spotty cell coverage, but as the data lines run on a separate system…" Mackenzie fidgeted as he rambled on and on about text messages sometimes getting through when a call cannot. "Look," he said as if she were in the room with him. She imagined he was pointing to the screen. "DeGraff's team is at the Washington/Oregon border and Foss is near the Canadian border. If he can stay ahead of them, maybe he can drag it out until we can get to him."

She told him about the gas situation.

"Damn, that doesn't give us much leeway."

"If I can get him downtown, can he come here?" The words flew out of her mouth almost as fast as she could form them. "Dom said once that this place is cloaked. I don't know how that works. Would my brother be able to find it? Would the Darkbloods be able to follow him inside?"

"He'd never find it. Neither could you if you were outside."

"What if I brought him to the loft?" Mackenzie brought a hand to her head, trying hard to control her desperation.

"Won't work. It's cloaked, too," Cordell said.

"What if I got him close? Would you be able to uncloak it to let him in?"

"The only way we could do that is if he's far enough ahead of them when he gets close. We'll need at least ten minutes to safely drop the shields and get them back up. And even then, I'd need Dom's authorization code."

If Dom hadn't been able to get far enough away from the Darkbloods chasing them the other night to uncloak the place, there was no way Corey would be able to do it in his piece of shit commuter car. She'd have to figure out a way to stall them. The beginning of an idea brewed in her head.

"I'll be in touch," she said and slammed down the phone.

She rubbed her temples when she felt a slight vibration inside. Dom.

It's the only way. He's my brother, Dom. I can't just stand by and let him be captured by those monsters like our father was. I love you. I'll be careful, I promise.

She wasn't sure how much of her thoughts he'd be able to pick up on from this distance, but what she did know was she needed to get the heck out of the loft before Dom was able to contact Cordell. He'd likely give him instructions to lock her up again, then her brother, with no one to help him, would meet with the same fate their father had. And Stacy. And Martin.

After double-checking that she had Cordell's number on speed dial, she ran out of the loft and took the stairs down to the building lobby, not wanting to wait for that ridiculously slow old elevator.

"Corey, how are you doing?" she asked as took the stairs down two at a time. "They still behind you?"

"Yeah. They dropped back a little, but they're still

there." He sounded more confused than worried, but at least he was doing what she'd told him.

"Where are you?"

"Going past Fife."

Damn. Still too far away. She startled the security goon at the front desk when she flew into the lobby.

"Wait, wait," he yelled.

She ignored him and ran for the exit. As she burst through the door onto the sidewalk, a shock of static electricity shot through her body. "What the—" She spun around, but the door she'd exited through was gone. All she saw was the side of a building.

OUTSIDE HER HOUSE, the street looked quiet enough, but she asked the taxi driver to circle around to the alley just to make sure. Except for Mr. Marsh's beat-up green Mustang propped up on jacks and the iridescent eyes of a cat on the prowl, the taxi's headlights illuminated nothing else. She paid the driver and climbed out, but when she turned to ask him to wait until she got inside, he drove away, oblivious to the fact that she hoped to God a pair of Darkbloods weren't lurking around for her. Pulling out the specially loaded Ruger from her purse, she took a deep breath and watched the taillights disappear around the corner. The textured grip fit tightly in her palm, giving her some measure of comfort.

Yes, I can do this thing. I must. Now hustle. Get in, get out, get Corey.

If only it wasn't so dark. She stepped onto an overturned milk crate and reached over the ivy-covered fence to unlatch the gate. Neighborhood kids must've busted out the bare bulb on the Marshes's toolshed again. The gate clicked shut behind her and a lonely-sounding dog barked in the distance.

All the lower windows of her house were black, but when she noticed the dim glow of the upstairs hallway light through the curtains, her heart stuttered with panic. It was the light Sam always left on. Crap, she wasn't home, was she? Mackenzie had gotten so used to Sam staying over at her boyfriend's place, sometimes she forgot she even had a roommate. Okay, whatever. She'd be in and out so fast it wouldn't matter.

She fumbled with her keychain, trying to find the large, oval-shaped key that unlocked the back garage door, when a sudden thought nagged her. What if Sam's loser boyfriend was staying here tonight? What if Sam hadn't dumped him after Dom beat the crap out of him? Sam had never brought him here before, but still... Even if the guy wasn't a loser, he was still evidently a vampire and Mackenzie was still Sangre Dulce. She gripped the gun tighter. Nothing she could do about that. She'd deal with it if she had to. All that mattered was Corey. With the key in her left hand, she awkwardly reached for the lock.

Branches rustled behind her. A twig cracked. She froze. The air was still—it wasn't the wind.

The hairs on her neck bristled when she heard another sound. A growl. Low at first, but it instantly escalated into a high-pitched cry. Cold panic seized every nerve. She lost her grip on Hello Kitty and the keys tumbled to the ground with a jangle.

But when another shriek joined the first one, she let out a heavy sigh and cursed.

A damn cat fight. *Stupid unfixed male cats.* They surprised her every time. A set of shiny eyes stared at her from under the bushes then disappeared.

Her hands were still shaking when she unlocked the door. Once inside the garage, she flicked on the light and there it was. Her motorcycle—alone—which meant no Sam, no boyfriend. The bike appeared to be in pristine condition. The pearlescent paint unmarred, the chrome shiny. Dom must've had it fixed for her, she thought as she dashed into the house.

Please let Sam's boxes still be in the dining room.

They were. She pawed through the contents, scattering tiny plastic bags everywhere, before she finally found what she was looking for. Yes. One of Sam's large, sterling silver, gothic crosses. She rubbed the pad of her thumb over the sharp points. *You have to have faith for that to work on me, Mr. Vincent.* God, she wished that was all it took. A cross, a little faith and the evil vampire would cringe and leave. But that was just a movie. This was real life. After saying a quick prayer, she looped the leather cord around her neck, tucked the cross inside her T-shirt, and within minutes, she had pushed the Triumph into the moonlight and was racing through her neighborhood.

Weeds grew from the cracks in the driveway leading up to Corey's old high school, unused since the area's two rival schools had been merged into one big high school on the other side of town. She had just finished stashing her bike in the bushes when her cell phone rang. Dom. Taking a deep breath to steel herself, she flipped it open.

"What the hell are you doing, Mackenzie?" His accent sounded a trace thicker than normal. "Where are you?"

"At the old Seaview High School near my house. In case I have to shoot, it's the only place I could think of that Corey could easily find. I didn't want them in our neighborhood or in a public place where people could get hurt."

"No. Do not take them on, Mackenzie. Get out of there. Leave. You're no match for them. I'll be there in less than an hour."

She tried to block out the desperation she heard in his voice, because she knew she couldn't do as he asked. "I don't have that much time. Corey's almost out of gas and the Darkbloods are right on his tail. They're too close for us to get Corey past the cloaking shields at the field office. Since he's not Sangre Dulce, they must want him for something else. If they get to him, we've got to assume they'll take him to their research facility, which you haven't—"

"Goddamn it. They don't want Corey. They want you."

"He's my brother, Dom. He's all I have. I can't just sit back and let those monsters take him."

"You have me. *Dios mio*, you have me. Don't do this, Mackenzie. Wait and we'll find him together."

She heard the sound of a ferry's horn through the phone line. He was too far away. "When Corey pulls up, I'll shoot the two Darkbloods, he'll jump on the back of my bike and I'll take him to the field office. Without the Darkbloods on our tail, Cordell can drop the cloak. This is the only way." A set of headlights flashed through the trees. "He's here. I'll call you when I have him. I love you." She snapped the phone shut and loaded a round into the chamber of the Ruger.

COREY WISHED HE could talk to Mackenzie one more time to double-check that she was in place and ready, but naturally his phone battery had died after he hung up with her a few minutes ago. For the millionth time he glanced in the rearview mirror. They were still there.

His sweaty hands slipped on the steering wheel as he turned onto the winding, tree-lined entrance of Seaview High School. He downshifted into second and the crappy little engine jerked him forward, rattling loudly as it accelerated up the hill. On both sides of the cracked pavement, the trees and brambles disappeared into the darkness beyond the twin glow of his headlights. Mackenzie should have plenty of places to hide, he thought as he scanned left and right. Nothing but black. He was halfway up when the Jeep's headlights flashed behind him. She'd better be here, otherwise they'd have him for sure.

At the top of the hill, the old gymnasium loomed ahead like a darkened hulking box and around back was the bus turnaround where he and his friends had spent many days smoking weed. Several pairs of fluorescent green eyes flashed in his headlights and two hunching shadows lumbered out from the covered walkway. Raccoons.

He whipped the car around the corner of the gym to face the direction he'd come from, parked it and opened the door. Before he could climb out, two quick staccatos cracked in the night air.

What the hell is going on? Was his sister totally nuts?

He jumped out and heard what he hoped was the low rumble of a motorcycle engine and not a Jeep coming up the driveway. For a split second, when light shined through the underbrush, he considered locking himself in the car. But he realized it was the single headlight of a motorcycle.

In a moment, she'd swung the bike around and was idling next to him.

"Kenzie, oh my God. Did you actually shoot those guys? Please tell me you didn't." He had a really bad feeling about this.

She whipped off her helmet and shoved it at him. "Here. Get on. Hurry."

"You just scared them off, right?" He put it on and started to reach into the car to turn off the ignition, but he stopped and turned back around. "Wait. Why can't I just drive myself out?"

"Forget about the car. Let's go."

"Tell me you didn't shoot them. You were just supposed to scare them off."

The whites of her eyes flashed with anger and she smacked him alongside the head with the palm of her hand. "I said get the hell on. Those guys following you are the same kind of guys who killed Dad. Now get your ass on the bike."

"Jesus, Kenzie." Both his ears vibrated painfully under the too-tight helmet.

What the hell did this have to do with their father? He'd never seen his normally calm and sensible sister like this. He climbed on behind her and held onto her waist. Dragging her inside foot, she cranked the throttle and leaned into a sharp turn. He did his best to lean with her.

Surprised to see the Jeep idling in the middle of the driveway, Corey could just make out a figure crouched over the steering wheel. *Oh God, she did shoot them. Mackenzie actually fucking shot that guy.*

"Don't look, Corey. Keep your eyes straight ahead."

Thank God, the guy was moving as they drove past. At least the dude wasn't dead. They could go and figure out—

Mackenzie's back slammed into his chest and the bike skidded to a stop. What the hell? His head, heavy from the helmet, cracked against hers.

A dark figure dressed in an ankle-grazing trench coat filled the driveway in front of them. Mackenzie patted the pocket of her leather coat, but it was too late.

Without seeing him move, the man suddenly appeared next to the bike, towering over them. Corey couldn't make out any of his features, but the dude's breath—or maybe something on his clothes—smelled rank and coppery, like blood. Corey's easily activated gag reflex made him choke and he tasted barf in the back of his throat.

Mackenzie cranked the throttle and the man grabbed the handlebars. The engine revved high in protest, the tires squealed on the pavement, but they remained immobile. No friggin' way. How was that even possible?

"Stupid bitch," the man growled. "Think you're clever with those silver bullets?" With one hand, he held the bike still and with the other, he twirled a gun, Mackenzie's gun, on his forefinger.

In one swift movement, he snatched them off the bike and dragged them along the pavement to the Jeep as if they were rag dolls. Corey tried to keep his feet under him, but he ended up being dragged on his knees over the asphalt. By the time they reached the vehicle, both pant legs had ripped and it felt as if a layer of his skin covered the driveway. His hands and knees stung with embedded bits of gravel.

Mackenzie hadn't fared much better. From what he could see in the pale light, her hands were raw and bleeding, too. He half-expected to hear her whimpering, but that sister of his was tough.

Their captor threw them on the floor of the Jeep and handcuffed them to the back of the seat. Mackenzie shoved her body against his until he was jammed tightly against the side, as if to shield him. Corey heard the stomp of the man's boots, a metallic click—*oh God, a knife?*— and then a dull thud right before the man climbed into the Jeep alone. Corey shivered as he managed to pull off the helmet with his free hand.

"You okay?" she mouthed in his ear.

Not able to form any words, he simply nodded.

"I'm sorry, my love," she whispered.

How bizarre. She'd never called him that before.

CHAPTER TWENTY-FIVE

MACKENZIE'S FEAR RUSHED through Dom like a flash flood. He stretched out his senses, trying to get something more from her—thoughts, a mental picture of what she was seeing, something concrete like he had before. But there was nothing. All he felt was her emotion. And even that was faint.

He roared out his frustration inside the armored SUV, pounded his fists on the dashboard. His enemies had her. She was frightened and scared. And here he was trapped on a goddamn ferry in the middle of Puget Sound, still unable to *vapor*. His only hope was that her attackers were taking her to the testing facility. If their intent was to drain her like they normally did…

By the time it docked a half-hour later, a cold rage had settled into his veins. He didn't give a shit about protocol or laws—vampire or human. No matter what it took, he'd find Mackenzie and destroy everyone responsible for her capture with his bare hands.

He vaguely remembered hearing brakes screeching and horns honking as he raced through the Seattle streets to the old high school. But when he saw Corey's car and the weak, almost-dead-battery glow of the headlights, his heart sank even deeper into the pit of his gut. With her motorcycle lying in the driveway, there went his last hope that she had escaped the Darkbloods and was simply hiding out somewhere.

Mackenzie, where are you?

He pressed his fingers to his temples and stilled his breath, worried he might miss the subtlest of signs. Faint chills of panic—her panic—coursed through him. Their bond was too weak to pick up anything more.

He grabbed his cell phone. "Lily, talk to me. Tell me you've heard something. They've definitely got Mackenzie."

"Oh, Dom, I'm so sorry. I've been texting my contact to see if he knows anything more, but I haven't heard back from him yet. Security within the Alliance is tight, but he promised to get ahold of me as soon as he heard something new. But that was days ago. And I'm worried, too, Dom. He's a…he's risking his life. If they find out about him, that he's been a mole inside the Alliance for years, they'll kill him."

"Where are you? How soon can you get back? You can track her scent."

"I'm at least two hours south. I won't be able to make it there by daybreak. Where's the scent-tracker from your team? Layman? Layton?"

"Too far away." *Guess I'll be going it alone.*

He tossed the phone on the passenger seat and careened back down the driveway. Maybe he could pick up her scent or energy trail from her bike. He jumped out of the SUV and canvassed the scene. Adjacent to the Bonnie's rear tire was a strip of fresh rubber on the pavement. Just beyond that was a pile of ash. Had she gotten off a shot and hit one of them with a silvie? It certainly wouldn't surprise him, given her performance at the gun range. Had she injured the other one as well?

Buoyed by this revelation, he gripped the handlebars of her bike and concentrated on her presence. He filtered the scents, focused inward on her latent energy trail. But he picked up nothing. Just the foul stink of a newly dead Darkblood.

She was gone, and so was their blood bond.

AFTER THEY'D BOUNCED around on the floor of the Jeep for what seemed like forever, rough hands grabbed Mackenzie and yanked her out of the rig. She barely had time to look around before she and Corey were shoved toward an ominous concrete building with barred windows that reminded her of gaping black teeth. What the hell was this place?

When an icy blast of wind hit, the thin layer of sweat under her hair conducted the cold straight to her bones and she shivered. Glancing around the darkness that surrounded them, she couldn't see any other lights except the sickly yellow from inside. She got the sense they were in the middle of an open area surrounded by nothing more than forest. Crickets chirped and a few wispy trees stood like skeleton sentries, but that was the only sign of life.

Inside it wasn't much better. Damp and musty, it was clear the place hadn't been used in years. In between the sound of their scuffling steps, she heard the sound of dripping water as they walked down a dingy hallway.

Their captor turned away, but not before she saw the pained look on his face. He was holding his breath. Her blood. Damn. Her hands were smeared with blood and gravel. She wished she weren't handcuffed so she could cram them into her pockets.

"Silver-tipped bullets?" he said. "Very clever. Your Guardian boyfriend help you with that?" When she didn't answer, he sneered and leaned in close. She almost choked when she smelled the blood on his breath. Had he just killed someone? "Looks like your luck has just run out. M'lord will be thrilled to finally meet you."

His gaze dropped to her neck as he spoke. She shrugged her hair forward and broke his trance.

"Do you know why a rancher has to shoot his own cows?" He was behind her now—thank God she wasn't breathing his air any longer. She walked faster, urging Corey forward. "Because when they smell the death of the butcher's van, they run. Adrenaline from their fear makes the meat tough. But I say it makes it much sweeter." He whispered the last word, drew it out longer on his tongue.

"Kenzie, what's going on? What's he talking about?" Corey sounded on the verge of hysteria.

"Shut the fuck up," their captor barked and Corey jumped.

Mackenzie took his handcuffed hands in hers as best she could, hoping that he found some measure of comfort in her touch.

They rode a battered elevator down to a lower level and the doors opened onto a long gray hallway. Only a few of the overhead lights worked and several of those flickered on and off, creating dark corners and eerie shadows on the walls. The hallway seemed more like a tunnel and they passed several other corridors that disappeared into blackness. What was it with vampires and tunnels anyway? Something scurried away as they passed, its toenails scrambling on the floor.

At the far end, a light shone from another hallway. Around the corner several ominous figures, outfitted in portable gas masks and dressed in hospital scrubs, flanked the doorway of a room, obviously awaiting their arrival. Their guard pushed them inside and her knees nearly buckled when she saw the metal gurneys, the overhead lights and the trays of medical tools.

What was she going to do now? Never in her life had she felt so hopeless, so incapable of handling things on her own. Being responsible for Corey, she should do something, but she could think of nothing. They were trapped and she had no idea what to do.

Is this what happened to Dad? Will Corey and I suffer the same fate? Oh please, Dom, where are you?

She felt a restless stirring inside. Was that him? She called to him with her mind, searching for his thoughts, but he didn't reply.

Maybe he was too far away. The sensation was weak, but it was definitely him she'd felt. Although it was nothing compared to what it had been, at least he was still inside of her somewhere. She tried to convey to him what little she knew of their location and hoped he'd be able to detect some of it. She tried not to think about the warmth and safety of his arms, but she couldn't help herself.

"Well, look what we have here."

Mackenzie spun around to see a gaunt man, his face hardly more than a skull with sallow skin pulled taut over bone. Although he was tall, his body appeared frail and his shoulders were rounded and hunched inward. Clasping his bony, ring-clad hands together, he appraised them like cattle going to market.

"Two members of the famous Shaw family. I'd say this is my lucky day."

"Kenzie, who are these people?" Corey crowded into her. She positioned her body slightly in front of his.

"Haven't you told him? Does he not know what we

are?" The man's eyes sparkled with twisted excitement. "About your family? About Sangre Dulce?"

"Shut up. Don't listen to him, Corey."

"What's he talking about?" Corey's voice cracked.

"Oh, my goodness. He doesn't know. What kind of big sister are you to keep such important secrets from your baby brother?" To the guard, he said, "Strap this young human male to the table. I'd like to give him a little hands-on demonstration."

She had to stall him. Every second brought Dom closer to her. "You seem to know a lot about us. So who the hell are you?"

The man tipped his head back and laughed, his large mouth gaping open like a macabre puppet and revealing long, yellow-stained teeth. "Yes, I suppose I do know quite a lot about you and your family. You're Mackenzie Shaw—forgive me—Foster-Shaw and this is your brother, Corey Shaw."

"Kenzie?" Corey looked as if he was going to throw up.

Skeletor continued. "Some know me as Pavlos, but, honestly, I prefer to be addressed as the Overlord." He bowed, swept his arm dramatically in front of him, and her breath clogged on a thick lump in her throat.

The one who killed Dom's parents.

Fury settled into her veins like a fast-acting poison and heat rushed to her face. This was who Dom had been searching for.

When Pavlos straightened, he snapped his fingers at the guard.

"You keep your filthy hands off him." She moved completely in front of Corey and widened her stance.

"Isn't that touching? I'd prefer to demonstrate on you,

but I'm afraid I'd be unable to stop." His hollow gray eyes darted hungrily from her face to both shoulders, or maybe both sides of her neck, then took a slow journey down her torso, finally stopping at her toes.

Instantly her skin felt dirty—she wanted to shed it like a snake.

"It's been weeks since I've had a sweetblood because we're saving those we find for our little experiment. Wait. I lied." He covered his mouth with one bony hand. "I did have one yesterday. She failed to pass our tests, so I disposed of her myself. Besides—" he crinkled up his nose "—you reek of *him*. I'd need to have you properly prepared for me before I'd consider partaking in you."

Corey's eyes widened, the whites showing all around.

Pavlos snapped his fingers again. "I can't wait all night."

Their guard grabbed Corey as if he weighed nothing. Although she knew it was no use, she clung to her brother as tightly as she could.

"Alfonso, get her, will you?"

Mackenzie gasped when a figure emerged from the shadows near the doorway. How could she not have noticed him standing there when they walked in? Had he come in later?

Wait. Did Pavlos say Alfonso? As the man drew closer, her eyes widened. Although the coloring was different, the strong jawline and the icy-blue stare were exactly the same.

CHAPTER TWENTY-SIX

"MISS SHAW, MEET your boyfriend's brother, Alfonso Serrano. He's one of my lieutenants and has been for years."

She shrank from Alfonso as he loomed above her. Before she knew what was happening, he clamped a strong hand on her shoulder and pulled her away from Corey. Like a mother bear protecting its young, she kicked at his legs, swung her handcuffed arms, but it was like hitting a steel pillar. He slid an arm around her neck and held her immobile.

"Bastard," she breathed.

"He doesn't subscribe to the apostasy of his brother—or his whole family, for that matter. Or the rest of the Council and their Agency lackeys. He believes in the supremacy of the vampire race, as do all those affiliated with the Darkblood Alliance. Isn't that right, Alfonso?"

"Yes, m'lord."

"Your boyfriend may have gotten the tenacity, but his brother here got the brains."

Alfonso dipped his head and kept his eyes on the ground as Pavlos continued.

"We are the superior race, Miss Shaw, and I'm afraid that you're just a delicious dietary requirement."

Mackenzie watched in horror as the guard strapped Corey to a gurney and Pavlos approached him. Although she couldn't be sure, it felt as though Alfonso's grip around her neck softened once Pavlos had turned away from her.

"Don't worry. He won't kill him right now." The words were spoken so softly against her ear that she thought she may have imagined them. She swiveled around as best she could, but Alfonso's expression was dark and guarded; only the muscle at the base of his jaw twitched.

Corey whimpered on the table as Pavlos took his hand.

"Unfortunately, Miss Shaw, as a sweetblood female in her childbearing years, you're too valuable to sate my temporary needs with right now. But if you don't pass our tests, we'll get to know each other a hell of a lot better. I promise."

Tests? A new round of panic shot through her. They'd find out she wasn't capable of getting pregnant and would be worthless to them. Either way, death would be a better alternative.

His wicked yellow smile made her gag; she didn't attempt to disguise her contempt. "But your brother on the other hand, he's just a bonus. Nice to have, but definitely not necessary. If I slip up, oh, well."

He brushed the tip of his nose along the inside of Corey's wrist and inhaled. "Mmm, you Shaws smell simply delectable. Even those without the sweetblood. Your father wasn't Sangre Dulce, did you know that?"

Her father? Mackenzie felt as if she had been punched. Pavlos kept talking but it took a moment for her auditory nerves to start functioning again.

"But he obviously carried the gene, as he passed it along to you. I do remember him being surprisingly sweet for a Standard. Let's see." He tapped his forehead. "San

Diego? Has it been twenty years yet?" Mackenzie gasped. "You see, your family and I go way back. I've been feeding off them for years. And I never forget a good one." He snapped his fingers and a guard produced a cluster of small cards on a three-inch metal ring. Pavlos sifted through what had to be thirty or forty before he opened the ring and flung one at her. "When I heard you were on your way, I fished that out of my mementos. Thought you'd enjoy seeing it."

The white card lay crooked at her feet. She toed it with her sneaker to straighten it. A California driver's license. The picture was small, but unmistakable.

It was the smiling face of her father.

DOM CRANKED THE steering wheel and brought the SUV to a halt on the side of Highway 2. Mackenzie's sudden agony struck him like a whip and he sucked in a deep breath. Since he'd been driving, he'd felt her a few other times, caught snippets of her thoughts, but this was the strongest. Could he be getting closer?

He sensed that she was crying and his arms ached to hold her. To protect her.

Kenz, are you out there? Am I getting close?

Dom...Corey... –doned old building...middle of nowhere...my father...

A few more words this time, but still not enough. His cell phone vibrated.

"Lily, talk to me."

"Just got a text from my contact. He's at the lab now, but he arrived on a day transport and isn't sure of the exact location. From downtown Seattle in rush hour, it took them an hour and fifteen. He thinks it's northeast of the city, but isn't sure."

Northeast? Dom was northeast of the city now, on the highway leading over Stevens Pass. An hour and fifteen? Was he north enough? Or east enough? Or had he gone too far? The night sky was beginning to lighten. Daybreak was less than an hour away. He didn't have much time.

"And, Dom?"

"Yeah?"

"Pavlos is there."

MACKENZIE'S BODY WENT boneless and her ears rang with the pain of growing up without a dad. No fatherly arms to comfort her. No one to protect her from spiders, or joke with her first date about inflicting bodily harm if she came home late. No one to teach her to drive or give her away at her wedding. No grandfather to hold her baby in his arms.

All because of *him*.

Her nostrils flared and a burning heat made her fingers and toes tingle. Flexing her fists, she narrowed her gaze on the monster who had destroyed her family. Her breath stilled and she wanted with all her heart to see him die. The ringing in her ears increased to freight train-like intensity until she exploded with rage.

She twisted, kicked, scratched, but Alfonso held her tight. She didn't care that if she had broken free, she'd still be no match for Pavlos or any of his people. She wanted to gouge his eyes out. To see his life ebb painfully away for what he had done to her family and Dom's. A stake would be too kind. She envisioned crushing his skull beneath her boot and peeling that hideous skin from his face with her nails.

"I'm going to kill you," she screamed at him when

she subsided enough to realize the only attack she could mount against him right now was a verbal one.

"Is she always this feisty?" Pavlos leaned comfortably against Corey's gurney as if he were being entertained, a hint of amusement in his expression. "I may have to rethink this whole experiment thing and keep her for myself anyway. Could be rather exciting. A veritable family affair."

He turned his attention back to Corey and leaned in close. "We're going to find out if you carry the gene, as well. We've preyed on your delicious family for genera-tions, but then…you probably figured that out."

"What the—" Corey choked, struggled against the bindings when he saw the fangs.

Mackenzie groaned and lunged again, but Alfonso's hands were twin vises on her arms.

With thick, drug-dealer-length nails, Pavlos stroked two fingers over the inside of Corey's wrist, tapping the skin lightly to locate the vein. "Your sister has been keep-ing a little secret from you. Actually, it's not quite a *little* secret. I'd consider it to be a big one. But I intend to inform you of the truth. All of it. At the moment, however, I'm a little thirsty. Talking does that to me." He brought Corey's hand up to his mouth and plunged his fangs into his wrist.

MACKENZIE WAS IN the same room as *him*. A coldness settled into Dom's bones and gripped his heart just like it had when he'd discovered his parents. The thought of Pavlos even breathing the same air as her made him want to kill something. And here he was, so goddamn helpless, not knowing if he was getting closer or farther away from her.

He grabbed his phone and called the field office. "Cordell, run a search for abandoned buildings—it'd be a large facility—northeast of Seattle. An hour and fifteen minutes away during rush hour…narrow your search to a ten- to twenty-five-mile radius and see what you come up with. I'm on Highway 2, just past Monroe and I'm feeling Mackenzie's presence a little stronger around here."

His phone beeped. Call waiting.

"I gotta take this. Call me the moment you have something." He pressed the touch screen. "Lily, anything?"

"No, haven't heard anything else from my contact. But that last text was pretty garbled, he must have been typing quickly. Dom, it's getting early. I'm in Kirkland right now, but I don't think I can make it up to where you are before daybreak. I'm going to have to find a safe house for the day. Know of any decent ones nearby?"

One who wouldn't mind housing a smart-ass vampire who talks like a truck driver? "Yeah, I know of a few."

"Sorry, I can't get there to help. At the end of the day, I'll head back out. And, Dom, if you find the place before I get there, be careful. And remember, I've…ah…got a guy on the inside and—"

"Yeah, you told me that already."

"Well, he means a lot to—"

The phone beeped again. Cordell.

"Gotta go, Lil." And he clicked over to the other call.

"Dom, there's an old prison," Cordell said. "It was abandoned years ago after a severe flood washed out the road, damaging most of the lower levels. A newer, more modern facility was built in nearby Monroe. That might be the place you're looking for."

"Give me the coordinates and I'll check it out."

As he waited for the information to transfer to his navigation system, he slipped into a Daysuit. Made from UV-resistant material, it was designed to offer emergency protection from the sun, though the effects were so transient the suits couldn't be relied on for everyday use. When the location came through, he did a double-take. He'd been down that road several times already. He remembered seeing a stand of cottonwoods near the road with a large sprawling pasture and forest behind it. Was that where the old prison was? Somewhere within the forest, cloaked by the Darkbloods?

Dom took the next exit and headed back to Trilby Road. Cordell had found a sketchy layout of the prison and a few photos online, all of which he forwarded to Dom's phone.

Ten minutes later, Dom swerved onto an overgrown, no longer maintained road. When he passed a bullet-ridden sign announcing the correctional facility was a quarter mile ahead, he parked the SUV in the bushes and jumped out. The smell of sweetbloods was thick in the air. He muttered a silent prayer of thanks and stretched out his thoughts to Mackenzie. A faint heartbeat thrummed behind his eardrums.

Kenz, can you hear me? I'm here, baby. I'm coming to get you out.

Dom? It was just a whisper, but it was all the confirmation he needed.

With single-minded focus, he strapped on his weapons, grabbed a duffel bag full of other goodies, and when he sprinted down the road, he clicked the headset.

"Cordell, this is it. Send the coordinates to the other field units."

"It's almost daybreak. They won't have enough time."

"Then use the goddamn Daytrans and tell them to suit up."

"But—"

"I don't care about protocol. I'm going in now." The Council could exile him to Siberia or revoke his Guardian status for all he cared. All that mattered was Mackenzie.

It wasn't until he was almost upon the cloaking field that he sensed the electric charge. The hairs on his arm stood up, and a high-pitched ringing—almost out of his hearing range—was barely audible. When the air shimmered in front of him in the early morning light, like a heat wave rising from the ground, he knew he'd reached his target.

He followed the perimeter of the field, looking for the perfect place to breach the shield. He'd have to be ready when he went through. For all he knew, there was an army of Darkbloods waiting for him on the other side.

With a blade in one hand and his Glock in the other, he took a running start and dove through with the telltale static snap of electricity. Crouched in a field of tall weeds, he quickly assessed his surroundings. Dark and deserted. No Darkbloods. Yet.

Behind a dilapidated wire fence, a crumbling brick monstrosity sat on a slight incline fifty yards in front of him, so it looked larger than it actually was. In its day, the fence would've been a huge deterrent, stretching fifteen feet with razor wire at the top. But today, many of the sections had been cut, most of the wire removed. He listened for guards, but didn't detect anything but the buzzing of a few insects and the chorus of early morning birds. Running low, he skirted through the fencing and over to a small side door hanging askew on its hinges. The air inside the dark hallway was almost colder than it was outside.

Kenz, I'm in. You okay? Can you hear me?

Oh, Dom...careful...Corey's been...

His heart pounded in his chest at the sound of her voice in his head, a little stronger now.

Describe where you are, how you got there.

When they...elevator...floors...old infirmary. Please hurry...they took...

I'm coming, Kenz. He'd find her somehow.

He made it through a series of doors onto a cell block. It appeared to be some sort of solitary confinement, as each cell was its own little room. He ran from door well to door well, flattening himself against each as he advanced. Voices. At the far end. He tried the door handle pressed to his back. Locked. Changing the hold on his blade to a throwing grip, he slowly peered around the corner. Two medical personnel in white lab coats walked through the intersection of the corridors and disappeared.

Were they coming or going? He counted to ten, then took a step in their direction. The pull of Mackenzie's presence weakened slightly. Going. They were definitely going away from her. He turned the other way and saw a stairwell leading down. The pull was definitely stronger this way.

He'd made it down three flights of stairs when he noted the sensation felt stronger than ever. She was somewhere on this floor. He opened the door a millimeter at a time and the strong smell of sweetbloods nearly knocked him to his knees. A few metal gurneys lined up against the wall and the sound of crying came from somewhere nearby. He glanced in both directions. The steel doors all had small barred windows.

Kenz, I'm on your floor. Can you stick your fingers out the bars of your door?

I'm not...individual room. I'm...exam...viewing window...strapped to a table. Dom, I...other room. Careful.

Damn. Where was she? He stepped out of the stairwell. The crying was louder and he heard the low murmur of voices. He looked through the bars of the nearest door.

It was a large cell with several groups of people huddled together in twos and threes. Corey stood alone, the only one dressed in street clothes. The rest were in hospital robes. Mackenzie wasn't inside.

"Hey," Dom whispered through the bars. "Corey, man, where's Kenz?"

A young Asian kid nearest the door jumped up. "Who are you?"

"I'm here to get you out." Dom rattled the door. It would easily cave, but he feared the noise would attract attention.

"Dom, thank God." Corey approached the door, dark circles under his eyes. He looked like shit. "Kenzie knew you'd find us."

"Where is she?"

"In the testing room."

"I'll be back." He turned to leave. He'd get them out later after he had Mackenzie.

"Wait, you can't just leave us here," someone said. "They could be back for any one of us at any time."

"What if something happens to you?" the Asian kid asked.

Dom turned around and saw the renewed terror in

everyone's eyes. Damn. "Where's the guard with the keys?"

"He comes off and on. They know we can't get out so they're not always outside."

"How many are there? Guards, medical staff, everyone."

"Five guards, one doctor—if you can call her that—two nurses, and that nightmare they call m'lord."

"Blake, don't forget the new guy," someone said.

"Oh, yeah," Blake said. "A new guy we hadn't seen before came in earlier today. Or maybe it was yesterday. We kind of lose track of time down here. He's tall and quiet. Watches everything, but doesn't say much."

"Ten total?"

Blake nodded his head. "Plus Marsha and Nick are down there, too. Marsha's been there awhile and Nick—they just came for him. They looked really excited when they took him away."

"Where are the guards stationed?"

"Around the corner to the left. Sometimes they're in the back room watching TV and other times they're sitting at the desk."

"I'll be back as soon as I can."

The guards' station was just where they said it was. A Darkblood sat behind the desk, his feet propped up, reading a newspaper. In a heartbeat, Dom was behind him, his blade unsheathed.

"Goodbye, asshole." He plunged the silver-tipped blade deep into the guard's sternum and twisted. The body slumped to the floor, where it darkened and began to char. Even the clothes disintegrated, until all that remained were the metal parts. Zippers, rivets, coins and a large set of keys.

He sprinted back to the cell and soon had the door open. "Hurry, but stay quiet." He gave them quick directions. Corey hung back with Blake. Dom unholstered a gun and checked the safety. "Either of you two know how to use this?"

"I do," Corey said.

"Why doesn't that surprise me? It's got silver-tipped bullets. Through the heart and the Darkblood is dead, anywhere else and he's wishing he were. Now, go." Seeing Corey hesitate, he added. "Leave with them. I'll find her. Now get the hell out of here."

Dom moved down the corridor quickly but methodically. He tried to reach Mackenzie, but she didn't answer. Why the hell had he wasted precious time freeing those people? He should've followed his gut and freed her first. If something happened to her because of that delay, he'd—

When he rounded the last corner, light from a cracked doorway spilled out into the dark hallway. A control panel was on the far side of the room, and the huge wall of windows overlooking another room reminded him of a surgery observation area. Was this the viewing room she'd mentioned?

Mackenzie?

No answer.

A door fifteen feet away hung open, as well, and he heard voices again. "Yes, m'lord," someone said.

Dom froze, hardly daring to breathe. It was *him.* Pavlos. Just a heartbeat away.

Random thoughts filled his head. The sound of his mother's scream. The terror in her eyes just before Pavlos killed her. His father, tied with silver chains to his chair, forced to watch. The draperies flapping in the open window. Never had he been this close to the monster who was the last one to see his parents alive. Not in the catacombs of Paris, on the hills outside Prague or down in the Florida Everglades. Not until now.

Revenge chilled him from head to toe as he palmed a blade. It took every ounce of willpower he had to stand his ground. He slipped into the viewing room instead. On the other side of the windows, Mackenzie was strapped to an exam table. With her arms out at right angles, an IV bag of blood at her side, she lay with her head turned away.

Oh God, she wasn't…gone…was she? Was he too late?

Just then, she turned her head and opened her eyes. He was at her side in an instant. She blinked a few times, as if unsure of what she was seeing. Then she smiled and her relief flowed into him.

"I knew you'd find me," she whispered.

He quickly unbuckled the leather straps and pulled her into his arms. After thinking he'd lost her, he wanted to hold her like this forever. Before he could get her out of the exam room, he needed to get the IV out of her arm. He tugged gently at the tape holding the thin tube to the inside of her elbow and slid the needle out. A small trickle of blood dribbled from the site. Without thinking, he dipped his head and sealed the wound.

Oh God, that taste. It sat on the back of his tongue. Sweet and enticing. He forced it out of his mind and pulled her off the table.

"Wait. I don't want those pricks to have this." She unhooked the half-full IV bag and tucked it in her pocket. "We've got to get to Corey."

"I already found him and the others. They're on their way to safety. Come on. Let's get you out of here, too."

Just before they exited the viewing room, they heard voices out in the hallway. He pulled Mackenzie down behind a gurney as two DBs entered.

Dom stealthily unsheathed two knives.

Close your eyes. This isn't going to be pretty.

In a single movement, he jumped out and knifed them both. A dual jerk and a twist. They collapsed to the ground in unison and began to disintegrate.

"Let's go."

Mackenzie was at his back. He was reaching for the door when the smell hit him. He tightened the grip on his knives, prepared to throw them. They were wrenched from his hands as if by magic and clattered to the floor. What the—

"What a delightful surprise." A tall, crane-like figure in a black robe was suddenly in front of Dom, his feet floating several inches above the floor. The overhead light glinted off Dom's knives, now held in his bony hands.

Pavlos.

Dom lunged at him, but Pavlos was faster. Before he knew what was going on, a cold metal band snapped around Dom's neck and jerked him off his feet.

"I figured you'd try to help out your girlfriend." Pavlos's dark, dead eyes leered above him. "You're good, Serrano, but as usual, you're not good enough. Alfonso, grab the girl."

CHAPTER TWENTY-SEVEN

MACKENZIE WATCHED IN agony as they stripped Dom of all his weapons before dragging both of them down the dingy hallway. Collared with a silver band around his neck, wrists and ankles, it was clear every step was an effort for Dom. He shuffled the little half-steps of a prisoner, chains clanking, as if he had heavy weights on each leg. Mackenzie knew the skin contact with all that silver was draining him of energy. Soon, he wouldn't be able to walk.

With Dom incapacitated, it was up to her now. She couldn't let them be taken back to that exam room. If she could just transfer some of her energy to him, that might help.

Dom, take my hand. Can you reach back with yours?

With her eyes down, she stretched out her arm, but rather than Dom's protective hand, she felt bony, ring-covered fingers instead. She jerked back, but Pavlos held on, pressing his moist palm to hers, leaching out her energy. Dom roared and lunged, but the guards didn't let go. As weakness compounded with her earlier blood loss, Mackenzie sank to the ground, her hand still clasped in his.

Pavlos's eyes danced with excitement and he licked the corner of his mouth. "What sweet energies you have, my dear. I can hardly wait to taste you on my tongue. Alfonso, carry her back."

"You stay away from her. Both of you." Dom's dark eyes narrowed to slits.

Taste her? What was he talking about? She thought he had other plans for her. The kind that involved testing first, buying them more time. Had he changed his mind?

In an instant, Mackenzie found herself slung over Alfonso's shoulder. She should've tried kicking him, but she was just too tired. The examination room was too bright when Alfonso set her down on the gurney again. A chain clanked as Dom was shackled to the wall. When she shielded her eyes from the light above her, she became aware of a lump in her coat pocket. The IV bag filled with her blood. She'd forgotten about it.

Dom, I still…bag of blood. If I can…are the effects immediate?

Yes.

Lemme just— As Alfonso fastened the ankle straps, she reached into her pocket and pulled out the IV bag. *Here, catch*, and she hurled it at Dom. But in her haste, she put too much power into her throw. The bag sailed past him, hit the floor, and blood splattered everywhere.

The Darkbloods leaped across the room in an instant, overcome by bloodlust. Pavlos didn't join them, although his balled fist flew to his mouth, yellowed fangs grazing his lower lip. Only Alfonso held back with his hands still tightly gripped around her ankles. She wrapped her arms over her head, trying to drown out the sounds of the snapping and snarling.

That blood was their last hope.

"Nice try, Miss Shaw," Pavlos said. "From the looks of

it, you're quite delectable. What a special treat this will be for you, Dominic. I've decided to let you watch as I have my way with your lady. I had planned to wait, but you know what? I'm suddenly hungry and I so enjoy a good fight when I take a woman. It makes life so much more interesting. Wonder if she'll be as fiery as your mother."

The instruments on the metal trays shook with the force of Dom's roar. He pulled at the chains like an enraged animal. They held tight and he sunk to the ground again. "How could you allow him to do what he did?" Dom said to his brother, his voice as thin and deadly as a stiletto. "Did you know this? That he...raped her, too?"

"Oh, your brother knows all right. He's the one who tipped me off on how to get to your parents. He just couldn't bear to do it himself, right, Alfonso?"

"Yes, m'lord," Alfonso said, his eyes cast down at his feet.

Pavlos clapped him on the back as a father would. With a jolt, Alfonso's gaze locked onto Mackenzie's. He held it for a moment before he looked away. Was that sorrow she saw reflected in his eyes? Desperation? Or maybe a combination of both?

"It's got to be frustrating, being so ineffectual and weak," Pavlos said to Dom. "To see the people you love get hurt because of your ineptitude and your misguided beliefs."

"When did being a monster become the ideal?" Dom said through his fangs.

"It's called being superior. And if you had realized it all those years ago, your parents would be alive today. Let's see. Your father would still be smoking those pipes of his, and he'd have his horses. And your mother— Well, she'd have continued to inspire great artists of the twenty-first century with her beauty. Did you know I bought one of the nude paintings she posed for back in—oh, when was it?—1870-something. It's one of my favorite mementos."

Dom continued to struggle even though she sensed his energy level was waning fast. Since it had been so long since he'd had any significant amounts of her blood, he probably wouldn't be able to *vapor* out of the chain, either.

"And now, here we are again," Pavlos continued. "I'm going to enjoy this as much as I did back then. In fact, I may enjoy this better. I do so love an audience. Let's get this little party started."

Alfonso double-checked the leather of her straps, taking care to count the holes as if to ensure they were tight enough. "M'lord, wouldn't you be more comfortable taking the woman into your quarters? The metal of the gurney can't be good with that bad knee of yours."

Pavlos twisted one of his jeweled rings. "Excellent idea. Always the thinker. Oh, and bring your brother, too."

Alfonso moved to the foot of her gurney, his expression devoid of all emotion. He snapped his head up when a Darkblood nurse entered the room.

"M'lord, I'm so sorry to interrupt you, but the blonde's ultrasound showed she's ovulating and I knew you wanted to watch the first mating."

"Yes, yes, I do want to watch, but I'm a little busy at the moment. Tell Dr. Skinner to wait. I'll be there shortly." He turned back to Mackenzie and ran his yellowed nails along her cheek. When she tried to turn away, he grabbed her cheeks. "You will look at me when I touch you."

"But, sir," the nurse said. "Dr. Skinner has already injected the young man with the erectile enhancement drug and he's ready to go."

Pavlos's eyes somehow managed to get blacker.

"M'lord, this is the first one." Alfonso set the foot brake on Mackenzie's gurney and joined the nurse near the door. "You need to witness this, sir. It's history in the making. Just think how much more ready for the woman you'll be after seeing your dreams come to fruition."

Pavlos stroked her cheek with the back of his hand. If only her eyes were daggers, she'd cut him to shreds. "Yes, you're absolutely right. No need to rush things with you, dear. We've got plenty of time."

They filed from the room, leaving a guard at the door, and Mackenzie heard multiple deadbolts slide into place.

With the excess chain wrapped around his forearm, Dom put his foot on the taut length and pulled. All the muscles in his arms bulged as he strained. Nothing.

"Nice try, asshole. You ain't going nowhere." The guard came down the three steps from the door and Mackenzie's heart quickened. But he pushed a chair over to the far wall underneath a tiny interior window and stood up on the seat. The other exam room must be over there. He wanted to watch, as well.

She turned back to Dom. *They don't know...my blood makes you stronger, do they?*

He shook his head almost imperceptibly.

Mackenzie tugged at the leather straps binding her limbs to the table and noticed that one of the wrist straps was buckled into the second to last hole, rather than the last one as it had been earlier. Alfonso? Was that what all the fuss with the straps was about?

She threw a glance at the guard. He had his hand down his pants. Carefully, she twisted her wrist and pulled. The band definitely shifted lower. Gritting her teeth, she folded her thumb against her palm and pulled her hand free.

Kenz!

Shit. The guard was looking straight at her.

"What the hell…" He jumped off the chair, but he was a moment too late.

Her fingers found the large silver cross under her T-shirt and she yanked it free. The guard lunged at her and she shoved the sharp point into his throat. With a hideous, breathy groan, he spun away, clutching his neck.

"He's down, but he's almost more dangerous," Dom whispered. "Get away from him or he'll attack you like I did at the cemetery to get at your blood."

She struggled to unfasten the rest of the buckles and when she jumped from the table the room began to spin. Oh God, she'd forgotten how weak she was. Grabbing for the edge of the gurney, she slipped anyway and the floor slammed up to meet her.

A flood of nausea washed over her as she tried to get her brain to work. Growing darkness surrounded her like a tunnel, but Dom's voice, although far away, gave her the strength she needed to keep going.

"I'll kill you, you bitch." From behind, the guard's voice was breathy. She'd punctured his windpipe.

Her head pounded as she stumbled to Dom and examined the cuffs. They were locked, and who knew where the key was. The chains were connected to the wall in a similar fashion. *It's solid. I can't get them undone.* She pulled his face close to hers, their noses almost touching.

Listen to me, Dom. It's the only way. You're not going to hurt me.

I'll kill you if I drink from you again. I can't.

She brushed his hair back from his face and kissed his forehead, his eyelids, his lips. *You must do this, sweetheart. I know you're worried, but I also have complete faith in you. And honestly, I'd rather die peacefully in the arms of the man I love than at the hands of him—* she inclined her head toward the guard—*or that monster Pavlos. Please, Dom. You must try. It's our only hope.*

Straddling his lap, she swept her hair behind her shoulder.

"Do it now," she whispered.

THE RHYTHM OF her heart rang in his head. It was the only way. He knew that. He had no other choice.

But what if he took too much as he had before? With all the blood they'd taken from her already, she couldn't spare much more. What if he couldn't stop this time? What made today any different?

He didn't care as much about himself. As a soldier in this war, he was prepared to die fighting for what he believed in. It was a possibility he faced every day. But she was innocent, caught in this dark web through no fault of her own. If he did nothing, she would be forced to endure the most unspeakable horrors and she would die anyway. Fury ran cold in his veins when he thought of Pavlos even laying a finger on this beautiful woman.

This was his woman. His life.

To die in the arms of the man she loved, she had said.

Mackenzie, I love you. If anything happens, if I'm not

*able to stop, with God as my witness, I pledge that I will
die with you.*

The skin of her neck was soft and delicate against his
lips. Running his tongue over her pulse, he felt the blood
rushing below the surface. With his hands chained, he
wouldn't be able to slip them up to her temple and put her
into the light calming trance they used when they fed.
She'll feel everything, he thought.

"Hurry, Dom. Just do it."

"I love you, Kenz." He closed his eyes and bit.

He heard a pop and her sharp intake of breath when
his teeth pierced her vein. As her sweet blood filled his
mouth, she leaned her body into his and relaxed against
him.

"Yes, love," she whispered, stroking his hair.

She was every bit as amazing as he had remembered.
Actually, more so. With every swallow, with every beat
of her heart, he could feel himself getting stronger and
more powerful. Her blood was transforming him into a
better version of himself. He yanked at the chains holding
his wrists and ankles, and they snapped like dry twigs.

Blackness loomed ahead, beckoning him, but it held
no sway over him. This woman in his arms was willing
to give herself to him completely, to trust him, to love
him. And he loved her. Wanted to complete her, to make
her happy, to be her everything.

Her pulse continued to flicker against his lips, filling
him with her lifeblood. His hunger was sated, his need
fulfilled. And he knew that he'd taken enough.

DOM SPRANG FROM the pile of silver chains and was
shocked at the speed and efficiency with which he killed
the guard. After *vaporing* under the door of the viewing

room, he solidified, strapped on his own weapons, and unlocked the door before Mackenzie had even managed to push herself to her feet. Was he really moving that fast? He did feel so much stronger with her blood in his system, maybe even stronger than when he'd drunk from her at the cemetery.

He swept her into his arms and in an instant he was running down the hallway again.

"Dom," Mackenzie whispered in his ear as she clung to his neck. "Where are you taking me? Aren't you going to kill Pavlos?"

"Your safety overrides everything. We are *Enlazado por la Sangre,* and you're the most important thing in my world. I will not leave you unprotected in order to seek out my revenge." For once, he was going to think before he acted.

"But, Dom, he killed my father and—"

"I have no intention of letting him slip away. It's daylight. He's not going anywhere. I will not leave you in order to get my revenge. I'll wait until the other teams arrive."

He sprinted up the stairs three at a time, his feet barely touching the treads, and burst into the upper hallway. The exit door loomed ahead at the end, hanging sideways in the jamb and casting a long, triangular beam of sunlight on the gray linoleum.

As he approached, the smell of rotten meat assailed him.

He skidded to a stop and Pavlos stepped out in front of him.

"Well, well, well. You are tenacious, aren't you, Serrano?"

He shoved Mackenzie behind him and palmed a short blade.

"I see you've finally discovered the profound effects human blood can have."

He was so fucking tired of hearing the sound of that voice. He took aim and threw the knife. Before it reached him, Pavlos sidestepped it with surprising agility.

But Dom was ready. With his left hand he threw another blade and grabbed the rawhide handle of the *brindmahl* with his right. He swung the coil once over his head, flicked his wrist and sent the long tail of the silver-laced leather flying. It circled around Pavlos's neck with a snap. Dom jerked his hand down, and Pavlos fell, clutching his throat. In the span of a heartbeat, Dom was on him. He pulled out a long blade, and in one downward motion, separated Pavlos's head from his shoulders.

FOOTSTEPS REVERBERATED behind Mackenzie as she lay on the floor. Dom slammed her into the doorway and covered her with his body. A man and woman in street clothes ran toward them.

"It's okay, Dom. It's two of the other captives."

His muscles relaxed and he scooped her into his arms again. Never had she felt so safe, so protected.

"Follow us," Dom told them.

"So how did you escape?" Mackenzie asked the woman.

"It was when the Overlord left. We were…" The woman choked back a sob while the man covered his ears.

"I'm so sorry," the man said over and over.

Oh, these poor people. Mackenzie's arms stiffened around Dom's neck as he carried her outside, into the sunlight.

They'll be all right, love, his voice soothed in her head. *Our doctor will check them, then we'll do a mind-wipe. They'll remember none of this.*

No more doctors, Dom. Given what they've been through, that could terrify them.

That's why Lily's mother is on her way down from Region. She's one of our top physicians. When Lily heard we'd located the facility, she sent for her. She's very compassionate.

Mackenzie relaxed. If Lily's mother was anything like her daughter, everyone would be well cared for.

The woman cleared her throat. "It was the tall man who helped us. The one with blue eyes. He brought us our clothes and told us how to find our way out."

Mackenzie looked over at the dark prison behind them. She caught a glimpse of a figure in an upper window. Alfonso. As she stared, an eerie orange light flickered behind him. Then he turned away from the window and was gone.

CHAPTER TWENTY-EIGHT

MACKENZIE COULDN'T BE sure if an hour or a week had passed when she woke up amidst a pile of pillows and beneath a golden down comforter. Bright light filtered through her eyelids as she yawned and arched like a cat, her back cracking several times. Although the thrumming of Dom's pulse was lighter than if he were in the same room, she still stretched her legs to the opposite side of the bed, hoping maybe he was buried away from the sunlight underneath the down. The sheets on his side were cool. He'd been up for a while, but she felt him nearby, elsewhere in the loft. Good. She needed to discuss something with him.

She slipped from the bed and walked naked to the wall of windows. He'd opened the blinds for her, and she smiled.

Absently she rubbed the tender bruises at her wrists and on the delicate skin inside her elbows as a container ship, guided by two tugboats, moved through Elliott Bay. She stretched her fingers through her hair, expecting to meet with the tangled resistance of major bedhead, but instead they slid right through. He must have brushed her hair again as she slept.

The thrilling heat of anticipation blasted through her veins and she felt Dom's presence getting stronger as he approached from somewhere else in the loft. Although she knew the light wouldn't bother him nearly as much now with her blood in his system, she hit the button for the automatic blinds and they droned closed.

Dom entered carrying a tray of breakfast food. As the air wafted in, the smell of bacon and coffee made her stomach rumble.

"Mmm. You're up." His eyes raked her from head to toe and a promising smile formed on his lips before he busied himself with setting the tray on the bed and fluffing her pillows. "Feeling better?"

She closed the distance between them and hooked her arms around his waist from behind. He was so warm, and she rubbed her cheek along his shoulder blades, inhaling the scent of his skin.

"Yes, much," she mumbled, not wanting to exhale. His low-slung pajama bottoms barely covered his hips and she wondered if they were the only article of clothing he wore. Slipping her fingers beneath the drawstring waistband, she confirmed her suspicions.

"Good morning to you, too." He turned to face her, brushing his lips against the hollow of her neck, his stubble tickling her skin, awakening her nerve endings like a blast of electricity, and she expelled the air in her lungs with a moan. "First things first." Gripping her shoulders, he turned her away. "Get in and eat."

She climbed back under the covers and he set the tray across her lap. Lifting her chin to him, she gave him her warmest smile as she let him attend to her. His hair fell forward, grazing the tops of his shoulders, and his brows furrowed with concentration as he first cranked the salt grinder over the scrambled eggs, then the peppermill. After opening her napkin, he sprawled out next to her on the bed to watch her eat. How could she concentrate? The closer he was, the harder he was to ignore. She fought the urge to push the tray aside.

"It looks and smells almost perfect. Thank you."

"Almost?"

Raising an eyebrow, she looked pointedly at him for a moment then blew him an air kiss before turning her attention back to her food. Did he know how much she loved him? He reached out an arm and his fingers twisted a lock of her hair.

Yes, I do, love.

Heavy emotion welled in her eyes and lodged in her throat as she took a sip of the mocha and surveyed the plate. His blood bond with her was much more acute now.

"How long since…how long have I been sleeping?" She stuffed a piece of bacon into her mouth. It tasted so good, it should be its own food group.

"You're going on fourteen hours now." He speared a forkful of scrambled eggs and fed her a bite.

They were tender and fluffy and she doubted even Tom Douglas could do better. "Everything tastes amazing. You're so good to me."

He reached over, brushing something from her lips and licked his finger. Whipped cream from the mocha, maybe?

Her heartbeat increased as she cleared her throat and sat up a little straighter, the sheet slipping down around her hips. Sensing her change in emotion, Dom looked up at her, but when he saw her exposed breasts, his eyes darkened with desire.

Oh, no, they couldn't go there. At least not right this minute. "Love, I need to discuss something that's been on my mind. Two things, actually."

He brushed a long finger lightly on the underside of her breast and the nipple tingled and hardened. "You're in love with someone else?"

"No, Dom, I'm serious."

"You want to join the circus?"

"Tempting, but no."

"You want a cat even though you know I'm allergic to them?"

She laughed. "No."

He sat up and nuzzled her neck. "You're embarrassed to bring it up, but you want to try a few kinkier sexual positions?"

Oh, for God's sake. "You should know me better by now. I'm not embarrassed about anything we do sexually."

"Then what, love?"

She looked into his warm blue eyes and brushed a stray hair from his face, but instead of letting go, she wound it around her finger first. "First, I want you to take my blood the next time we make love."

"But—"

"No arguing. Just say yes."

He twirled a finger around her nipple. "Next."

"Next, I want to go through the conversion process. I want you to change me. Before you can protest, I've gotten all the details from Shirl. I know it requires approval by the Council."

"Yes, and it's excruciatingly painful." His brows knitted together and he turned away.

"Dom, I love you and want to spend the rest of my life with you. If I stay as I am, we'll always worry about Darkbloods and you'll outlive me by at least a hundred years."

"I love you, too. So much that it feels as if my heart will break when we're apart. But change you? I just don't know, Kenz."

Shirl had also told her that only when a couple had been married for a year would the Council consider it. A gnawing ache formed at the base of her neck. Could that be the problem? Maybe Dom didn't want to get married.

EXCEPT FOR A couple of grapes and a half-piece of bacon, Mackenzie had eaten everything he had prepared for her. His chest swelled with warm satisfaction as he popped a grape into his mouth and folded his hands behind his head. He was glad to see she was feeling like her old sassy self as he wanted to discuss some serious matters with her, too, but now was not the time. Out of habit, he rubbed his forefingers over his thumbs, but there were no rings to twist. He smiled. Now that she was feeling better, he needed to make one last trip to the jewelry store.

He heard a splash of water and a soft moan as she slid into the tub. Not surprisingly, he became aroused as he thought about her naked in the warm water. She chuckled from the other room as he reached beneath his pajama bottoms and straightened his erection out on his belly.

"Come on in, love," she called to him. "I know you want to. I can feel it." He heard the water ripple as he walked into the master bathroom. "I'm surprised you lasted this long." Green eyes peered at him through dampened lashes as she stretched out in the large soaking tub before him.

Sweet Jesus. She was so stunningly beautiful.

"Why don't you have the blinds open? I know how

much you love the view." He reached for the button, but she sat up and grabbed his wrist.

"No, don't. I kept them closed because I want you in here with me, silly."

"I'm okay in the UV light since I've got you inside me." That still sounded so strange to say.

"Maybe so, but your strength wanes much faster and I want you strong right now." She gripped the fabric of his pajama bottoms, slipping them down over his hips.

Before he could even fantasize about what he wanted her to do, she slipped her hands behind his buttocks, pulled his hips forward and took him into her mouth in one motion.

"Oh God, Kenz." Hardly able to get the words out, he fisted his fingers in her hair as her lips moved up and down his shaft. Somehow she magically balanced rough and gentle and an epic surge coursed from his fingers and toes, ramming into him like a tidal wave. He was about ready to crash a monster orgasm.

Grasping at the thinnest thread of his self-control, he pulled free and stepped into the water. He pushed her knees wide with his thighs and positioned himself between her legs. The green of her eyes darkened with desire and rivulets of water trickled between her breasts. He dipped forward and took a nipple into his mouth and she sucked in a breath between her teeth.

With a low growl, he slid inside her in one powerful thrust. Water sloshed over the side of the tub as he flexed his hips and her tight channel gripped him like a vise. Her inner muscles began to clench; he pushed further but couldn't gain any traction in the slippery tub.

Damn. The water kept them too buoyant. Maybe this was fine for slow and easy, but he wanted to drive in deep.

He wanted to take her hard. He could feel the passion mounting inside her as her heart blasted in his head like a jackhammer. She gripped his forearms with desperate abandon. She wanted it that way, as well.

Without breaking their connection, he stood from the tub. With her legs around his waist, she clung to him as he grabbed a towel and marched to the bed.

Her nails dug deep into the skin of his buttocks, keeping him seated deep inside her as he laid her down on the duvet and covered her delicate body with his own. But he needed to be careful; she was still recovering.

"I'm not breakable, Dom," she said, reading his mind. Her voice was low and sultry in his ear as he began to thrust. "I want you and I want it hard."

"*Dios mio,* Kenz." He pushed in until the base of his erection ground against her engorged flesh. *Open for me, my love.* Harder and faster he coaxed until he felt the pleasure tighten her muscles around him.

Remember your promise? Her voice caressed his soul like velvet.

He brushed the locks of brown hair from her neck and stroked a finger over the skin there, locating her pulse. Yes, it waited for him. His gums throbbed as his fangs elongated and he opened his mouth to accommodate them. His beautiful angel looked up into his face and smiled.

My glorious savior. I am yours.

As he arched his head back, he caught a glimpse of the painting over the headboard. He had never noticed the depiction of a slight smile on Mackenzie's face or the flush on her cheeks until now. It was as if she were basking in the afterglow of their lovemaking.

An animalistic sound spilled from his lips as heat

rushed through him. Dipping his head to her neck, he ran his tongue over the delicate skin covering her artery. With her orgasm, she opened fully for him and he pushed himself inside that little piece of heaven just as his teeth plunged into her flesh. Over and over he pumped into her as he swallowed her sweet essence and she held his head tightly to her throat.

I love you, my darling. Her voice whispered to his soul and she clamped herself impossibly tighter around him.

CHAPTER TWENTY-NINE

One year later.

DETERMINED TO PRY more than just the obligatory smile from her friend, at least for a moment, Mackenzie wrapped her arms around Lily and kissed her on the cheek.

"Careful," Lily said, pushing her away. "You're going to eff up your makeup and I don't want to redo it again. No more hugs and kisses until it's time for you to kiss Dom. Then you can smear it all to hell. What was that for, anyway?"

"In case the night gets away from me and I forget to thank you later."

Lily straightened the peach-colored satin bow on Mackenzie's velvet wedding jacket and adjusted the lapel. Although her eyes looked a little hollow and drawn, she scrutinized Mackenzie from head to toe, picking off little bits of lint and stray threads. "This dress is abso-fucking-lutely amazing. Shit—shoot—sorry. You look fabulous and smell even better. Are you back one hundred percent yet?"

"Try two hundred percent. Lil, how can I ever thank you enough for everything? You're like the sister I never had."

"Well, with my blood helping in your conversion, we

are sisters. Blood sisters. We're practically related now."
Lily laughed, but it still didn't quite reach her eyes.

Mackenzie took her friend's hand in hers, noticed
Lily's signature red French manicure had a few unchar-
acteristic chips. "He just needs some time, Lil. He's lived
a century masquerading as someone he wasn't, trying to
make amends for some poor decisions he made as a young
man. Dom said Darkbloods used to lace Sweet with opi-
ates. It's no wonder Alfonso got so addicted and didn't
realize what was going on back then. It's bound to take
a while for him to find out who he really is. It can take a
long time to forgive yourself for something like that."

"I know, but it still doesn't make it any easier."

"Would you be interested in going up there to visit him
at his new place? Alfonso commissioned me to do some
paintings of their childhood estate in Madrid and I should
have them finished pretty soon. It'd give you a chance to
see him again. Maybe the two of you could talk."

"He hasn't returned any of my calls or emails. You
should probably just take Dom."

"Well, I'm not sure he's ready for a social call with his
brother, either, although I'm hopeful that day will come.
Stubbornness seems to be a Serrano family trait. But
if there's one thing I've learned, you need to love your
family while you have them."

Lily walked around Mackenzie again, straightening
the tiered lace layers of her wedding gown. "Speaking of
families, your mother cracks me up. She was convinced
Jackson was trying to look up her skirt earlier."

They looked at each other and laughed. "He probably
was."

Corey burst through the doors, his skater shoes a stark
contrast to his slightly wrinkled tuxedo. "Kenzie, Shirl

wanted me to tell you that it's almost midnight. Everyone's waiting. It's time to— Wow, you look fantastic."

"She cleans up well, eh?" Lily said. "Okay, let's get a move on."

WITH HIS CHIN held high, knowing all eyes were on him, Dom waited at one end of the red velvet carpet that stretched down the center of the expansive lawn. The other end covered the stairs of the lodge's veranda, disappearing into the ornate doorway, and a small gathering of people lined up along the side near the center. They watched him now, but he knew that at any moment their heads would crane around to see *her*. The steady but slightly elevated sound of her heartbeat caressed his mind, reassuring him she was very near. For probably the millionth time, he reached up to smooth down his ponytail. He wasn't accustomed to wearing the stiff-collared cloak of his ancestors.

"Would you stand still?" Chuck laid a hand on his shoulder. "It's almost time."

As if on cue, the sound of a single chime broke the silence, and Dom felt his heart pound even harder against his ribs. When he rubbed his forefingers along his thumbs, he had to force himself to stop. For the past year his father's ring had sat on his own wedding ring finger and the other, his mother's, after some adjustments, had sat on Mackenzie's. Tonight, in the tradition of his people, would be the ceremony that celebrated their now-eternal bond. Squaring his shoulders as the chiming continued its midnight countdown, Dom peeled his gaze from the doors and glanced over at Chuck, standing to his right.

"You've made a wise choice, son. Your father would be very proud of you."

As the twelfth gong sounded, the double doors at the far end of the red carpet opened and there, in the doorway, she stood. With her dark curls fanned out over her shoulders, she wore a flowing ivory dress and matching hip-length coat with velvet collar and cuffs and sheer sleeves. She had told him it was covered in gold French embroidery, but he hadn't seen it until now.

His breath caught in his throat as a hush descended over the guests. Her form was almost ethereal, shimmering in the light of hundreds of candles. Although he would never have thought it possible, she was even more beautiful to him after going through the change seven nights ago. That she went through the agonizing blood ritual for him, to become like him, when he was perfectly happy with her as a human, still amazed him. This woman had sacrificed everything for him, and he vowed to cherish her every day for the rest of his life. At the top of the stairs, she paused and his soul reached out for hers.

When the humming of the soloist began, he lifted his arm in a loving command and Mackenzie descended the steps toward him. After piano notes joined the hauntingly beautiful singing, he started walking toward her and they met in the middle.

As he looked down upon her upturned face and felt the heady warmth rolling off her body, he was struck with the desire to bow at her feet. She'd called him her savior, but it was he who should be worshipping her. She was the one who'd saved him and brought him out of the darkness.

Eres la luz que ilumina la oscuridad de mi vida. Thank you, Lord. He lifted his eyes to the heavens.

Mackenzie untied the silk ribbon of her coat and slipped it off her shoulders. A sweet fragrance wafted up from her skin and hair, somewhat familiar and yet different. It was gloriously musky and he closed his eyes for a moment as it invaded his nostrils. Was it from the ritual oils anointing her body or the smell of her since her change? They had not lain together yet so he couldn't be sure.

When she bent on one knee, her pale peach toenails peeked out from the hem of her dress. Dropping her coat at his feet, she looked up into his eyes and began to speak.

"All that I was, all that I am, all that I will be, I surrender myself to you." Her voice, though soft, rang out through the still night air for all to hear.

He grasped both of her hands and pulled her back to her feet. With a shrug, he slipped off his cloak, revealing his bare chest, and wrapped it around her shoulders as a sign of his protection. From his pocket, he pulled out a princess-cut diamond solitaire, flanked with tiny emeralds. She gasped as he slipped it on her finger, where it nestled against her filigreed wedding ring.

Oh my God, Dom, it's absolutely beautiful.

She twisted it around and watched as it sparkled in the candlelight, shooting tiny prisms onto her gown. Moisture tinged her dark lashes as she looked up at him and his heart soared. Exactly the reaction he had hoped for when he had it designed. He'd purposely not told her about this little detail of the ceremony.

Then, after turning to take the ornately carved sword from its scabbard, which Chuck held in outstretched hands, Dom bent on one knee at her feet. He repeated the same vow to her and offered her the weapon.

"I give to you my strength and power. Your enemies

are my enemies and I will give my life to protect you and our family."

He stood and with his hand over hers, pulled the blade across the palm of his hand. Then he did the same to hers, careful to barely knick her skin. Chuck took the weapon from him and sheathed it without wiping off the blood.

His hand still joined with hers, Dom was bending his head to kiss his wife, his mate, his forever, when he heard her sharp intake of breath.

She was looking at her coat, still crumpled at his feet.

What is it, love? he started to say until his thoughts to her stopped. Several drops of their mingled blood had dripped onto the coat, marring the delicate ivory fabric. His knees almost collapsed at the sight.

Dios mio.

How was this—? His heart swelled impossibly larger in his chest and his hands, clasped over hers, began to shake. When she lifted her chin to him, he felt her concern but couldn't see it etched on her face. Everything was a blur through his warm tears.

What's wrong? I'm not upset about the coat, just surprised.

He lifted his eyes to the night sky. *Lord, how is this even possible?*

Dom, what?

He blinked a few times and saw confusion reflected in her fiery green eyes. Of course, she had no idea. Running a finger down the side of her face, he freed a wisp of her hair that, as usual, had tangled in her earring. He wanted to laugh, to twirl her around.

A child, my love. Oh my God, a child. The blood on

your marriage coat signifies you will bless me with a child.

That's not possible. You know the doctors have told me my womb is unable to carry a baby.

Going through the conversion repairs many physical imperfections. I didn't tell you because I didn't want to raise your hopes. But my darling, you were meant to carry my child.

Without waiting for the official, Dom pulled her into his arms. When her lips parted for him and he tasted her intoxicating sweetness, the world around him seemed to dissolve until it was just the two of them in the cool night air. Oh God, that beautiful scent was hers. This angel in his arms was his. What could he possibly have done to deserve—

Shouts of encouragement from the onlookers brought him out of his mesmerizing reverie. As waves lapped gently against the rocky shore, he scooped her into his arms and carried her to the bridal suite to get started on their future.

* * * * *

MILLS & BOON Book Club

Free Book!

Get your free book now at
www.millsandboon.co.uk/freebookoffer

Or fill in the form below and post it back to us

THE MILLS & BOON® BOOK CLUB™—HERE'S HOW IT WORKS: Accepting your free book places you under no obligation to buy anything. You may keep the book and return the despatch note marked 'Cancel'. If we do not hear from you, about a month later we'll send you 3 brand-new stories from the Nocturne™ series, two priced at £4.99 and a third, larger, version priced at £6.99 each. There is no extra charge for post and packaging. You may cancel at any time, otherwise we will send you 3 stories a month which you may purchase or return to us—the choice is yours. *Terms and prices subject to change without notice. Offer valid in UK only. Applicants must be 18 or over. Offer expires 31st July 2012. **For full terms and conditions, please go to www.millsandboon.co.uk**

Mrs/Miss/Ms/Mr (please circle)

First Name

Surname

Address

_____

Postcode

E-mail

Send this completed page to: Mills & Boon Book Club, Free Book Offer, FREEPOST NAT 10298, Richmond, Surrey, TW9 1BR

Find out more at
www.millsandboon.co.uk/freebookoffer

Visit us Online

0112/T2XEA

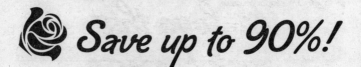

Special Offers

Every month we put together collections and longer reads written by your favourite authors.

Here are some of next month's highlights— and don't miss our fabulous discount online!

   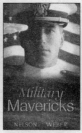

| On sale | On sale | On sale | On sale |
| 17th February | 17th February | 17th February | 2nd March |

Find out more at
www.millsandboon.co.uk/specialreleases

 Visit us Online

0212/ST/MB363